COLD AS ICE

Center Point
Large Print

Also by M. K. Gilroy and available from
Center Point Large Print:

Cuts Like a Knife
Every Breath You Take

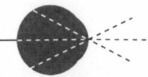

A Kristen Conner Mystery—Book 3

COLD AS ICE

M. K. Gilroy

CENTER POINT LARGE PRINT
THORNDIKE, MAINE

16 March 28
Center Point
34.95 (26.21)

This Center Point Large Print edition is published
in the year 2016 by arrangement with
Mark Gilroy Creative, LLC.

This novel is a work of fiction. Any references to real
events, businesses, celebrities, or locales are used only for a
sense of authenticity. Any resemblance to actual persons
is entirely coincidental.

The text of this Large Print edition is unabridged.
In other aspects, this book may vary
from the original edition.
Printed in the United States of America
on permanent paper.
Set in 16-point Times New Roman type.

ISBN: 978-1-62899-831-3

Library of Congress Cataloging-in-Publication Data

Names: Gilroy, M. K.
Title: Cold as ice : a Kristen Conner mystery / M. K. Gilroy.
Description: Center Point Large Print edition. | Thorndike, Maine :
Center Point Large Print, 2016. | ©2015
Identifiers: LCCN 2015042180 | ISBN 9781628998313
   (hardcover : alk. paper)
Subjects: LCSH: Women detectives—Fiction. | Large type books. |
GSAFD: Mystery fiction.
Classification: LCC PS3607.I45525 C65 2016 | DDC 813/.6—dc23
LC record available at http://lccn.loc.gov/2015042180

Dedicated to my sisters
Cheri and Susan
Who never fought with each other like
Kristen and Klarissa

PART ONE

Accidents happen.

Phineas Fogg

❄ 1 ❄

It was four in the morning in New York City, the city's quietest hour—perhaps only quiet hour. Francis "Frank" Nelson, Jr., stepped off the curb in front of the Dexter Arms on West 58th Street, and looked left and right. A cab was idling across the street, but still no driver behind the wheel. He had crossed the street a few minutes earlier to rap on the driver's window, but the car was empty then, too. That seemed odd, but what isn't odd at four in the morning in New York City? He looked left and right again, but still saw no sign of another cab. Preferably one with a driver.

Where is the driver?

He had been freezing his butt off for almost ten minutes now, and his impatience was beginning to ball up into a tight, throbbing knot in the base of his stomach. He wasn't a New Yorker, but he did enough business in the city to embrace the cynical and sometimes too true belief that the only time you can't find a taxi or a cop is when you need one.

Stage two hypertension. Doctor says I've got to manage stress better. If I don't get out of here I'm going to stroke out tonight.

He was tired and anxious to get back to the second floor of the brownstone on the east side of Central Park. Very nice but at twenty-five thousand dollars for the week it cost too much under the circumstances—his company was on the ropes financially. So was he. Everything he had was sunk in the company.

That is why I had to do what I did tonight.

Nelson was ready to scream with the tension. He was already irritated that no one was working the bell stand at the Dexter to make a cab appear right away. The young lady attending the registration desk, barely able to speak English and barely awake, he thought with a snort, assured him that she could get a cab in no time. Right. He paced inside the lobby and then paced outside on the street for as long as he could stand the cold. Not very long.

He had hired his own car and driver for the week, but he was cabbing it tonight because he didn't want his activities known. Nor did the people he was meeting with. The man in charge— not what he was expecting—said it would be much less conspicuous to catch a cab back to the brownstone at this time of night. He agreed. But where was the cab? Just how hard was it to get an open cab at four in the morning?

Okay, I know the cab across the street is open, but how about an open cab with a driver?

He was late to say the least, and if his wife, Justine, was awake or woke up with him coming back now, she would kill him. She would accuse him of cheating and drinking. Neither was true, of course. At least not tonight and not in the sense she would assume it.

But things could get bad, very bad, if she or anyone else began asking questions about why he was at the Dexter Arms throughout the night.

Nelson told her not to come this trip. That only made Justine more set on travelling with him.

She loves to disagree. I should have begged her to come.

"Kristen, what are you doing? Tell me you aren't going out in this weather."

"It's my last chance to run in Central Park."

"It's below zero."

"Don't exaggerate, Klarissa. The weather guy said it would be at least five degrees this morning."

I can't understand what my sister just mumbled from under the covers but I don't think it was very nice.

Her head pops into view. "Really, Kristen? Really?"

I'm tugging my leggings up. "We grew up in Chicago, Sis, this is child's play."

"It's not even four in the morning, Kristen. Go back to sleep. Or at least get out of here and let me sleep."

"I'm going. Give me a sec. I'm going."

"Good."

"But not for real long. I've got to pack for my

11

flight later this morning. Mom will be calling fairly soon to make sure I've given myself plenty of time to get to LaGuardia."

Klarissa finally sits up to glare at me. I stifle a smile. Her glorious mane of golden blonde hair looks as beautiful mussed as when it's done up for her television work. Women pay big bucks to have a stylist try to make their hair look like Klarissa's does with a simple toss of her head when she wakes up. My hair is pulled back in a tight ponytail for my run. Same as I wear it for work. Life's not fair.

"Okay, Kristen," she says. "You're right—like always. Far be it from me to argue. We grew up in a freezing cold city. So I guess that makes your obsessive . . . your obsessive stupidity toward physical activity understandable. Since you're crazy enough to run in this weather, at least be quiet about it so one of us gets some sleep," she finishes in disgust, rolling away from the night-stand light and putting a pillow over her head. "And stay warm!" she adds, muffled but loud enough to wake our wing of the Hilton.

I look over at Klarissa, her hair cascading from underneath the pillow. So beautiful. Always the princess. I'll never understand my sister. I lift the pillow, give her a quick kiss on the top of her head, smile when she mumbles something else, nice or otherwise, and head for the door.

Hey, what did she say about me being obsessive

and stupid? And what's with giving me the business on being noisy? I was being quiet. I think. And what's with her claiming I always have to be right?

I've got to run. I'll argue with her later.

After the door shuts behind Kristen, Klarissa sighs and gets up to go to the bathroom.

My sister. Is it possible one of us got put into our family by mistake? Detective. Workout warrior. *Fighter.* Kristen isn't happy unless she's fighting or getting ready to fight. Or sweating. She doesn't have a clue how beautiful she is. I'll never understand my sister.

❄ 2 ❄

Edward Keltto's breath was ragged and raspy, white clouds of breath glimmering in the pale yellow light of the side entrance to his garage. Another five inches of snow had blanketed Chicago while the city slept. He got up to shovel the narrow driveway beside his red brick row house. Then the sidewalk and front stoop. He knew his next-door neighbor, Mrs. DeGenares, a widow for a couple years now, would need help. She was living off her husband's small pension and he didn't want her to pay someone else to clear the snow, so Keltto repeated the

13

process around the front skirt of her home too.

He looked at his watch. He needed to get ready for work. He would have liked to take care of Mrs. Conner's drive and walk as well. Another widow. She was married to a policeman. Her daughter was a cop, too. Nice people. He would take care of Mrs. Conner later. He had to get ready for school. He had a couple of students coming in early for tutoring. It was the first day for the kids to be back in school after winter break, but some were already behind.

He returned the shovel to the garage, filled a bucket with rock salt, and quickly scattered it along the paths he had cleared. After another glance at his watch, he trudged over to the DeGenares house. He didn't like to leave a job half done.

He would be exhausted teaching his class of 5th graders today. School would be cancelled outside the city. But it took a lot more from Mother Nature than half a foot of snow to close Chicago Public Schools. Keltto didn't mind. If you got too many snow days off during the school year, the district would add days at the end of the year. He was looking forward to a long drive out west to see a part of the country he had never visited. He had been saving up for a couple years. No easy task as an elementary school teacher.

Keltto opened the door to put the bucket in its place. Everything was always in place in his garage. He felt for the light switch and flipped it to the on position. No light. That was strange. The light was working just fine less than ten minutes ago. No problem. He had started extra early this morning and still had just enough time to get ready and catch the bus to Lincoln Elementary School, his home away from home for the past twenty-five years. He would go inside the house, get the replacement bulb from the closet, and change it so his wife, Nancy, wouldn't have to fumble around when she came out to get in the car to drive to the suburban office park where she worked.

Medved Kublanov, a shaggy, burly bear of a man, urinated on a shrub. The plastic Gatorade bottle he carried on the floorboard of his cab to take care of business when he was on shift was full. Probably because the vodka bottle he kept under the passenger seat was conversely empty.

The cold was so bitter that amber yellow icicles formed on the shrub almost immediately. That's actually kind of pretty, Medved thought with a smile.

He had gotten a call less than an hour ago to pick up a man somewhere between four and four-fifteen across the street at the Dexter Arms. Pasha Boyarov told him not to be late and to not let anyone else near the cab—or the man. He told him to be off the books and to make sure the cab's GPS was disabled. No problem on any of those counts. He didn't care if Pasha told him to play an accordion and sing love songs from the homeland with a dancing monkey. Pasha was not someone you wanted to disappoint. And he paid well. A whole lot better than the cab company. But Medved's parole terms required him to hold a job. He didn't mind driving.

It would have been nice to use indoor facilities, but if you walked in one of the fancy lobbies of a midtown hotel, there was a decent chance you would be reported by someone behind the front desk or working the bell stand at the front door. Most of them were immigrants too. What made them better than him?

Oh well. Nothing he could do. He couldn't afford to lose another honest job. He kind of liked it. Less stress than his work as a *krysha*. He didn't mind roughing people up who got behind on debts, but he seemed to be the one that always ended up in jail.

❄ 3 ❄

The knot in Frank Nelson's gut tightened another twist. Unable to stand the wait, unable to manage the stress another minute—*where is that driver?* —against every objection of his better judgment, and despite a quick somersault of uneasiness in

16

his stomach, the handsome silver haired man trotted across the street and into the southwest entrance of Central Park off Columbus Circle. He knew better. But he figured he'd just jog north half a mile and catch a path running east before he hit the path leading past the zoo and out the east side of the park. Then once out on Park Avenue, he would cut over half a block, and be in the toasty warm brownstone. Two miles tops. Shouldn't take more than fifteen minutes. I won't freeze to death in fifteen minutes.

Unless the wife is still awake, he thought. Then it's going to get even icier in a hurry. When it's hot it's hot, he mused. But when things got cold, Justine could make it snow inside.

Now in his early sixties, he was very fit. A little jog was nothing. He ran three, sometimes four miles a couple of days a week. Of course that was in sunny California.

It was a bitterly cold January morning; hovering just above zero actual temperature, but ten below with the wind chill factor. Not even a thick wool overcoat with the new synthetic fleece lining skiers used and another three layers of clothing underneath, including a cashmere sweater Justine had just given him at Christmas, could keep that kind of cold from piercing him to the bone with a simple gust of wind. His throat burned from taking too big of a gulp of air. Each time he exhaled it appeared as if he was smoking a cigar.

That was something else that displeased Justine. But a man has to have a few vices.

Too cold he thought. Just go back inside and wait. The driver will show up. His cab is running after all. Stay with the plan. Surely the girl at the front desk can find another cab. People get started early in New York City.

He hesitated, then hunkered his shoulders and kept going. With his first step down the steep decline of the path into Central Park, he knew that for certain this was a mistake. He had let his impatience get the better of him. He remembered a Jack London short story one of his teachers— Sister Anne, to be exact—had read aloud to his fifth grade class.

More than fifty years ago—what a memory!

What was it? Oh yeah, *To Build a Fire*. A gold prospector, impatient to meet up with his buddies, ventured solo into the Alaskan—or maybe it was the Canadian—Yukon Territory, despite repeated warnings from an old-timer that nothing good could come of traveling alone in Arctic conditions. He hadn't thought of that story—or Sister Anne—in what seemed to be a hundred years.

Why am I in Central Park at four in the morning? Bad idea.

Nelson remembered that the prospector didn't survive in London's story. The old man had been right. After a few bad breaks and a few bad decisions, the prospector took a long, winter nap that stretched into eternity. He couldn't remember all the details, but he thought the guy tried to kill his dog and use the inside of its guts to warm his freezing hands. The dog had smelled danger and danced out of his reach. Well, it might not be seventy below zero in Central Park, he thought, but what I am doing might be just about as stupid as the character in a Jack London short story.

Why am I thinking about Sister Anne and Jack London? I know why I'm thinking of Sister Anne. Growing up in a parochial school you never get rid of the sense of guilt. And I do feel guilty.

But a whole lot richer.

Near the bottom of the slope, he stopped to return up the path. He would head back in the warm lobby of the Dexter to have the girl at the front desk—might be from Brazil or possibly the Cape Verde Islands—call the dispatcher again. He wished he had listened to his youngest son and got the Uber app on his phone. One way or another, he'd eventually get a cab.

Then it happened.

Okay, this is the coldest weather I've ever run in. Klarissa might have been right that this was a stupid idea. But just this once. I'll never admit it, which isn't the same as having to be right all the time. Or is it?

I entered the southeast corner of Central Park

feeling pretty good. I mapped out a four-mile route in the shape of a horseshoe. I'll exit the park out the southwest corner at Columbus Circle, and then do a final sprint down 59th Street and back to the hotel. If the streets are clear of ice, that is. I tore my left ACL when I played soccer for Northern Illinois, had my wrist broken by a serial killer—you should see what I did to him— and have a few other battle scars from life. I'd rather not add a broken tailbone from slipping on ice to my checklist of injuries.

I really have wanted to try out the new Gore-Tex cold weather running gear I got for Christmas. My niece and nephew got me a new fleece hat with a hole in the back for my ponytail. Good kids. Even James who has learned at the ripe young age of six that flatulence is a real attention getter—and he is apparently crazy about attention. My sister Kaylen needs to check his diet. But he and Kendra got me exactly what I wanted.

Mom came through big this year and got me what I asked for rather than the annual Sunday-go-to-church dress she gives me that I never wear. She gave me high performance compression leggings and gloves that are rated for subzero weather. Whoever did the rating is either a member of the Polar Bear Club or might have exaggerated a little. Mom did good even if my legs and fingers are freezing. But they aren't hurting as much as they were earlier, namely because I can't feel them anymore. Is that good or bad?

I slowly squeeze my hand into a fist. Ouch. Okay, I can still feel them.

I wasn't sure what Austin was going to get me. I told him that if he felt the need to give me something for Christmas, I wanted something practical, not romantic. He asked what gave me the idea he would give me something romantic. I've always seen him be spot with how he interacts with people, but he overplayed that line about the fifth time he threw it out there. Sheesh. I finally let him have it. If I did happen to use an inappropriate phrase about where he could put his gift, he quickly regained his usual aplomb and dropped the teasing.

I think the real reason we're still a couple is we live a thousand miles apart. I seem to be much better at long distance relationships. Austin did go big for me at Christmas—and did good. Very good. He bought me an arctic grade Patagonia running coat that might have cost a fortune. Klarissa looked up the list price online and told me, "He does like you; a lot." I told her not to tell me the actual damages. But I would kind of like to know. I have to tip my Gore-Tex hat to FBI Special Agent Austin Reynolds, an ex-Army Ranger and rumor has it, member of Delta Force, for good measure. He was a good soldier for Christmas.

I bought him a silk tie, which I thought was quite nice—and if it hadn't been half off list price would have cost way more than a tie should cost —but didn't seem nearly as impressive after tearing wrapping paper off a large box and seeing the coat.

Kaylen and Jimmy got me a beautiful fleece sweat top that I've layered under the Patagonia. I think my upper body is the only thing warm on me. I hope they didn't spend too much. They just had their third kid and I don't think his pastor salary goes too far. I gave them what they would get from me even if it wasn't Christmas. I made a coupon book that committed me to babysitting my nephew and nieces once a month. I could spend what I suspect Reynolds spent on me and never do half as well for them.

Count on Klarissa to steal the show. She gave me a balaclava—a fancy word for ski mask— something I hadn't requested but could use right now. Of course James ran off with it immediately to play cops and robbers. I hate to see a six-year-old on the wrong side of the law already. If he keeps passing gas every time he's next to me one of us may be going to jail anyway. What is that kid eating? He's got to be saving it up for me.

I should have just told Klarissa thanks. But I tried to be funny, which usually doesn't work with me, and asked her, "Are you telling me something about my looks, Sis? You could have saved money and bought me a paper bag."

For once, everyone laughed at my attempt at humor—except Klarissa. She sulked whenever she was around me the rest of Christmas day. I would have felt bad but she seemed to have a twinkle in her eyes at the same time she was pouting. Drama queen. Who knows if she was gigging me like I suspect or I hurt her feelings? Or both? Our relationship is complicated.

I didn't wear the balaclava this morning. Was that me being petty and having to be right? Big mistake either way. Pulling a wool gator up to cover half my face isn't getting the job done. This can't be good for my skin. I'm no Klarissa in the looks department but I do have good skin.

Okay, time to pick up the pace. I need to get out of this cold, despite my new gear, which may have met its match in Central Park.

The guy at the bell stand warned me not to go in the park while it is still dark, that it is dangerous even in bad weather—"there are many bad people in there when it's dark," he told me. I don't think he's right about it being dangerous due to bad people this morning. Who else is idiotic enough to be out in this weather besides me? And I do know how to handle myself when things get rough. I alternate a krav maga and Brazilian jujitsu workout every week. My handgun scores are only up to average, even using the Sig Sauer

23

the FBI let me keep. But pound-for-pound I can fight with anyone.

It might be a problem that I only weigh 115 pounds.

❄ 4 ❄

Frank Nelson's left foot hit a patch of black ice and flew forward and to the side. He swung his arms to catch himself from falling, but his body was already catapulting violently backward. He felt and heard a ripping in his groin muscle from the thrust and angle of his left leg. Nearly airborne, he flailed to get his hands behind him to break the fall, but still thudded on his tailbone violently, the back of his head smacking the pavement a nanosecond later. His momentum carried him into a heels-over-head half-somersault. It would have been a full somersault if his head hadn't got in the way to break the move. Excruciating stabs of pain shot up and down his right and left arms and all the way up his back as if they were in a race to reach his cerebral cortex and be the first to scream out in agony.

Swimming—no drowning—in pain, he knew that climbing back up the slope to the warmth of the Dexter Arms lobby had just become much, much harder. Impossibly harder?

Bad break. Bad decision. Nothing good can

come from traveling in Arctic conditions alone, he heard echoing in the recesses of his mind. He could almost see the old timer, chewing thoughtfully on a plug of tobacco, slowly shake his head from side to side to warn the impatient prospector about venturing into the Yukon without a partner.

That's what he had done, he realized, even before entering Central Park. Rationalization is amazing, he thought. Everything seems good, then you fall and realize you sold your soul to the devil.

Sprawled on the ground, his leg corkscrewed at a gruesome angle, he alternated between gasping for air and releasing soft moans. He could not remember a time in his life when he hurt more. Nothing came remotely close. He knew he blacked out when his head hit the ground, but he didn't think it had been for long. Maybe a couple seconds.

"Dear God in Heaven, I don't know if I can get up. But if I don't, I'm going to freeze to death out here," he prayed with all the sincerity and desperation he could muster. *There are no atheists in foxholes* echoed in his mind and he felt a sharper stab of guilt. There are no atheists splattered on a patch of ice either. If this is karma, then karma is brutal. So much for slipping inconspicuously into bed next to Justine.

He remembered the idling cab on the street above. His mind went back to London's Yukon prospector, and then the thought of his own death, but he immediately chased the specter away with a shudder and a soft but audible moan.

You don't think about death when you close a deal that results in $25 million being wired to an account you own in the Cayman Islands. It might not be enough to save his company from bankruptcy but it would be enough to fund the retirement he promised Justine.

I just have to get a couple hundred feet back up the path and I'm set, he thought. I'll go straight to the hospital. I might not be able to get a cab, but surely I can get an ambulance. Justine can meet me there. Then after I get better, she can kill me. The thought warmed him. They could barb, bait, and banter with the best of them, but dear God, he truly loved that raven-haired dynamo. They were supposed to be sunning on the beach in Cayo Espanto, a private island off the coast of Belize in a week. Might have to delay plans. Nelson thought of death again.

"Shut up, Jack London! I'm not dead yet!" he screamed in his mind.

Ascending the slope was going to be the hardest thing he ever did in his life. But he could do it. He grew up in a blue-collar working class neighborhood in Cleveland, Ohio, called Brooklyn—an easy icebreaker when meeting New Yorkers.

Where you from?

I'm from Brooklyn.

You don't sound like you're from Brooklyn.

Brooklyn, Ohio.

Not real funny, but it elicited appropriate courtesy laughs.

His life and career were based on grit and determination. He hadn't been born with a silver spoon in his mouth. *I can do this.*

First he rolled back to his left side to avoid the avalanche of pain on the right side of his backside, the area that had sustained the brunt of his fall. But that released a tidal wave of angry sensory messages letting him know that the damage to his left leg was significant, too. He knew if he stopped midway, however, he might not have the courage to turn either way, so he rolled all the way back, sobbing as his hip touched icy pavement, and on over until he was facedown. He pushed himself up with his weight on his right knee, which might be the only joint to get off fairly easily in this tangled mess called his body.

Tears streamed down his cheeks. They froze before reaching his chin. He felt ice forming below his lip as well, and realized he had bitten all the way through it. The ice was his blood. He thought that might be something that happened in London's story as well, but couldn't remember for sure.

Crying and groaning loudly now, doing all he could to keep his shattered right hand and arm off the ground, he straightened his back, and made it up to a kneeling position on both knees.

It took every ounce of effort not to keel over. He nearly fainted from the exertion.

Dear God, I think I'm going to vomit. Please help me not to vomit. Hail Mary, full of grace . . .

He breathed in deeply and nearly gagged, but was able to stifle the reflex and relax for a second.

Then he vomited a toxic mixture of pinkish blood, too much coffee, and last night's steak he ate at Peter Luger's.

He nearly fell back to his side, but somehow held onto his balance. As he exhaled with a sputter, he realized at a near subconscious level that he was not alone.

What the . . . what did I just see? Medved Kublanov had just finished zipping his fly up when he saw the man go airborne. Other than throwing a man off a fourth story balcony that was the worst fall I've ever seen in my life. Med ambled over to take a look. He went down on one knee to see the man who was sputtering and groaning on all fours. His eyes widened and he froze in place. He looked up into the azure sky, a few snowflakes swirling. He looked closer at the man's face. No. No. This can't be. I think it is the guy I'm supposed to drive to Pasha Boyarov. What is he doing down here? Medved looked at his watch. Only one minute after four. *Chert poberi!* I should have peed in the street. I shouldn't have drunk so much vodka. But why

28

would he walk into the park alone? It was fifteen below zero Celsius. That was foolish. And it wasn't part of Pasha's plan.

Pasha likes things to go a certain way. What do I do now?

More than halfway. Past the point of no return. Stop whining. Just keep running. You hate it when people whine. Don't be one of them.

But this is miserable. It feels like that moment when you eat a big spoonful of ice cream too fast and get brain freeze. The only problem is the freeze isn't going away. My temples are throbbing. It feels like my head is going to burst. I turned thirty this past year. Isn't that too young to stroke out, even under extreme conditions?

I slathered Vaseline on my lips in the hotel lobby. Seemed like a good idea, but it's making the gator stick to my mouth and I feel like I can hardly breathe. Every time I pull the gator away I get stabbed with icy needles on my face. I wish I had worn that balaclava Klarissa got me. I'll probably even admit it to her. Not today. But at some point. See, I don't always have to be right.

My mom asks me why I never cry. Not even at my dad's funeral. If she could see me now, she'd know I have tear ducts that are in perfect working order. The problem is my tears have turned to ice and are frozen to my face.

Just run. Stop whining!

•••

Ed Keltto took two steps into the darkness to put the bucket in its place—he didn't need a light to know where it went. Then he heard a sound behind him. Maybe a footstep on crunchy snow.

Before he could turn to investigate he heard a whoosh through the air. Then he felt a momentary explosion of pain on the back of his head. By the time he fell forward and his head bounced on the rear panel of Nancy's Chevy Malibu, he was out cold and felt no pain.

The attacker hissed a curse in the darkness. The plan was to move quick enough to catch Keltto before he fell forward. This had to look like an accident. But the single blow with the heavy steel crow bar with what was hoped to be just enough force to mirror cracking one's head on icy concrete had done its work well—maybe too well. The attacker wedged between Keltto and the car bumper, secured his limp body in a bear hug before Keltto slumped all the way to the ground, hoisted him upright—a limp body feels heavier than a ton of bricks—turned 180 degrees and duck walked him back a few feet until Keltto's heels touched the wood threshold. The next part was easy. Just let go and watch him fall backward out the side garage door. However he sprawled was fine. It just had to look natural. A lot of people slip on ice and hit their head. Some die.

When Keltto fell backward his head actually

did bounce off the ground. How many blows to the back of the head was normal when someone fell?

The attacker looked around. The body looked good. Just like it should. But Keltto's face was a worry. Would he have a bruise from hitting the bumper? It was ice cold, which should inhibit swelling. Good.

Killing a man. Wow. Is there a bigger leap you can make? Killing. It's so final. What should I be feeling? Guilt? I don't. Fear? Maybe a little. Okay, maybe a lot. But I don't see how I can get caught.

The killer looked at Keltto again. Was he even dead yet? Better double check. If not, just squeeze his nostrils and cover his face until the deed was done. The killer had seen Tony Soprano do that to Christopher on a *Sopranos* rerun. It wasn't necessary. There was no pulse on Edward Keltto's neck. Good. One less thing to worry about.

At this temperature the ground was frozen so solid that footprints shouldn't be much of a problem. But walking backward in soft moccasins, the attacker used a small mop to brush away any possible trace that a second person had walked beside the garage this morning—the idea came while watching curling in the Olympics—then took one last careful look back to make sure everything seemed natural. Don't want this to turn into a murder investigation.

Edward Keltto, beloved teacher, father, husband, church deacon, and good neighbor—the kind that shoveled the walk for widows—was dead.

Nancy Keltto looked out the back door of the small house. Edward. Sweet Eddy. He'd probably shoveled snow and ice for half the neighborhood. He was obsessed with being the nicest person in the world. It drove her crazy sometimes. Okay, it drove her crazy all the time. Is it possible for a person to be too nice? And not just for public consumption. He treated her like a queen. He deserves better than me, she thought.

She ground the coffee beans and poured them in the triangular brown filter she had ready. The water was already added to the Mr. Coffee machine. She hit the button and listened to the first gurgle of water working its way through the system.

She put the sliced bagel halves in the toaster. Should I start Eddy's?

She had on a bathrobe and slippers but was still cold. Ed lowered the house temperature to the low sixties when they went to bed. Mr. Green. He was going to save the whole world.

She took another sip of coffee and walked back to look through one of the windowpanes on the back door. It was still dark. What had Ed left by the garage? And why did he leave the side door open? He never leaves anything out or open.

She felt a twist of nerves in her stomach. Today was the day. The papers were prepared. The Cook County Sherriff's office was to deliver them to him after school let out.

How many times in our marriage have I put this moment off? But now is different. I've found someone who makes me feel alive. Is it wrong to want to be madly in love—something Eddy and I never had?

He says he can't live another day without me.

But how can I do this to Eddy?

I'm a horrible person.

❄ 5 ❄

"Can you give me a hand?" the silvery white-haired man croaked out, he hoped to a savior.

No answer came.

"Who's there? I need some help." Frank Nelson knew he was speaking words, but was not sure whether they were making any sound. If they were, why wouldn't someone answer? Am I hallucinating? Don't people hallucinate just before they freeze to death?

Hail Mary, full of grace . . . when was the last time he had prayed that? Too long. As soon as he got out of the hospital he would go to mass and thank God for not punching his ticket yet. And make his confession. That was going to take some time. He had fast-talked his way out of jams his entire life. Was it possible to fast-talk God?

He heard slow, heavy, crunching footsteps circle around him. He heard a low guttural voice say something, but couldn't make out the words.

"Can you help me?" he tried again.

"*Nyet*," was the answer, which he heard clearly this time. Russian? He felt a hand on his shoulder. And then a push that toppled him on his back. Every fiber of his being screamed in agony.

He opened his eyes and tried to focus but it was dark and his vision was blurred from the fall. I probably have a concussion. He squinted and made out a shape with two eyes peering at him. His head cleared a little. He was looking in the curious eyes of a big man. A mountain of a man. Maybe the man would lift him and carry him to warmth and help. But why did he just flip me on my back?

"You are not doing well, my friend," the man said to him.

He called me friend. That's good. He'll help me. Nelson fought hard in his mind to keep tethered to reality in face of the pain and bitter cold. He kept feeling like he was slipping away. You grew up in Brooklyn—even if it was in Cleveland, Ohio. You are tough. Keep fighting.

But the man just stood there pondering him.

"Can you help me?" he asked again, desperation rising in his voice and mind.

"Don't talk. You only make things harder. I am having a think. I can't think when you talk."

What was there to think about? Couldn't the idiot see he needed help? He hoped he didn't say that out loud.

The shaggy man's eyes narrowed and he nodded as if he had come to a decision.

Thank God, Sasquatch is going to save me. Nelson tried to smile in gratitude.

The man knelt down to him and began to push him halfway to one side, sending new waves of pain up and down his mangled leg. The man slowly patted down his pockets on that side. What is he doing? Is this what it feels like to be tortured? Nelson was beyond trying to scream. I'm slipping.

He was pushed roughly the other way. Oh, Mary, Mother of Jesus. That brought him back to a full awareness of his misery.

The man mountain grunted when he felt the lump of a wallet that was in Nelson's left jacket pocket. He pulled up hard on the left side of the outer jacket and three buttons popped. He reached inside and lifted out the black calfskin billfold.

"Take the money," Nelson gurgled. "Just save me. I'll give you more. Anything you want."

There must be a couple thousand dollars cash in there. Enough to satisfy a petty thief. And credit cards. He could have them too. But there was a long set of numbers written down that he desperately needed—and that no one else could see. He and Justine's future depended on it. I have to stay alive.

"You should not have come out it in the cold. You should not have set eyes on me. You make it impossible for me to follow my orders."

Orders? Why was the man saying that? I didn't see you, Nelson wanted to say, but the effort was too great and he had just enough awareness to know he was fading into shock. Too cold; too much pain. He could feel whatever fight he had left in him evaporating into the frigid New York City air. Who is idiotic enough to enter Central Park when it's zero Fahrenheit outside?

He relaxed. Not good. That's what happens before you die. You get comfortable. Don't let Jack London be right. Keep fighting. But Nelson wasn't sure he meant it.

If he could have raised his head he would have seen the man make a lightning quick violent movement of his arm in a sideward trajectory, a finely honed blade of metal comfortably held in his hand. The sight would have struck terror in Frank Nelson's heart. He was too delirious to see or hear anything. The sixty-three-year-old CEO of PathoGen, a biotech company he had founded in Redwood Shores, California, had his throat slashed at 4:10 a.m.

The huge man wiped the sides of the blade of his *pika* against the man's outer coat. He pushed the

36

button on the switchblade and folded the blade into the ivory handle and put it back in his pocket.

I've got to be getting close to the Columbus Circle entrance. At least my legs have warmed up some and my body is still comfortable. Don't think about your fingers and toes. Definitely don't think about your face. I can barely feel my extremities. It's going to hurt so bad all over again when I thaw out. I think Klarissa and the bellman were right. Only an idiot goes running in Central Park in zero degree weather.

I'm whining. Stop it!

Medved stuffed the dying man's wallet into the side pocket of his parka. He looked down. The man's face contorted in a desperate effort to get air. His body began to spasm. What the . . . how was he still alive? Medved thought he should put him out of his misery. But it was too much effort to pull out the *pika* again. His fingers were freezing. And the white-haired man would be dead in a minute or less anyway. He pushed him into a small cropping of bushes, looking around to make sure there were no witnesses.

No one was going to discover the body for another hour or two even if he left it in the middle of the path, he thought. But better to be driving, or better yet, asleep, in his hell-hole of an apartment in Coney Island—with Ilsa, purring like a kitty cat next to him—when the investigation started.

Then he realized again, a police investigation was the least of his worries. I have to think this through carefully. Why did I drink two bottles of vodka? All my problems start with vodka. I already have problems with thinking and the vodka makes it worse.

Pasha wanted Medved to bring the man to a small warehouse he owned in Queens. No one was to know what he was doing. He himself was to forget what he had done and about the existence of the warehouse once he made the delivery. Pasha didn't care how rough he had to get to put the man in the cab and keep him there, but he was to make sure he was alive and able to answer questions. At the end of the call Pasha asked if he had been drinking. Medved told him no, he had been driving all evening. Not a total lie. He left out the drinking but it was true, he had been driving.

This was no good. Pasha would not be happy with what had just happened. He would know he had been drinking.

I guess I could have just carried him to the cab, but then I would have had to explain why I wasn't waiting for him outside the Dexter Arms and Pasha would fly into one of his rages. With the way he fell, the man might have died anyway.

Think. Think. All I have to do is tell Pasha the man ran and he had a weapon, so I had to kill him. Would Pasha be satisfied with that answer? Probably not. Pasha doesn't like excuses, but he hates weakness even more. It would sound like I was afraid of an old man half my size. And this man doesn't look like the kind of guy who carries a weapon.

I shouldn't have killed him. I could have told Pasha that the man ran and got hurt when I chased him. But who is to say the man would have backed my story if he didn't end up dying? Calling Medved a liar might not have helped the man save his own skin, but if he let Pasha know I wasn't in place when I was supposed to be, I would have still been screwed.

I used to know what to do. I could have moved up and become a *boyevik* with my own gang. Life in the *bratva* has passed me by. Driving a cab makes me happier.

Medved looked down at the broken body. Red bubbles continued to form at the man's mouth. He stifled a smile. How is he still alive?

Medved's plan after he picked up the man in his cab in front of the Dexter was to jam on the brakes hard at an intersection on 57th past the Plaza Hotel. The man's head would slam into the metal and acrylic divider between front and back seats. He had thought enough ahead to stuff the seat-belts in between cushions so the man wouldn't be braced. Then, quick as a cat, before the man's mind cleared, Medved would put him face down on the back seat, cuff him with plastic ties, and put a bag over his head. This should have been very simple.

Maybe I'm not quick as a cat, but I surprise people with my speed. Like a bear. And bears are a lot faster than people know. Medved's real name was Nazar. Medved was his *klichka*, his nickname, the Russian word for bear, after all. Most just called him Med. He went by Nazar at home because it was what his mother had called him. But once you are given a *klichka* and it seemed to fit, it usually stuck. Med. The Bear.

But he lost his nerve when the man looked him in the face. That was not supposed to happen. If he hadn't had to urinate so badly—and if he hadn't sipped too much vodka—the man would have opened the back door, hopped in the back seat, and Med would have driven off. He had removed the license with his picture on it, even though it didn't look much like him anymore. All the man could have done was describe the back of his head. But back in the park they had looked in each other's eyes. The man had seen his size. It would not be hard to describe Med—the Bear—to police. That changed everything.

Med had been to prison back in Russia—Butryka in Moscow—and for a short time in the relative comfort of Riker's Island in New York before getting cut loose on a technicality—namely the only witness in his murder charges had gone missing. He was still given parole based on an earlier plea where he promised to avoid all appearances of evil. Parole was fine. Incarceration wasn't. A bear wasn't meant to be kept in a cage. He didn't plan to go back. No more *sidet* for him.

Maybe Pasha was going to kill the man after he was finished questioning him and it didn't matter that he saw his face. But what if he wasn't planning to kill him?

Nobody tells me anything. They take one look at my size and assume I'm stupid. That's a prejudice nobody talks about. But maybe they are right. The vodka doesn't help.

Pasha is cunning. Who was to say he wasn't planning to set me up the whole time? It is easy to let the Bear take the fall. Or maybe the plan was for me to be dead no matter what. This is too confusing.

Med thought of the empty bottle underneath his front seat. He wished there was just a sip left to clear his thoughts.

Medved looked down at the dying man one last time. He felt no compassion or remorse. Maybe a twinge of admiration that the guy was still fighting to breathe. He did note with amusement that the blood below his knife stroke was freezing into the shape of a smile on his throat. Life's too short not to smile. He smiled at his own cleverness.

The Bear started up the path, chuckling at the

thought of the man's theatrical fall. He had looked like the circus clown who slips on a banana peel. No one thinks how bad a fall like that must really hurt, he thought. The whole family squeals in delight.

He cursed when his own foot started to slip on a patch of ice. But he managed to keep on his feet after a brief stumble.

He looked northward up the path on the west side of the park and froze in place. He could see a ghostly figure running toward him. What the . . . who would be out on a morning like this? Do I stay and take care of him too? But if I can't see what he looks like he can't see me either. Right? Just get out of here.

Nancy Keltto hugged her arms around herself as far as they would go to fight the cold. The wind was blowing in gusts and she wasn't dressed to go outside just wearing a bathrobe. But the garage was only fifteen steps away from the small back door stoop. Eddy was going to miss his bus if he didn't get inside and get ready. Just make a dash for it.

She'd pop her head in the garage door, tell him to get a move on it—and he would dutifully obey—and then hustle back into the warmth of the house.

The cold hit her like a sledgehammer but she kept going, head down. Nancy tripped over the lump in front of her. *Eddy?* She knelt down and looked into his lifeless, staring eyes.

Nancy fell backward, stumbled to her feet. All she could do was stare. She was done with Eddy . . . today was the day she would tell him she was filing for divorce. She desperately wanted a new life away from him . . . but not like this. What had happened?

Nancy Keltto opened her eyes wide in horror. She screamed loud enough to awaken Mrs. DeGenares in the house next door and startle Bradley Starks, a teenager that lived with his mom in the house on the other side, into spilling his orange juice.

She ran for the backdoor to call 911, almost slipping on the ice.

❄ 6 ❄

Nelson was not dead when I arrived. His throat was slashed, opening his trachea and cutting into the jugular vein, but not all the way through. The tenuous strands of tissue were enough to keep his blood from spurting out immediately. But the gurgling fountain didn't bode well for his survival. He was going to bleed out soon. The blade didn't cut all the way through the interior carotid artery, so his brain was getting a little oxygen.

With the wound he received, it was a miracle the man was alive.

As I neared the crime scene, I saw a man stumble up the sloped pathway to exit Central Park—even from my distance it appeared to be someone huge. That got me excited. Seeing the incline meant I was almost done with my icy run. I still had to cut east to the other side of the park and the warmth of my hotel lobby, but the end was in sight.

The brain is pretty smart whether we're awake or asleep. It gave an order for Nelson's body to scream. Since his windpipe wasn't in one piece, it did the best it could and let out a shrill kerning wail that I will never forget as long as I live.

I had already picked up speed to get my ill-advised run over with when the undulating, piercing shriek from Hell shattered the relative quiet of the park. I broke into a sprint. Nelson's brain did the right thing to get me moving faster than I would have thought possible a few minutes earlier. I think I moved as fast as when I ran track in high school or played forward for the Northern Illinois soccer team.

I took one look at the victim and knew his ticket to eternity was punched or about to be punched. My mind raced to my EMT training.

ABC. ABC. ABC. Airway. Breathing. Circulation. ABC.

Adrenaline coursed through my body and my

frozen fingers could suddenly work. I got my phone out, punched 911 somehow, and stuck the aluminum casing in the crook between my neck and shoulder while it rang. I brought my hands to his gaping throat, got my two pointer fingers and thumbs on the separated pieces of ringed cartilage, muscle, and connective tissue that formed the four-inch tube that allowed him to breathe. I could see the top and bottom holes that needed to be joined. A moist gooey mucous dripped from each end.

God, you are going to have to help me, was all the prayer I could muster.

I pressed the two tubes together and held them as I heard an operator ask calmly, "What is your emergency?"

Be calm. Be steady. Keep the airway together. Don't drop the phone.

"Victim has been slashed across the throat. Condition is critical. I am down the slope from the Columbus Circle entrance to Central Park. I need a medical emergency team immediately. I also need police backup."

"Are you NYPD?"

"No."

"I need your name and phone number."

"I repeat. Emergency medical unit needed now."

"My procedure is to get a name and number first."

"Detective Kristen Conner. You have my number."

"You said you weren't NYPD."

"I'll explain anything you want later. Listen to me. A man is about to die. You need to get EMTs moving now. And blood. Bring blood."

"What type?"

"I have no clue. Whatever you got, everything you got, bring it. Now!"

The phone slid off my shoulder, hit the ice, and slid a few feet from me. I hoped and prayed she got that. Legally she has no choice but to act. The only way I could have held onto the phone any longer was to have let go of his severed airway. It was a miracle I held onto the phone as long as I did.

This guy was dying and I only had one set of hands. What next? Was help on the way? Was he even still alive? I took a gulp of air. It burned going into my lungs but I calmed down and got back to working on trying to save a life. It had taken too long to get to B: Breathing. How long since his last connected breath? A minute? Probably longer.

I leaned forward and began to blow softly between his blue lips. I heard a hiss of air escape out a gap in the mangled trachea I was trying to hold together. I lifted my head from his mouth. I looked down at the gory mess at his throat and pressed the two white pieces together a little

46

tighter. But I didn't want to squeeze the carotid artery and cut off the blood supply to his brain. I bent back down to his face and blew three more times. I could still hear air escape but it wasn't as loud. Some air was getting through. That's as good as I could do.

I started to shiver. Hard. Not good. The adrenaline was wearing off. I couldn't keep doing this. I suddenly heard a glorious sound; sirens from several directions. They were heading my way. I was heartened. I knew I could keep going until they arrived.

I was overdue to check what was happening with C: Circulation. He had lost so much blood already. I couldn't see anything coming from what was once a gurgling fountain. Had he bled out? I know a little about exsanguination from a case I worked—the serial killer. I still don't know how anyone can get comfortable with the coppery smell of the gooey substance that keeps us alive. My fingers were going numb and getting clumsy again. I couldn't feel a pulse. But I lowered my head and saw there was just enough trickle to assume—to pray—his heart was still pumping blood.

The gooey, freezing puddle beside us said he didn't have much left in his body to donate at the blood drive. Just focus and stay positive, I told myself. Help is on the way. Keep working. I blew into his lips again, trying to figure out how to stop the bleeding. If I pressed too hard on the jugular I'd cut his airflow—and I was barely keeping the trachea held together as it was.

The sirens were closer. Please hurry.

I kept my thumbs and pointer fingers on the trachea. I worked my pinky and ring fingers of both hands up and down each side of his neck. I was sure I felt a pulse this time. The exterior jugulars are on each side of the neck so I pressed in. I lowered my lips to his and continued to breathe for him. I thought, if this guy has AIDS or Ebola or another communicable disease, I've got it.

Some people question whether I can do one thing at a time. Apparently I can do three things at the same time.

I thought about my ruined Christmas presents and immediately felt guilty for wondering if the NYPD or some other city agency would reimburse me for my blood-soaked outdoor running gear I only got to wear one time.

Sirens were wailing closer and closer. I just had to keep going another minute or two.

What if I hadn't run this morning? I don't like to blame God for my stupid decisions, but is it possible, on this occasion, He sent me out to save a life?

Focus. Push the ends of the tube together. Press in where you think a pulse should be. Breathe into his lungs. Repeat. Stop thinking.

I felt the icy cold return like a sledgehammer. I told myself to breath. I was near the point of fainting when I heard the rush of footsteps and knew the cavalry had arrived.

Pasha Boyarov looked into her pleading, terrified eyes. She knew nothing but someone had to pay. He raised a fist as she sobbed and whimpered.

"Careful, Pasha," Vladimir Zheglov, his right-hand man said. "We need her. The best way to catch a bear is with a pot of honey."

You wanted it all, Pasha thought to himself, barely able to contain his rage and hold the punch.

Spittle flew from his mouth as he leaned forward, eye-to-eye with Ilsa.

"If I find you are holding back . . . if I find there is anything you aren't telling us, I will kill you with my bare hands. Do you understand?"

She nodded her head yes, trying to avoid the cold black reptilian eyes that were boring into her.

"He always comes home after work. I swear. I don't know where he is. He's told me nothing."

Pasha spun, grabbed a wooden chair, and smashed it against his desk. He beat the chair until only a splintered club was in his hand.

He looked at Vladimir, who looked back at him impassively. If I go down, Pasha thought, at least I know I have Vlad at my side. The only man Pasha considered more deadly than himself was his lifelong friend, Vlad.

Less than one hour earlier a door to multiplied power and wealth stood open to him, only to have a bumbling bear kick it shut. There had to be a way to kick it back open. Doors are made to be destroyed. He had been doing that most of his life.

❄ 7 ❄

I have needed time to shut the world out. I have needed to think about what happened, as painful as the experience itself was, and as painful as it is to relive it, which I have, every moment of every day spent here.

It could be worse. The Metropolitan Correction Center in downtown Chicago is a modern prison. The architects have thought of everything it seems, even giving me a room with a view. The window is seven feet high, but alas, only five inches wide. But even if it were wider and the glass wasn't too thick to break, it wouldn't offer any hope for escape. I'm on the 27th floor.

But I've been able to look through that slit in the wall at the possibility of freedom, even as I have been forced to face up to my mistakes. Yes, I now realize they were my mistakes. I own them. I have risen above the hubris that put me here. What happened was not bad luck or the work of others. I allowed it to happen. I was not true to my code. I fell short of the perfection that I thought I had attained—and perhaps had—but let slip away due to carelessness.

I'm not one for religion, but it's true, pride precedes the fall.

It is only through brutal self-examination and honesty that I can begin to write the story of my life again.

Detective Conner. Dear Kristen. I confess I underestimated you. I own that, too. You were my only mistake in seven years of living life in full. I wrote and directed all of my encounters—until you.

Why you? Even if neither of us understands the bond I felt—that I discovered—the moment I first set eyes on you, just know that my response to you is the ultimate compliment you have ever been paid. Consider it grace; something you don't deserve. You are flawed. But my eyes, my mind, still can't turn from you. I should have recognized this; embraced this; and pursued this reality. My mistake was to keep you at a distance. I will move quicker and directly next time. Be assured of that.

No, you wouldn't understand our bond, for I don't understand it myself. We only met face-to-face one time, a painful encounter for both of us, but devastating for me.

The FBI profiler continues to visit me often, praying to me for the words she longs to hear.

Dr. Leslie Van Guten is one of those people who love to prove they are the smartest person in the room. But not my room. She is so easy to read. She dreams of being famous for analyzing me and writing about her discoveries. I can see her gazing at the awards on her wall and her picture on magazine covers. She is cold, arrogant, and persistent. She let something slip that I doubt she remembers. It has offered me a glimmer of hope. I must use her arrogance if I am to reengage with the world, free from constraints. She will be of use to me. I will tease her with a gift of my thoughts—just enough for one paper or article to show her masters that her time with me is not in vain.

I've asked for an attorney. Such worthless societal parasites. But I must stay positive. I will need him too.

But ultimately it's you who will save me, Detective Kristen Conner. The thought of being with you as it was supposed to be keeps me going. You will die for what you've done, but not until you see those you love die at my hand. Only then will I grant you escape from the world—the Hell—I will create for you.

Thank you, Kristen. The thought of you is enough to keep me going.

❄ **8** ❄

The fact that I was running in zero-degree weather huddled over a man who was bleeding out made me an immediate suspect. I was walked up the hill and led into a van with no inside door handles for questioning. It was so toasty it hurt. I felt prickly, itching jabs as my fingers and toes partially thawed. But I wasn't complaining—until I warmed up enough that the jabs turned to icy stabs.

When I reached for my fanny pack to pull out my detective shield, I was ordered to stop and was promptly cuffed. That got me wide awake and my blood started to boil. Five minutes later I was able to get an officer to fish through the crowded pack and pull out my badge. The cuffs came off quickly. My anger was turning to steam but I kept my cool. I get in enough trouble with CPD for my temper, why make enemies with the NYPD?

After the uniform left to find a detective, I asked a techie who stuck his head in the back of the van the million-dollar question: "Is he going to make it?"

"Is who going to make it?" he asked.

"The guy I was giving CPR to. Who do you think I was asking about?"

"Make it? What are you talking about?"

"Did he live?" I nearly hollered.

I didn't call the techie what went through my mind. I thought I was doing so much better with my temper.

"Not unless his name is Lazarus. He's dead."

"On the way to the hospital?"

"No. He was dead when we got to you."

Okay. So maybe I didn't feel a pulse. I wonder how long I blew air into the broken airway of a dead man?

I'm a homicide detective. I've seen death. It's never pleasant. Sometimes it's horrific. I was at the murder scene where a twelve-year-old was beaten to death by kids his own age. I heard his mother scream to God for it not to be so. That case—that moment—will never go away. Neither will this one.

I followed in my dad's footsteps and became a Chicago policeman. He warned me before my first day at CPD Academy that sometimes you have to forget what you just saw with your own two eyes and move on. Compartmentalization. I understand the word in my head. I do compartmentalize. I think everyone does. But sometimes the dividers let things slip through.

Someone has to deal with bad people. You don't wallow in mud without getting muddy. You just hope a hot shower can get you clean enough to interact positively with the people you love.

My dad got shot on the job. I still wonder what he was thinking before he breathed his last. He knew I would be the first one to reach him. He set it up that way. Was I supposed to take that as a compliment?

I don't understand what he did but I still agree with him on compartmentalization. Some things have to be left behind and forgotten as much as possible. His death is one of those things—even if finding the man who shot him isn't. I carry this with me every day even if I don't like to talk about it. People want me to open up and discuss my feelings. But what's the point? What happened, happened. Dead is dead.

Life requires that we move on. Some things have to be locked away. That's what my dad said and I'm sticking with it.

❄ 9 ❄

Nazar Kublanov, Medved, the Bear, drove across the Brooklyn Bridge and pulled up to a 24-hour convenience store. He stared straight ahead, the engine idling roughly. Not the route he was supposed to be on to take the silver-haired man to an unmarked warehouse in Queens. Not the place he was supposed to be. He looked at his cheap cell phone. Eleven missed calls. The number was blocked but he knew who was calling.

Pasha. A legend in the *bratva* for his brutality combined with a businessman's style. He could beat a man to death for breakfast and then change into a tailored suit for lunch at a fancy restaurant, all smiles and charm. He would be Pakhan one day.

Med replayed all that had happened. He went on his shift at eleven the night before. It was a slow night because of winter storm conditions. That didn't keep everyone inside. He picked up a few fares. Tips were decent. Then business fell off. He sat in a line of cabs outside the only throbbing, crowded club in the Meat Packing District. No one was in a hurry to leave. He got bored. He sipped vodka. He might have dozed off a few minutes. A little after three o'clock, Pasha called him. A first. Not someone who worked for Pasha, but the man himself.

Medved was over thirty but was still the lowest-level street soldier. He got called from time to time to apply some muscle when a shop owner got behind on insurance payments, but nothing more. Not since his time on Riker Island. That's when he started drinking all day and all night long. His age and his position were a bad combination. It meant he wasn't going anywhere in the *bratva*. He'd get table scraps, but he was far from the real money that guys younger than him were now making.

He knew his days with Ilsa were numbered. She

looked too good. She had loyally waited for him to get out of Riker, but no way would she stick around with the man he had become.

Pasha's call represented a big opportunity. Problem was he had been sipping vodka. He couldn't tell Pasha that and miss out on a chance to show his value to the *bratva*, the family. So he grabbed a cup of coffee at an all-night Dunkin' Donuts and headed for the Dexter. But he lost track of time when he went down into Central Park to pee.

Now everything was a mess. The question wasn't promotion and getting back in the action. The question was staying alive.

His phone rang again. He looked at the flashing number with a dawning sense of dread. It wasn't blocked. It was Ilsa. Ilsa never got up this early. She worked graveyard shift at a bakery. She had been home less than an hour. She was always asleep by now.

He hit the green answer button.

"You okay, *konfetka*?" he asked quickly.

"Med," a gravelly voice responded. "You are there. I was getting worried about you. Very worried. You didn't show up and you haven't been answering."

It was Pasha Boyarov.

"I can explain, Pasha."

"Good. I hope you can explain things to me and to your lovely wife. Your *konfetka*. Neither

Ilsa nor I are very happy with you right now."

"I'll come explain. Where do I head? The warehouse or my apartment? Just tell me where."

"Are you alone?"

"Yes."

"I was afraid you would say that." A pause. "Where is the man? Answer me truthfully. It will make Ilsa and me happy."

Med heard Ilsa scream in pain.

"Pasha, I can explain. He ran. Into the park."

"He escaped then?"

"He fell. Bad. He's . . ."

"Yes?"

"He's dead."

"Who has him? Where is the body?"

"I don't know. Maybe he's at the morgue. Just tell me where to meet you. This has nothing to do with Ilsa."

"Do you have the man's wallet?"

Med hesitated and then lied, "No, I just take the cash."

Pasha sighed. "You found no small sheet of paper with numbers on it?"

"No, Pasha. Just the cash."

"What am I to do with you Med?"

"Do as you will. Just don't hurt Ilsa."

"Come to the office."

"I'm on my way, Pasha."

"Good. Be fast. We are on a tight schedule and you have messed it up."

"Can I talk to Ilsa?"

"Of course."

Med waited for her voice. But it was Pasha who spoke.

"You can talk to your *konfetka* when you get here."

"So tell me again. What were you doing alone in the Park at four in the morning?"

"Like I told you, I wanted to get a run in before flying back to Chicago."

"In zero degree weather? Who does that?"

Lots of people. Okay, maybe a few people. But either way, I'm not answering this guy. I don't like his condescending attitude. Of course I'm a cop and nobody likes my attitude when I'm asking the questions either.

"So you're a Chicago detective?"

I'm not covering old ground. Best way to put an end to this repetitive nonsense is to say nothing.

"I'm just trying to work with you, hon."

Hon? What year is this? If that is supposed to be the good cop half of his one-man shtick, it's pretty pathetic.

"You checked out," he says after another long pause. "And based on what I've been told I guess I'm supposed to be impressed. You've closed some big cases the last couple years. You're the one who broke the case on that serial killer guy. What'd they call him?"

I'm not answering. I know he already knows. Some guy with a popular website—the ChiTownBlogger—dubbed our infamous serial killer the Cutter Shark. It was a stupid name but it stuck. I hate that name but we all use it. Some nicknames just stick. This guy is just trying to get a rise out of me. I got a lot of press busting the Cutter. My sister did an exclusive interview with me that probably got her the job offer with WolfNews, a national network headquartered in New York.

"Still not feeling talkative?"

"I'm thinking about how I've missed my flight and I need to get rebooked on a later one. I'm soaked in blood. I need a shower. I've got to get packed. Is that talkative enough?"

He smiles and shakes his head. "Might as well put all that packing and rebooking stuff out of your mind and just relax. You're not going anywhere anytime soon."

"I'm due in the bullpen tomorrow morning. My vacation in New York City is over. Let me thank you for a grand finale."

"We aim to please. And since you aren't leaving the warm embrace of our hospitality today, better call in and tell your boss you'll be late."

That gives me pause for thought. Who is my boss? Captain Zaworski retired because he was diagnosed with prostate cancer. He was doing chemo or maybe it was radiation last I heard. I haven't checked to see how he's doing since . . . more than a month. I feel a pang of guilt. One of my colleagues on the Cutter Shark case, Bob Blackshear, was named acting head of homicide detectives in the Second Precinct. We busted a huge case with him in charge, which should count for something, but bad luck for him, it was discovered someone in our department was feeding the murderer information the whole time. That reflects bad on all of us, but Blackshear was boss so he took the fall. He's back at the Fourth.

I went into Christmas holiday not knowing who my new boss would be. I think they should look at my partner, Don Squires. He's put up with me for going on three years. Everything else should be a snap in comparison.

"You really aren't going to talk to me are you?"

"Sorry, I was thinking. I do need to make a couple calls, but you or one of your pals still has my phone."

He fishes in his pocket and hands me my iPhone. I should probably say thanks but seeing his smug face, I don't. I hope I haven't scratched the glass face when I dropped it. I keep meaning to get one of those plastic covers.

I stare at the screen—can't tell if it's scratched because of the bloody smudges on it—wondering who I should call first. I put it on my lap and look up to organize my thoughts to make a list, not sure where to start.

"Ready to talk now?"

Here we go again.

"I've talked and talked," I say. "You know as well as I do I can't be of any help here."

"Not my call."

"Whose call is it?"

"Up the food chain. Way above my pay grade."

"Just because I found a dead guy?"

"You solved the case where the billionaire's kid got whacked, too, didn't you?"

Yes I did. I give Barnes a sideways look. We've moved from the van to the back of a patrol car. The heater is blasting away and I'm sweating in my Gore-Tex and fleece running gear but my toes are still tingling. I've already shed the Patagonia coat. There is no way the blood is coming out of the fabric. I doubt I can sell it on Craig's List, even though I can honestly claim it is only slightly used.

"How long you had your detective shield?" he asks.

I think about saying nothing, but answer, "A little over two years. Actually, it might be closer to three now."

"I've had mine for twenty years and I've made a few decent take downs. But I've never landed a whale. You, Detective Kirsten Conner, have just landed in the middle of a case with whale number three. Keep it up and you'll have your own TV show."

"It's Kristen."

"That's better. My name is Tommy."

"I was just correcting you for calling me by the wrong name."

"Huh?"

"You said Kirsten. My name's Kristen."

I've corrected my barista at JavaStar for the same thing for five years with no success. Why do I even try?

"Glad we got that settled," he says. "But either way, sounds like you're finally ready to be friendly and you want me to call you by your first name."

Funny guy. I'd say something sarcastic back to him but now I'm wondering about what he just said. A whale? Who did I find dead? Actually, I found him alive. He died in my arms. I hope. Who was he?

"If you ever consider a move to New York City," he continues, "let's partner up. I'm spinning my wheels and need a promotion or I need to get rich writing a true crime book. Or maybe I could do a documentary. Either way I could use the press."

"So what's going on, Barnes?" I refuse to use his first name. "Who did I find?"

He's looking forward now and it's his turn to dish out the silent treatment. Touché. I deserve it. Although he could cut me a break after what I just went through. A guy died in my arms. That should count for a little sympathy.

"I didn't have time to look for an ID when I found him," I say. "You'd think trying to keep a guy alive counts for something."

No answer.

Okay, I'll play ball. "Tommy, who was the victim?"

"His wallet was already gone when I got there. I didn't get to check for an ID either."

I sigh. "So how do you know he's a whale? How'd you come up with a positive identification so fast? *Tommy*."

Hearing his first name a second time satisfies him and he answers, "The ID is not officially confirmed but strongly believed to be known. We know who he is because he's known."

"Okay . . . he's known because he's known," I say, confused.

"You'll figure it out later." He's still holding out.

"Looked like a politician to me. Is he someone I should recognize if I paid more attention to the news?"

"Nice guess. But no cigar."

"Are we going to play twenty questions?" I ask.

"You sure you didn't get a look at the guy leaving the park?" He isn't giving me anything until I give him something first.

"I don't even know if I saw a guy," I answer. "Might have been a three hundred-pound woman. It was dark and someone was stumbling up the path. I just caught a glimpse when he—and note that 'he' is an assumption—passed under the light pole. I was at least a hundred yards away— probably farther—I wasn't even thinking there was anything wrong because I hadn't heard the scream yet."

"I would have liked to hear that scream," he says. "The medical techie told me you weren't lying. When someone with a severed windpipe screams, it's like nothing else you'll ever hear."

Really, Tommy? You just said that? I stare forward. He drums his fingers on the door handle and knows to hold his tongue.

"Okay, Detective Barnes—"

"Call me Tommy since we're on a first name basis," he interrupts, almost with a snarl. He's giving me that New York attitude. A little exaggerated if you ask me. Am I supposed to be intimidated?

"Okay, Detective Tommy, I know the routine. You're just doing your job. You're asking the same questions over and over because it might jog a memory. But I'm telling you I have zilch."

His fingers continue to drum in a broken pattern of threes.

"So, Tommy. Who did I find?"

He turns to me and I can see him debating with himself. He finally says, "The victim was a big tuna in the business world." He pauses and holds up a hand. "Let me correct that. Not a tuna but a whale. The kind of guy that gets his picture on the cover of Forbes. But what made the ID come up so fast was he was on an FBI watch list."

"FBI—really?"

"Yeah."

"What's he into?"

"That's above my pay grade too," he answers and pauses. He decides to end our battle of who can respond the least to the other's questions and continues, "He's the CEO of some biotech company. From what I picked up, Homeland Security, the FBI, CDC, and some other agencies with initials I've never heard of think he's into some very deep and dangerous territory. When Homeland Security is in the same sentence as biotech, my mind starts thinking things it isn't getting paid to think. So I'm leaving it at that. You know everything I know now. You're a detective. You figure it out. I still expect some reciprocity when you know more."

"I'm going to make a call," I say.

"It's a free country," Barnes snaps. "So have at it."

"Where do we go from here?" I ask as I start scrolling through names on my phone.

"Our relationship?" he asks, putting his hand on my arm.

I shrug it off. I'm used to guys flirting with me on the job. It never gets old. Right? I give him a dirty look.

"We're on hold," he answers. "We're going to

drive you to wherever 'what's next' is as soon as the brass tells us where that is."

"Can I at least get a shower and change?"

"I've been told you aren't going anywhere between points A and B. Apparently you've got the reputation of being a lone ranger who doesn't always play team ball."

"Who said that?"

He smiles and holds up his hands, palms face up, in the universal "can't say" sign. I glare at him, but not because I'm mad. I'm wanting him to feel he won something, so he'll give me what I want later.

I need to let Klarissa know there's been a change of plans and I won't be checking out of the hotel. I look at my phone again. Five missed calls from my mom. No surprise. A bunch from my partner, Don Squires. Very surprising. He compartmentalizes work and home better than any other cop I know. I'm still technically on vacation until morning. So this is out of character for him to intrude across boundaries. I have missed calls from Klarissa, Kaylen, and then someone calling from a number inside CPD. Wish I knew who but all I have on my log is the main switchboard number. Squires from work? Maybe he's the new boss. I have five voice mails.

I'd like to clear them but I need to call Austin Reynolds first. My sort of boyfriend, ex-Special Forces for the US Army Rangers, and agent-at-large for the FBI is the one who has all the connections and who can tell me what I've gotten myself into. This time.

The blood from the dead man has thawed out. I don't get grossed out easily, but the goo is definitely getting to me. I'm starting to itch.

I wonder again if I can get someone from the NYPD to replace my ruined cold weather gear.

❄ 10 ❄

Med loved Ilsa as much as he loved anyone in the world but his mother. But she was dead or as good as dead. His fault. Nothing he could do to save her. Even if he tried to be a hero, Pasha or, worse yet, his *byki*, Vladimir Zheglov, would beat him like a dog and then tear him apart, limb by limb. No point dying to save someone who was already dead.

As he went through his options all Medved could come up with was that there was someone who trumped Pasha. The Pakhan. Pasha's boss. When Pasha told him no one else in the *bratva* could ever hear of this night, Med suspected Pasha was doing something he didn't want the Pakhan to know about. Could he go directly to Genken without getting killed? Maybe. Would Pasha kill him for screwing up a simple task of delivering a man to Queens? Almost for certain.

Medved wasn't clever or cunning but he knew "maybe" was a better option than "for certain." The code of the Russian Mafiya demanded he follow chain of command. But what if he brought the Pakhan a gift? Information he needed? Med opened Frank Nelson's wallet. There on top of the bills was a sheet of paper with a series of numbers on it. He sensed this was the only way to save his life—and it might work.

He looked at the gas gauge hovering near E. He backed the yellow cab to the fueling island and filled the tank with the company card. Instead of turning right and continuing into the heart of Brooklyn and then up to Queens, he swung out to the left and headed back across the bridge. Change of plans. He would head out to Long Island. Ilsa was dead but there was one man that might save his life. The Pakhan. Aleksei Genken. The most powerful man in the American *bratva*.

"Where are you Conner?"

I'd recognize that growl anywhere. Zaworski. Why's he calling me? He's retired. At least his call saved me from pulling a muscle in my brain trying to figure out who to call after Reynolds.

"New York City, sir."

"I know."

Then why did you ask?

"You're scheduled to be in the office at

eight sharp," he says. "You going to be here?"

Why do I suspect he already knows the answer? Is it my crack instincts as a detective?

"Doesn't look like it, sir. Are you?"

A good offense can be the best defense. But when I try it, it usually just makes people mad.

"Indeed I am. Our good friend, Commander Czaka, along with other members of the executive leadership team of the Chicago Police Department, in their infinite wisdom, have asked me to return to active duty to clean up some messes."

"That's good, sir. That means you're doing good, right?"

I feel another pang of guilt for not checking up on him while he was in cancer treatment.

"Don't worry about me. The only reason it is good is the Second Precinct homicide department is a mess since I've been gone and the powers that be still think I can fix problems. I might add that a lot of the mess I'm coming back to is due to the daughter of my good friend, Michael Conner."

Okay. That hurts. Not fair play.

"With all due respect sir, I don't appreciate you throwing my dad's name in my face."

Did I just say that? I told myself to let it pass. My mouth didn't listen.

Zaworski has always scared me half to death. Now he's silent. I've thrown him for a loop.

70

Inconceivable. Klarissa and I watched *Princess Bride* on Netflix last night. I'll be using the word inconceivable for the next year.

Zaworski and I were starting to get along at the end of the Cutter Shark case. On my next case, he supported and defended me when I disobeyed orders and followed a lead. *Maybe I don't play team ball all the time.* Seems like we are back to square one, where every time he scolds me I feel like a fifteen year old who gets called to the principal's office. Heck, he's known me since I was younger than that and tagging along with my dad when he caught up on paperwork at the precinct on a Saturday morning.

"Okay, Conner. You're right. I should not have mentioned your dad the way I did. May he rest in peace. Heck of a cop."

"Yes, he was."

"And the fruit doesn't fall far from the tree, Conner. You're good. Almost great. It's those messes that hold you back."

I don't know what to say. Am I supposed to respond?

"Now listen carefully, Conner."

"Yes sir."

"I have chewed you up one side and down the other since you've worked for me. Right?"

"Yes sir."

"I'm going to tell you a secret . . . if you ever tell anyone what I'm about to tell you, I'll swear to

71

them you are a liar with an active imagination. Are you ready?"

"Yes sir."

"When I'm chewing you out you have nothing to worry about. I chew you out because I care. Because I believe in you. It's when I stop chewing you out that you need to worry. Because it's going to get ugly. Real ugly. I'm old school. I do things one way. Direct. No cream and sugar needed. Understand?"

"Yes sir."

I think I know what he's saying but my mind wanders to the glorious thought of a hot cup of coffee with cream, no sugar.

"Okay, good. Back to where we are. I'm back on active duty because the Second is a mess. And you are a big part of the mess. What's the deal? You didn't like Blackshear? Did you work to get him bounced from leadership?"

Wow. I guess he really does believe in me. Here we go.

"I did, sir."

"You tried to get him demoted?"

"No. What I meant was yes, I liked Blackshear a lot. I thought he did great."

"So you liked him better than me?"

Okay, he's busting my chops. He's got to be joking. I think. I just had a man die in my arms. This isn't a good time to gig me. I don't answer.

"I'm going to ignore that silence. What is going

on there? All I know is you found a dead guy."

"Then you know about as much as I do."

"About?"

"I'm about to find out more. Unofficially I've been told the victim was on an FBI watch list. This is apparently a pretty big deal."

I can hear him blowing into the phone. "Everything's a big deal with you, Conner."

That's not fair. I don't answer. I did eight years of grunt work for the CPD. No one knew who I was unless they knew my dad. Then one day, things, big things, started happening. I didn't ask for it. I got it. I can't help it if I busted a serial killer. Or the murderer of a trust fund billionaire. Big cases are messy. That's why I leave messes.

"Let me know what's going on when you know. Then figure out how to get on the next flight to Chicago. We got to get some problems fixed here."

"I'm sorry to ask sir. You've made it clear that things are a mess. But what kind of real problems am I looking at?"

"I'm not sure I can cover all of them on the phone but I'll just give you one example. Have you attended mandatory counseling sessions since being involved in not one, but two violent and lethal altercations with the public?"

"Uh . . ."

"I didn't think so."

"I thought my three months with the FBI counted for that."

"Did you go to counseling?"

"No, but I was in rehab."

I'll admit that is a pretty feeble response.

"Exercising your knee and pretending to capture terrorists doesn't count toward what is needed to fix your mental health," he says with a sigh. "And by the way, even though my doctors have beaten me like a rented mule with radiation and chemo and my memory is still a little blurry at times, I know that you were required to meet with a CPD counselor before violent altercation number two occurred. If I read the reports and newspapers correctly, that second altercation included a dead body."

"You're the boss of homicide. Are you blaming me for working with murderers?"

"Don't get cute with me, Conner. At issue is counseling. Believe it or not we take your well-being seriously. That's why I want to know why you haven't seen a counselor."

"I don't know."

"Do you know that the psych department can suspend you from active duty?"

"I guess I did . . . I guess I do."

"Well you need to start doing more than guessing. You are officially suspended from street duty until you follow the rules."

"They can't do that, sir."

"Really? That's a good one, Conner. In fact they can and they have. And this is just the first problem I have returned to that has your name written all over it."

"Is there something that can be done? With the psych people?"

"Of course there is. Follow the rules. When you get back, you will present yourself to my office. Once we cover some other messes that need to be cleaned up, you will head directly to your first counseling appointment. I had you scheduled for ten tomorrow. I need to know when you're going to find your way back home so I can reschedule for you."

Ugh. I was hoping they had forgotten about the counseling. Does it make me a bad person to not want to beat a dead horse to death by spilling my guts over things I've experienced? What's wrong with moving on?

"Conner, I didn't return to active duty to be your scheduling secretary. Get things figured out there and call me back immediately."

"Yes sir. Any other mess I should know about ahead of time?"

"Probably. But it's more than I'm going to put on you at the moment."

Huh? I'd rather know. My stomach balls into a knot.

Barnes pokes his head out a conference room down the hall from where I'm on the phone with Zaworski. He whistles and jabs his head sideways. No doubt, Tommy-boy is a charmer.

I realize I haven't been able to get back to my partner, Don Squires. I have to call him next, even if he's not the new boss.

I sign off with Zaworski and hustle toward where we are going to meet on the murder of Frank Nelson.

More than I'm going to put on you at the moment? What does that mean?

❄ 11 ❄

Where was the Bear, Pasha wondered through clenched teeth. Time to put some of his troops on the ground and look for him. The problem was with the PathoGen deal falling apart, he was going to need every soldier he had to fight what was coming his way. Medved could have amounted to something if he hadn't lost his mind in prison and given in to the bottle. Every good Russian was supposed to love his vodka, but Med had drowned in it.

Pasha looked at the bloodied face of Ilsa and made a slashing motion across his throat. Vladimir Zheglov arched his eyebrows in response. Pasha glared and Vlad nodded, then cut the woman's throat. Too bad, Pasha thought. Ilsa wasn't half-bad looking. How did she end up with an idiot like the Bear?

"Get rid of the body and get the place cleaned up," Pasha growled to the other man in the room.

Nazar. Medved. Bear. Why did I call you of all people? Why did I put my life in your hands? You're a drunk. I curse you and you will die by my own hands if it is the last thing I do.

"Vlad do you know what has happened? Do you understand?"

Vladimir met Pasha's gaze. The problem was he did know what just happened and it was bad. Life as a soldier in the *bratva* taught Vlad it was almost always better to say too little than too much. One had to be especially careful when Pasha was mad. The two men were lifelong friends but that meant nothing when Pasha went into a rage. Vlad could read Pasha very well. He was about to explode.

"You're not saying anything Vlad. Tell me."

"You seized on an opportunity, Pasha," he answered carefully.

"No. That's not quite right. Tell me. Make me hear it."

"You saw an opportunity and were bold, Pasha," Vlad said calmly but carefully.

"You still aren't answering me, Vlad," Pasha said as he spit. "What just happened? What happened?!"

Vlad didn't answer. Pasha looked at Georgie, busy putting Ilsa in a body bag.

"Georgie!" Pasha yelled.

The man looked up, scared.

"Tell Vlad what happened."

"I don't know nothing, Pasha."

Pasha walked over to him.

"Tell him, Georgie."

"I think things went bad. Very bad."

"You are right, Georgie. Now tell Vlad whose fault it was."

"Medved's," Georgie answered quickly. "The Bear messed it up."

"Don't tell me. Tell Vlad."

"Med made a mess of things, Vlad," Georgie said, doing his best to remain calm, his eyes darting between the two men.

"But I gave him the job, Georgie. Doesn't that make it my fault?" Pasha asked.

Georgie shifted from foot to foot, nervously. Don't answer, Vlad thought.

"I guess it is your fault then."

Pasha sprang forward and got his hands on Georgie's throat as quick as a cobra hitting a rat before it darts out of reach. Vlad watched impassively as Pasha choked the man's life from him, his eyes clouding and then shutting tight.

"No need to clean up, Vlad. We won't be coming back here," Pasha said. "Get me the can of gasoline from the garage."

"Conner, could you pick him out of a lineup?"

Ten sets of eyes are bearing down on me.

"I was too far away. No chance. Not if every-one in the line was the same relative size. Like I said, all I can confirm is I saw a large person, I assume a man, lumber up the incline that leads to Columbus Circle."

The guy asking questions is the NYPD's version of Zaworski. White hair cut close. Thin—almost gaunt. He also looks very unhappy with me.

"Let us know if you think of anything else," he says with an exasperated sigh. "You've got Barnes' contact info?"

"Yes."

"Okay. Work through Tommy. We appreciate your help and what you tried to do for the vic. Best to cut you loose so you can get cleaned up."

That's it? I'm done. I wait for something else. No one says anything. That's my answer. I get up, knock the guy next to me's coffee cup off the table, and make my typical awkward departure.

I can't believe I'm done. I wanted to hear about the whale.

Vladimir Zheglov exited the room, relieved and concerned. Pasha had to get his mind right because he knew exactly what happened. He had witnessed it with his own eyes. He tromped down the stairs, thinking. It was Frank Nelson, the Swiss intermediary, Heinrich Hiller, Pasha, and him in the room at the Dexter.

There were only a few details to be ironed out between Pasha and Nelson but it took longer than expected. Once done, Hiller took off his headphones that were playing classical music, opened his computer, and inputted a series of commands and instructions. This kind of deal wasn't based on trust. That's why Hiller was there.

It is a new world, Vlad thought, scratching the stubble on his chin as he looked for the large can of gas. He couldn't follow Hiller's explanation of how he provided a two-factor exchange server. But he understood too well that both men were required to login and punch in individual codes within a set time—less than twenty-four hours from now—for either to get what they wanted. If both security codes weren't activated by the pre-arranged time, the deal was off.

So Pasha provided Hiller with the account numbers that would fund a wire transfer of $25 million to Nelson. Then he burned the numbers in the bathroom sink. Nelson was to provide a single document with detailed schematics on a pathogen along with instructions on shipping five small vials from an undisclosed location to a drop box— also unknown—Pasha had supplied. He read off detailed instructions on how to download the document and initiate the shipment.

Hiller explained again that the transaction would not go through until both parties went to the hidden website and supplied codes. Once the locked system verified that both parties had supplied their part of the bargain, it would insure and initiate the deliverables.

Vlad kicked a crate out of the way, picked up the gasoline can, and shook his head. How could a man as smart as Frank Nelson be so stupid? He could see what happened next in his mind in slow motion. Apparently this scientist and business-man could not memorize the series of numbers and letters for his code so he wrote them down. In front of everyone. Vlad watched Hiller turn his head. He knew what was happening but wanted to maintain his deniability. Vlad didn't have to look over to know what Pasha was thinking. If he had the man's code he could get the files and vials—and keep the money that the man from Moscow had given him to buy them.

This would be a huge coup. It was a typical bold and brilliant move by Pasha, except then Boyarov stepped out of the room and called the Bear. It made sense to pull someone else in to snatch Nelson. They couldn't let Hiller see them grab Nelson or, technically, it was his duty to scuttle the exchange. Plus they needed to get out of the area and on the move as soon as possible. Pasha suspected they were being monitored. They had stayed in one location too long. But why call the Bear? Bad mistake. Sure Med was close—and expendable—but the Bear simply wasn't reliable. He'd been okay to work with before Riker, but not since.

Where was the Bear now? Did he have Nelson's code? If he did, he wouldn't have a clue how much power he had in his hands. Pasha needed to settle down and work out a deal with Med. The Bear might not be bright but he knew what awaited him if he showed up in Pasha's presence. Georgie got off easy in comparison.

Things were so bad that Pasha was about to torch his own office. Where did that leave him?

In between calls to the Bear, Pasha had made inquiries through his NYPD contacts. No wallet had been found on Frank Nelson. That meant the Bear had it. Had to have it. That meant there was a glimmer of hope Pasha could salvage the deal. It would have helped to have Ilsa alive.

Vlad walked through the door to the office carefully, a hand on his Glock. If it was just him and Pasha, no weapons, who would walk out alive? Hard to say. It could go either way. If Pasha's blood lust wasn't sated on Georgie, he didn't intend to find out. They had been friends since childhood and always fought on the same side. But when Pasha was crazy, who knows?

He looked at Pasha who just nodded at him. He might be okay. Now was the time to say it.

"Pasha. Reach out to Med. Give him a way to leave the numbers for you. Promise him something—Ilsa, the money, anything he wants. You can find and kill him later. He's easy to spot."

"I've been trying. No answer. I overestimated his ability to do a simple muscle job, but maybe I underestimated his ability to think through where he stood with me. He was smart not to come home."

He handed a small box of files to Vlad.

"This is all we need from here. Go ahead and warm up the car."

Once out of striking distance, Vlad said, "Keep trying, Pasha. It is the only way."

Pasha nodded and started pouring the gasoline on the two dead bodies and then all around the office.

"Mom, are you okay?"

"Why haven't you answered?" Mom says with that accusing tone—just a hint of hysteria mixed in—that drives me crazy. Do I tell her about trying to hold a severed windpipe together?

"Sorry Mom, something came up."

"Something always comes up when I call."

"Well something really did come up that was life and death."

"You always say that, Kristen."

I'm about to blow a gasket.

"What's going on Mom? Is everything okay there?"

"No, everything is not okay, Kristen. Something awful happened."

She sounds like she's about to start crying. My stomach does a somersault as I think of my sister Kaylen and her husband Jimmy and the three kids.

"Is the baby okay? Is Kaylen alright?"

"Your sister and Baby Kelsey are fine. It's the neighborhood. We've had a murder."

"What?!"

"You remember the Kelttos."

Yeah. I remember the Kelttos. Mom's struggling to continue.

"Did something happen to her? I can't remember her first name."

"Nancy. No, Nancy is fine. It's Eddy. Such a nice man. He's cleared my sidewalk twice this winter. Someone killed him."

Ed Keltto? She's right. He is a nice guy . . . was a nice guy. Mr. Keltto always reminded me a little of the neighbor on the Simpsons. Ned something-or-other. They looked a little alike and Ed rhymes with Ned. Ed, Mr. Keltto, was old school gosh and golly. He is . . . or he was a grade school teacher.

"What happened Mom? Was it a break-in?"

She's crying and I'll have to wait. Give her a second to pull it together.

I grew up on the near west side in West Lawn, a Chicago neighborhood near Midway Airport that was a mix of blue and white collar. Our house was small and definitely in the blue collar section of the village. I never thought of it as dangerous. It helped that my dad was a cop, which meant the rougher kids knew better than to mess with the Conner sisters. With Mom alone, I've begun to wonder if it's time for her to move. She's a

84

librarian, which doesn't necessarily make her helpless, but I still worry. All three of us have brought up to her that it might be time to move. She's been very adamant she is staying in her house.

"I don't think it was a break-in," she says, clearing her throat. "It happened outside."

Maybe this is why Squires has been calling— for sure it's why Kaylen called.

"But you're okay, right, Mom?"

"I'm not hurt, if that's what you mean. But my heart keeps racing and my mind is going a million directions."

"Does this make you think about moving?" I ask hopefully.

"Of course not," she answers quickly. "Your daddy and I got this house right after we got married. I could never leave our home."

I have no answer for that. It's sweet. Not many people left who put down such deep roots.

"What's got my mind racing," she continues, "is I'm afraid the police are going to treat Eddy's murder as an accident."

Okay. What's going on? If Mr. Keltto was murdered, why would CPD treat it as an accident?

"Who's working the scene, Mom?"

"Someone you've worked with. Detective Blackshear."

"Blackshear is top drawer, Mom. You have no worries. He'll get it right."

"But I only got to talk to him for a second. He didn't interview me. He came by and introduced himself, told me he knew you, and then left a couple kids to take my statement."

"Kids?"

"You know what I mean Kristen. They're all so young now. Even you."

Even me? I'm only thirty but I sometimes feel like a grizzled veteran—whatever grizzled means.

"Listen Mom, Blackshear is good. If he says it's an accident it's an accident."

"But he doesn't know everything going on at the Keltto house."

"And you do?"

"I know something."

"Did you tell the uniforms?"

"I tried to, but I don't think they were listening. One of them kept closing his book before I'd finish a sentence. He said they had a lot of people to talk to and would stop back if they had more questions. I'm not sure he meant it."

This is getting stranger by the minute.

"What'd you tell them Mom? What weren't they listening to?"

"Something I've seen a couple of times."

Is my mom going to make me put her in an interrogation room and sweat this out of her? No wonder the uniforms weren't listening. They did have a lot of people to talk to and needed to keep moving.

"What'd you see Mom?"

"I hate to say it out loud. Maybe it's nothing. I was going to talk to Jimmy about what I should do anyway. Then this happened."

I'm a cop. Jimmy is a preacher. And she was going to sort it out with him?

"Mom, what did you see? And by the way, how did Mr. Keltto actually die?"

"It looks like he slipped on ice and hit the back of his head on the ground."

"Maybe that's what happened, Mom."

"I'm not so sure after what I've been seeing."

She leaves that hanging. Her dramatic pause is pushing my impatient button, which doesn't require too much pressure to ignite.

I got booted out of the meeting after thirty minutes by the group of NYPD officers and FBI agents who wanted to confirm what I told Tommy Barnes. I hated getting kicked to the curb but it did give me a glimmer of hope that I can get back to Chicago tonight—and possibly get a hot shower to clean off the gooey mess that still hasn't completely dried on my clothes and skin. I need to get off the call with Mom if that's going to happen. Actually, that's not quite fair to her. I'm hanging around the precinct because Austin Reynolds called to say he's close and wants to see me before I take off.

But I need to work the phone. I've got to book another flight. Then I've got to get packed. I've got callbacks to make. I need Mom to pick up the pace. But I'm not asking her what she saw again. I'll wait her out because she's not going to be pushed. I let her gather her thoughts.

"Ed leaves for work earlier than Nancy and gets home later most days."

Yes? I wait.

"I get home from the library after she's already home but before he gets home."

And? The silence is deafening.

"The same car has been parked on our street a couple times now."

"In front of their house?"

"No. About four doors down. In front of the Yaconelli's house."

"So what does that have to do with the Kelttos?"

"I've seen the same man walk from Nancy's side yard and go straight to the car. He always takes a look around and then walks fast. I thought it looked suspicious."

"Are you watching her house?"

A slight pause and Mom answers, "Maybe a little bit the last couple weeks. But it didn't start that way. I'd get home, go inside the back door, and then come out the front door to get mail and the newspaper off the front steps. I didn't think anything about seeing him the first or second time. The third time, I started thinking something wasn't quite right. I'm not surveying their house or whatever the word for it is."

"Surveillance."

"Right. I'm not doing that. But I do take a look out the front window about the same time every day now. It's not every day he's there. But it's pretty regular that he leaves her backyard and walks down the street to get his car by the Yaconelli's. Does that not sound suspicious to you?"

I might argue with her for doing surveillance on the neighbor's house—even if she says she isn't—though as an officer of the peace I know that is actually a great crime deterrent that is on its death throes. But I can't argue with her conclusion. Mom's right. It does sound suspicious.

"Did you get the make and model?"

"I did better than that," she answers, now sounding triumphant. "I've written down the license plate number."

Keeping an eye on her street is a good thing. But recording license plate numbers? I stifle a laugh.

"You're not saying anything, Kristen. Do you think I did something wrong?"

"Not at all, Mom. You did great. Listen, I have to get to the airport and see if I can catch the last flight out of JFK or LaGuardia. I'll talk to Blackshear about what you saw tomorrow. He'll make sure it gets followed up on."

"You will?"

"Absolutely. Email or text me the license

number and the description of the car. Anything else you can remember about him."

"I will. But I thought you were catching a morning flight back to Midway."

"It was O'Hare and I missed it."

"You need to pay more attention, Kristen. I told you New York City traffic would be bad on the way to the airport."

"It's a long story, Mom. I'll catch you up when I get home."

I need to pay more attention?

❄ 12 ❄

It would have been easier to head east from Brooklyn through Queens to Oyster Bay. Med didn't want to risk being spotted by Pasha, so he cut back and forth in a northwest pattern through Manhattan and jumped on I-87. The roads were still lousy but he could be there in less than two hours.

The phone blared again. Pasha. Always Pasha. He lowered the window to throw the phone to the side of the road. With more snow coming tonight plus the road crews laying down ice and pushing the slush into embankments on either side of the concrete thread, it would be a month or two before anyone found it. He needed the names and numbers that were stored in it. He held down the red button and powered it off.

Better to forget the phone for now. Having it on might allow someone to trace his location. It didn't matter if it was the NYPD or Pasha—if he was found it would mean prison or death. Plus if he answered, Pasha would promise him everything was okay and all was forgiven. But a man like Pasha never forgave. It had been a couple hours since Med had taken a sip of vodka and he realized he was thinking clearer. He had gone through the dead man's wallet. He had found what Pasha wanted. But why work with a man who had undoubtedly killed Ilsa and who would kill him with his bare hands?

If Pasha wanted the numbers there was a good chance the Pakhan did too.

"What were you thinking? Seriously, Kristen, what was going through your mind?"

Reynolds is mad, something I've never seen from him.

"Central Park in the dark in subzero weather? Are you kidding me?" he continues.

The park in the dark. I just learned something. Reynolds is a poet. I'm a little surprised at how mad he is. I've never really noticed before but nostrils really do flare when someone is ranting. Check it out for yourself. No big biggie for me. I'm used to getting scolded. This is the third time

91

I've been chewed out in one morning, counting Barnes and Zaworski.

I just look at Reynolds, waiting for him to get the lecture out of his system. I would think I am due for a hug or some other sign of comfort. I did just perform CPR on a dying man. No way was he dead when I found him. Impossible. Inconceivable. Reynolds isn't making a move my way. Maybe it's my blood-soaked ensemble. I wouldn't want to hug me either.

I actually shouldn't be surprised about the lack of bodily contact. Our relationship has been strictly platonic. I'm not great with affection under most circumstances—unless it's my niece and nephew—and James doesn't count because if I get a hold of him, he's wriggling and moving like a greased pig and releasing appropriate smells that make this a great analogy. Maybe I have arrested development. Should I bring it up with the shrink that Zaworski is making me see? I've got to stop thinking the word shrink or I'll end up saying it out loud.

Austin has seemed fine with my reserve. The perfect gentleman. I've assumed this works out for him because he wants to take things slow after going through a divorce. His ex is a colleague he has to work with on a case basis. I've met her. The ice queen. You can catch a whiff of her aura of condescension before she enters a room. If I had lived with her, I might volunteer for counseling.

Maybe I'm not being fair to her. How well do I really know Reynolds? He may be too much like me. Just keep active, keep moving—we can talk about our feelings later.

He knows I'm old school and don't sleep around. I know that makes me a dinosaur and Klarissa says I'm repressed and will die a spinster. Anyone that uses the word spinster might have a few issues of her own.

I grew up in a warm and affectionate family. I've never been abused. So why do I keep people at arm's length—and I'm not just talking about jumping in the sack with someone? I keep a protective wall up. I'd like to blame it on my dad's death. But it was there before. Is it possible that that's just the way I am? Is that a crime?

Right now, even if Austin isn't the right guy for me—and I suspect, the truth is, I'm not the right girl for him—I feel a need to be held and comforted.

I guess you can't push somebody away for months and expect him to read your mind when things change and you need him close.

We're in a coffee shop across the street from the 54th Street Precinct where Barnes brought me to meet on the Frank Nelson murder. When I called Reynolds from Barnes' car to ask what was going on, he said he was already on the way and would talk when we both got there. If he considered being in the same meeting the equivalent of us having a talk, then I guess we'll have to put our talk on hold since only one of us has a ticket to get in. Spilling coffee as I exited probably guarantees whoever is in charge won't reconsider and invite me back.

Reynolds drums his fingers on the table and repeats, "What were you thinking? You're not talking."

"Hey Austin, I heard you the first time and I think it was obvious what I was thinking. I just wanted to get a short run in the park before I flew back to Chicago. Simple as that. You're making way too big a deal out of this."

"In zero weather? In the dark?"

"You're sounding like Klarissa," I say, resisting the urge to rhyme dark with park.

"If she said you were out of your mind, then good. I hope I sound exactly like her."

"Okay, Austin, I'll check in with you next time I want to do a cold-weather run and make sure I have permission."

"Very cute. I figured you could do better than that."

"Hey, you bought me cold weather gear so blame yourself for tempting me to actually use it."

"That's a little better."

"Listen, I don't need this," I say, fed up with everyone getting in my grill for the crime of finding a murder victim. "Next time you try to hold a guy's windpipe together while you keep him from bleeding out and give him mouth-to-mouth and he dies as an added bonus, let me know, and I'll find something to grind you on."

"You can deflect and counter all you want but this isn't about me grinding you. It's about you jumping into things before you think."

Now he sounds like Zaworski. If they have the same belief about what it means to chew someone out then I guess this is his way of saying he really *really* cares.

This is the point when I'm supposed to stomp out. We just glare at each other. I wonder if we're causing a scene in the crowded JavaStar. I think my comment that he died as an added bonus insured that.

"How do you do it Detective Kristen Conner?" he asks, a bemused smile slowly appearing on his face.

"I have an instinct for trouble?" I ask back.

"That you do."

"And I might add I have a flair for getting out of trouble."

"But never for long."

He folds his arms, shakes his head, and laughs.

"You okay?" he asks.

Am I okay? Is no one listening? I just had someone die in my arms while I tried to save his life. Everyone I know bugs me to death about opening up and sharing my feelings. Now they're surprised I have emotions? I guess I'm supposed to save that for the counselor.

"I'm fine, Austin. I'll be a lot better after a shower. I think I'm ready to get Frank Nelson's blood and body tissue washed off."

Was that enough of a hint to lay off and give me a little sympathy—and maybe a hug? Last chance to read the tea leaves, soldier.

"Good, because I got to hustle over and get in that meeting."

A swing and a miss. Thank you for your tender concern, Austin. He's preoccupied. The only reason we're not yelling at each other with me stomping off is he has more important things on his mind. No more time to lecture me on not running in the park in the dark.

I do think of myself as self-aware and empathetic to the world around me. I'm just not good at this romance thing. And people wonder why I'm single and never dated much. My last reasonably long-term relationship was when I was in college. I was on the soccer team and he played football—we were both too busy to spend much time together. There it is again. I do well in a relationship as long as I don't have to regularly interact with someone. I guess I'm good at relationships as long as they aren't really relationships.

I've been told I'm good looking. But when you grow up with a sister that looks like Klarissa, you learn early on that good looking is a very relative term. She's breathtaking. When I walk with her down a busy street, men nearly break their necks to make sure they get a good look. Not at me.

I met Reynolds on the Cutter Shark case, which went almost half a year. We ended up going out for dinner a couple times. Things didn't end well between us; par for the course in my personal history of dating. Halfway through my work on the Jack Durham murder—another one of those "whales" that Barnes alluded to—Reynolds showed back up in Chicago and we made up. We've sort of been an item since. I think. I'm never sure what is up or down when it comes to my love life.

He flew to Chicago and spent Christmas Day with the Conner family—my mom, my media star younger sister, Klarissa, and my older sister, Kaylen, and her husband, Jimmy, and three children, Kendra, James, and baby Kelsey.

I still haven't figured out why the grown-up male in my sister's family is Jimmy and the kid is James, but I need to let that one go. There are more important things to figure out that I'm still clueless on.

Spending time with my family is usually enough to scare anyone off, but Austin invited me to Schenectady, New York, to meet his parents. That was interesting if you like long discussions about the history of Schenectady and why the New York

State economy north of the City is a sleeping giant while plowing seconds of Yankee Pot Pie, followed up by a huge bowl of Aunt Sylvia's apple crumble with ice cream.

I went to the Y with Austin the next day and did a hard two-hour workout to burn off a few pounds of dead cow.

I survived a three-thousand-calorie dinner and that awkward moment when Austin's mom was trying to figure out if we needed one room or two. I like Austin. More than any guy I've dated. Doesn't mean he's the one. Heck, my previous item—who really wasn't an item—bought me a diamond ring after I'd told him I wasn't going to see him anymore. He still didn't believe me after I refused the ring. He said I could hold onto it in case I changed my mind. So not quite trusting my ability to spot a winner is a valid perspective on my part. When Austin and I worked the Cutter Shark case together with his ex-wife, a small detail he decided wasn't something I needed to know, I pushed him away. Hard. I disagreed strongly with his decision that I didn't need to know that Van Guten was his ex. He hung in there and I finally accepted his explanation and apologies.

But that doesn't mean I don't have reservations about him. He is smart. He has a good personality. He is good looking. He is successful. He seems to like being with me without putting any demands on me.

Maybe that's what I like most. No demands.

Klarissa is a free agent these days. I wonder why he hasn't dumped me and made a move in her direction. Apparently they are in absolute agreement that I'm out of my mind. Not quite up to both of them kind of liking the movie, *Breakfast at Tiffany's*, but it's a start.

Would that bother me? Of course it would. But the fact that I'm even wondering something like that doesn't bode well for the dashing FBI Agent and me. That and him not knowing the one time in our relationship I really need a hug.

Klarissa begged me to come with her to NYC while she interviewed and did guest appearances for the gig with WolfNews. I think it's a done deal if they agree on the money. Her agent is in New York and pushing hard to get Klarissa there. She's done just enough modeling to generously supplement her pretty good salary, but not so much as to seem too shallow to report hard news stories. I'm guessing he sees more opportunities for enriching her and himself in New York. She just bought a condo in Chicago. She wants me to stay in it so she doesn't have to sell. She says I can pay what I've been paying on my not-nearly-so-nice place. How do you turn down a deal like that?

I had some vacation time I had to use or lose, so here I am in New York, soaked in blood.

I do wonder what Reynolds' parents think of me. Nice people. But more to the point, what does

Reynolds really think of me? He will tell me, I'm sure, when he thinks I need to know.

Reynolds starts to stand, looking at his watch again. That breaks my reverie.

"I got a few questions before you roll," I say, all business.

"Gotta keep it quick," he says.

"Yes sir," I salute. He wants to protest but I hit my first question before he can say anything. "Why was Frank Nelson on an FBI watch list?"

"You remember all that media junk on the NSA listening in on domestic phone conversations?" he asks back.

"I'm not a news junkie but sure, I remember."

"What are your thoughts on it?" he asks.

"I guess I haven't given it much thought."

"You should," he says. "It's a big deal. And both sides of the debate are one hundred percent correct. In this case, score one for the NSA. Some algorithms in the computers out in Nevada started noticing that Mr. Nelson was talking to some nasty people who don't have the best interests of the United States in mind."

"Middle East?"

"Close enough."

"Who?"

"Russians."

"Russians? Like Putin?"

"Maybe. Maybe not. What we do know for sure

is that Nelson was working a deal with some Russian-American mobsters. The Red Mafiya. At least entertaining a deal. Once the judge signs off on our California warrants we'll know more. We're tearing apart the place where he was staying. We might find what we need in New York City, but I'm guessing he didn't travel with the smoking gun."

"I thought the Russian mafiya in America was made up of Eastern Bloc dissidents and are anti-Russian government."

"That was the assumption for years. We still haven't completely figured out who works with who and who is connected to who back home—and this is twenty-five years after the breakup of the Soviet Union. It's a tight knit family. A lot of the gangsters are ex-KGB and Putin is ex-KGB and it's no secret that Putin has dreams of reassembling all or a big part of the old Soviet Empire. Ukraine is just the start. So some old enemies—or distant cousins—may have been reconnected, even if informally."

"What kind of deal was Nelson working?"

"He got degrees in molecular biology from Case Western in Cleveland, where he grew up, and Stanford. He was a research scientist early in his career but ended up on the management side of biomedicine. He's earned and lost a few fortunes with a couple biotech companies. He is primary shareholder in his own company, PathoGen.

Anything else I say is speculative, off the record, and absolutely confidential."

"Aye, aye, Captain," I say with a salute.

He arches his eyebrows and shakes his head at me.

"And I'm having this conversation with you so you can be a smart ass?" he asks.

"My sincere apologies." I agree, I'm being juvenile. "So what does PathoGen do?"

He stops glaring and continues, "They've sold a couple of patents to pharmaceuticals, but nothing has monetized like planned. The company is in serious financial trouble. We think he's got something in the lab that he was trying to sell to the Russians to feather his own nest."

"Why would Russian mobsters buy something Nelson can't sell to a pharmaceutical company? Are the bad guys planning to cure a Third World disease?"

"There's a pretty simple rule of thumb when it comes to biotech," Austin says. "Anything strong enough to cure is strong enough to kill, in proportionate measure. He was working on an Ebola vaccine but we suspect he discovered a better delivery system in the process."

Anything strong enough to cure is strong enough to kill, in proportionate measure. I need to remember that. I've never had a way with words. Maybe I can throw that into a conversation sometime with inconceivable, which this whole conversation has become now that the word Ebola has been used.

Austin is looking at his watch, which means he's desperate to get away from me and join the meeting. He's looking at me like I would have been looking at my mom if we had talked face-to-face. Yep, he's preoccupied. And seriously uninterested in me.

"Listen, I got to get in there, Kristen. In the morning I'll be on a plane to California to turn the PathoGen offices in Redwood Shores upside down. But I need to make sure I'm up to speed on what happened here before leaving town."

He'll be on a military jet to California and I'll be on a flight back to Chicago; my love life in a nutshell. I can't help but wonder again if I made a mistake when I turned down an offer to work for the FBI and decided to stay with Chicago PD. This is big stuff. I hate not being back in that conference room.

I look at my own watch. I'm running out of time if I want to get back to Chicago tonight. I have to roll, too.

Reynolds and I stand up and walk toward the front door, putting on our coats.

"Why don't you stay over another night?" Reynolds asks. "Let me take you to dinner at Peter Luger's, the best steak house in America."

No hug, but he does know my prodigious and legendary appetite.

"I'm getting chewed out by the boss. Zaworski is back and I'm in a little trouble. I've got to get back."

"Well, we need to figure another time to sit down and talk. We really do need to talk."

"About?"

"A lot of things . . . but now isn't a good time."

He looks at his watch yet again and pushes the door open. We walk out. I stay in the doorway out of the wind. He steps on the sidewalk and I watch him pull his coat up to cover his neck and face.

"Catch you later Special Agent Reynolds."

I wasn't trying to be dramatic but my tone stops him from stepping off the curb and jaywalking through a break in the traffic to the front door of the precinct. He walks back over and gives me a peck on the cheek.

"We gotta talk," he says one more time over his shoulder.

We gotta talk? That sounds ominous, same as Zaworski saying there are things I'm not going to burden you with. We gotta talk. What does that mean? If he's calling it quits, I don't blame him. How do I feel about that?

I'm standing on the street, still soaked in blood, feeling sorry for myself. I never did get that hug. Just get moving, I tell myself.

Time to get back to the hotel and pack. I look at my phone. Two missed calls from Klarissa. She wants to know what the heck is going on with my stuff cluttering the room, I'm sure. I've got to call her back. I am incredulous that I've missed another call from Don as well. Something must be up for my partner to call all weekend and on a Sunday afternoon. He's probably going to clue me in on what Zaworski didn't want to burden me with.

The screen lights up and I see a New York number.

"Conner," I answer.

❄ 13 ❄

"So things didn't go as planned this morning. That happens. But why are you here in my home, Medved? What makes you think you can come here?"

"I found something that I thought you might want to see, Pakhan."

"Then you take it to Pasha. Pasha brings it to me if he feels I should see it. You know how we work. You are never to come to my home. Med, are you listening? Look at me."

The Bear looked up. "Pasha wouldn't listen."

Aleksei Genken was about to dismiss him with a nod to his bodyguard but paused. He traced the scar under his right eye, a physical habit that helped him think. Genken was longtime Pakhan of New York City, which made him the most powerful Russian Mafiya boss in the United States, the greatest among equals. You don't hold power in a Russian *bratva* through trust. It came through knowledge. So he kept at least two spies in each of the cells that reported to him to make sure his brigadiers weren't skimming from his profits or planning a coup d'état.

"Show me."

Medved handed him a folded sheet of paper. Genken opened it and read the words and numbers carefully. The long string of numbers meant nothing. But the note underneath did. *Password to deposit $25,000,000!!!*

"What is this Med?"

"It is something Pasha wanted."

"Why didn't you give it to him?"

Med wasn't sure how to word it.

"Just say it, Medved."

"When things didn't go as planned, he got very mad. He took my Ilsa."

Genken looked at the Bear and thought.

"Where does he have Ilsa?"

"I think maybe at his office. Maybe at a warehouse he has in Queens."

"In Queens?"

"Yes," Med answered. "Pasha was very angry with me and he was hurting Ilsa. This had nothing to do with her."

"It is not good for a man to hurt a woman. *'Kazhdyy chelovek imeyet mat'*."

Medved nodded. *Every man has a mother.* He loved his mother very much. And Ilsa almost as much.

"A man should protect his woman, too, Med," Genken said.

"I would die a million deaths for my Ilsa, but I can't defend what is no longer alive."

Genken nodded. What was going on? He first assumed it was a low level operation gone wrong. But $25 million indicated an operation that was a lot bigger than anything Pasha had ever worked on—and much bigger than Pasha would do without his full knowledge. Unless . . .

"Where did this come from, Med?"

"The man on the news had it. His name is Frank Nelson. He was murdered by somebody in Central Park."

"Somebody?" Genken asked.

Med could barely breathe.

"Tell me more," the Pakhan ordered.

"He was the man I was to bring to Pasha. It is the paper that Pasha really wanted. That's what he asked me about."

"Did you give him the numbers?"

"No," Med said, hanging his head. "He took Ilsa."

Genken thought. He knew nothing of this. He was certain Med had screwed up something Pasha was working on. But what? More importantly, why wasn't he informed?

Pasha? He was youngest and boldest of his brigadiers. Genken wouldn't show it, but Pasha was also his favorite. He was undoubtedly ambitious. That was a good thing and a bad thing. How had he got involved in a deal that involved that sum of money? Who was backing him? And who was this man he was making a deal with? And why don't I know about any of this?

No doubt. This was a coup. Pasha was the edge of the sword that others were wielding. Probably Moscow ready to assert more control, something Genken had not let happen in his years as Pakhan. He remembered Soviet rule too well.

The problem in Genken's line of business was there was no safe retirement or succession plan. At seventy-three, he was feeling his mortality. He was tired of following the part of the *vory v zakone* code that demanded he forsake all relatives and family for the apparatchik. Genken would like to tend his garden and play with his grandchildren. He liked that scene in the first Godfather movie where Don Corleone had a stroke or a heart attack or whatever while playing with his grandkid. Not the heart attack. The family time. He couldn't show love to his family or it would put them in danger as a lever against him.

He felt the jagged scar tissue beneath his eye. He had sewn up the bullet wound himself.

None of his men inside Boyarov's camp had reported anything unusual with Pasha. But in addition to being bold, Pasha was smart. He had figured out who Genken's spies were and paid them off. The two men did not have much time to live. Pasha maybe had a little longer. There were things Genken wanted to learn from him. His like for the young man aside, he knew just how to make him talk.

Too bad. No question in Genken's mind Pasha would have taken his place as Pakhan. But it was obvious from the sheet of paper in front of him that Pasha wasn't willing to wait for him to die, but had already begun his move to grab power. Genken frowned. The Americans had a saying about athletes when they got a little bit older: "He's lost a step." Unfortunately, it seemed to be true of him at this moment.

He looked at the big man in front of him, shifting his balance uncomfortably from foot to foot. Medved was a loud oaf that drank too much. He was too unreliable to move up the hierarchy from anything other than a foot soldier. Genkin would never trust the Bear with anything important. So why was Pasha using him for such a big deal?

He pursed his lips and shrugged. It was obvious. Pasha planned to knock off Medved after he finished his assignment.

"Medved, I have been rude. Sit. Sit. I'll have someone bring you a cup of coffee—or maybe you need a glass of vodka?"

The Bear nodded.

"Which?"

"A small vodka might be good right now."

Genken got up from his desk, walked to a sideboard, and poured a large measure of iced vodka in a crystal tumbler. He brought it over to the man who was trembling with nervousness.

"Relax, Medved. We're going to talk. But first I need you to answer a couple of questions. Then maybe I will have you do something for me."

"Yes Pakhan."

"Drink, Med. Then tell me everything. Leave nothing out. If you tell me everything you will live. If you lie to me I will know. And you will die."

Medved was warmed by the fiery clear liquid and the hope of life. When they tell you, "I will know," is it true? Do men like the Pakhan have special powers of discernment? Or is it just a bluff?

"Conner, we didn't get off to a great start and I want to apologize," Barnes says.

We shake hands.

"No problem, Tommy, you were just doing your job."

"Thanks. Listen, I'm glad I caught you before you left the area."

We're in the lobby of the 54th Street Precinct. If he'd called me a minute later I would have already been in a cab to the Sheraton on 6th Avenue.

"So what do you need, Tommy?"

"Don't punch me, but I need you to take your clothes off."

I glare and he laughs.

"You think I'm kidding," he says, "but you know it's true. Everything you're wearing needs to go to the lab and get checked into the evidence box."

I shake my head. What a day. And unfortunately he's right.

"You didn't hear it from me," he says, "but we've not done right by you. You know the drill. No way should you still be soaked in someone else's blood. Way off protocol for a potential biohazard. If you want to file a grievance, have at it. It wasn't my call so no skin off my back."

"I'll think about that," I say, wondering if I can get the NYPD to replace my gear. "But just in case you haven't noticed, it's still under ten degrees out there and I didn't bring a change of clothes."

He smiles real big at that. Funny guy. Do I put him in a hammerlock now or later?

"Any suggestions?" I ask with all the patience I can muster.

"Don't get worked up, Conner. We've got you covered—literally."

I don't smile and he continues, "I'll walk you back to the squad room. A couple of the girls have found a spare uniform and coat that might fit

111

you. Don't worry about sending them back—they're compliments of the friendly NYPD. One of the girls will bag your clothes, you can grab a shower, change, and get on your way. Who knows, you might hook another whale today."

The girls? One of the girls? I'm in New York City, the center of US culture, and I'm hearing this. I really don't get caught up in political correctness or worry about whether my gender is being disrespected—except when it really is—but if Tommy Barnes wants to improve his career track he's going to have to work on his language and attitudes.

"I appreciate it, Tommy. Why aren't you in the meeting?"

"Same reason as you. They didn't need me when the Feds showed up. It's their show now."

"Are you still working the murder?"

"Nominally, yes. I'm not sure they actually care about the murder at this point."

"But we do and that's why they pay us the big bucks."

"No argument on that point, Kirsten."

Kirsten? Do I even try to correct him? Nah.

"Let's get this over with, Tommy."

I'm suddenly very tired. The only thing on my mind is the promise of a warm shower.

❄ 14 ❄

Pasha was in trouble and he knew it. Time to look strong or even his own men would turn on him. He had assured his backers in Moscow he could handle the PathoGen deal with Frank Nelson with no problem. They believed him and were ready to hand him the keys to the *bratva* that Genken had ruled with an iron fist for almost three decades. Pasha liked and respected Genken. He owed all his success to the man. It wasn't personal. But his time was over. The *bratva* needed fresh leader-ship. The *bratva* needed him.

Moscow's twenty-five million bucks would not be lost, but Hiller said if the transaction aborted, it could take up to a month for it to be laundered from the escrow account back to the original account in Moscow. The sum was a drop in the bucket to his sponsors, but his failure was huge.

Pasha ran his hands through his close-cropped hair. Where would the Bear have gone to hide? He had twenty soldiers out looking for him. He hadn't been seen at any of his regular haunts. A thought came to him.

"Vladimir."

"Yes, Pasha?"

"I have a suspicion where we might find Med."

Vlad looked at him but said nothing. Vlad is smart, Pasha thought.

"If you knew I wanted to find you and was going to kill you, where would you go?"

Vladimir said nothing.

"Come on old friend, humor me. Where would you go?"

"A place no one else knows about," Vlad answered.

"Do you think the Bear has such a place?"

"I doubt it."

"So where?"

"Me? I'd find such a place and stay there."

"Okay, Vlad, since you refuse to humor me, I'll tell you where I think he's gone."

"You think he's gone to Genken?" Vlad asked.

"Finally you speak. That's exactly where I think the Bear has gone."

"And that means you want to move our plans forward."

"You read my mind," Pasha said. "Can you make the move tonight?"

Vladimir Zheglov thought a moment.

"You got a few of my men out looking for Med," he answered.

"We'll call them home. Can you do it?"

"Sure. The plan is set. The men have never known the exact target or the exact night it happens. With the Bear on the loose there will be a lot of chatter. The sooner we act the better in my opinion. We don't want to lose surprise because of whispers on the street. It's always better to strike first."

"Make it happen, Vlad. Go now. Everything rides on it."

Vlad nodded and the two childhood friends hugged.

It's time for war, Pasha thought. I better change locations again. That's the way it will be until I fix this.

I couldn't believe how lucky I was to book the last flight to Chicago. But then it started snowing again and traffic was a tangled mess. I started sweating in the back of the cab, looking down at my watch every minute, wondering if I was going to miss it after calling Captain Zaworski and letting him know I was going to be at the office in the morning after all. Then the traffic jam didn't matter. I got a text message from Southwest. My flight was canceled due to weather. They rolled me over to the first flight in the morning. I let the driver know I needed to go back to the Sheraton. He shrugged and got off at the next exit.

I decided to eat the frog first and called Zaworski to let him know I wasn't going to make it after calling to let him know I was going to make it after all. No answer—a big relief—so I left him a message and let him know I'd be in by early afternoon. I'm praying I'm not actually suspended because I didn't meet with the counselor after the Cutter Shark case—or the Jack Durham case.

Maybe Zaworski was just lighting a fire under me to make sure I got the point. Or maybe not.

I called Mom to check on her and she sounded fine. She reminded me that I had promised to call Blackshear and let him know about the mystery man that had been visiting Nancy Keltto. I found Blackshear in my contact list, hit the number, and he picked up. I gave him the skinny on what Mom saw as quick as I could so I could follow up on some other callbacks. But he was in the mood to talk and I couldn't get off. We talked about Keltto's death and whether it might just be an accident. That's his initial suspicion but he takes down the license plate number my mom supplied. Then we end up swapping updates on other cases and office politics, including the return of Zaworski.

I wanted to catch Don who called a seventh time and Klarissa to let her know she's stuck with me as roommate one more night, but I couldn't get off the call with Blackshear and now the cab is pulling up to the doors of the Sheraton. I swipe my card and punch in a fifteen percent tip. The driver looks at his screen in the front seat and scowls. I guess driving on icy streets calls for a higher percentage. This trip has gone way over my budget. Rice and beans and bumming meals at Mom's and Kaylen's the rest of January.

The doorman out front offers to have my bags carried in, but I'm out of cash and have done all the tipping I plan to do in New York City.

I sling my backpack over a shoulder and pull my roller board behind me. I snag it on the rounded corner of the revolving doors and for a nanosecond fear I'm going to jam the motors.

There's a long line of tired, irritable travelers in the reception desk line that snakes through a maze of velvet ropes. I wonder how many are here for the same reason as me; cancelled travel plans.

I weave through the mob to get where I can fish out my phone to call Klarissa. Hopefully she's in the room. I didn't keep a key and it's going to take an hour to get to the front of the line and ask for one.

It's late enough in the day that there is a guy in a fancy uniform in front of the corridor to the elevators who won't let anyone pass without a key. Klarissa is on the club floor and you need a key to access it anyway. I'd have to get lucky someone else was going to the top floor or ride up and down until someone did.

I look to the left at the open bar. A cozy couple is laughing and clinking martini glasses together.

My lungs don't ask my permission and gulp in a big breath of air and let it out slowly. They do it of their own volition. I'm suddenly tired. I might even feel faint. I need to sit down.

The cozy couple is Austin and Klarissa. They look good together.

You are right Austin. We gotta talk.

PART TWO

We have to distrust each other.
It is our only defense against betrayal.

TENNESSEE WILLIAMS

❄ 15 ❄

Medved woke from a nightmare. He was in the woods outside of Vologdsa, the grimy, crumbling, industrial city he grew up in until his mom moved he and his three sisters to Moscow.

It had started so pleasantly. He was walking with his mom, hunting for mushrooms. But then his mom was no longer there and he was with Ilsa. Then he was with his roommate from Riker Island. Bobby.

Even when he was awake, Med could never remember his last name. Bobby was from Highpoint, North Carolina. He got into a bar fight on his first and only trip to New York City. He swore he killed the man in self-defense. He stabbed and slashed the man with a hunting knife he kept strapped to his lower right leg. Fifteen times. The judge and jury decided the last fourteen stabs and slashes put into question his plea of self-defense.

Then it was suddenly dark and Med was alone. He was lost. He heard the howl of a wolf and started lumbering the opposite direction. But another howl sounded ahead. He went down another path and there was a third wolf. It didn't look like him but in his dream he knew it was Vladimir Zheglov. Pasha's death angel. Waiting for him.

Then the Bear was awake, sweating and trembling. Pasha will have Vladimir hunt me until the day I die, he thought. Med was staying in a small guest room over the detached garage at the Pakhan's estate. They had talked late into the night. The Pakhan wanted to know everything about Pasha's operation; who was moving up or down the ladder of influence. Genken kept coming back to the warehouse in Queens. Medved had never been there. He had been given the general area but was to call for final directions while in route. Med wanted to be more helpful. But you can't tell what you don't know.

Better not to lie. Maybe the Pakhan does have special powers to know.

Med stood up and scratched his shaggy beard. A bead of sweat rolled down his spine into the small of his back. He shivered. He rarely dreamed or, if he did, he rarely remembered one so clearly. The doctor said he had sleep apnea that needed to be treated. He wasn't sleeping well enough to sink into REM, the place where dreams begin and come alive.

Doctors don't know everything. Maybe I don't want to sleep better.

He reached over to turn on a light but as his hand neared the pull chain, he heard an explosion of sounds from the main house. He wet his pants. He moved to the window and saw—and felt—a kaleidoscope of flames from the muzzles of automatic rifles. Kalashnikov AK-47s. What the . . .

Med had gone to sleep thinking he might survive the wrath of Pasha, though the shadow of Zheglov would follow him everywhere. He was with Aleksei Genken after all. The Pakhan.

In a nauseating flood of dread, Med realized that maybe not even Genken could save him.

Could it be? Would Pasha be so bold? Would he move against the man?

Med peaked through the window slats as an explosion opened a gaping hole in the side of Genken's house. The Bear fell backwards.

No question. Pasha was making his move. Would the other brigadiers of the *bratva* follow him? They would if he succeeded.

I can't sleep. Is it the music with the pounding bass in the room next door? Or is it the couple going at it in the room on the other side of me? Or is it the fear of contemplating just how many germs are in this dirty, dingy room? I finally found a vacancy at a motel on the edge of Manhattan and Harlem. No way could I stay with Klarissa after what I saw.

Did I just see what I think I did in the lobby of the Sheraton? Would my sister do that to me?

I consider pounding on the walls on each side of me. I don't have the energy to be ignored.

"Nazar, you are now my Medved—my Bear. I have work for you to do."

The Pakhan had been so reassuring. Med's head spun as men came and went and Genken worked the phones.

Before dismissing him to get some sleep in his guest room . . . or was it a prison room? . . . Genken took a call and roared in laughter, looking at Med the whole time. When he hung up, he walked over to his fax machine that had sprung to life. He picked up the single page and handed it to him.

"Med . . . the runner in the park . . . of all things . . . it was a detective from Chicago. You have a problem. And since you are now my bear, we've got a problem. Your runner was police. That is a bad thing. A very bad thing. It's always better to be friends with the police, not enemies."

"What must I do to fix this?" Med asked, eager to please—and stay alive.

"We will instruct you in the morning. Tonight, study the paper I have given you. Memorize every detail. Make sure you can recognize her face no matter what she is wearing."

Med nodded numbly as he looked in the dark eyes of Detective Kristen Conner.

"Med, look at me," Genken said.

Medved looked in his eyes.

"I don't have to tell you. You already know what you must do. We will find a way to get you to Chicago. But realize you will never be safe until she is dead. That is rule number one in the *bratva*."

Med nodded in agreement.

"Consider this a test. Do the deed. Then come home and we will see what else that we have for you."

That's when Med was finally escorted to his room. They hadn't armed him—and the door to his room was locked from the outside. Not good signs, he knew, but he was alive and death would wait at least another day.

Another explosion and round of automatic gunfire sounded. He got off the floor and lumbered across the room and checked the handle. Locked, just like he knew it would be. Now what? Sporadic shouts, screams, and gunfire continued across the driveway.

I am not a lucky man, he thought with a sigh. I suppose I was lucky when I married Ilsa and we made it to America. But nothing ever changed. My entire life has been a battle to survive.

Med could barely breathe from fear. He cursed his bad luck again. But he had to admit his troubles tonight were his own doing. He had drunk two bottles of vodka. He had to pee. So he had trudged down the path into Central Park to relieve himself and missed picking the man up.

Who knows, he might be with Pasha, carrying a Kalashnikov, right now.

The gunfire died down and picked back up.

You are alone in the woods. The wolves are before and behind you. What do you do now?

The answer was easy. A bear would stop running and climb a tree. He looked at the ceiling. In the corner was a small wood-framed square. Could it be? He moved a chair over, stood on it, and pushed. A miracle. It was unlocked. The attic door opened with a spring release. A small ladder was folded into the opening. He pulled the end of a rope and lowered it. He quickly ducked when an explosion boomed and a ball of flame lit up the night sky. Staying low, he looked around the room. He opened the door of the small bathroom, grabbed the towel, he had used, and wiped everything down. He crawled over to the bed and straightened sheets, pillows, and bedspread. He moved the chair back in place and picked up his filthy, smelly clothes. He started up the ladder, tossed the clothes through the opening above him, and squeezed through the hatch. He reached down and pulled up the ladder, folding it one section at a time. He fumbled around until he found a small handle and clicked the door in place, something the last person up here hadn't done. He breathed slowly. It was completely black in the attic.

He poked around with his foot and located a piece of plywood resting on ceiling joists. It wouldn't be comfortable and his wet pants were itching him. But there was adequate heat so no problem. He was alive. He was Russian. That made him a survivor. He just might live to see another day. He would miss Ilsa, but there was nothing he could have done to save her.

What about the detective in Chicago? He had her name. She identified him. He would have to do something about her. The Pakhan said he would never be safe with her alive.

Herr Hiller drummed his fingers on his polished oak desk. He looked at the clock on his bookshelf. Four in the morning. Eleven o'clock at night in New York City.

He had arrived in Geneva on the last flight from JFK, landing at almost midnight. He knew he would not be able to sleep so he had his chauffeur bring him straight to his office on the Rue de la Servette to watch the completion of his services.

The name of the street described the man and his work. He was a servant. He had created a small fortune for himself and his family by handling certain types of transactions, where two or more parties didn't want a transaction to be known—and didn't trust each other. He served as the bridge of trust and circumspection. People were happy to pay his exorbitant fees.

It did not matter if the two parties failed to meet the conditions of the final transfer . . . his fee was paid up front and was nonrefundable.

Somehow he was not surprised that neither the American nor Russian had punched in the code.

As a servant, it was not his job to judge. But he saw signs of trouble when he was called into the room to activate a sequence that would download to the Russian a large file and initiate shipment of a small package, while wiring to the American what he assumed was a large sum of money. Once done, his server would be wiped clean with a sophisticated electronic scrubbing program. Retrieval of what had transpired would be impossible no matter what level and sophistication of tools were used.

Hiller had explained slowly and carefully that if either party failed to input the required code, there was nothing he could do to rectify such an unfortunate error, not by choice, but due to the design of the system. That was the beauty of his service. He knew nothing and could do nothing once the wheels were set in motion. That fact kept him safe.

The clock was silently ticking. He felt an uncustomary sense of unease.

It is impossible to judge what you don't know. But he would be glad when this business was done.

Perhaps it was time to take his wife on an island vacation.

He looked at the screen. He heard the sound of

a tiny blip and the whir of fans as the scrubbing program went into effect. That was only the tip of the iceberg. The real data was in the deep web. Not all the intelligence services of the world could put together what had just been torn apart and scattered in an ocean of non-indexed data.

Somewhere warm and sunny. That is what he would do.

❄ **16** ❄

"So Kristen, what has brought you here today?"

My eyes narrow. Is she being polite or is she really asking why I am here? CPD is outsourcing more and more services, including psychological testing and therapy. Surely they provided her with a report on why I am required to be here.

"CPD policy," I answer tersely.

She pauses with raised eyebrows. Zaworski warned me to at least pretend to appear warm, open, healthy, and normal. "We need you working," he said.

"Which I think is good," I quickly add. "I'm way overdue. I'm glad to be here."

How stilted did that sound?

"Okay. And what do you hope to see happen in our sessions?"

"Uh, basically I want to . . . uh . . ." What I want to say is get this over with, but I behave myself

129

and say, "make sure I've properly processed a couple violent incidents that have been part of my job experience."

"Do you want to tell me about them?" she asks, perhaps a faint smile at the corners of her mouth.

"Just to clarify, are you telling me to tell you about them in question form or actually asking if I want to?"

"Which should it be?" she asks primly, looking me in the eyes serenely, though she is starting to give little kicks with her high heeled right foot that is dangling from her crossed legs. That means I am irritating her or making her nervous. I'm not a psychologist but I do have some psychological insights.

I try not to let her see I've noticed, but she does, and stops. She recrosses her legs with left on top and smooths an imaginary wrinkle from her black skirt. We are sitting in two facing chairs, leather on wood, ergonomic design, probably very expensive. I'm thinking she is late thirties or early forties. Black hair—might be some subtle hints of red and purple from a bottle—pulled back in a loose French braid. Knee-length black skirt, white blouse with a Peter Pan collar, and a lovely purple cardigan. Or eggplant. Nice. Maybe I should look at upgrading my wardrobe. She is holding an electronic tablet with a thin stylus poised over the screen for taking notes. Or she's watching screaming goats with the sound turned off and is pretending to listen to me.

I hear Zaworski's growl echoing in my mind: "Behave. This is serious."

"I think I'm getting off to a bad start and being difficult," I say contritely. "It's an occupational hazard. I'm used to being the one who does the questioning. I apologize."

"No need to apologize."

"Sorry about that."

Now she's really making me nervous.

"Where should I start?"

"Where would you like to start?"

Just tell me what you want lady. I'm exasperated but trying not to show it. Just hit it, Kristen, I say to myself. I walk through the main points of the Cutter Shark case in the next fifteen minutes, concluding with our violent encounter. For some crazy reason I show her the scar on my wrist and knee and then spend the next twenty minutes talking about my soccer career. She looks like she might ask a question so I keep momentum and plow right into my last case, the murder of billionaire heir Jack Durham, which ended with me in an apartment with a dead body. It takes fifteen minutes.

"I think that's everything," I say, coming up for air.

"I understand you were witness to a murder yesterday morning as well?"

131

"Not exactly a witness. The murderer fled before I got there."

She watches me.

"That really wasn't CPD business."

Her look remains impassive but she jots down another note. That might not have been the right thing to say.

A soft ping sounds from her desk. She looks at her oversize man watch. I wonder if that might signify she is more motivated by control and power in her dealings with clients, but I stifle the temptation to broach the subject.

"I'm afraid that our time is up."

Whew. I'm relieved. That wasn't so bad.

"Shall we make this our regular time to meet each week?"

Uh oh.

"Ummm . . . earlier is actually better for me. Once I hit the office and we get rolling on things it's sometimes hard to pull away from a case."

"Are you planning to go back to work?" The eyebrows are back doing their thing.

"I was certainly hoping to. I had quite a bit of down time last year after the Cutter Shark case. I took a couple months off."

"I thought you were part of a training program at the FBI Headquarters in Quantico."

"Well, I was. But I spent a lot of time rehabbing my knee and then I went to classes so it kind of felt like a vacation."

"I see."

I wish I did. I'm pretty good at reading people. She has the therapeutic neutral look down to perfection.

"Is there a problem with that? I really would feel better working than sitting around."

"You love what you do, don't you?"

"I do."

"I'll see what I can do. I should have an initial report to your Human Resources Department by early next week. It will be up to them."

It's Tuesday. I landed at 10:30, took a cab to the Second, met with Zaworksi for fifteen minutes, then headed to Dr. Jeana Andrews' office in Wrigleyville for our two o'clock appointment. I can't believe I'll be sitting the pine the rest of the week.

"Is there any way we can expedite the report?"

"Why the hurry?"

"I do better when I'm moving, when I'm busy."

"Is it possible that slowing down right now might not be a better idea?"

"Look . . ." I take a deep breath. Slow down. Don't attack. "I will confess I'm not the most expressive person, though that doesn't mean I'm not introspective and self-aware. But I know myself. I love my job. I have no qualms about my actions in putting away a serial killer. I have no qualms about defending myself against a murderer."

"What about your dad's death?"

Oh boy . . . she did read her notes. I'm not going to tell her that my sister is dating a guy I thought I was dating less than twenty-four hours ago.

"That hurts every minute of every day. But I deal with it and am dealing with it. All the more reason to work."

She looks at me long and hard. She glances at her watch.

"I'll see what I can do, Detective Conner."

"Thank you, Dr. Andrews."

"Next Tuesday at . . . ?"

"Is eight too early?"

"Let's say nine."

"Sounds good."

I was actually hoping to be in the office by nine but don't want to seem difficult. I add the appointment to the calendar on my iPhone.

"I'll be here with bells on."

We shake hands and I exit her office into the empty waiting room. I wonder why we couldn't have kept going if no one else is waiting to meet with her. Next week might not have been necessary. It then occurs to me that this is not going to be finished to her satisfaction in two or three weeks. How long is she expecting us to meet?

I exit the waiting room and walk down the hall to the bank of elevators. I put on my coat in the lobby. It's a gray, windy, freezing Chicago day.

Lake Michigan is threatening to dump another load of snow overnight.

With bells on? What does that even mean?

Am I really going to be in therapy for an extended period of time? Inconceivable.

❄ 17 ❄

"Good tip, Conner, tell your mom thanks. She rocks."

My mom rocks?

Blackshear called as soon as I pulled into traffic. I'm still driving Klarissa's Nissan GTR, which will do 160 miles-per-hour—though not advisable in Chicago's winter land. It has Bluetooth and I'm hands-free. My beat-up Miata with a couple plugs on the dashboard that don't work is in the shop. I was planning to drive Klarissa's car for a week. Not after what I saw. I wanted to drop it off at her condo and then get a cab to the shop before it closes tonight. It was kind of settled that I'd live in Klarissa's place for however long she is in New York or until she wants to sell the place. After her betrayal? No way. I'll pack my stuff and go to Mom's house tonight. I wish I hadn't given up the lease on my apartment. I've never felt quite right there since I discovered I had an electronic stalker. But this new arrangement is unacceptable.

"So there's something to what my mom saw?" I respond.

"There's a lot to what she saw."

"You don't think it's weird my mom was monitoring Nancy Keltto?"

"Hadn't thought about it being weird or not weird. I'm glad she noticed something amiss in the neighborhood. Your mom delivered a gold mine. Things are not looking good for Nancy Keltto—except to us. We're driving over right now to read her rights and bring her in."

"Mom's lead was that good? Oh man. What have you found?"

"She's been having multiple affairs the past five years. She's been with her latest lover for a couple months. She actually had divorce papers ready to be served to Mr. Keltto today."

Mr. Keltto. Ed. Rhymes with Ned. Seemed like an awfully nice guy. Nancy seemed okay, too. What happened to those two?

"Are you looking at the boyfriend, too, Bob?"

"No, Conner. We don't think of things like that unless you are on the case with us. We're idiots."

"Sorry, Bob. Just checking. Don't blow a gasket."

"Yeah, sorry, Conner. It's been a lousy few months after getting busted back down to lieutenant and put through the ringer over the Durham case."

"None of that was your fault."

136

"Tell that to Czaka."

Maybe I will. We've had a few run-ins over my dad's shooting. Czaka put the investigation into the cold case files.

"But to answer your question, Conner, yes we're looking at him. The boyfriend. I could definitely see him being an accessory. He is in LA on business so he'll have a convenient and iron-clad alibi for the time of the murder. I'll be disappointed in him if he doesn't.

"When I got him on the phone he tried to bluff me that he didn't even really know Nancy Keltto. I'm not sure why potential suspects think lying on something we can check on easily or already know is going to help them. It only and always makes them look worse. The same with Nancy telling us there were no problems with her and her Edward. If she'd told us straight out they were on the ropes we'd at least give her the benefit of being forthcoming."

"So you are going to for sure read her her rights?"

"I think we need to. She's crossed the line from person of interest to suspect with this affair your mom handed us. I don't want Nancy Keltto saying anything else incriminating that a lawyer will argue later on was coerced or otherwise inadmissible."

"How about the guy? You going to read him his rights?"

"We're not going to charge him yet. He's flying back from LAX tonight. We'll pick him up for formal questioning when he lands. But the talk will be voluntary, at least this once. No Miranda yet. He didn't indicate he felt the need for an attorney to be present. I'd like to keep it that way for our first sit-down."

"You know this is really strange for me, Bob. This is my growing up neighborhood. We weren't close with the Kelttos or anything, but I saw them around. Nancy always seemed fine to me. Now she's a murder suspect."

"She was a suspect the day her husband was killed. You know as well as I do the spouse is going to be the first suspect."

"Maybe there's a reason I'm single," I say with a laugh.

"Sad but true, the vast majority of murders in America are at the hands of someone close to us. We have a funny way of showing love."

"So you like the two of them on this?"

"Why not? I'll say it the other way around. I would be surprised if we found they were *not* in this thing together."

"Any forensic help?"

"A couple things. Again, tell your mom her lead was solid gold. We went back to the crime scene and looked at things a little differently and, hate to admit it, a little more closely. The ground was frozen solid but there were just enough flurries that we were able to trace Edward Keltto's movements the morning he died. He shoveled his walk and drive and the neighbor lady's. But then we discovered something strange. We couldn't find his footprints from the house to the garage. But guess whose slippers we do have?"

I don't even have to answer.

"But Nancy found him," I say.

"Right. But what happened to his footsteps to the garage that morning? We think someone might have done some sweeping."

"Which means someone else might have been there."

"True. But how did they get there?"

"And you don't think he just slipped and fell?"

"That's where it gets interesting. We asked the ME to take a closer look. Apparently Keltto's got bruising on his front left cheek and two contusions to the back of his head. The ME is digging a little deeper on it. At first glance he said either of the contusions would match up with falling backward and hitting the back of his head. But not both. He isn't confirming anything yet but he thinks he was hit in the back of the head twice, once from a blunt object and once from the concrete. You add that with no other footprints but Nancy's—and her having motive—and I think I might have a righteous case."

"Sounds good."

It actually sounds horrible. Ed Keltto—Mr.

Ed—he was a nice guy and now he's dead.

"I'm just playing devil's advocate here, Bob, but if she was planning to murder her husband, knowing she'd be a suspect, wouldn't Nancy have thought through all this? She sounds good for it but I would like her even more if she had an alibi. Seems almost too easy doesn't it?"

"This job is tough enough not to take a gift. I'll take easy every now and then and be grateful."

"No argument there. On a personal level, this is just sad. I was planning to head over to Mom's house tonight anyway. Now I will for sure. She'll be freaking out when word gets out that Nancy has been arrested."

"Thanks for reminding me. That's why I called. I'm heading to your old neighborhood in a few minutes. You want to join me for the arrest? My new partner, Michael Shepherd, has got this flu that's going around and went home early. I need a second. Then you can go over to your mom's."

"It would be weird to arrest the lady down the street I grew up with."

"I understand. I'll find someone."

"Forget it. It's part of the job. I'm on my way."

"Good. You're a life-saver, Conner."

One part of this mess will actually work out good for me. It will save me having to explain to Mom why I am moving out of Klarissa's place and in with her. I'm not ready to deal with Klarissa and Austin. Truth is, I have no clue how

140

I'm going to handle that personally, much less with the family.

Klarissa. Klarissa. You could have had him. All you had to do is wait for Austin to break things off with me. I don't know where things stood with us, but common sense and family loyalty would tell you to give it a few months. I would have been fine with that.

I arch my back, which is aching. That usually means I need to stretch out my hamstrings. My bed in Harlem was awful.

The phone chirps. Austin Reynolds calling. I let it go into voice mail. We really do need to talk. Just not yet.

❆ **18** ❆

I finally call my partner, Don Squires. He gave up trying to reach me. I didn't see him on my way in and out of Zaworski's office on my way to Andrews' office.

"I can't believe you decided to call back. So you are still alive?" he answers.

"I am indeed. Sorry to be the bearer of bad news."

"How'd your meeting with Captain Z go?"

"Hard to say. Have you heard anything?"

He pauses. Not a good answer.

"Spill it, Don."

141

"Let's just say Zaworski has not had anything good to say to anybody or about anybody since he returned. You saw what he looks like. He's lost about thirty pounds and he was already thin. He looks like an extra on *The Walking Dead*."

"I can tell when you're evading, Don. Have you heard anything specific on my situation?"

"Right before I left the office he said I'm still flying solo until you are cleared to return to duty."

"I met with the psychologist this afternoon. I was hoping I would be good to go today."

"You aren't being very realistic on this counseling," he says. "You know, the more you fight it, the more your doctor is going to assume you need it."

"You're probably right," I say, thinking he does have a really good point. "So Zaworski was still there when you left?"

"As of ten minutes ago."

"I might call him. Maybe he's heard from HR and I'm cleared. The therapist said she'd work on it."

Don laughs and says, "You aren't listening and you just won't give up. He actually just got off the phone with HR when he called Martinez, Green, and me in to let us know we're still down a man—or in your case, a crazy woman."

"Ha ha."

"Do you want me to tell you I told you so on the counseling now or later?"

"Have at it," I say. "I deserve it. But I don't think that's why you tried to call me fifty times. What's up with you?"

I hear him clear his throat and suddenly realize what I've done out of habit. How stupid could I be?

"Uh, Don," I interrupt before he can start his first word.

"Yeah?"

"I might have a problem."

"We've already established that."

"Funny guy. I mean a CPD problem. I'm on my way to meet Blackshear to arrest Nancy Keltto."

"KC . . . what the . . . are you out of your mind?"

"Possibly."

We're silent for a moment.

"Don, you still there?"

"Yes. Just tell me you're not going over and then I am going to hang up. We can talk tomorrow. Devon has a hoops practice tonight and I told Vanessa I'd get him there. I'm coaching his team."

I'm scrambling to think of how I can ask him.

"You're not saying anything, KC."

Just eat the frog and do it. "Don, I need you to help me out."

143

❄ **19** ❄

We're all just one happy family. Mom is in the kitchen with my sister, Kaylen. She's been crying the last hour. Squires cancelled his family plans and partnered with Blackshear on the arrest. She was taken in a squad car, complete with whirling blue lights and a couple siren squawks on the way out of the neighborhood, to the booking room at the Fourth. The case might be coming to the Second because apparently they are experiencing the Plague this winter.

Blackshear followed in his car. Squires is eating a piece of blackberry cobbler and just listening to Mom and Kaylen talk without comment. I've been in and out of my seat at the table. He's better at providing that reassuring presence than me.

I helped Kendra with her homework for fifteen minutes and she is watching a talent show on TV. She's decided she wants to be an international soccer star and a pop singer and a detective like me. I'm not going to be the one to tell her that dreams have to be at least a little realistic. She'll be ten in a couple months.

I've ended up sprawled on the living room floor playing toy soldiers with James, wondering when they are going to stop shooting each other and call a truce for the night. He's tired but don't tell a six-year-old that—in his case, he'll get a second wind. He is slurring his machine gun rat-a-tats. I want to tell him to say it, not spray it, but that, too, will have an opposite effect.

I look over at Kendra who is lip-syncing with the performers while cradling Kelsey on her lap. Great baby. She is sleeping peacefully despite the battle her brother is staging.

I'm happy with the setup. Keeps me from thinking about what to do with Klarissa. I've got enough secrets in life. Would one more hurt? Can I just pretend I never saw her and Reynolds in the lobby bar of the Sheraton on Seventh Avenue? Austin says we need to talk. Fine. I agree. And I think I might be ready because I might have figured out how to handle this. He can break things off with me. I'll act surprised and appro-priately hurt—for a day or two. Then he and Klarissa can make a show of just happening to discover their mutual attraction after a couple months. Two months should suffice. It might be a little awkward if they become a couple and she brings him to Chicago, but certainly not the disaster we have brewing. If Reynolds needs some prompts I'll provide them. No one would be the wiser except for me. It wouldn't be the first time I kept a secret to protect my family.

I start to stand and James immediately begins to protest that he's not tired and wants to play more.

"Shhh. You'll wake the baby. I'll be right back, General. I need to check on the grown-ups."

"Tell mommy I'm not tired," he says earnestly. His eyes have dark circles smudged around them.

I'm tired myself. I meet with Captain Z at eight sharp in the morning, with an emphasis on sharp. The kids have school. Mom has work. Time to wrap things up.

My phone goes off again and Kelsey is immediately awake and in full lung. I'm about to block what I assume is another call from Reynolds— I'm ready to talk but not right now—when I see a New York number pop up. It's almost eleven, so that makes it midnight there.

"This is Detective Conner."

"Kristen. It's Tommy."

I pause. Oh, Barnes.

"Yes, Lieutenant? You're working late tonight. Or is it early?"

"Both. Have you watched the news?"

"I've been running all day and have a family situation I'm dealing with. Can this wait until tomorrow?"

"Absolutely not."

"Really?"

"Not if I want to keep my job and you want to stay alive."

"What's that supposed to mean?"

"We've got World War III going on over here—

and apparently you are part of it. I'm serious. This is big, Kristen."

"Hold on a sec, Barnes. I'm going to get my partner and put you on speaker, if that's okay."

"You're out awfully late with your partner aren't you, Conner?"

"Save it, Barnes. Give me a sec."

"Take your time, Conner. All I'm trying to do is save your life and you get prickly about a little kidding."

I hit mute. Prickly? Me? I guess I better start calling him Tommy if I don't want him to pout.

"Kaylen, we've got it all under control here. You need to get those kids home."

"You said you'd play more!" James shouts.

Kelsey lets out a scream. I give James the I'm-not-messing-around eyeball and he shuts it down. Kaylen looks tired. She nods and stands up to bundle everyone up.

"Yeah, I need to get going, too," Don says.

"Don, I need you to stay just a second," I say.

He looks at me in disbelief, taps his watch face, and shakes his head, but sits back down.

"What's the matter, honey?" Mom asks me. She looks drained.

"Detective Squires and I need to handle a call. I'll tell you what's up if you're still awake. But you need to start getting ready for bed."

Who is the parent here?

I kiss Kendra and Kelsey and hug my sister.

James is mad and tries to escape, but I snag him long enough to give him a bear hug and loud smooch kiss.

"Gross!"

Now that's what I call a prickly attitude. Maybe he'll work for the NYPD some day.

"Don, let's head into the dining room. I need you to listen in."

"Can I pour another cup of coffee?" Mom asks.

Don shakes his head no.

"Half of one for me," I say. "Then you need to head to bed."

Was that enough of a hint?

Don and I ended the call with Barnes an hour later. My battery is about dead. I've missed more calls. Klarissa. Reynolds. They can talk to each other while they wait to connect with me. They're the least of my worries now.

Barnes wasn't lying. New York City is in the middle of a war. A whole lot of Russians with names I can't follow have been shooting each other all day. The mayor hasn't been on good terms with NYPD and is about to drop another notch or two in their esteem. He's ordered mandatory double shifts and is threatening to initiate a curfew to commence tomorrow night at six if the bullets are still flying.

We had to clue Don in to what happened with me in Central Park less than twenty-four hours earlier since he just got bits and pieces out of Zaworski. Don loves to gig me. But to his credit, he just listened and asked a few pertinent questions. No trash talk toward his partner.

When I asked Barnes to clarify how I figured in all of this, he said they made an arrest of one known foot-soldier in the New York *bratva*—I guess that's their version of mafia. When they searched his car they found an AK-47, a sniper rifle, and my picture—along with my work and home addresses, my cell number, and a list of frequent haunts, including church and two health clubs. That is scary even if they have my old apartment address, not Klarissa's condo.

It is suspected, with good reason, there is a death warrant out on me.

I think I do need to call Reynolds. I need to find out everything he knows and he is higher up the law enforcement food chain than Barnes.

Don watches as I hit speed dial. Reynolds doesn't answer. Then I think of Klarissa. I wonder if it is known she is my sister. I call Barnes back and ask him to put a security detail on her.

"Good call, Conner. We should have done that already."

"Thanks, Tommy. I appreciate it."

Nothing is going to keep me from being mad at her and Reynolds. But I love my sister. I already had one case put her in harm's way. Dear God, please don't let that happen again.

"You better call the Big Z," Don says.

"You said it yourself. He looks awful. I'll let him sleep. This can wait for morning."

"This is serious business, KC. Call him now."

"But they got the guy with my picture so it might be over. You heard Barnes say that yourself."

"What I heard him say very clearly is that this might not be over."

"Don, you need to go home and show your face and tell Vanessa how sorry I am I screwed up family plans."

Don ignores me and points at my phone. On cue the battery dies and gives a death beep. Don sighs and calls Zaworski himself.

I walk down the tiny hall and peek in my mom's room. She is fast asleep. Good. Hopefully she'll forget that I told her I'd let her know what was going on in New York. She doesn't need to hear this.

Don and I drive separate cars to the Second. Zaworski took Don's call and is convening a late night meeting.

❄ **20** ❄

The Bear waited as long as he could. He lay on a sheet of plywood someone had put on top of some roofing joists for a full eighteen hours. The gunfire had stopped about fifteen minutes after it started. Then came the sirens. Then came the muffled sounds of police searching around the house for evidence and banging in and out of Genken's estate house for hours. Then there were two sets of footsteps on the floor below him and the sound of furniture being moved around. He was sure someone would say something, point to his hiding place, and one of them would scrabble up the folding ladder.

He hadn't decided whether to surrender or kill anyone who poked a head through the opening— it would be like the whack-a-mole arcade game he liked—when a radio squawked. Both sets of footsteps left the room and went downstairs.

He was still alive and free at the moment. What more could you ask for?

After it was quiet for a couple hours, he finally pushed down on the latch with a quick jab and the ceiling door popped up. He pulled it open with a loud squeak of unoiled springs. He held his breath for what felt like a full minute. No response. He lowered the ladder and climbed down stiffly. It was much easier to squeeze through the opening on the trip down. He took care of an urgent matter first and visited the toilet, cleaning himself up after lying in urine and excrement. He walked over to his prison door. Whoever had been there to check for signs of life was considerate and left it unlocked.

He went back to the window, pulled the corner

of a curtain, and scanned the driveway. There were three black and whites parked there but no one was outside, at least not in his range of vision. He exited the garage through a rear door and wended through the trees to the back of the grounds where a wall awaited him. Was the security system still activated? With all the coming and going, quite possibly not. Heck, it might have been blown up in the battle. It didn't matter. He had to at least try to get out of the area.

The stone wall blocking his escape was ten feet tall. Not good. At six-seven he was tall enough to reach the top with just a little jump. But with his weight, no way could he pull himself up and over. He looked around. In a small clearing there was a decorative concrete—heck it might be marble—birdbath, resting on a pedestal. He pushed the basin off the pedestal, trying to keep it from falling. The sound of it hitting tile seemed to echo for miles. He looked around. No movement. He heard no sound of footsteps running his direction. Sorry, birds, you'll have to land somewhere else for a drink.

He gripped the pedestal in two hands. It must weigh three or four hundred pounds. But he was Medved. He couldn't do a pull up with his body weight but he was the Bear, and everyone knows a bear is quite strong. He bent his knees, keeping his back as straight as possible, and hoisted it to his body. He duck-walked it over to the wall.

Was there wire and cut glass on top of it? Didn't matter. He couldn't walk out the front gate.

Two minutes later he fell to the ground on the other side, turning his ankle. He hopped around in pain but bit back the urge to yell.

He was free. What next?

Yes, I did a bad thing. But I'm a good guy.

Everybody thought Kellto was a saint. But will the world miss him? His wife won't.

He was so holier-than-thou. Religious do-gooders love to put on a show of humility, but I think deep down inside, they want to let the world know how much better they are than the rest of us. In the end, they are just as selfish and controlling as anybody. No way was I going to let him control my life.

❄ **21** ❄

It finally hits me. I'm exhausted. I barely slept my last night in New York City—and that was after a long day that included administering CPR to a dead man and running through the arctic tundra of Central Park. I was up before four to catch a six o'clock flight. I hit the ground running and then ended up in an all-night meeting at the Second that included Commander Czaka, Captain Zaworski, Sargent Konkade, Don—no good deed goes unpunished, the captain of our CPD internal security—a man named Frank Nelson—how is that for coincidences?—one of his lieutenants, Beverly Sams, and two FBI agents, Heather Torgerson and Carl Doornbusch. Detective Tommy Barnes and Austin Reynolds were added to the meeting by our video conferencing system—Reynolds looked as dapper as ever in sport jacket and open collar, but Barnes looked like a man who has been up for two straight days without sleep, which he had.

When Heather Torgerson said to Reynolds, "With what you have going on in California, I think we have this under control," Reynolds answered tightly, "take it up with Deputy Willingham; he insists I participate." She reddened and didn't say much the rest of the meeting. I've stepped on enough social and professional landmines and been put in my place accordingly to know the feeling. I felt sorry for her.

We only stumbled a couple times on which Frank Nelson we were referring to; the New York City murder victim or the captain of internal security at CPD. We started calling the victim by his given name, Francis Nelson.

I only had one concern and question—my family's safety.

"Is my sister or anyone else in my family in danger?" I asked for the tenth time.

"I don't think so," Reynolds said.

That's not very reassuring.

"My understanding is the Russian Mafiya is notorious for going after family members," Frank Nelson said.

That's what I thought.

"They are," Reynolds answered. "But here is why the FBI thinks . . . let me say that stronger . . . why we strongly believe Conner's family is not currently in danger."

I wondered if he was going to say it is because he, personally, will keep a very vigilant eye on Klarissa. There I am picking at a scab that hasn't even formed.

"If this was a matter of vengeance, then yes," Reynolds said, "the FBI would need to put security detail on all members of Detective Conner's family. But Detective Conner is being targeted as a potential witness. So we feel very satisfied in putting protection strictly on Kristen herself."

"We can watch out for our own," Nelson interjected. I think Czaka gave him a dirty look.

"We appreciate any support you might provide," Reynolds said smoothly. "But this is a federal case. If you're going to add backup, we need to coordinate so everyone knows who the good guys are and no one gets shot with friendly fire."

"We'll discuss details in a separate meeting and get back to you," Czaka said, giving Nelson a pointed look.

If I know how things work with CPD, I'm guessing anybody assigned to babysit me and my family comes out of his budget.

"How concerned should we be about Conner?" Zaworski asked.

"Concerned, but not overly," Reynolds answered. "Aleksei Genken and his praetorian guard are dead. No question Pasha Boyarov is responsible. He has been Genken's top brigadier and protégé. Apparently he felt it was his time to take command. That's why he was meeting with Frank Nelson."

Everyone looked up.

"Sorry. Francis Nelson," he corrected. "Bottom line, Boyarov has gone underground and hasn't surfaced. Whatever was supposed to happen between him and Francis Nelson went wrong. He hasn't grabbed control of the *bratva* and it is now in the middle of a family war he probably can't win. We don't think Detective Conner will be his top priority. And that's assuming he called the hit. If it was Genken, he's already dead and his shooter is scooped up. We're squeezing the shooter hard but he's not singing yet. But unless Genken gave the job to multiple contractors, no one is going to risk shooting a police officer without getting paid for it. And like I said, Boyarov has bigger worries than to order a hit, even if he could."

Hard to argue with his logic. Should I feel better?

"How does a biotech guy get involved with the Russian Mafiya?" Barnes asked.

I know he already suspected the answer but wanted it confirmed.

"We think he was trying to—" Heather Torgerson began.

"That's classified," Reynolds interrupted. "Suffice it to say, Frank . . . Francis . . . Nelson was not a central figure in Russian Mafiya politics. This was a one-off deal. Someone, we believe in Moscow, connected Nelson with Boyarov. I'm only speculating, but I would guess that Boyarov's reward was control of New York. He was to become Pakhan. But whatever happened in the moments before Detective Conner arrived on the scene had already gone so wrong that he is a hunted man—and not just by the NYPD and FBI. Again, let me reiterate, that's why we think Conner is safe. She represents a low level risk to him in light of his other problems. He won't be sending anyone after her."

"But why do I represent any risk to Boyarov or Genken or anyone else?" I asked. "I know nothing. I saw nothing. I'm not a witness."

"They obviously don't know that," Reynolds answered. "All they know is a detective showed up in the middle of a high level deal. If they know you spent time with the FBI—and they have informers everywhere, so they do or eventually will—it would just confirm in their minds you were there for a reason and saw everything or something."

"That's what worries me," Frank Nelson said. "There's nothing we can do about what they think. This threat could go on indefinitely."

That cheered me up.

"Actually there is something we can do." Reynolds answered, "We're working with the NYPD to make sure the fact that this was a chance encounter and that Conner saw nothing is well known. Detective Barnes will help us on that. We want that circulated throughout NYPD far and wide, not as a rumor, but as fact. Word will get out organically. Genken's brigadiers will get word. If Boyarov is alive and in the picture, one of his informants will let him know. I'm just guessing, but it's an educated guess, that a hit was ordered on Conner before it was known she wasn't a witness to the crime. If that's the case, she can get back to normal sooner than later."

I wouldn't be so sure of that, Agent Reynolds. But I'm not thinking about something as inconceivable as a contract to kill me being out there. I'm not used to normal anyway.

"If Moscow is involved, why isn't the CIA represented in this meeting?" Don asked.

Reynolds paused and his eyebrows knitted together, larger than life in HD. Maybe that was an oversight.

"Deputy Director Robert Willingham is personally briefing the Directors of the FBI and CIA as we speak," he said smoothly.

"So this threat on Conner might blow over in a few hours?" Czaka asked.

Was his hopeful tone due to protecting the budget or my well-being? I'm sure I'm not being fair to the man. He was my dad's partner and then boss. I've known him since I was a little girl. But everyone in the Second knows he and I had a major falling out when he moved the investigation into my dad's shooting to the cold case files.

"That's exactly what we are hoping and expecting," Reynolds answered. "But to quote someone, 'hope for the best, plan for the worst.' "

He and Barnes signed off as an early breakfast was brought in. Bagels and a tub of coffee from JavaStar. Czaka scowled at Nelson, probably for putting another thirty-dollar dent in his budget.

We ended the meeting after a few minutes so everyone could follow up on their assignments. Torgerson and Doornbusch are in charge of my security and were assigned first shift. They were given a small interrogation room to work from so they could coordinate additional FBI staff and shifts and be close to Frank Nelson. The CPD's Frank Nelson.

Don Squires was cut loose to go home and sleep.

"We need to talk," he said, holding up his hand

in the shape of a phone and wiggling it on his way out. It seems everyone needs to talk to me about something scary and mysterious. Zaworski still hasn't hit the subject that was too big to put on me over the phone.

I spent the next three hours with Torgerson and Doornbusch going over my daily routines.

After twenty-eight hours of no sleep, I am ready to head back to my mom's house and catch some sleep. As I head for the door, Zaworski motions for me to come into his office. He points to a chair and shuts the door.

"Hold calls, Shelly."

Uh oh. This is it. I know my expense report is in order—I'm a cheap date for the CPD. I know what others turn in. I haven't been sneaking into the file room to find the box with the case files for my dad's shooting—namely because I haven't been around. What could I be in trouble over?

"I need to mention one more thing," he says.

"Did they clear me for active duty?" I ask as a delay tactic.

"This Russian crap changes everything. I actually think it would be better to have you here than home. So I'll work on that. But something else came up while you were on vacation."

My trip to New York doesn't feel like a vacation anymore.

"The Cutter Shark," he says.

That wakes me up. The Cutter Shark. The

nickname that just won't die. The serial killer I put behind bars at the Metropolitan Correction Center in downtown Chicago. Is it wrong to wish he fell out a window too narrow for anyone to fit through?

"Is he finally talking?"

"Yes he is. And he's hired a lawyer."

"That shouldn't be a big deal. Not hiring a lawyer probably slowed things down more than if he had one."

"Just hear me out, Conner. He's hired a high powered defense attorney who has agreed to take his case pro bono."

"We have everything needed to give him the needle or life without parole."

"Agreed. We do."

So why does Zaworski look concerned?

"But here's the deal. His attorney is Joseph Abrams—have you heard of him?"

I shake my head no.

"I'm surprised. He's a professor at University of Chicago and a spokesman for the ACLU. He's on TV a lot. He's a big deal. The ACLU funds him when he takes cases on. And he never loses."

"There's a first time for everything. We have so much evidence that Houdini couldn't get the Cutter out of the cage we have him in."

"You mentioned evidence. Mr. Abrams has filed a motion of appeal to have all evidence thrown out."

"What?! On what grounds?"

"Illegal search and seizure."

"Reynolds and the FBI took care of that. No way was anything illegally searched or seized."

"They indeed got all the proper warrants. But Abrams is arguing that they did so on the basis of his rights being violated."

"No judge will hear that."

"A judge has agreed to hear it."

"Who?"

"Probably the only who would. Bernard Jankowitz. He's no friend to law enforcement."

"But not even he would cut a serial killer loose."

"I don't think so, but we have to take this seriously and carefully."

"How were his civil rights supposedly violated?" I ask.

"When you broke down a door, without a warrant, to apprehend him."

"Are you kidding me? To save a life? Whatever happened to Imminent Danger?"

"That's our argument and we think it will prevail. But defense is arguing you had no probable cause to enter the home where you found him."

"But I knew he was holding another victim. I think that gave me the right to break into the White House to find him."

"We know that, Conner. The law has always recognized Imminent Danger as a clear cut exigent circumstance that supersedes a need for warrant."

He's obviously been meeting with the attorneys on this. I've never heard him speak so formally.

"Then we're good," I say.

"Here's the tricky part. Your report, confirmed by the testimony of the witness who pointed you where to go, indicates that he really didn't know where the Cutter was. It was a lucky guess. They are arguing that breaking into a home on the basis of a lucky guess is not covered by Imminent Danger."

"I never used the phrase *lucky guess*. And my witness was right and so was I."

"I'm not the one arguing with you. It's gonna work out okay."

"He also confirmed the Cutter had another potential hostage," I nearly shout. "I worked with facts I had in front of me on the basis of Imminent Danger—and no one can ever question how imminent that danger was."

"Correct. That should settle it. But don't kid yourself, you're still going to come under attack by Abrams."

I am steaming. I look down. My hand is shaking.

"Listen, Kristen," Zaworski says, raising a hand to stop me from saying more. "No one thinks you did wrong and no one thinks this appeal is going anywhere. But you are going to be deposed. I'm just giving you a heads up."

"When and where? I'll do it now."

He snorts. "No. Not now. You're going home to get some sleep. We don't know when. It could be days, weeks, or months. Probably weeks. But believe me, you'll be prepping with our legal team and will have had a good night's sleep."

Is this for real? I'm in counseling. I have a security detail. My sister cheated on me. Now it looks like I will be spending hours with the CPD legal team. I feel like my life is under siege. I think of the David Bowie and Queen song, "Under Pressure." Maybe I'll turn that up loud on my drive home.

What did Reynolds say about my situation? We should be *concerned but not overly.* Is that like saying, I want to be your boyfriend as long as I can see your sister?

❄ **22** ❄

I throw off the covers, stand up, and stretch my back. I'm finally awake. I head out to the kitchen. Mom isn't home. It's church night for her. If the doors are open and the lights are on, she's there.

She's left a note for me on the kitchen table letting me know I just need to turn on the burner to heat up vegetable soup. I've been asleep for seven hours. It's after eight. I look at my phone and have a text: *Meet us for dinner?*

Vanessa Squires sent me the text a couple hours ago.

Just woke up, I text back.

Her response is almost immediate: *We have a babysitter. Just leaving now. Meet us!*

Do I really want to go out? I realize I'm starving. I missed lunch. I can live with soup and I would like to stay in and catch up with Mom when she gets home to make sure she's okay. Don and Vanessa do dine in a style that is a couple major upgrades from soup. They do everything in style. You can't live like they do on a detective's salary. But Don has a secret that he'd like to stay that way. Call it male pride. But his wife makes a boatload of money as a real estate agent. A lot more than he does.

He didn't like it when I teased him about being a kept man so I dropped it. I'm not always obnoxious. I can actually be very sensitive to the feelings of others. But even if he doesn't like being teased, Don dresses more like a business mogul with his sharp suits—I can actually recognize a Hugo Boss now—his designer ties, and expensive shoes—he loves his Allen Edmonds. He's been after me almost three years to upgrade my wardrobe from the same black slacks and jacket I wear all winter. If I ever figure out what my style is outside of the workout gear I prefer, I'll try.

Tell me where.

Alinea. North Halstead. Lincoln Park.

I speak the name to Siri. A lot of five-star reviews pop up with all the dollar signs lit up and gleaming. Alinea must be expensive. Figures. I'm not even going to pretend I'm paying for my meal tonight. Don might let me, but Vanessa won't. That does mean I have to dress up at least a little.

I'm glad I took a shower before I went to bed until I look at my hair in the bathroom mirror. I wonder what I did with the balaclava Klarissa got me for Christmas. It might be an improvement. I need to get it back from James. No way do I have time for the curling iron. I go back to my room and open a couple dresser drawers. Mom hasn't thrown away the stuff I left behind more than ten years ago. I spot a plastic tortoise shell hair clip I used to wear in high school. Maybe it's retro night at Alinea. I push my hair back with it. Who knows, it might actually work. Don will tell me if it doesn't.

I wash and towel-dry my face. I add a hint of red lipstick. I start digging in my suitcase and find a knee-length fitted dress, which Klarissa said was too long.

To each their own, including boyfriends, Baby Sis. That almost makes me smile. Humor is my defense mechanism. Maybe that's a positive sign that I'll figure out how to handle this. Or maybe I'm as emotionally repressed as Klarissa claims I am.

As a cop, I can tell you first hand, there are some people who could use a little repression.

I pull on my leggings—it's freezing outside—and grab a pair of pumps with two-inch heels. Klarissa would roll her eyes. It's all I've got.

Why am I worried about what Klarissa would think?

I write Mom a quick note.

Fifteen minutes after emerging from a deep slumber, I'm on the road. Maybe I can get my own car back tomorrow. Driving Klarissa's GTR has lost its thrill. But at least I'll show up at Alinea in style—at least until I enter the front door.

You don't order at Alinea. Each season they present a new tasting menu. You get what they bring you. I have a healthy appetite and was worried when the first plate arrived with enough food to feed a baby squirrel.

Don sees my expression and fights not to laugh.

"There are twenty-one courses, KC, so you don't have to lick the plate."

"Don, be sweet!" Vanessa scolds.

She might be suppressing a smile herself. Talk about feeling awkward. I probably look like one of the Clampetts arriving in Beverly Hills.

There are no prices on the menu. I don't want to know what this is costing. I didn't grow up with money. Dad was a cop. Mom worked and still works at the library. Three kids. We never went without necessities, but our clothes were from Walmart and family vacation was visiting relatives who were within driving distance. I get paid pretty good. More than enough for my single life. I really don't spend a lot of money. Maybe it is time to upgrade my image a bit. I am still feeling very self-conscious about my hair and what I have on.

As the fourth or fifth course arrives, Vanessa tells me I look fabulous for maybe the tenth time. She wants to know where I found my hair clip. She has to have one. She just has to. I think compliments numbers two through ten have been to bolster my confidence and now border on overkill. Don has smirked the entire dinner. How out of place do I look?

On a quick trip to the ladies' room, I overheard the waiting list to get a table at Alinea is six months. I think Don and Vanessa shoehorned me in on a special occasion. I'm afraid to ask if this is their anniversary.

We're on dessert when I say, "Okay, this is maybe the best meal I have ever had in my life with two of my favorite people in the world. But you shouldn't have. What gives? I love being with you guys but is this a sympathy treat?"

Don is poking at the last vestiges of a dessert made with lemon, pine nut, and caramelized white chocolate. Maybe I'll tell him to go ahead and lick the plate. He says nothing.

"Maybe a little," Vanessa answers. "You've had a tough week. But the real reason we asked you out is we have some big news to share . . . I should say Don has some big news to share . . . and with everything going on we figured the only way to properly tell you was to get you away from the office and everything else going on."

If she's pregnant, she's not showing. Don told me that two kids were enough. If they're having relationship troubles—and they sure don't act like it—I doubt I'd be on the shortlist for counseling. I look at Don. He's still poking at a few crumbs.

"You get a tryout with the Bears?" I ask.

No smile. He takes a deep breath and looks up quick. I wonder if Vanessa just kicked him.

"We've talked about this before, partner. But now it's real."

Uh oh. I know where this is going. I try to keep a smile frozen on my face.

"The timing is crummy but it was always going to be hard."

Three servers appear at our table, remove the dessert plates and present each of us with . . . a second dessert. This has to be plate number twenty-one. I've lost count.

"Chocolate with menthol, coconut, and hyssop for your pleasure," we are solemnly told.

Don takes a bite of the chocolate and chews thoughtfully.

"Come on, Don. What's up?" I ask. "Just say it."

"I wanted you to know before it happens. I turn in my papers on Friday. I'm resigning. I'm done."

I knew he was going to say that but it still feels like the wind has been knocked out of me. I'm not great with relationships. We've had our fights as partners the last three years. But it's been safe and comfortable. I respect Don as a family man and professional as much as . . . well as much as anyone I've ever known. I might drive him crazy but I think he feels the same kind of respect for me. We've been a good team.

I'm afraid to say anything. I might cry and as my mom can tell you, I don't shed tears.

"You're not saying anything, Kristen," Vanessa says, putting a hand on my shoulder.

"It's been a tough couple days. I'm not going to do my usual shtick and try to say something funny that isn't very funny. I'll just be honest. This is hard."

"Don's told me what you've been through this week," Vanessa says, her eyes glistening with what might turn into tears. "But it's not just been the last few days. It's been nonstop for over a couple years now. Your dad. That serial killer. The Durham murder. Then this crazy thing in New York."

She realizes she isn't cheering me up and stops. She tries to say something but I lean over and give her a hug and she hugs me back hard.

Are we making a scene? I'm not sure I care.

"Okay, what's next Squires?" I ask Don, rubbing the back of my hand over the corner of my eye. There are times when not wearing much makeup is a plus.

"You know my brother, Rodney, has been trying to get me to move to LA and finish law school. Become a partner with him. I think we're going to do it."

I met Rodney last year. I know he's been pushing Don to partner up with him for the past few years. It's interesting that Squires said, I *think* we're going to do this, rather than, we *are* going to do this.

"You happy with that?"

"I've always wanted to be a lawyer, so yeah."

"Then I'm happy for you. I'm happy."

"You'll finally get a partner that can keep up with you," he says, eyes on his coffee.

"Right. I figured I would have a new partner sooner or later—after you became the boss."

"I haven't held my breath on a promotion."

"It's always been just a matter of time."

"If it was going to happen, it would have happened when Captain Z went down with the Big C. They looked outside our squad."

I didn't realize how much Blackshear getting the nod bothered him. I've been afraid the messes I get in have held him back for promotion.

"Zaworski is only acting captain," I say. "He's

doing it as a favor to Czaka. He's not going to be in the chair that much longer."

"You trying to talk me into staying?"

Vanessa gives Don a look I can't miss and I shut my mouth. I know she has wanted him out of CPD for some time. Not because of the unpredictable hours. Not because of the microscope we get put under by citizens, bureaucrats, the judicial system, and the press. Not because of the modest pay. It's what everyone married to a homicide detective in a big city thinks about. When am I going to get the dreaded call? I can't argue with that. My mom got the call. My whole family did.

There's something I want to ask but know I can't. Don's sister, Debbie, still lives in Chicago. Crack head. Hooker. Homeless. Rodney flies out once a year and the brothers make a trek through the gutters of Chicago to find her, in hopes she'll agree to go to a rehab center. Money's no object. Rodney's rich and Don isn't doing bad because of Vanessa. Last time I saw Debbie was last Thanksgiving. She seems too far gone to know what she's turning her back on to me. They found a very nice facility that had an opening that week. I went with them to pick her up. She disappeared in the middle of the night. Don told me that convinced Rodney to put in a deposit at one of Chicago metro's best facilities to guarantee an immediate spot.

Vanessa is dabbing at her eyes with a napkin.

Don is watching me closely. He knows what I'm thinking. I don't think inviting me to dinner was his idea. I'm sure there will be another conversation that includes the topic of Debbie.

Maybe I do need counseling. Everyone seems to think I've been through a lot of trauma. I've always thought the good outweighed the bad in my life. Is that suppressing my feelings?

What I want to do now is a workout. That always helps me sort things out.

❄ **23** ❄

Mom is already asleep as I enter the back door. Good. I'm talked out for the day. Reynolds latest message let me know he is still at the PathoGen offices in Redwood Shores, California. He said to call no matter how late since he is on West Coast time. He stresses *we need to talk.*

To call or not to call? I figured after sleeping seven hours in the middle of the day—and drinking a couple cups of coffee with dinner—I would be too wired to go back to sleep. But I was wrong. My eyelids are drooping.

We can talk tomorrow.

"No word on the Bear?"

"No word, Pasha."

"Turn off the phone, Vladimir. You idiot. I told

you, we only turn on the phones for three minutes every hour. Do you want to send a signal to the FBI to tell them where to find us?"

Zheglov gave Boyarov a hard stare and held the phone up high so Pasha could see him switching it off. When had Pasha ever shown him disrespect? He knew better. And when had he ever seen him this nervous? Never.

They were using throwaway phones with no ID. But with the software the NSA was running, including voice recognition, who knew when the listeners would figure out who was on the phone.

Vladimir watched Pasha run a hand over his freshly shaved scalp. He was propped up against the headboard on an uncomfortable bed. He reached over to the nightstand and grabbed a half-empty bottle of vodka. He fumbled for a glass, knocked it off the stand, swore, and took a swig straight from the bottle.

He held it up for Vlad. Vlad took it and tipped his head back but only allowed himself a very small swallow. *One of us better keep our wits.* There was a smoldering tension in the air. There should be. Vlad had led the attack party on Genken. He expected to come home a hero—with Pasha in charge of the New York *bratva* and him as Pasha's number two man. It hadn't worked out that way.

Pasha took the bottle back and slugged back another drink. He shook it at Vladimir. Vlad shook his head no.

"How has it gone so wrong, Vlad? I finally get everything I wanted. Genken is dead. I'm the Pakhan. The problem is no one else knows that."

Pasha is not in good shape, Vladimir thought. He hadn't been anywhere near Genken's estate yesterday. That had been the plan so that Pasha had an airtight alibi when he assumed command of the *bratva*. Now not being there made Pasha look weak.

With US law enforcement and Genken's other brigadiers racing to find Pasha, word was out. How long could he and Pasha convince the gang to stay loyal? Not much longer, he thought. Soon they would be switching sides.

After delivering the formula, Pasha had been told he had a green light to take out Genken and become the new Pakhan. Everyone but Genken knew this day was coming sooner than later. He was an old man. He had lost his ruthless edge. With Moscow's blessing behind Pasha, the other brigadiers would have fallen in line beneath him. They wouldn't like it—there was no love lost for the favorite son—but they would bow or they would die.

Everything had depended on securing a top-secret formula, the price for Moscow's blessing. That ship had sailed when the deal with PathoGen imploded. Vlad's attack was their last chance to get the code and it, too, had failed.

Akulov, Yerokhin, Korablin, Ishutin, and

Luytov. They were turning the city upside down looking for Pasha—and undoubtedly him—systematically picking off their soldiers and disabling the organization. Vlad ordered reprisals while Pasha raged. Not good.

Who will get to us first and pull the trigger? Probably Ishutin. He was oldest and had been in the Genken inner circle longest. He was considered too old to succeed Genken as Pakhan—that would go to Luytov now. But Ishutin was old school and would forgive no break in the code of *vory v zakone*. His group was biggest and best organized.

"*Chert!*" Pasha seethed, taking another swallow of vodka.

"Easy, Pasha. We need clear heads."

It worried Vlad that Pasha simply nodded his head in agreement.

"Vlad, do we have a way of hitting Ishutin?"

"He would be hard to get to, Pasha. What do you have in mind?"

"If we could buy some time, I could get things squared away with Moscow."

"Will that do any good?"

"Nyet."

Pasha had made promises to powerful people and failed to deliver. His last chance to salvage a simple operation went up in smoke, literally, when Genken set his safe room on fire during the attack. Aleksei wasn't going to leave behind anything that would help Pasha take his spot. He burned the security code to activate the PathoGen deal rather than let Pasha win. When Vlad and his men finally broke into the Pakhan's safe room, Genken had swallowed the cyanide tablet.

Pasha had paid off one of Genken's bykis to help plan the attack. Pasha thought they might snatch victory from defeat when he suspected Medved had run to the estate in Oyster Bay to beg Aleksei for his life. There was no sign of the Bear, but Vlad was sure Pasha was right. Informants had confirmed there was no wallet on Nelson. Who else could have taken it but Med? How else could Genken have it in hand if the Bear hadn't come to him?

Old news. What came next?

❄ **24** ❄

"Kristen, I thought we agreed that you would let us know your schedule at the beginning of the day."

"I did give you my schedule at the beginning of the day. It just changed."

FBI Agent Heather Torgerson is not amused.

"It's understood things change. But we need more time than you gave us to check out an unfamiliar venue."

She is quite unhappy with my last-minute decision to join Don and Vanessa for dinner.

Maybe she's mad they couldn't get a table.

"Yesterday morning was the first time we talked, Agent Torgerson. Things are a little up in the air with me just getting back in town."

"Listen, Kristen . . . call me Heather . . . I don't disagree with anything Special Agent Reynolds said and I don't want to be an alarmist. But this is serious. These are dangerous people. If they still have designs on you, they'll exploit what you are calling 'up in the air' moments."

"I hear and obey. I can't promise that plans won't change. But I'll try to give you more warning when they do."

"Calling while you are driving to a restaurant is not adequate time."

"I get it. I get what you're saying."

"Lunch today?" she asks.

"Was that on my list?" I ask innocently.

"Very funny."

"I'm skipping lunch—I ate enough last night to hibernate the rest of the winter. I'm working out with our fight instructor and trainer, Barry Soto. You're welcome to join me."

She purses her lips and says, "Thank you. I might."

This is serious. Do I not look like I am taking things seriously? Everyone keeps using the word "serious" with me.

It's still hard to imagine someone has a contract on me. Inconceivable.

Pasha took another slug from a new bottle. Only one drink left. He handed it to Vlad, who looked like he might decline, but took another sip of the fiery liquid.

I'm swigging and he's sipping. Not a good sign.

Pasha finally came back to the sad, painful conclusion that went against everything he believed. The ultimate betrayal. A complete breach of *vory v zakone.*

His only escape from Moscow and the other brigadiers was the US Government. They would jump at a chance to make a deal with him.

His mind began to chew on how to do it. It could not look like he had surrendered. It had to be an authentic-looking takedown.

The only way to do that was if Vladimir was not involved. No way would he agree to it. That meant he, too, had to be taken or killed. Everyone knew Vladimir Zheglov and Pasha Boyarov were lifelong friends—and that neither would betray the other. Which meant that was exactly what he must do. It had to look real.

"What is it, Pasha?"

"I'm just working on what comes next, Vlad."

Pasha Boyarov in Witness Protection. What a thought.

❄ **25** ❄

Life is good on the road, Medved thought to himself, contentedly sipping coffee and eating a third donut at a Dunkin' Donuts just off the exit of the Keystone Shortway in Stroudsburg, Pennsylvania.

Now he could no longer say he never got lucky. First he limped out the back of Genken's Long Island estate in Oyster Bay Cove unnoticed. He knew that remaining undetected wouldn't last long in the mansion district, even without increased police traffic. Wealthy people notice when someone who looked like him walked on their streets—he stuck out like a sumo wrestler at a beauty pageant. But everyone was huddled inside against the icy cold and no one reported him to the police as he walked along the street. His next break was that construction had come to a halt less than a mile from the back of the Pakhan's residence. The crew had left equipment outside, including a dump truck, while they took a break and headed indoors due to the ferocious freeze that had settled on the Northeast corridor of the United States.

Med could drive anything. The three-year-old Western Star 4700 with a Detroit engine was love at first sight for him. He kicked in the door of the construction trailer. He then broke the lock on the manager's desk to find the metal box with the equipment keys. They were all there, including the keys to the Western Star, all conveniently labeled for him.

Med knew there would be cash around. You couldn't keep construction going in New York City without paying neighborhood insurance fees. He knew this firsthand because he had sometimes collected dues before his short stay on Riker Island. After prying open the lock box, he whistled. Close to ten grand was neatly stacked in tens, twenties, fifties, and hundreds. That would supplement the three grand he got from the white-haired man's wallet nicely. Lady Udacha was smiling on him.

The great thing about driving a dump truck in a major metropolitan area—and maybe anywhere else—is no matter how big you are, you are invisible. He liked the feeling. He drove back to Coney Island, parked a street over from his apartment, and went up the back stairs from the alley. He knew it was a risk but he needed a few things, including a small Byzantine silver cross that had been his mother's. He was wearing it now as he considered getting one more donut. He liked the jelly-filled.

When he went through his apartment—undoubtedly for the last time—his first priority was getting into his safe that had close to a thousand bucks and a couple of Glocks. He had an old Remington shotgun in the back of his closet along with a short-barreled Kalishnikov he for sure wanted to take as well. He knew Ilsa kept some money stashed too. She wouldn't be needing it. He ransacked her stuff and found another thousand dollars—maybe more—in bills of all denominations—there was Lady Udacha again. Ilsa had been a prostitute when he first met her. She worked in a bakery now. Either baking bread paid more than she let on or she had been up to old tricks. Yesterday he would have beat her until she confessed. No point in even getting mad now. He would miss her. She deserved better than him.

He grabbed a lock box with his important papers and packed two suitcases. He looked at Ilsa's stuff one more time and saw something that gave him an idea. He really shouldn't risk being in the apartment any longer than he had to, but it might help. It was a clipper set she had used when she worked at a barbershop. He stripped down and starting with the widest guard, he began cutting his hair and beard. It took him thirty minutes but he got to bare scalp. He barely recognized himself in the mirror. He showered, ran a razor over his face and head, and quickly headed out the door. It took two trips to load up the Western Star. No one seemed to notice him— except Lady Udacha.

He made a stop at yet another deserted construction site. He removed the license plate from a dump truck at the back of the lot that looked unused, and put the plates from his Western Star on it and then those plates on his Western Star.

He drove onto the Verrazano Narrows Bridge, exited west on Interstate 278, and drove slowly out of the city toward I-80 west. Once traffic thinned, he was able to relax and think.

He knew it was possible to get new identification that was good enough to get a job and a license in a new state—but it would be expensive. He didn't know how much. He was sure he could do the same thing with the truck. The Western Star was probably worth a hundred-fifty grand but he'd never get that much without a bill of sale and valid registration. But the idea of owning his own truck and becoming an independent contractor—maybe somewhere warmer—suddenly seemed very appealing to him. He wasn't cut out for life in the *bratva* anymore. He was tired of killing. Why not a new life? A respectable life?

But he still had one loose end to tie up. The Chicago detective. Genken said she had positively ID'd him, which put him at risk for the rest of his life. Something as simple as a friendly fight in a bar and having his identity probed could put his picture and presence back in circulation with the police. There were a lot of things he had done in his past that couldn't be proved. But an eye-witness to a murder was a different matter. Especially if she was a cop.

If he was going to start over, why not do it all the way? Or at least as much as possible. Pasha and his death angel, Vladimir Zheglov, would always be there. But who was to say either would survive? But a witness—a detective witness—would never go away unless he made it so.

❄ 26 ❄

"Okay, Conner, how bad do you want to be back on active duty?"

"Very."

I might have said that too quickly. There has to be a catch.

"Then listen close."

There obviously is.

"You can't work any cases until you've completed your first three counseling sessions. Without scaring the good doctor off, I would add."

"Sir . . . sir . . . that's two more weeks."

"Did I ask you to comment or to listen?"

I gulp and shut up.

"Your therapist has agreed to meet with you this afternoon and tomorrow morning to help us out. If Czaka or me had leaned in, she would have rightfully pushed back. Your old buddy from Internal Affairs, Tom Gray, went to bat for you."

"Really? I didn't think he liked me."

"You don't think anyone likes you. One day you'll get old and wise enough to realize no one is paying enough attention to you to come up with dislike."

Ouch. That hurts. Am I really paranoid?

"Stop thinking, Conner."

"You don't even know what I'm thinking."

"But I can see it and it's hurting my brain. Let's deal with one thing at a time. You do the sessions today and tomorrow, then you go back on your Tuesday schedule next week."

"You mean I'm not done after three sessions? What the heck are we going to talk about?"

If looks could turn you into a block of salt, they'd be using me to clear ice and snow from the streets of the Windy City within the hour.

"Who said three?" he asks.

"Uh . . . you said three would clear me."

"Clear you to get back on active duty, but not stay on active duty. Are you taking this seriously? Did you really think a single session with a shrink was going to settle this?"

"I assumed it was one and done with the therapist. If you're ready to work, you're ready to work. Sir."

I note in my mind that it was Zaworski that called Dr. Andrews a shrink, not me.

"When was the last time you read the employee bible, Conner?"

I splutter but can't think of an answer. Probably my first year on the job.

"Conner. Do me a favor."

"Yes, sir."

"Since you've got a couple hours before you meet with the doc, I want you to spend some time reading the section of the manual that specifies procedures for when an officer is involved in a shooting."

"I can do that."

I start to rise and he holds up his hand.

"Hold on. I want to make sure we're on the same page. I blame myself for not being more specific in what I just told you to do. When I say, 'spend some time,' what I mean is the next hour. At least. Is that too much to ask?"

"No, sir."

"Good. Because I'm not asking."

"I'm on it, sir," I say as I pop out of my seat.

"Hold your horses, KC."

Sit or stand? I want to get my workout in. That gives me an hour to read, hustle downstairs to go through a Barry Soto torture session, and shower quickly before driving over to Dr. Andrews' office. I stay standing. He waits for eye contact.

"What's up with Squires?" he asks.

"Sir?" I ask as innocently as I can muster. We look at each other for at least twenty seconds—an eternity with my attention span.

"I figured you'd clam up for your partner. That's fine. I'll know when I know."

"Yes sir."

"You sure you have nothing to say that might illuminate my suspicion that Detective Squires is unhappy?"

"Uh . . . no, sir."

"Go read your bible. If you don't know where your desk copy is, it's also on the website."

"Yes, sir."

The Chicago Police Department realizes that our most valuable resource is you, an officer in the field. We know that it is common to experience stress from post-shooting trauma that can sometimes feel overwhelming, which can affect how you feel and relate on the job and in non-work-related environments. It is with your well-being and complete recovery from the psychological stress you have endured in situations involving deadly force that we have created a series of coping strategies in order for you to work functionally through the impact of the trauma.

We have outlined numerous post-trauma interventions and support processes, first of which is a safe, confidential, psychological evaluation and therapeutic process with a professional therapist.

Okay, maybe something is wrong with me. I don't feel stressed out any more than usual. Except for my sister cheating with my boyfriend, Russians wanting to kill me, and a serial killer seeking to have all evidence against him thrown out. Being involved in a shooting doesn't even faze me. Is that so abnormal?

I didn't grow up wanting to be an accountant or a fashion model or a teacher or even a fireman. I guess that's a fireperson. I think I'd like to be married and have kids some day, but what I've always wanted to be, as long as I remember, was a police officer. I wouldn't have minded playing soccer for Team USA first. But getting my detective shield before my twenty-eighth birthday was one of the happiest days of my life.

I wanted to be in the field. I knew that meant I would probably find myself in some dangerous situations and might even have to use the gun I've been trained to use.

I know that the popular perception is us cops are looking for a reason to shoot someone. That's not even close to the truth. I personally don't know anyone looking to use lethal force of any kind at any time. But we train for it in case it is required.

In the past year I've had a knife pulled on me by a punk who is still roaming the streets of Chicago. It bothers me that he went free because someone screwed up his processing papers and let him walk by accident. But I don't feel bad that I put him on the ground and cuffed him. I've also had a psychopath attempt to murder me. There was no question in my heart and mind when I raised a gun to stop him. Unfortunately he slammed my wrist in a door and I lost the gun, which turned it into hand-to-hand combat. I've never lost a minute of sleep over that either. I was also in a life or death skirmish where a man was shot and killed. Not by me. But I was there. Traumatic? Sure. It could have been me that went down. But I didn't. So I feel pretty good on that count too.

I read through the interventions, which include group therapy with other officers involved in deadly force.

I resolve to take the counseling with Dr. Andrews very seriously.

Maybe there is something wrong with me for not feeling betrayed and angry and isolated. Again, no more than usual. I was taught to pray and ask God to help me with my problems. That's what I do. Isn't that counseling?

Maybe I should have PTSD. If I do, it's because of my dad's death, not for hand-to-hand combat with a serial killer. I'll ask Andrews straight out if I'm the one with the problem for feeling the way I do. Plus maybe she can help me come up with a way to deal with the Klarissa and Austin situation.

What I won't tell her is I don't want to go to group therapy. I have a feeling that if I did, she would be sure to make that a requirement.

❄ 27 ❄

"You told me two hours. Now you say you'se got seventy-five minutes tops. You're going soft on me, Kristen. Soft. How am I gonna keep you'se alive if you're soft?"

I warned Torgerson about Barry Soto, our fight instructor at the Second. I can't remember his exact age but I know he trained my dad. I'm pretty sure he's over retirement age, maybe seventy, but he's still ripped. Short. Big chest and arms from five hundred dips and pushups a day. His legs look small in comparison but he can jump and kick like a man forty years younger than him. He's bald on top with a ring of red hair that always made me think of Bozo the Clown from when I was a kid. When he lost his hair up top it found its way to his ears, nostrils, and arms.

"C'mon, Kristen. Keep up with your pal. Act like you want to be here. I don't got time for your dawdling."

Dawdling?

We have jumped rope for almost ten minutes. Sometimes fast, sometimes slow, sometimes on one leg . . . whatever he barks.

"Stop! Put the ropes up. Where you found them, Kristen. Don't teach your pal bad habits and make a mess of my palace."

Cinder blocks and a slab floor. Some palace.

I'd bark back at him but I can't breathe enough to speak. I put my rope on the exact hook I got it from. I lean over to get a drink of water and that gets him going again.

"So that's how it's going to be? A sip of water every time you want to take a rest?"

I hustle back on the mat in the middle of Mr. Soto's palace of pain. Concrete floors, bare walls, and only a couple machines that plug into a wall.

"Where's the love, Mr. Soto?" I gasp out.

"When you stay alive you'll know how much I love you, Kristen. I told your dad I'd keep you alive, so it's my cross to bear. Now enough of chitchat. This isn't a tea party. On your backs ladies!"

Chitchat? A tea party? He's in rare form. I think he's showing off for Torgerson. He must think she's cute. She is.

"I want you standing up. No hands. Keep 'em folded on your chest."

"How many?" Heather asks.

"You been hanging around Kristen too much, FBI tough girl. Keep doing them until I tell you to stop."

Go ahead. Try it. Standing up without any assistance isn't easy. You rock, arch, explode forward, and still fall on your butt two out of three times. By my sixth successful trip to get two feet on the floor, my abs and glutes are on fire. I pause.

"Keep going!"

I love Soto. Does that make me a masochist? He pushes and badgers us for an hour of exercises on the mat before pulling out the gloves and punching pads. Heather and I alternate three-minute sets of punching and blocking. Heavy crosses and straights are followed by rapid-fire jabs. Soto believes in body weight and balance. If the punch isn't popping it's because the feet are getting lazy. My arms are thin but by the time we call it quits so I could make my appointment, they feel like lead weights.

I shower and dress quickly. Heather is still sitting on the bench in front of her locker.

She looks at me and says, "Is he always like that?"

"Nah. He was in a good mood today."

Maybe I'm trying to show off now.

"So your dad was a cop?"

"Yes, he was. The CPD has him to blame for putting up with me."

"I think everyone feels lucky to have you."

"I hope you're right, but some days it doesn't feel that way."

"Looks to me like everyone loves you."

"I need to ponder that. Because it sure doesn't feel like it."

Maybe I do need counseling. I'll add what Heather said to the list for Dr. Andrews.

❄ **28** ❄

"Nancy is back home. I saw her pick up the newspaper off the front sidewalk this morning. Is she out of trouble?"

Just how close of an eye is mom keeping on the neighborhood?

"It's not my case and I don't know anything past last night, Mom. But even if I did, you know I can't tell you. Besides, I'm guessing you already know more than I do."

She gives a little snort and rolls her eyes.

I'm thirty, living at home—even if only for a few days—and eating tuna casserole with my mom. They write articles in the *New York Times* about what's wrong with America when they describe my current profile. I've got to find a new apartment. I'm not going to live in Klarissa's place. I'm mad at her. It would feel dishonest to turn around and accept a sweetheart deal from her. Kind of like I feel driving her GTR.

Mom added canned peas to the tuna casserole, something I protested vigorously as a kid, to no avail. I still don't love the mushy texture but at least she covered them up in a lot of gooey cheese. Other than the peas I'm not complaining about dinner.

"I feel terrible," she says. "I feel responsible

because I told you about the man who was spending time with her."

"You aren't responsible for anything good or bad in Nancy Keltto's life, Mom. You did the right thing. You were a good citizen who supplied an important tip in a homicide."

"So she is in trouble . . . and I'm responsible."

"You can't look at it that way. People are responsible for their own actions. That's how you and dad raised me. You just reported what you saw. You weren't involved."

"I know. It's just so surreal. I can't believe Eddy is dead. The thought that his wife . . . that Nancy was involved is almost overwhelming."

I've got to find my own place. I love my mom. But if this is what we are going to talk about every night I am going to go crazy. Plus she does have a habit of adding canned vegetables to otherwise delicious recipes.

"You've not talked about your visit with Austin and his parents. How did that go?"

Talking about Nancy Keltto as a murder suspect is suddenly quite appealing.

"Let me ask you this Mom, what do you think of Austin?"

She gets an amused expression on her face. "Are you asking your mom for advice?"

"I always appreciate your thoughts, Mom."

She laughs. I can't help myself. I have to laugh too. I suddenly feel better. Good endorphins can do that. It won't last long. I saw my sister with the guy I was dating. I'm not officially cleared for active duty until Dr. Andrews says so—hopefully tomorrow. An evil guy I put in jail is trying to get out on a technical error in the investigation, an error that is being pinned on me.

I chew thoughtfully. I've been trying to pick my bites carefully to even out the number of peas. They overwhelmed the noodles and tuna on this one and I grimace.

"Am I really that difficult Mom?"

Mom pauses. Is that an answer?

"I love all three of my daughters. Exactly the same amount."

Of course. What else can a parent say?

"But you three couldn't be more different. Of the three of you, you were born determined and ready for action. You had your own mind and were going to do things your way. You couldn't sit still. Kaylen and Klarissa would sit on my lap and I could read a storybook to them for an hour before bedtime. You wanted to look at the pictures and would turn the pages before I could finish the first sentence. Then you were off to climb on the kitchen counter or get into something you weren't supposed to."

"So does that mean I've always been difficult?"

"No, honey. Different. You've always been who God made you."

Last time I heard Jimmy preach he said God

has a sense of humor. I might be living proof of that.

Maybe I should have been a counselor. People accuse me of answering questions with questions of my own. Andrews is obviously the Ph.D. on that tactic.

I had a lot of questions for Andrews. Her answers were pretty consistent: "What do you think, Kristen? How does that make you feel, Kristen?"

At one point I told her that when my dad's case was moved to the back burner it made me angry . . . really angry with CPD and particularly Commander Czaka. She asked me how that made me feel. Uh . . . angry.

I guess the point is I'm supposed to dig deep and get in touch with what I think about seeing people get killed and personally being in harm's way and pulling a trigger. But what if there is nothing deeper inside of me than what I've already said?

I would really have liked to talk to Dr. Andrews about Klarissa and Austin—not just my feelings— I know I'm pissed off—but what to do about them. It would be nice to know if there are some tricks of the trade where I can confront my sister for sneaking behind my back without destroying the relationship forever. A month or two of mad would be fine.

Heck, that brings me back to where I started

with Andrews. I'm a church girl. I know the right answers spiritually even if it takes a while to apply them. I'm going to have to forgive her . . . at some point.

So how does that make you feel, Kristen?

❄ **29** ❄

I go out for an early walk. My mom said I was crazy as I stepped outside and got hit by a blast of wind. The temperature is still in single digits. Last time someone said I was crazy for going out on a bitterly cold morning it didn't turn out well. What can happen in my old neighborhood? Besides murder, of course.

I get to the end of the block, trying not to look at the Keltto house. How sad. I want to call Blackshear and ask what's going on. Zaworski has made it clear I need to keep my nose out of anything and everything that has to do with police business until cleared for active duty. Hopefully that changes this afternoon when Andrews sends her report to our HR people.

There's a young teenager standing on the corner. That's a blast from the past. My old school bus stop.

"How's it going?" I ask as I walk up.

"Not bad," he mumbles.

"Which house you live in?"

"Over there," he says with a jerk of his head, which I think is pointing to the house next door to the Kelttos.

"Too bad what happened on Monday," I say.

"Yeah. Ed was a nice guy."

"Did you know him well?"

"I guess. He was my scout leader when I was a kid. We started doing some projects this year."

"What kind of projects?"

"I'd go over there and do woodworking stuff in the garage. He was teaching me how to use all the tools he's got."

"Even in the winter?"

"He puts the car in the driveway and turns on a kerosene heater he's got. It gave us room to work and the cold wasn't too bad."

"Very nice. You build anything cool?"

"I don't know," he answers. "I guess some of it was getting okay. I made my mom a couple bird houses and a stepladder for the pantry. Just little stuff. Nothing big."

"Sounds big to me."

He just nods with a shrug.

"I'm gonna keep walking," I say. "Hope your bus gets here soon. You can freeze standing around out here."

He nods. On cue, I can hear the brakes on his bus squeal about a block away. As I turn he asks, "Are you the lady cop that grew up down the street?"

Lady cop?

"I am."

"You working on finding who killed Ed?"

"It's not my case."

"Do you know whose it is? Who is looking for the killer?"

"Yes. A friend of mine is in charge. Detective Blackshear."

"Is that a guy cop?"

"Ah . . . yes . . . Blackshear is a guy cop. By the way, what's your name?"

"Bradley."

"I'm Kristen."

He nods. I want to ask his last name but the bus pulls up and the door hisses open. He puts a foot on the first step, pauses, and looks at me. "You need to tell him, the guy detective, it wasn't Mrs. Keltto. It was her boyfriend."

He hustles up the last two steps and into the warmth of the bus. After giving me a suspicious scowl for possibly trying to corrupt America's youth, the driver pulls the lever to shut the door with another hiss. I stand there and watch as he releases the brakes, shifts into gear, and rounds the corner.

Did Blackshear's team talk to the kid? I'm sure they did. I wish I'd got his last name. I want to call Bob right now but there are two problems. My hands are frozen and I'm not sure I can work my phone. Second, I think I just put my nose in police business, even if by accident. Better wait until I am officially cleared for duty this afternoon. See, I'm following the rules.

Nothing is going to happen in the next six or seven hours. Whatever the kid might know, which might be nothing, can wait until then.

❄ 30 ❄

"What you hauling? Wait. Don't tell me. Rock salt."

Med wanted to tell the guy fueling his big SUV at the next pump aisle to mind his own business but that wouldn't be fitting in. Fitting in was important if he wanted to stay out of a cage.

"Nothing now. Heading over to Chicago for a job."

"Chicago is in a deep freeze. Not much work there. What do they have you doing? Has to be the salt."

"You got it. They can't keep up with it."

"That wasn't really a guess. I am in construction up in Chicago. About the only thing getting hauled and dumped is salt."

"That's why they called. They're paying good."

"Make sure you get your check up front. The city's broke."

"Good advice."

Why is this man so curious? Do I look like I

want to talk? And why does he have to be from Chicago?

The Bear had slept in a cheap motel in Gary, Indiana, last night. He wasn't on a set deadline, so he pulled off early so he could catch up on the news. The Russian Mafiya war in New York City—CNN was calling it Red Storm Rising—was getting nonstop coverage. There were five more murders and an explosion the day before. The Mayor had ordered a citywide curfew and called for federal help. The next story was an outbreak of flu. He switched stations, looking for more news.

A pretty blonde was reporting:

Day two of hostilities have raised the tally of dead to at least twenty-six known members of organized crime, in what is called the American bratva. That is the largest total of homicides in a two-day period in New York City's history. The number of arrests will not be confirmed by the New York Police Department or the FBI, but there are independent reports that the number now tops one hundred and is rising every hour.

There is much speculation as to what the catalyst was for this outbreak of violence that is pitting different factions of the American bratva against itself.

In an exclusive WolfNews interview, the

director of the New York FBI station had this to say.

Blah blah, Med had thought as the man droned on. I want to see the pretty blonde. Fortunately the man in the dark suit and red tie didn't take long to say nothing. Then she was back:

The man who is considered priority number one in a manhunt by the police and FBI alike is named Pasha Boyarov. He was widely believed to be the heir apparent to Aleksei Genken, who was killed two nights ago in an attack on his home that police describe as an unprecedented use of heavy weapons on American soil. When we return from a commercial break we will provide an in-depth profile of a man who is reputed to be one of the most ruthless killers in the American bratva—and reasons why he may have turned on his boss.

Could Lady Udacha be smiling on him yet again? Pasha out of the picture?

When the commercials ended, Med was disappointed on what the blonde and her interviewees had to say about Pasha. They obviously knew little about Boyarov. Most of the talk was of Genken. Then the network showed pictures of the twenty-six dead—Med knew some of them by face and a few of them on a first name basis. The first twenty on the list looked like an even split between Genken's personal army and Pasha's gang. The last six were Ishutin's men. Unfortunately, Vladimir Zheglov, the angel of death, was not pictured.

So the other brigadiers went to war with Pasha. That meant he was fighting the NYPD, FBI, and other brigadiers. Pasha was lethal and dangerous, but no way could he win against those odds.

But the shooting hadn't stopped so he was still fighting. If Vladimir Zheglov was still alive and at large, he would be at Pasha's side and those two men would not go down easily.

The one thing the news people got right, maybe by accident, was that Pasha was the mastermind behind the coup on Genken.

As long as Boyarov was alive, Med would never be safe. But what could Pasha do now? Unless he seized control of the *bratva*, Pasha's days were numbered. Could I get so lucky? The thought of delivering gravel in Phoenix or San Antonio or Dallas warmed his heart.

The gas nozzle shut off with a clump. He had prepaid three hundred in cash. It was going to take some time to get the truck legally registered in his name so he had to watch his funds. The Western Star was great but it was a gas-guzzler.

He climbed in the cab, started the engine, shifted into first, and rolled it over to the parking lot next door. He might as well start the day with a big breakfast. He'd find a cheap motel in Chicago and figure out how best to hit Detective Conner over the next few days.

Shoot her, hope Pasha and Vlad get gunned down, and you are a free man.

"What's up, Pasha?"

"Just waiting another ten minutes to use the phone again. I'm going to send Yuri to hit Ishutin's grandson—I know where the kid hides his mistress. If Ishutin thinks I'm going to roll over, he's going to learn the hard way not to mess with Pasha."

"Good," Vlad said. "Make them think hard about how far they want to take this."

"Exactly," Pasha responded.

Pasha did know where Ishutin's grandson kept his mistress and he would send Yuri to kill him. But it was show. If Vladimir only knew what he had really been working on it would get ugly. The deed was done. Basic terms were agreed upon and being reviewed by attorneys from the US Justice Department. He, Pasha Boyarov, would voluntarily walk into custody sometime late afternoon. It wouldn't look voluntary—couldn't look voluntary. That was part of the deal. To get what he wanted, Pasha had to offer up his lifelong friend, Vladimir Zheglov.

It was in everyone's best interest if he and Vlad

went down together. Vlad would be okay in prison. He was a ferocious killer. He would be left alone or people would die. He had to maneuver him carefully in the next few hours.

"Vlad, I think we need to move hotels again."

"We moved this morning, Pasha."

"Something doesn't feel right here."

Vlad shrugged and asked, "When?"

"Let me think about that after I send Yuri."

That was fast. They weren't supposed to arrest Nancy. It's her own fault. She panicked. I've got to save her—and myself. I guess if it comes down to her or me, it'll have to be her. But there should be something I can do to send this investigation a different direction.

Problem is, there wasn't supposed to be an investigation. Why couldn't the police take the situation at face value? The guy slipped on ice and hit his head.

In the few months we've sort of been seeing each other, Reynolds and I go days without talking. It's the nature of our profession. I'm not sure all Agent Reynolds does for the FBI, but he does disappear for days and even weeks at a time.

He's calling again. I'm not sure what to say, but I better answer.

"Conner."

"Reynolds," he says, matching my tone. Then he laughs and says, "with everything you've got going on and everything I've got going on, I wasn't sure when we were going to get a chance to talk again. Without a committee present."

How do I play this? I decide aloof and cool.

"I am absolutely buried. What do you need?"

Okay, that might have been abrupt and semi-rude.

"Why do I get the feeling that something I don't understand is going on in that lovely mind of yours?"

"Get in line to fathom the depths of how my brain works," I answer.

"Am I in trouble for not checking on you? If so, I promise it was not by choice or design."

"You are not in trouble for not checking up on me," I answer him more warmly than I feel.

He misses the implication, which is good, since I'm not ready to confront things with him and Klarissa.

"Listen, we need to talk," he says. "But right now I'm catching a flight to New York and will be out of pocket for a day or two."

I'm relieved.

"But I wanted to be the one who gives you some good news."

"Good news is always welcome here."

"You're going to like this—and no applause necessary—just throw kisses until I can see you in person. Then you don't have to throw them. You ready for this?"

"I'm on the edge of my seat with bated breath."

"Is that for the news or the kisses?"

"Austin! Spill it."

I wasn't going to call him by his first name.

"It's official. You are no longer a target. We confirmed it was Genken that ordered the hit on you. The shooter we picked up finally talked, knowing that his boss is dead."

"So this is over?"

"We believe so. And the good news keeps coming."

"Yeah?"

"Pasha Boyarov, the man who started this internecine war within the Red Mafiya, is turning himself in. He's struck a deal to roll over on his comrades and then disappear into Witness Protection."

"So he gets off?"

"Yes, which is unfortunate. But we will get the information to shut down or at least severely disrupt operations that include extortion, prostitution, and drugs."

"So it's putting a big hurt on the bad guys?"

"Definitely. They're already hurting with this civil war they're waging."

"So what's in New York for you?"

"Yours truly is going to kick off the Pasha Boyarov debriefing."

Yours? Truly? We do need to talk. Now? Nah. Not yet.

"Congratulations. I'm glad for you. What about the mountain man that cut Frank Nelson's throat?"

"That's Nazar Kublanov. They call him Medved; the Bear. No sign of him. I'm looking forward to finding out where he fit in Boyarov's plans. I'm guessing he's at the bottom of the East River if they managed to cut a hole in the ice big enough to push him through. He's officially a missing person but is presumed dead. He's the least of our worries."

I can hear engines roar in the background.

"I need to sign off. I'll call when I can," he says.

"Sounds good."

Take your time.

So no one is planning to kill me at the moment. That's one step toward normalcy. Next on my agenda is making sure I keep a serial killer incarcerated so he faces trial. I'll worry about Austin and my sister later.

No sooner had Reynolds hung up when my phone chirped again. Zaworski. Could this be good news? Or bad?

I can't believe I'm back on active duty. I need to send Tom Gray a thank you note for going to bat for me with his neighbors in the psych division. Gray is an investigator in Internal Affairs and he and I had a run-in last year back when a perp accused me of excessive force.

Now that I'm official again, I can stick my

nose into the Keltto case. Time to call Blackshear.

"This is Blackshear."

"Bob, this is Conner," I say.

"What trouble you in this time?"

"More than you can imagine, but I might have something good for you on the Keltto case."

"As long as it makes it even easier to convict the person we all know did it, I'm all ears."

"We all know who killed Ed Keltto?"

"I hope we all do. What you got, Conner?"

"I'm sure you got to talk to the kid living next door. I had an interesting chat with him this morning."

"What are you doing working my case without my permission—and, last I heard, while still suspended from street duty?"

"It just happened, Bob. I can explain. I wasn't nosing into your case."

"Okay," he says, not sounding convinced. "What'd you get from the kid?"

Blackshear and I get along pretty easily. He's as exasperated as everyone else that has to deal with me regularly.

I have to stop going out in the cold.

❄ 31 ❄

"*Y así, la hija pródiga ha vuelto a casa. Ven a saludar a papá!*"

I should have taken Spanish as my second language. Who knows? Maybe it's not too late. They have online courses. Spanish would help me on the job, though there are so many language groups in Chicago, it would only be a start. However, it would definitely help me know what Detective Antonio Martinez is yammering about, with his eyebrows rising and lowering faster than the elevators at the Hancock Building, his eyes sparkling, a smirk on his face, his straw fedora perched at a jaunty angle.

"I hear you're fighting the Russians in New York City now. Brave girl." He whistles and shakes his head.

"Who said I'm fighting Russians?"

"I can't remember but I think it was . . . *everybody*. Kristen, you are our *princesa guerrera*."

"I'm your what?"

"You are our princess warrior," Don deadpans. "Lay off, Antonio," he adds.

Did I ask for help?

"Oh brother," I say, blowing a loose strand of hair from my face that has escaped my tightly pulled ponytail. Klarissa says tying your hair too

210

tight damages it. Not sure she's right but it seems to be coming loose more often so I'm at least listening at a subconscious level. Who says I have to be right on everything?

I'm enrolling in a Spanish class tomorrow. Maybe CPD will pay for it if I haven't broken the budget on a security detail. I was fighting with Mom when I signed up for classes my freshman year of high school and took French instead of Spanish, which she was pushing. *Je suis Kristen. Quel est votre nom*? I've said to nobody. Ever.

I give Don a narrow look. Who's been talking? He just shrugs.

Martinez is partnered up with a new kid who looks about fifteen. He enters the conference room, sees me, walks over and puts out a hand to shake.

"You must be Detective Conner. I'm Detective Smith."

"Call me Kristen," I say, shaking hands with him.

He's now supposed to tell me to call him by his first name but goes a different direction: "I've heard a lot about you."

"All good I hope."

Sergeant Konkade, the man who keeps our department running, has walked in with two other detectives that alternate night and day shifts, Sandy Green—new since the Durham murder—and Gabe Fletcher.

"*Sólo decimos cosas buenas de nuestra princesa guerrera!*" Martinez says to me and everyone laughs.

Now what?

"All good," Smith resumes, oblivious to what Martinez is saying as I am. "I heard you got into a fight with a Russian hit man while you were in New York City."

I look back at Martinez and Squires. Both raise their hands with expressions of innocence that look much too sincere to be true.

The door opens and Blackshear, Frank Nelson—our CPD security guy, not the murder victim—and Zaworski walk in. Zaworski doesn't look up but automatically says, "Stop fighting ladies." I'm guessing that is politically incorrect and could earn him a reprimand and some sensitivity training. I'm not going to report him but I glance over at Green. Don't know her very well yet. Some people look for opportunities to file a grievance with the union early and often. Used to be that would hurt your career. Now it sometimes helps because it puts you in a protected category. Didn't get a promotion? Just say that it was payback from a superior you reported.

"Conner, do you know Green and Smith?"

"Green was here when I left, sir. I just met Smith."

"Collin," he says.

About time.

"Collin who?" Zaworski asks.

"Uh, Collin Smith. Me, sir."

I have to remember that Zaworski has only been back in the office for a couple days before I got back from vacation.

He looks at Collin and says, "Okay, that's good to know, Smith."

Smith is beat red. Ha! Nice to see someone else on the hot seat.

"I've only got a few minutes before I'm due to meet with Czaka. So I'm going to hit two items personally and then turn it over to Konkade."

We are meeting in a small battered battleship-gray conference room on the fifth floor of the Second Precinct. I got here early enough that I nabbed a chair with the green vinyl still in one piece.

"Conner, both items deal with you. First, have you got word from your FBI contact that you are no longer believed to be the target of a Russian hit man?"

"Yes sir," I answer, turning slightly red at his reference to my FBI contact. Everyone but Collin Smith knows I've been seeing Reynolds. With Martinez in the department I bet Collin knows about us too.

"Listen careful," Zaworski says, sweeping the whole group with a glance. "If you don't live under a rock and turn on the news, this Russian gang war going on in New York is crazy. I've never seen anything like it. This is Al Capone stuff. Frank"—he glances at Nelson—"tells me two cops got shot this morning in a Mexican standoff."

A Mexican standoff? Zaworski really is old school. I never noticed much before. Even I know you can't say things like that and I am the master of the *faux pas*. There, my high school French did come in handy. I look over at Green. Either she has indigestion or she is offended by Zaworski.

"I have no reason to doubt that the FBI knows what they are doing . . ."

Zaworski leaves it hanging long enough to get gratuitous snickers and laughs. Law enforcement agents from different agencies don't always play nice together.

"You can call me old school and paranoid and you would be correct in both statements," he says. "But Captain Nelson and I aren't as confident as the Feds are that this thing with Conner is dead. So everyone is going to stay alert when she is around."

"Nothing new there," Martinez interjects.

"No joking today, Antonio, this is serious stuff," Zaworski cuts him off gruffly.

Martinez takes the rebuff in stride—he got the smiles from the group he was looking for.

"Frank is going to share some pictures and set some protocol." He nods to Nelson.

"Thanks, Karl."

They must be old buddies. I've never heard anyone call Zaworski by his first name. Don calls him Z-Man—but not to his face. Nelson opens a folder and sends a stack of stapled briefs around the circle.

"There's only two pictures I want you to get a good look at," he says. "First two pages. The main guy is Nazar Kublanov. He goes by the name Medved, which means the Bear. Good nickname. He looks like a bear. He's a low level thug that NYPD has on camera going into Central Park before and after the murder of Francis Nelson. No relation to me."

He looks up to see if anyone thinks it's funny. Everyone is staring at the shaggy mountain of a man who sliced Nelson's throat. He tells a joke as good as I do.

What was the giant's name in *Princess Bride*? All I can remember is that Andre the Giant played the part. He and the Bear could be brothers.

"The guy might be dead or alive," Nelson continues. "There have been no reported sightings of him since D-Day. One of the survivors from the Genken Massacre says he was there the day of the murder. Might have even spent the night. But no body was found there. He might have been taken and killed later. We just don't know.

"The second picture is of Vladimir Zheglov. He is the right-hand man of Pasha Boyarov and his major enforcer. Same thing with him as with

Nazar Kublanov. He might be dead. Might be alive. If he's alive, he's dangerous. We're more worried about him. He's a nasty piece of work. At least eleven known kills."

"If there are that many known kills, then why isn't he in jail?" Martinez asks.

"No witness will testify," Nelson answers. "But let me keep going. Ask questions later. The Feds now have Boyarov. My understanding is they were supposed to bring in Zheglov at the same time. We don't have confirmation. If the Feds have him, everyone needs to say a prayer of thanks."

He crosses himself.

I think back to my short conversation with Reynolds. He mentioned Boyarov. Nothing about Zheglov.

"So who got Boyarov, the Feds or NYPD?" Martinez asks.

"The Feds," Nelson says. "The Russians don't tend to talk. If the Feds have worked a deal that gets Boyarov to sing then that is a major coup. They'll learn the ins and outs of Russian operations up and down the East Coast, from New York to Miami."

Don whistles. I just nod my head, thinking Nelson was included in a briefing with someone from the FBI and is saying way more than he's supposed to, even if he's couching it as personal speculation.

If Reynolds is flying cross-country to work

Boyarov then Deputy Director Robert Willingham is undoubtedly running the show. Austin is his sharp edge of the blade. After Reynolds cut loose from the Army he went to law school. Brains and brawn.

Nelson drones on about other players, including unknown operatives who are in the country from Moscow. No one knows who is working for whom or fighting with whom at the moment, so Vladimir or Med could be tied to any of the warring groups.

"We hope the FBI is right and Conner is no longer on the radar screen. But the Russian mobsters are a different breed and have long memories if they perceive she has moved against them. Bottom line—stay alert. If you see someone who is showing undue interest in Conner that fits either description, you don't engage, but you call a special number we have set up and, if possible, maintain visual contact. Don't get yourself killed being a hero."

Frank's a bit melodramatic if you ask me.

We go through the details of keeping me alive, which takes longer than Zaworski planned, so he stands up before we're done and says, "As soon as Frank is finished, Blackshear is up to discuss a murder that landed in the Fourth but that's been moved to the Second. Konkade can brief me on how you want to proceed this afternoon."

A few minutes later, Nelson gives Blackshear the floor.

"We've got a homicide that occurred on Monday morning down the street from where Conner grew up. Kristen's mom, the widow of Detective Michael Conner, gave Kristen a tip that has yielded some good results. Conner spent the night at her mom's and had interaction the following morning with a juvenile who may or may not know something that will help us further the investigation. I met with Commander Czaka and Captain Zaworski and we determined the Fourth and Second will share responsibility on this one because of Conner's proximity to the murder site."

"You just can't stay away from us, *amigo*," Martinez interrupts.

"There is that," Blackshear says with a smile. "Oh, and I might add my partner, Mike Shepherd, is down with a bad case of this nasty flu. So we're down a man and up a murder on you guys, so this makes sense."

"Always good to work with you, Bob," Don says. "We miss you."

I think they're trying to cheer the guy up for having been knocked down a level. He's smiling. Might be working.

"I miss you guys, too. It's more fun over here— probably because we do all the work in the Fourth."

That gets a groan.

"Of course you have Conner to stir the pot and I know that keeps you jumping," Blackshear adds.

That gets a big laugh. Way too big of a laugh. *Et tu* Bob? The things I put up with just because I keep finding myself in the middle of big cases.

"Okay, sorry Conner," he says, the smile gone. "This shared case will mostly involve just Squires and Conner and me, but we thought everyone needs to be aware of what's happening so Konkade can move cases around—and because it's unique with a potential juvenile witness."

Things get interesting when a juvenile is involved as a potential witness. Not as bad as when he or she is a potential suspect, but it gets dicey nonetheless.

In 2011 the Supreme Court affirmed that special considerations must be in place when we interrogate a child. The reasoning was children aren't able to understand the full significance of cooperating with the police. Justice Sonia Sotomayor wrote the majority opinion and every cop knows what she said even before Blackshear reads it: "A reasonable child subjected to police questioning will sometimes feel pressured to submit when a reasonable adult would feel free to go."

The ruling dealt with the reading of a simplified and amplified version of the Miranda Rights so it shouldn't affect our questioning of Bradley Starks.

But it does. Like every other new law, it starts specific and then starts getting applied with broader strokes. So all questioning of juveniles is something we plan and conduct carefully. The other factor at hand is parental permission. Do we have to ask Karen Starks permission to interview her fourteen-year-old? There is no state or federal law that prohibits police from questioning a minor without parental consent. But for a time CPD adopted a policy that we wouldn't interview kids in connection to a crime without permission. Last year—at least I think it was last year—the policy was rescinded, for obvious reasons. Too many parents said no. But even without the rule, new standard protocol requires that we get approval from a captain before we make the move. It slows things down but beats the policy we had.

"Zaworski will sign the form on whatever we decide," Konkade says, "whether you get permission or not."

He smooths his nonexistent hair on his bald scalp, a nervous habit he picked up during the Cutter Shark case. We all picked up a few nervous habits back then.

We debate whether to ask or not ask and determine to ask Mrs. Starks for permission . . . with a soft ambiguity. We'll see how cooperative she is. The concern is she might go into a defensive stance based on what we already know—she didn't come home the night before the murder. Someone dropped her off with Blackshear and his team already on the scene.

If she looks like she wants to help, we'll ask, assuming she won't say no. If she does say no— or it looks like she might be so inclined—we'll interview Bradley anyway. Blackshear will hint that we might have to call Social Services to let them know about her leaving a fourteen-year-old home alone at night.

This is the part of being a cop that eats at you. You have to get the job done—and sometimes that means getting heavy-handed.

"What about the kid?" Sandy Green asks. "Shouldn't we be calling Social Services either way?"

"If the kid helps us find a killer we don't want to put his competency in question," Blackshear answers.

"That's what it comes down to?" she snorts.

"In this case, it does. Welcome to Homicide," he answers.

"I'll ask around the neighborhood to get the score," I say. "If the kid is in a vulnerable situation, we can deal with it."

"I think we already know the answer to that," Sandy says.

"Listen, we might get lucky and the mom tells us to come in, serves us milk and cookies, and tells us to spend as much time talking to Junior as we want," Blackshear answers, glaring at Green.

"His name is Bradley," she says, undaunted.

If approaching Mrs. Starks goes anything like this, it's going to be a tough interview.

We move on and finalize the plan. We start with the mom, in person, with no advance warning. Squires, Blackshear, and I will set up shop at my mom's house and watch for her. Heck, my mom is keeping an eye on the neighborhood already—she can probably tell us when Karen Starks gets home. Second, it will be Blackshear and me doing the interview, but Konkade insists that will only be after we spend an hour with a child witness specialist.

"We got to do this right folks," he says. "I want to make sure there are no new policies we aren't aware of, and it sure wouldn't hurt to get a briefing on the best way to connect with a fourteen-year-old."

As we exit the conference room an hour later, I see Agent Torgenson standing by my cubicle. I walk over and she puts out a hand to shake.

"Kristen, I am glad this contract killer thing is over."

"Not as much as me."

"Probably true. But now I head back to the FBI office and that means no more workouts with Barry Soto. I figured I would help keep you safe and lose ten pounds in the process."

"You don't have ten pounds to lose," I answer. "But you're welcome to join me in Soto's torture chamber anytime you want."

"I may take you up on that." She smiles. "I was told you are a unique individual, and the reports were correct."

"Reports?"

"The background summary we got before we came over."

"Any chance I can get a look at that report?"

"Not a chance in the world," she says with a laugh. "I shouldn't have brought it up. Sharing sensitive personal data, even with the subject, is definitely off limits."

"Sensitive personal data?"

"I'm making this sound awful. I'm sorry. Don't worry about it. It's all good. You're a rock star."

We exchange a few pleasantries. We promise to say in touch. She has offices on the Loop. She says again that we definitely have to work out together.

So the FBI has a subject file on me?

❄ **32** ❄

"So how's the place? You haven't burned it down yet?" Klarissa asks.

"Uh . . . I should have called. I actually haven't been there yet."

"What?"

"I've been staying with Mom. We had a murder in the old neighborhood."

"You are kidding me. Who was killed?"

"Do you remember Ed Keltto?"

"Mr. Ed? The school teacher? Of course I do. He was a nice man."

"That's what everyone seems to say about him, which makes finding his killer even harder."

"Are you on the case?"

"As of this morning, yes."

"That is terrible. Just terrible. How's Mom doing?"

"She's upset. That's why I've been staying at the house."

"Good for you, Kristen. That's sweet. Do you think you can at least drive by the condo and make sure no pipes have burst in this weather or anything?"

"Sure. I need to get some stuff anyway."

"Really? How long you planning to stay at Mom's?"

"I don't know. Long enough to . . . listen, I'm actually prepping for an interview and don't want to get into stuff now."

"What stuff?"

"Just stuff."

"You're not planning to abandon the condo are you? We agreed you could stay there for the same amount you were paying for your dump."

"Now's not the time to talk, Klarissa," I answer, sounding a lot like Zaworski and Reynolds.

"You are! I can't believe it. Do you know how good a deal you are getting?"

"I know it's a great deal. But—"

"But what?"

"I don't have time to talk now."

"Okay. Your loss. But I didn't want the hassle of vetting a renter. And I would have brought my furniture if I suspected you were going to bail on me."

"We just need to talk, Klarissa."

"That sounds ominous."

I don't answer.

"What is up with you, Kristen? I call because I'm in the middle of a huge story that is putting me on-air nonstop and now I have to deal with you and your moods?"

The drama queen is accusing me of having moods?

"What story are you covering, Klarissa?"

"The only story there is. The Russian mob wars. Don't you watch the news?"

"I should have figured."

"What does that mean?"

"Nothing. It means nothing. I know that's the big story in New York so I should have figured you were covering it. That's all."

"So what's stuck in your craw?"

"I told you, I'm prepping for a witness interview. I just don't have time to get into anything right now."

"So you *are* mad about something."

"I'm not mad."

That might not be exactly true. But I'm hurt more than mad and telling her that will put things on the table and now isn't the time.

"Have you talked to Austin?" she asks, piquing my interest.

"Not much. He's on a case and I'm on a case."

We don't say anything. Maybe he was supposed to have broken up with me by now and she's investigating whether he's done the deed yet.

"Okay. I thought you'd want to talk about this Russian gang war—CNN is calling it Red Storm Rising, which is pretty weak if you ask me. We're calling it the Red Mafiya Wars with the letter y added to mafia. Much stronger I think. But hey, sorry I called. Let me know when you have time to talk about *stuff.*"

I'm about to let her know what I think about stuff but realize she's hung up.

Klarissa and I were close growing up. Then when she moved to Springfield, Illinois, and Kansas City, Missouri, for her first news gigs, we drifted apart. Then we reconnected during the Cutter Shark case, which made me very happy. Now I don't know what happens next.

Thank God for Kaylen. Everybody loves Kaylen and she loves everybody. She is the mother of my nieces and nephew. I told her I would pick up Kendra and James tomorrow and keep them overnight and then bring them to church with me on Sunday morning. Baby Kelsey is too young to be away from mommy, but I know Kaylen is probably ready for some downtime, which doesn't happen much when James is in the vicinity. I miss Kendra terribly. I coach her soccer team, the Snowflakes. We are two months away from the start of season. Yes, we will still be in our yellow uniform—the girls chose the team name and color, not me. Maybe spending time with sweet nine-year-old girls will get me back to normalcy so I can handle *stuff* better.

I think about the Cutter hiring an attorney to appeal his arrest. My stomach clenches in a knot. Normalcy isn't in the picture at the moment.

❄ **33** ❄

We walked through our notes on young adolescent males again.

- Growing interest in girls, but still very uncertain how to interact positively with opposite sex.
- Prefers to be in same sex groupings.
- Less conflict with parents.
- More independent. Strong desire for self-directed choices and activities.
- Despite desire for independence, struggles to plan and organize; still needs boundaries and direction.

- Less literal, growing ability to think in abstract terms.
- Very body conscious, particularly if he perceives himself to be bigger, smaller, more mature, less mature, or different than peers.
- Might struggle to understand and articulate emotions.
- Media saturated: music, movies, games.

Okay. I think that could describe a few twenty and thirty-something males, too. Blackshear and Squires didn't laugh when I pointed that out. Mom made a big pot of chili and we ate in the kitchen. She thought Karen Starks was home from work by seven most days. She said she would watch for us while we ate. We looked at each other and shrugged. Why not?

Understanding generic profiles is great. But how do you get a fourteen-year-old to open up? I pointed out to our child witness specialist that I thought Bradley might be a little immature for his age. Not physically. He looked bigger and thicker than average—maybe 5'10" or so. But he seemed a bit self-conscious and shy.

We brainstormed a list of ice-breakers.

- What's your favorite band? Sports team? Movie?
- What's your favorite class at school? Have

you started to think about what you might want to do for a living?
- What activities are you in at school?
- What are your friends like? Do you have a best friend?

We decided to stay away from the subject of his parents. If he felt neglected or alienated from them in any way, he might shut down. Dad's in Florida and mom is gone all the time. That might do it.

Mom was right. Karen got off the bus and walked up the front steps of her house at seven sharp. We were pretty certain Bradley was home from the time he exited the school bus.

You can live without a car in Chicago with the El and the bus system. But a lot of people still own one. No car for the Starks probably means money is tight. Duh.

Our approach was a disaster. No, we could not talk to Bradley—he wasn't even home. *So who was playing the music upstairs? He must have left it on. It was Blackshear's show so I watched.* When she ordered us out of the house he let her know we would be back with a judge's order and that the interview would take place at the Second Precinct. I thought she might attack him and moved on to the balls of my feet. She wheeled at me and let me know what a crummy neighbor I was. I kept my mouth shut and didn't point out that I hadn't lived in the neighborhood for more than ten years.

Blackshear went for the jugular: "We know you weren't here the night or morning of the murder and that your son was all alone. I'm starting to get the idea that you might have something to hide. It might be time for me to make a call to Social Services."

She folded her arms in defiance and then signed a permission form he pulled out smoothly. I felt sorry for her. I felt sorry for Bradley. I felt sorry for all the things that happen to make people shut down and put up barriers to keep the world out.

Is that what I'm doing?

Bradley didn't have a favorite band, movie, book, sports team, or subject at school. I threw color into the mix. He didn't have a favorite color either. No activities at school. No idea what he might want to do for a living or if he wanted to go to college after high school.

He didn't remember telling me to tell Blackshear that Mrs. Nancy didn't kill Ed, either. We're sitting at the dining room table. Karen is banging pans and dishes around in the kitchen. After Blackshear insisted we talk with Bradley alone, she insisted she would be in the next room taking care of housework. I'm racking my brain to figure out a way to get this conversation going.

"How long were you in the Scouts?" I ask.

"Couple of years," Bradley answers.

"I know you don't like the word 'cool,' but I'll use it anyway. What was the coolest thing you did in Scouts?"

"I liked the campouts."

Blackshear and I nod our heads vigorously and without looking at each other, realize we are way too eager, and back off.

"Where'd you guys camp?" I ask.

"A couple times we went to a state park on the Kankakee River," he answers.

We wait.

"That was okay. But my last year we went up to Wisconsin."

Patience . . .

"That was on a lake. It was really . . . cool."

He smiles.

"Was Mr. Keltto your leader?" Blackshear asks.

The smile is gone. He nods, shrugs, and folds his arms.

"What kind of things did you do?" I ask.

"I know you guys don't care about my stupid scout campout or what classes I like."

Before I can protest, he continues, "You want to know if I saw something to help you find who murdered Ed."

It's interesting he referred to Keltto on a first name basis. Do I assure him we care or let him

231

continue what he started? He makes the question a moot point.

"Mrs. Nancy has a boyfriend. Not her husband. I wasn't watching or anything, but every now and then I would look outside and she would be . . ."

She would be . . . ? I can hear the second-hand on an old-fashioned wind-up mantle clock tick.

He shrugs and says, "She would be hugging and kissing him at the back door when he got there or was leaving."

"Did she know you saw her?"

"Yeah. I walked up the driveway to start working on one of the birdhouses before Ed got home. They were there. I tried to stop and get back to the side of the house but they already saw me."

"Did she say anything? Did he?"

"She just put a finger to her lips and blew like she was saying, 'shhhh,' " he said, looking absolutely miserable.

So far, he's told us nothing my mom hasn't already tipped us to. How will this clear Mrs. Nancy? Makes her look guiltier.

Tick. Tick. Tick. Tick.

I think I have a new understanding of Edgar Allen Poe's *Pit and the Pendulum*. I didn't quite get it when I had to read it in high school.

He looks up. "On the morning Ed was killed, I saw the man. He was there."

"Where Bradley?" Blackshear asks. "In the

house? Outside the house? Did you see something happen?"

Blackshear might be leading the witness.

"Take your time, Bradley," I say. "Just tell us what you saw."

"It was before Mrs. Nancy found Mr. Ed and screamed. I woke up early because I had to finish some homework I didn't do the night before. I looked out the front window. He was walking down the street and got in his car and drove off."

"So you didn't see him murder Mr. Kellto?" Blackshear asks.

Bradley shakes his head no.

Blackshear takes his time and probes what Bradley did and didn't see. Bradley described the car in detail. Even though it was dark, he got a good enough look at the man that he was certain it was the same guy Nancy had been seeing. The man passed under a streetlight between the Keltto home and his car—which was in the same place my mom said he usually parked—and he got a good look at him. The same hair. The same coat. The same walk. The same car. He was sure of it.

Blackshear asked Bradley if he could tell the whole story again with a tape recorder on. He nodded yes. By this time Karen Starks was seated at the table. No one objected.

When he was done, she burst into tears and hugged him fiercely. It was sweet. Maybe something good can come out of something rotten.

"Mrs. Starks," Blackshear said at the door, "you should be very proud of that young man of yours. He did good. He helped us tremendously."

"Yeah. He's a good boy. Deserves better than I can give him."

Bradley is watching from the dining room doorway. I walk over and hand him my card.

"We do care. Call if you think of anything else or need anything."

"I thought our man was in California when Keltto was murdered," I say.

Blackshear, Don, and I are huddled at a table in a matching tiny dining room at my mom's house.

"I got a young pup working on tracking his movements, so it's not confirmed," Blackshear says with a sigh.

"Can you move him along? We need to know," Squires says.

"He is a she. Alyson. Alyson moves at her own pace. And she doesn't work past five. If the mayor was on fire and it was one minute after five, she'd politely let him know she would put him out tomorrow morning."

"Did you get a feel for him?" I ask.

"He landed two nights ago about seven. I met him at the airport. He came straight up to us like he was told. TSA let us use one of their offices to take his statement. He was very forthcoming. Admitted to the affair if you call meeting for sex an affair. But he didn't admit to having plans to leave the missus to run off with Nancy Keltto. In fact, he all but promised to show up anytime, anywhere to talk about anything if it would mean we wouldn't have to be at his house where his wife would learn about his extra-curricular activities. Nothing he said cleared him as a suspect from complicity with Mrs. Keltto in this. But the vibe I got was he was telling the truth. He was afraid his wife was going to find out and he would lose her. He didn't sound like a guy who was ready to have his wife served with papers so he could run off with the love of his life. He didn't look much like a killer either."

"Most don't," Don says.

"So you cut him loose after his statement?" I ask.

"I did," Blackshear says unhappily. "I told him not to leave town or see, speak to, or otherwise communicate with Nancy Keltto without calling me, but that was it. I didn't see him as a flight risk."

"You didn't Miranda him?" Don asks.

"No. That would have shut him up fast. I felt like I was okay treating him like a person of interest, not an official suspect."

"I would have done the same thing," Don says. "But tonight changes everything. We gotta get his movements checked out and confirm his whereabouts on the morning of the murder."

235

"Do we bring him in and talk to him tonight?" I ask. "It'd be good to test his willingness to be anywhere at any time to talk about anything."

It's been a long day. All of us are ready to call it quits. No one says anything for a minute.

"On one hand it would be good to punch him in the nose tonight," Blackshear says. "It would mess up his equilibrium. But on the other hand, we can do the same thing early morning. Do you all see a problem sleeping on this?"

We don't.

"I'll set my alarm for six," Blackshear continues. "I'll call and set up a pickup at seven in a black and white. I think it's time Leslie's wife knows what's going on."

"Whose wife?" I ask.

"Leslie. That's the guy. Leslie Levin."

We make plans to meet up at the Second at eight to interview him. The two men leave. Mom is already in bed again—I'm not much of a support to her. I'm too tired to talk anyway.

"They gone?" I hear her ask.

She pads into the living room where I've locked the front door. I think she's wearing the same bathrobe she's had since I was a little girl. She gives me a tired smile.

"Your daddy would be so proud."

"Ah, Mom."

She hugs me tight.

"I'm proud too. And I love you. And I pray for

you every day you're on the job. It still scares me to death sometimes. But I know you're doing what you love and you're good at it. Like your daddy."

"I love you too, Mom." I hug her back hard.

"Go to bed, you look tired honey. It sounds like you guys are starting early."

"Mom?"

"Yes, Kristen?"

"With everything going on, you okay?"

"Maybe not tonight, but I will be. God always looks after me. So yeah, I'm okay. Besides, what choice is there?"

She gives me another hug and heads back for her bedroom. There for a moment I thought she was going to see a few tears roll down my cheeks. Then she basically let me know she was eavesdropping the whole time.

Maybe Mom should have been a cop.

I brush my teeth, consider a shower, but settle for washing my face. I plop into the bed that has been mine since my earliest memories. I consider reading. I'm halfway through an Ian Rankin novel that features an Edinburgh detective that is always in and out of trouble. I wonder why I like the Inspector John Rebus books so much. I'm too tired.

I look at my iPhone, flip to a Bible app, and read the verse of the day: "Make every effort to live in peace with everyone and to be holy; without holiness no one will see the Lord." Does that count for devotions?

Lord, I'm not sure how well I'm doing in the peace with everyone department. Can I blame it on the job?

Not much of a prayer tonight.

My mind is still working. Nancy, how do you throw away your marriage and run off with a guy named Leslie?

Then I think of what mom said. *What choice is there?* I always assumed I got my attitude about counseling from my dad. Maybe I learned you have to move on, no matter what life throws at you, from my mom.

❄ **34** ❄

The carpet was worn and there were cigarette burn holes on the bedspread and the upholstery of the two chairs on either side of a battered table or desk or whatever else you needed it for. The walls were thin and the room next to his was apparently rented by the hour. The TV set was a big cubed monstrosity that might be twenty years old. The bathtub was stained with years of dirt. It was a dull watermelon color that might not be made anymore.

Medved sighed. It was perfect. The old steam radiator put out plenty of heat and the nightly rate was cheap. Best of all, the owner, probably Pakistani or Indian, Med figured, had a spot in the back of the lot where he could park his truck.

"Anyone going to mess with my truck?" he demanded gruffly.

"No sir. I have a spot where our trash dumpsters used to be. We can pull the gate shut and lock it. But it will cost extra."

Perfect. He liked that the man called him sir. He figured it would take three or four days at most to figure how to hit Detective Kristen Conner. Then he'd be on his way. He went ahead and paid for a full week because the owner offered him a twenty-five percent discount. He added ten bucks a day for the truck and that went in the man's pocket instead of the cash register. Everyone was happy.

"Any good breakfast spots?" The Bear asked.

"We serve pastries and coffee in the morning. Complimentary of course, sir."

"Nah. I want something hot. I'm a meat eater."

"Yes, of course. Two blocks down you will find fast food and local restaurants. One that is very popular is in an old railroad car. It is called the Silver Palm. But it is a little further away and you will not find a spot to park your truck."

"No problem. I like to walk."

Med liked the idea of eating in a railroad car.

"It is very cold sir."

"That's how I grew up. I might not even wear a coat."

The two men found that hilarious and laughed hard together.

"You don't look like you grew up in the cold," Medved said.

"No. It was always hot in Mumbai. Near the Indian Ocean."

"Let me ask you a favor," Med said. "Any chance I can borrow your key to the gate lock for a few days? I'll be sure to return it to you and you alone. That way if I get called on a local job and have to drive it, I can let myself out—and you don't have to freeze your butt off opening the gate."

The man asked for an extra twenty-dollars as a deposit, which Med was glad to pay. He handed him the bill, they shook hands, and the deal was done.

After parking the truck and dumping his stuff in his room, he bundled up to walk down to the Silver Palm for breakfast.

❄ **35** ❄

Vladimir Zheglov rubbed the grease black stubble on his chin. He was sitting in a horrible little apartment in upper Harlem. It was his hidey-hole. No one, not even Pasha, knew about it. He rarely slept there but made an appearance once a month to pay the landlord his rent in cash. It was the kind of place where people didn't ask questions or look at you.

Something was wrong. Everything was wrong. Pasha was supposed to be Pakhan of New York City and run the East Coast Bravta. It was set up with Moscow. Zheglov was to be the Sovietnik, Pasha's chief counselor. It was all agreed. Then all hell broke loose when the Bear failed to deliver Frank Reynolds, Jr. to the warehouse in Queens.

That was the past. Now Pasha was arrested. That was all wrong, too.

Pasha told him he needed a few minutes alone with a girl he had coming over. He told Vlad to disappear for an hour, then come back and they would switch hotels. Vladimir told him it was a bad idea. No one could be trusted. This is how he would be caught. Pasha got angry and told him he knew what he was doing and calling for a little comfort wasn't going to get them killed.

Pasha barked, "Be back in an hour sharp. We're moving."

Vlad ignored the disrespect—for the last time. But his antennae went up. He disappeared like Pasha asked but stayed close. He found a spot in a janitor's closet across the street to watch. The window was up high and he had to stand on a ladder but it gave him the perfect angle to cover the hotel entrance and most of the front desk.

He saw a girl enter the lobby of their boutique hotel. Even bundled up she smelled like FBI to him. But then she came back to the front desk with her coat off, wearing a knee-length professional dress and high heels. The lady working the desk handed her a key. She didn't look quite right for Pasha. Too sophisticated. Definitely not hard enough. But maybe his imagination was playing tricks on him.

Foot traffic was almost nonexistent. People weren't venturing outside unless they absolutely had to. He saw next to nothing for the next hour, including the kind of girl Pasha would send for.

He wondered if he was being paranoid. Of course he was. How could you not be paranoid with NYPD, FBI, and the *vory y zakone* after you?

He thought about walking back over. But a little lizard in the back of his brain said to wait. Five minutes after he was scheduled to return, agents with automatic rifles, wearing black body armor, flooded from an armored transport, and stormed the place. It was an impressive display of power. Pasha was a dead man.

Vlad listened with full concentration for the inevitable gunfire. But the only sounds he heard were from the street. Where was the fight? Would Pasha allow himself to be taken without trying to shoot his way out? Not the Pasha he knew. The two had discussed if it was better to go out in a blaze of glory or be taken into custody. Pasha said a blaze of glory. Vlad understood that beliefs sometimes changed when situations moved from hypothetical to reality. But not even one gunshot?

A black delivery truck rumbled onto the sidewalk behind the assault vehicle. He got a good look at a hand-cuffed Pasha, surrounded by men in black, being pushed inside before both vehicles roared off.

Vlad still didn't move and kept watching. Twenty excruciating minutes later the girl in the short skirt entered the lobby, talking solemnly with a man in a suit and overcoat. The two looked like law enforcement all the way.

So what just happened?

Anyone who survived in this business had a hidey-hole no one else knew about. Vladimir exited an adjacent building a street over from his watching spot and had headed straight there to ponder all he had seen.

Now he sipped a cup of strong black coffee, sitting alone in the dark. It burned going down and warmed him.

The arrest . . . it didn't look right. The more he thought of Pasha's instructions to him an hour before it happened . . . the girl in the lobby . . . no gun shots . . . the more it reeked of betrayal.

Pasha, what have you done? What was supposed to happen to your old friend, Vlad?

Suspicion gnawed at him until it turned to certainty.

No gun. No knife. Bare hands. He would kill Pasha himself.

❋ 36 ❋

Finally stuffed after devouring two orders of the Three Little Piggy sandwich, Med returned to his room, shaved his face and head, and plopped on the bed. He slept most of the day. When he woke the sky was turning from dark gray to a smudgy black. He turned on the TV and laid back down.

The picture on the screen wasn't clear but it was cable so he got the national news stations. He flipped the channel to WolfNews and almost gasped. There was his face along with five others from Pasha's gang. Under his picture was his name and in bold letters, the words, AT LARGE.

He watched with fascination as the news anchor talked about another day of murders in New York City as more faces and names were shown. Under each name was one of a couple statements: Killed; In Custody; At Large; Presumed Dead. It was crazy. Pasha's gang was still taking the brunt of the deaths, but all the brigadiers were losing soldiers.

Did I do all this? He began to laugh uncontrollably until he sucked saliva down his windpipe and choked and gagged for a minute. Someone in the room next door pounded on the wall. Maybe I will pound on you, my friend. Watch that you don't make the Bear angry. He started laughing again.

When the newsman switched to warnings about

another wave of freezing weather being churned up and hurtled south by the polar vortex, he started cleaning his guns, but he kept listening to hear if the blonde was on the air tonight.

As he threaded the black bristles of the brush through the barrel of his Glock, he thought about his current status. At Large. That meant he was being hunted. When he looked in the cracked glass mirror earlier to shave his head again, he still barely recognized himself. He looked nothing like the bearded, bushy-haired man with his name under it.

But tomorrow he would still go to Dollar General to buy new clothes. It was not easy to find pants, shirts, and shoes that fit him. But he needed to get rid of what he brought from home. He had to do everything possible to make the old Bear disappear. No one here would recognize him, but better safe than sorry.

A thought crossed his mind. Why not just drive to Dallas or Phoenix or even Los Angeles now? No. Listen to the Pakhan. He was right. Even a new ID won't protect you from a live witness.

He still needed to get rid of Detective Kristen Conner. Genken had given him a one-page information sheet on her. He needed to get a city map and study the lay of the land.

He looked up to see the pretty young reporter, Klarissa Conner, back on. She solemnly announced breaking news:

"This just in. Notorious Red Mafiya leader, Pasha Boyarov, the man believed to be responsible for this killing spree that has left more than thirty dead in New York City, has been apprehended and taken into custody by FBI agents. He will be held in the Metropolitan Detention Center in Brooklyn in solitary confinement."

The screen showed a man under a blanket being escorted by a small army of FBI agents in what looked like a cargo loading area.

Unbelievable, Med thought. To think, all of this is happening because I was drinking vodka and went outside to relieve myself. Genken—the Pakhan, the big boss—and thirty others dead. More than a hundred arrested.

And now Pasha was captured? Could it be? Was Lady Udacha smiling so brightly on him? The only shadow was that Vladimir Zheglov's name wasn't mentioned in the report.

He looked at the array of weapons he had out on the table for cleaning. Just focus on the detective and forget the death angel. His rifle would be great for a long-range shot, but it could take weeks or months to find the right location—and the weather would have to clear. Not even an option. A handgun would insure the job was done. Her death would have to come from close quarters. He looked at his *pika*. He could slice her throat.

The knife or handgun. Up close.

❄ **37** ❄

"Aunt Kristen!"

I give Princess Kendra a bear hug. I make a move for James, but he escapes my grasp and yells, "No smoochies!" at the top of his lungs.

"James!" his father, Jimmy yells.

It may only last for a brief moment, but life feels normal.

"Hey, James," I say. "No smoochies for me means no pizza for you."

He gives me his hard guy stare, weighs the options in his mind, purses his lips into a tight line, and delivers his kiss with a head-butt before running off.

I rub my forehead. That might leave a bruise. Kaylen tells me I wind James up too much. She's looking at me now with an I-told-you-so expression.

"Are we going to Aunt Klarissa's house or Grandma's house?" the princess asks.

"Grandma's," I say.

"Her house smells funny!" James yells, well out of his dad's arm-reach.

"James!" Kaylen and James yell in unison.

It's good to see family love in action.

"It does! It smells funny," he yells from the stairway, poised for a quick escape.

James, of all people, should not be passing judgment on what smells.

"Does not," Kendra says.

"Does too," James says, his volume one decibel beneath the legal yelling limit.

"I need to give Kelsey a kiss and then it's time to roll gang."

It's one o'clock. I'm only an hour late. I head for the nursery to hold Kelsey for a little while. I need to be with someone sweet and innocent.

I spent the morning in a conference room with Blackshear and Squires interviewing Leslie Levin.

Good looking guy. He was humble and contrite but found numerous and subtle ways to let us know he was a player. "Nancy was nothing. I've had better," was his classic line. What a creep.

Halfway through the interview he quit trying to pretend he wasn't looking at my chest. I didn't get the big genes, so maybe he was just trying to determine if anything is there. But I somehow suspect Leslie ogles anything and everything in his path. Definitely a creep.

Leslie and Nancy hooked up through an online service that I guess qualifies as a dating service. But I think the idea is to skip dinner and movie and maybe any chitchat. Apparently Ed Keltto took care of everyone but his wife. At least that's what Nancy told Les—according to him. His assertion that Mr. Keltto was inattentive is hearsay, of course, but at this point, Nancy isn't talking. She has lawyered. The lawyer isn't letting Nancy talk to us again until he has time to review the facts and have an in-depth discussion with her client.

Leslie corrected me several times after I called him Les. "It's Leslie." That only encouraged me until Squires gave me a look that said knock-it-off.

If Mr. Keltto carried himself with angel wings and a halo, you can see devil horns and a red tail on Leslie from a mile away. I'm being judgmental. Is that a crime? I guess it is to some people.

Nancy hooked up with the wrong guy. He threw her under the bus throughout the interview. He insisted he has no idea where Nancy got the notion he was leaving his wife to be with her. It was just sex for him. Free—he made sure we knew.

Bottom line, he doesn't want to be charged in Edward Keltto's murder as an accomplice. He was doing everything in his power to distance himself from her. In the end it won't work if he's lying. Everybody rolls on everybody.

We still haven't confirmed he was out of town. Blackshear wasn't lying when he said his research assistant is slow. It shouldn't take Alyson more than a day or two to check out the guy's alibi. You get his airline and parking receipts to start with. You ask him where he parked. You call security at O'Hare and have them email the digital video surveillance files. You watch mind-numbing footage until you want to pull your hair out. You confirm that Leslie wasn't lying when he said he drove his car to the airport, the same car Bradley said was parked a couple doors down from the Keltto's house right around the time Ed Keltto was murdered.

Not only does Alyson not work late, she apparently calls in sick a lot. She's been out Thursday and Friday. I'm probably being harsh. The flu is going around.

I told Blackshear I'd look at the video myself. Problem is Alyson didn't put it on the CPD server—a major violation of IT and procedural policy—and she isn't answering the phone from her deathbed. So now we have to wait until Monday unless she picks up the phone and loads the files on the server from her VPN connection.

You can't just fire someone in a union heavy system like the CPD. Alyson has been written up with one formal reprimand. If she gets a second over this, it shouldn't take too long to cut her loose. But you never know.

If Bradley is wrong and Leslie Levin's alibi holds up, we're wasting time we could spend combing through Nancy's life. If she isn't the killer, we're wasting time not looking for other leads.

When we were through with Leslie Levin all I could think is life is difficult enough already, why do some people seek out more complications and problems? Nancy, Nancy, Nancy. Did you even try to work things out with Ed? Did you ever tell him you needed more attention? Who am I to talk? I couldn't tell Austin I wanted a hug after attempting to resuscitate a dead man.

Rachmaninoff's Concerto No. 2 in C Minor played in the background. Vladimir had barely moved in the past few hours. The small living room was dark except for a faint glow from a dull yellow streetlight, which cast shadows that matched his mood.

He stood, cracked his neck and lower back, and pulled out his wallet. He slid out a small stack of cards he kept squirrelled in one of the slots. He turned each one over slowly until he came to the name Arkady Ruchkin.

He slowly ran the edge against the stubble on his cheekbones, up and down, the rasp blending with the music.

Ruchkin. Assistant Attaché Agricultural Affairs with the Russian Embassy. Pasha's contact with Moscow.

Could he call him without getting himself caught?

He would try in the morning.

Chuck E. Cheese works for me about twice a year. Once for my birthday celebration and one other night I have the kids stay over. It ends up being more like four times. I'm not complaining. The kids have fun, though I suspect the allure of the giant piano-playing gorilla and singing rat is wearing off for Kendra. I've got this little ritual where I tell Kendra and James I don't know where I want to go for my birthday dinner. They yell, "Chuck E. Cheese!" and I remember it is my favorite place in the world. Honestly, it works out for me. I can pound out the reward tickets playing Shoot the Moon fast enough to get both of them a prize. Wish my handgun scores on the CPD range were half as good as what I can do on Shoot the Moon.

After a couple hours of pizza and games we went swimming at the Y. My goal was to wear James out so he'd go to bed early. When we got bundled up for the run to the car, my eyes were bloodshot from the chlorine overdose and drooping with weariness. James looked like he was ready for a night on the town.

I drove the kids home in the GTR. He squawked the whole way for getting stuck in the tiny backseat. I've got to get my car back from the garage. I haven't had time to get over there to pick it up. Since finding out my repairs cost more than seven hundred bucks, I haven't been in such a hurry, no matter how mad I am at Klarissa.

We pulled into Mom's tiny driveway and sprinted the few frozen feet to the back kitchen door. I couldn't help myself. I started sniffing. Maybe James is right. Maybe mom's house does smell a little funny. I look at upholstered furniture that has been there since I was a kid. That would do it.

James fumed that Kendra was sleeping with me and he was imprisoned in his mom's old room.

"It isn't fair!"

Life isn't fair, James. You'll learn that sooner or later. Mom, the librarian, went in and read to him for an hour with the patience of Job. I know he—Job—had some terrible things happen to him, but I'm still not sure how patience got associated with his name. It's something my parents said, so it just pops out. I need to read my Bible more.

Mom reading to James worked out great because it gave me time with Princess Kendra without watching out for a head-butt from James.

After church in the morning I'll drive over to Klarissa's condo. Hopefully it hasn't burned down. In five days Mom seems to have got her equilibrium back from a neighborhood murder. Maybe I should just move back in there.

I feel betrayed. It wasn't like I had figured Austin was my one true love. In fact, I'm pretty sure I don't see it working out. I've talked to him just twice this week. Once in a video conference call and once when he let me know no Russian was trying to kill me. Maybe I work for him the same way he has worked out for me. Low demand and maintenance. Maybe he's ready for more. A relationship with Klarissa won't be a walk in the park, but probably not as difficult as one with me, and she's definitely more engaged.

So if Klarissa and Austin make each other happy, I think I'm fine with that.

I'm just mad about them getting started behind my back. You just don't do that. I'll have to get over it. I'll have to forgive. Maybe I'll hash it out with Klarissa tomorrow. She sure isn't going to fess up to it unless I bring it up.

Last time we talked she asked, "What's got in your craw?"

What is a craw anyway?

❆ **38** ❆

So this is the detective who puts my life in such risk? She is skinny. No meat on her. I should have waited for her in the Park. I could have snapped her neck like a twig.

I don't like that she has children. Why did Anasenko Sadowsky not tell me she is a mother? I did not like it when my mother died. Those two are younger than me. But this is America. Everyone gets divorced. There is a daddy somewhere. So they are better off than me. I never knew my father. He was killed in prison before I was born.

They will be fine. It's time they learned life isn't American commercials and TV shows where everyone smiles and has only nice things. In Russia we know death is always around the corner.

How can she afford that nice car on a cop salary? She's probably crooked. Maybe her children are better off without her.

Med drove the Western Star to Conner's address on the information sheet he had been given. It was still day so he had got out and poked around. There was a different name on the mail slot. She'd moved. Wrong address. He'd have to find her for himself.

It didn't take long for Medved to realize there were too many Conners in the encyclopedic Chicago phonebook—with none showing the first name Kristen—for him to find her on his own. He considered calling the switchboard at the Chicago Police Department, but with his heavy Slavic accent, he didn't want to set off any warning bells that someone had come to call on one of their finest with everything going on in the news. They would know she was at risk. They would be keeping an eye on her with everything happening in New York City.

Why would the FBI or NYPD use a Chicago

detective to track Pasha? That didn't make sense to him.

He'd never been in a position of making decisions and taking the initiative, but the Bear wanted as clean a slate as possible.

He thought back to the news reports. Genken dead. He already knew that. Pasha Boyarov in prison. That was new and that was big.

Med gnawed on an idea. Maybe he could . . . No . . . It wouldn't work . . . Don't think about it . . . But why not?

There was only one name he knew in Chicago. Anasenko Sadowsky. Everybody knew Sadowsky. He ran Chicago. Sadowsky visited New York to meet with Genken. Years ago, back when he was still on the rise, he had heard Pasha brag that he had been included. Med assumed Sadowsky and Genken continued to meet and that Pasha was sometimes in the meetings. But what about Vladimir Zheglov? He was important to Pasha's gang but was he high enough in the New York *bratva* to be in strategy meetings between the cities. He hoped not.

Could he do it? He could try.

After changing into a new set of clothes at Dollar General—thank Lady Udacha they carried large sizes—he took a bus to the Holy Trinity Russian Orthodox Cathedral on Leavitt Street in the Humboldt neighborhood. He stepped off the bus into swirling winds. He began walking the streets in a three-block radius around the cathedral, looking at each bar he passed. He came to one named Minsky's. It looked right to him. He entered and sat at the near empty bar.

"What can I get you?" the bartender asked in Russian.

"Are you Minsky?"

"Maybe. Maybe not," the man answered with a scowl. The response was right. Anyone who grew up in Russia knew that answering questions was rarely a good thing to do.

Med matched the man's scowl and said, "I need to speak to Anasenko Sadowsky."

"Don't know him."

"Mr. Sadowsky will want to speak to me."

"That's great. But I don't know him. Never heard the name."

Play this right. What would Vladimir Zheglov do?

"Bring me a bottle of Stolichnaya, my friend. Cold. Ice cold. I need a couple of glasses. I will sit over there," Med said, pointing to a booth.

"I am not your friend," the man answered. "I will bring you a bottle when you show me money."

Med pealed a hundred dollar bill from his wad and left it on the counter before walking over to the booth.

Minsky brought him the bottle and four glasses. Med didn't look up but gave a nod and said softly, "If you remember meeting Mr. Sadowsky, give him a call and tell him that Vladimir Zheglov would like to talk to him."

The bartender never said another word to him but an hour later a Cadillac Escalade pulled up and parked in front of a fire hydrant.

Two men walked in and nodded to him. He stood up. They patted him down thoroughly and none too gently. It was noon and there were maybe thirty men present now. Heads stayed down and no one took notice. After removing the *pika* strapped to his left shin—it would have been suspicious if he wasn't carrying some weapon—and satisfied he was not wearing a wire, one man sat across the booth from him and stared. The other went outside and opened the back door of the Escalade.

A short stocky man with white hair emerged. Now is the time to stay cool, the Bear told himself. Say little. Russians don't like talkers. Think like Zheglov. Be Zheglov. You are not the Bear. You are a powerful man. You are feared and respected.

The white haired man sat across from him and the second bodyguard slid into the booth next to him.

Shut up, he said to himself again. Don't ask questions. Don't answer questions. That's how Pasha and Vlad handled things. Just tell the man what you need.

Nobody said anything. I'll speak first but only one time, Med said to himself.

"I need information on a Chicago detective and I need a car."

The man stared at him for a full minute. Who would break the silence? He finally asked, "What is going on in New York?"

Medved shrugged.

Another stony minute went by. Maybe I could have been a brigadier, Med thought. I am doing this right.

"Who am I helping?"

Now it was going to get very tricky.

"You are helping Vladimir Zheglov and you are helping the *bratva*. You are helping friends who will sort all things in New York out very soon."

"Moscow?" Sadowsky asked.

Med shrugged.

"Genken is really dead?" Sadowsky asked.

Med gave a small nod. He poured four glasses of vodka and lifted his glass. The men did nothing. He shut his mouth and waited. They brought the glasses up slowly and the four men toasted.

"To Genken," Med said.

Another excruciating pause.

"I heard you pulled the trigger," Sadowsky said, eying him warily with perhaps a hint of hostility.

Med stared. He didn't know what to say, which was good. It made him tough like Vlad. He couldn't speak until Sadowsky said something else.

"What will Boyarov tell the Americans?" the man asked.

"Don't worry about Pasha. He will be handled."

Where did that come from? It was a good answer.

"Tell me the name," Sadowsky said, holding his hand out.

Med slid the sheet of paper across the table.

"From the Pakhan's own hand," Med said. "But the information is out of date."

Sadowsky let his hand rest on it and stared at the Bear. Med had done prison time. He knew the game. He stared back. Sadowsky finally looked down at the paper and handed it to the man sitting next to Med, who got up and walked to the back of the bar.

Now is not the time to drink too much, Med told himself. You say too much when you drink. You get too friendly. He sipped on a single glass of vodka for the next thirty minutes, despite his urge to pour the whole bottle down his throat.

The bodyguard returned and handed a clean sheet of paper to Sadowsky. Sadowsky slid it across to Med, face down. Med wanted to snatch it up but told himself, don't touch it. Be cool. You are a powerful man. You are Vladimir Zheglov. Don't show eagerness or nervousness. Be patient.

"Where do you want the car delivered?"

Med almost looked up with a smile. Vlad would not smile. He fought it down and looked at the table. You can do this. Your problem is you drink too much Stolichnaya. Not another drop until Kristen Conner is dead and you are hundreds of miles away. Med had mapped his route toward the south. His next stop would be St. Louis at the earliest and maybe as far as Tulsa. I-55 south out of the city and pick up I-44 westbound in St. Louis.

"Here," Med answered.

Another long pause and Sadowsky said, "We work well with Chicago Police. Many friends there. We don't bother them and they don't bother us."

Med looked up slowly. What would Vladimir do? They wouldn't care what the Chicago *bratva* thought.

"Chicago is a dangerous city," he said with a shrug. "High murder rate. People die every day."

The bodyguard whispered in Sadowski's ear.

Medved knew life and death hung in the balance for him. He held his tongue.

Another tediously long pause slipped by before Sadowski said, "You will remind our friends that we helped."

Med wanted to dance on the table and shout, yes, I will say anything you want me to. But that was not what men of power did.

He looked Anasenko Sadowsky in the eyes and gave the smallest nod he was capable of.

Ten minutes later he drove away in a five-year-old, nondescript Chevy Malibu. It was too small for his liking but it was perfect for what he had to do next. No way could he have kept looking for Kristen Conner in a dump truck. One thing he knew how to do without trying was drive a car in heavy, confusing traffic, even if his days of driving a cab were over.

Med pulled into a filling station two miles from the Holy Trinity Cathedral. I'm a different man. Maybe it is owning a valuable truck. Lady Udacha has given me a new reason to live. I will be a successful businessman. Maybe I will have many trucks one day. Men will answer to me, the boss. I will marry a new girl in Texas or California. I will have kids.

He spent the next forty-five minutes looking for the transmitter. He almost gave up but found it in the inside flap of the Malibu's owner's manual. He went inside the Gas and Grub and bought a small tube of Gorilla Glue. He went back to his car and watched the flow of customers sliding credit cards in and out of the slots on the gas pumps next to a small TV screen with commercials about all the things that could be purchased while fueling up their cars. Every now and then someone pulled up, went inside to prepay his or her gas in cash. He counted how many seconds it took.

I am getting good at this thinking. He waited for

the perfect moment. When have I had patience like this? When a line formed at the single cash register and a man in a beat up pickup truck went inside to pay, he made his move. He slipped the transmitter under the lip of the front bumper with enough glue to hold it in place for years. If Sadowsky finds out I'm not Vladimir, no matter how much power I have shown, he will find me and kill me.

The Bear ambled slowly and confidently back to the Malibu, got in, and returned to his motel. After checking that his Western Star was fine, he went to his room. He pulled out a map of Chicago and compared it against the sheet of paper that Anasenko Sadowsky had given him. He plotted out places he would watch Kristen Conner to find the best place to kill her.

He followed her from the Second Precinct to her sister's house and then to the game arcade. He had never seen a Chuck E. Cheese. A couple times he wondered if he could go inside. The games looked fun. He wanted to play whack-a-mole.

But he was not the old Bear. For a couple more days he was Zheglov, the death angel.

It was Sunday morning. Medved overslept. He had drank a bottle of Stolichnaya while watching TV the night before. He only meant to take one, maybe two drinks, to take the edge off a long, stressful day. It was only a temporary slip, he thought. Not another drop until Tulsa. Time to pick up the trail of Detective Conner again. I do wish I didn't have to kill the kids' mother. Very sad for them. I know. I know. But it must be done. Perhaps she is not a good mother.

❄ **39** ❄

Vladimir Zheglov arrived at the meeting spot three hours early, as was his custom when sailing in uncharted waters.

He made the call to the man in the Russian Embassy that was Boyarov's contact. It took five attempts—the man was too busy to talk to just anyone. Vlad finally said the words he wanted to avoid saying at all costs: "Tell Arkady Ruchkin that Vladimir Zheglov would like to speak to him."

He looked at his watch. With the FBI monitoring calls through NSA eavesdropping technology, he had three minutes to stay online tops. Ruchkin was on the phone almost immediately. They concluded the business of setting a meeting place and time in less than ninety seconds. Zheglov wasn't happy it took that long. He knew what he was doing. He could tell Ruchkin didn't.

"Never call here again," Ruchkin hissed as they hung up.

The meeting was set for the Time Warner

Building on Columbus Circle. He shook his head. He was just a couple hundred yards from where this all had begun.

His preparation began hours before he set foot in the Time Warner Building.

First he went to a barbershop at the corner of Eighth Avenue and Fifty-First. At forty, his hair was turning salt and pepper and was all white at the temple. He asked for a businessman's haircut and to have his hair died black, along with a straight edge shave to have all stubble removed.

"You must have a job interview young man," the elderly barber said with a laugh.

"You are correct on that. Got to look my best and the guys I'm competing against look like teens. Everyone wants to hire young guys, right?"

"You aren't lying," the barber said. "Young guys cost less money. That's what those turds do to save a few bucks. But I guarantee you'll look your best when I am done with you. How old are you?"

"Forty."

"People won't believe you're thirty when I'm done with you."

When the man was done, Vlad looked in the mirror and had to admit, he did look good. Would people believe he was thirty? Nyet. He still looked close enough to forty.

Next he headed south a couple blocks, went into an optometrist's showroom and purchased a pair of stylish turtle shell glasses with clear lenses.

The effect was good if you wanted to look like someone different. Very good.

His next stop was H&M department store. He rode a cab to Rockefeller Plaza and walked five blocks south, following every counter-surveillance maneuver he knew. Walk fast. Walk slow. Use the reflections in windows as mirrors to spot followers. Keep an eye across the street—and ahead. But don't let anyone know what you are doing. Easier in spy novels than real life, he thought.

A suit? No. He wanted to be ready to move fast. He picked out a nice pair of slim fit twill pants. Not warm enough for this weather but if he was outside he would be running and it wouldn't matter.

He picked out a jacquard-knit sweater and a mock turtle to go under it. Next he bought a pair of soft-soled desert boots. Not much protection against the polar vortex but he could run in them if needed and better than sneakers or deck shoes against the slushy streets of wintery New York. He picked out a stylish quilted jacket, continuing to make sure he selected clothes he would never otherwise buy. When he was done, he bundled what he was wearing in the small duffel he was carrying. He took a look in the mirror. Not bad. Not until we're up close will Ruchkin know it is me. From more than a couple yards, I have a whole different look.

He walked north, monitoring his surroundings, and went into the Tumi store and bought a large canvas tote with leather handles and edging. He eyeballed the dimensions until he was comfortable it would hold what he needed to bring to the meeting.

He took a cab to Penn Station. In a bathroom stall he transferred a custom Remington sawed off shotgun into the bag. The barrel was less than eighteen inches long and illegal in just about every state. Didn't matter. Everything was illegal in New York City. If he was going to be ambushed, people would die with him. He added two Springfield .45s with the maximum number of shells in the clip. He put a third Springfield in his left pocket and a fourth in his right pocket. He strapped a Gerber LMF II survival knife at his belt and a second on his right leg.

He took the shotgun out, added a pillow to the tote so the gun was positioned close to the zipper opening. He added four more clips of .45 bullets to a side pocket.

Pasha laughed at him and said he packed too much when they were preparing for field work. Better safe than sorry. Pasha is in custody and I'm not.

If I'm walking into a trap, Arkady Ruchkin and whoever is backing him up will die. I might too. But not without a fight. I won't go like Pasha did.

Zheglov checked every public egress and exit

point in and around the meeting area. He then wandered in and out of shops to check escape routes not visible to the public. He went to a coffee shop a couple blocks away, sketched out ambush points and exit routes from memory. He studied his chart for thirty minutes and returned to the Time Warner Building. He had picked a lookout spot two levels above the large basement level atrium where he and Ruchkin were to meet. It was densely congested with shoppers on a Sunday afternoon. No one wanted to venture out in the frigid air. Better to hide in a crowd anyway, Zheglov thought.

Ruchkin was to come alone. That didn't mean he would. He probably wouldn't. So Vladimir watched to know who else might be studying the area to identify his threats.

A few minutes before the meeting time Zheglov spotted Ruchkin, a mid-level attaché in the agricultural department, who supposedly held a much higher level in a field that paid much more lucratively than tracking wheat, corn, and soy beans.

He had already spotted a man across the atrium floor that looked like a good candidate. He looked back over at him. Sure enough, he watched Ruchkin as he neared the meeting spot. Then the two men gave one another small, barely perceptible nods. Vladimir almost smiled. Amateurs. They were handlers, not field men. They needed to get out more often and get their hands dirty tilling the soil of their profession.

The agreed signal was Ruchkin would order one cup of coffee if he thought their meeting was in anyway compromised. Don't come. Two cups of coffee meant it was fine to join him at the table.

Vladimir's eyes swept the crowd for another five minutes. He couldn't find a second man. Another mistake. Ruchkin was now in place, two cups of coffee on the table.

Vlad took the escalators down one level. Ruchkin's watcher never saw him coming. It was too easy. He slid the stiletto between two ribs in the back and pushed to where he knew the heart was.

He caught him around the waist before he could fall forward and put one of his arms over his shoulder. He half carried, half dragged the man to the door of the men's restroom. A young punk with about twenty facial piercings gave him a hard look. Trying to be a tough guy.

"Excuse me. My friend is sick. He is about to vomit again."

The kid made room for him to pass through the door.

A stall was open. He got inside with him, undid the man's belt, dropped his trousers, and sat him on the toilet seat. He pulled out a roll of duct tape, wrapped it around the man's torso four times and then around the toilet tank until the roll was empty. The man had died instantly and wasn't going to stand up and leave. But Vladimir didn't want him falling forward. He checked the tape and stood up. The man's bowels released. A rancid stench filled the space. Good. More realistic.

The whole process took less than two minutes, from stopping his heart to taping him to toilet tank.

He yanked the ear bud out of the man's ear, found the transmitter, and stuffed both in his jacket pocket.

He exited the restroom and strode confidently to Ruchkin's table. The man looked slightly surprised. He was expecting a heads up from his compatriot.

"Sorry I am late. I got detained. Thank you for the coffee."

"No problem and my pleasure," Ruchkin answered.

"Were you followed?"

"No. I'm certain of it. I took precautions. With everything going on, I was very, very careful."

"And you came alone?"

"Of course. We agreed."

"Good. Tell me what is happening."

"I was hoping you could tell me."

Zheglov reached across the table and calmly pulled the listening device from Ruchkin's ear.

"You won't be needing that. Now give me the transmitter."

Ruchkin looked shocked.

"If I have to ask you again you won't like what happens next."

Ruchkin pulled a matching device from inside his coat pocket and handed it to Vlad.

"Let's walk Andy. That is what Pasha calls you, Andy, not Arkady, correct?"

He nodded and asked, "Where?"

Zheglov's look told Ruchkin he wasn't going to ask a second time. The two men walked together to a cigar shop. When Ruchkin paused in the doorway, Vladimir said, "Keep walking. Past the counter."

They passed the cash register where a dapper gentleman with flowing white hair began to mouth a protest. He saw the Springfield .45 DMX in Vladimir's hand and closed his lips tight. They went through the back room. Vlad pushed open a service door that opened to a wide hall where deliveries were made.

"Move and be quiet."

They passed the loading bay and the two men descended the steps and walked up an incline to Ninth Avenue. Vlad raised his hand for a cab.

"We will tell each other all we know. If you cooperate, you go home to your family tonight. I am sure your wife and three lovely children would like that. Understood?"

Ruchkin gulped and nodded.

Zheglov knew that Ruchkin was an amateur being used by professionals. Arkady knew nothing he wanted to know except one thing. A name and how he could be reached.

❄ **40** ❄

I love my sister and brother-in-law—and not just because they have provided me with sweet nieces and a hyperactive nephew.

I do wish Jimmy would end his sermons at noon, but fidgeting the last ten minutes of a church service is a small price to pay for being around good, kind, gentle people like them.

I know I'm sounding like a Marine, but I realize I do what I do so that they can do what they do without being jaded by the ugliness of life. I have no problem with that. I am glad they are sweet and effervescent and everything I was taught to be. I love God. I'm a good girl. I'm a church girl. But a lot of my life is spent interacting with the worst of humanity. It didn't start when I got bumped to homicide with a detective shield. Since the first time I spent a Saturday morning with my dad in a police station, seeing good and bad people come through the doors, all with a story of violence or debauchery, I knew I wanted to be a cop, to battle injustice at the street level.

Okay, now I'm sounding like a comic book

character. I somehow don't think I'd look good in a cape—though Klarissa already got me a mask I can wear.

Jimmy preached on the power of positive thinking today. It was a good sermon, even if he got carried away for an extra fifteen minutes, when he had already said everything we needed to hear. His verse was: "I can do all things through Christ who strengthens me." I did need to hear that. I have a lot of things to do. I have to make sure the Cutter stays in prison. I want to help clear what looks like a pretty simple murder case that is starting to drag. I have to figure out how I'm going to handle the Klarissa and Austin situation. Dear God, I do need strength.

By ten after twelve my head was bobbing, my eyelids were closing shut, and I was unsuccess-fully stifling a series of jawbreaker yawns. Kaylen elbowed me. Okay, she's not always sweet. Then my phone vibrated and against better judgment, I sneaked a look—Kaylen caught me and gave me another jab and another disapproving look. It was a text from Blackshear letting me know the deathly ill and very slow Alyson had put the O'Hare surveillance tapes on the server. It was all I could think about for the final few minutes of church service.

I hugged my precious Princess Kendra in the church foyer, breathed in the fragrance of baby Kelsey, and captured squirming James in a bear hug—me thinks thou dost protest too much—and ventured into a blinding sunny day that promised more than it could deliver. The bright shining light couldn't mask the bitter cold. I fired up the GTR, intent to work on the surveillance tapes at Klarissa's place.

At a red light I looked down to double check Blackshear's text and respond: *All son uploaded fillets. Stuck at famine event. Do you have thyme?*

It's possible I interpreted this wrong and he wants us to cook together to end world hunger.

I text back: *Yech!* at a red light. I meant to say *Yes*. If he isn't editing his voice-to-text than neither am I.

We have to get moving on the Ed Keltto murder. We think we have what we need to at least charge Nancy Keltto with murder-one.

She is very predictable. Not smart when someone wants to kill you, though she doesn't know that. She left her kids with other people. She is probably not a very good mother.

Med kept three cars between his Malibu and the little sports car she was driving.

Maybe Lady Udacha is smiling on me again. I don't want the kids to see their mother die. If I follow the skinny detective to the right place, I'll do it now and be on the road tonight. He patted his pockets. The gun and knife were where he left them.

Got it. Leslie Levin wasn't lying. I'm watching grainy black and white footage. I see his make and model enter the parking lot. I get a good look at the license plates and confirm it is his black Infiniti. I note the file number and time stamp. I do the math in my head. Was there any way he could have driven from West Lawn where Keltto was murdered and get to O'Hare at 6:30? I wouldn't cut it that close if I was flying out of town but it seems possible. Someone will have to make the drive based on the presumed time of the murder. The most likely route would be to take Cicero or Harlem to I-290 and then I-294. It would be close.

Now I want to verify that it was actually Levin in the car.

I look at the menu of cameras to see if I can spot his creepy face entering O'Hare. One of the most likely cameras is missing from the menu. Alyson is slow—and not very careful. Not a great combination for police work.

I stand up. Can't do this anymore. I need a break. But I do want to put a checkmark that Levin was at the crime scene or not at the crime scene. I plop back down. I watch another hour of video and spot him. I move the image back and forth at least five times. Yep. It's him.

I'm back in Klarissa's condo. A week ago I was calling it my condo. It's a very nice place just off

Lake Shore Drive with a beautiful view of Lake Michigan, a private parking garage, and a doorman from six a.m. to midnight. Bernard works a few evenings during the week and one of the weekend nights. He is my favorite. After parking the car, I went in the lobby to say hi. How old is he? Maybe seventy, maybe eighty. His snowy white hair and deeply creased face are timeless. He is the only doorman that is allowed to eschew the dark uniforms and wear his own outfits. I can't help but smile. His yellow tuxedo will wake you up and put a smile on your face. The purple suit with bright teal bowtie he had on tonight is maybe my favorite. Bernard is a showman whose beaming smile makes you feel good even on a bad day. He won't call me Kristen, only Miss Kristen, so I return the favor and call him Mr. Bernard.

"Well, well . . . Miss Kristen is back. It is so good to see you young lady," he said to me when I popped out to greet him.

It will be tough to give this up.

Klarissa got rid of her townhome after a bad experience with a stalker and moved in with mom for a couple months. After interviews in Atlanta and LA didn't pan out for a promotion to a national news show, she bought the condo. Then New York came calling. If she inks the deal, she'll have her own primetime news show. She's only twenty-eight. Not a bad career path.

I think about what I'm paying her. I doubt it

covers half the mortgage payment. No way. I have wondered if Klarissa will be able to maintain the arrangement when she finally gets a place of her own in New York City. There's nothing cheap there—and she obviously won't stay in a dump that I would find perfectly acceptable. After recent events, I'll make it easy for her. She can sell the place or find a renter at fair market value.

I think about sprawling on the elegant Queen Anne couch and watching some TV. But I've had enough excitement watching surveillance footage. I need some exercise.

I head over to the marble foyer, drop down, and start pounding out twenty-five burpees with double pushups and jumps. I am red faced and panting heavy before fifteen. My arms are shaking by twenty-one. I roll on my back and start on fifty pikes—alternating ten fast and ten incredibly slow. My stomach is a knot by thirty. I jump up, put my hands behind my head and do lunges, starting at the doorway, crossing the living room floor, swiveling, and crossing back. I lose count but my butt and quads are burning.

It hurts so good.

I drop down for another twenty-five burpees—but no double pushups and jumps this time. I collapse at ten. I hate to be a quitter. When I stand up I realize I need to mop sweat off the floor. It can wait. No visitors tonight.

I head to the master bedroom for a shower.

There was no food in the refrigerator. I'll order delivery if any drivers are willing to brave the weather. If not, I think there are some cans of soup in the small walk-in pantry. No canned peas—which is good. That will have to work if I can't get delivery.

I detour back to the kitchen and pull the Golden Palace menu off the refrigerator magnetic clip and order cashew chicken. Yes, they are delivering, the order taker tells me. My lucky night.

As I towel-dry my hair after a quick shower the doorbell rings.

That was fast. This really is my lucky night. I throw on a pair of pajama bottoms and my lucky Northern Illinois Husky sweatshirt that has seen its better days. The bell rings again.

"I'm coming," I yell.

I can taste the chicken now. I forgot lunch and I'm starving. They aren't going to brave the cold and leave quick I hope. I head for the door. Dang. I need my wallet. I head back into the bedroom to find it.

Hurry. How often do you get this lucky? Must be a slow night for Chinese food to arrive this quickly.

❄ **41** ❄

"I wondered how I might reach you Vladimir," Teplov said. "You have saved me the trouble and found me yourself."

The two men stared at each other, each with a gun pointed at the other's chest. Zheglov said nothing.

"Vladimir Zheglov. I've heard good things about you. Pasha Boyavov said you are very good. I can see that for myself. What you did at Genken's was very impressive. Let me guess how you found me. Ruchkin was always a weak link."

He looked for confirmation. Zheglov's eyes never left his eyes or blinked. The stare was disconcerting.

"Let me assure you," Teplov said, "We are on the same side of this unfortunate set of circumstances. It is time we put down our weapons of mutually assured destruction and figure out what to do next. Together. There is a place for you in the new order."

"You put down your gun first," Vlad said.

Teplov sighed and lowered his Makarov, confident . . . almost . . . that Zheglov would work with him. The truth was, he was looking for Vladimir and did need him—and there was a future for him in the *bratva*, which would now be under total control of Moscow. None of the five active brigadiers had been selected as next Pakhan. But he could make sure Zheglov was part of the deal. Have him tie up a few loose ends, then send him overseas for a year until things cooled. When he came back he could report to the new Pakhan and become eyes and ears for him in Moscow.

Or he could just have him killed for his role in killing Genken.

"Sit, Vladimir. Let's talk. Then we will toast a bright future."

The two men sat across from each other in comfortable leather chairs in his suite at the London Hotel. Their guns sat on a coffee table in front of them. I am good but Zheglov might be better, Teplov thought. As he prepared to speak his phone buzzed.

"Vladimir, I am going to reach in my top pocket and accept this call. If you would like to pick up your gun to feel comfortable, you may do so."

Zheglov picked up his Springfield XDM 45, a nice handgun the Springfield Armory had manu-factured by HS Produkt in Carlovac, Croatia. It was based on a model the Croats commissioned for their war with the Bosnians. It was reliable, which was all the trust Vladimir needed.

"This is Sergei," Teplov answered.

The volume was set high and Vlad could hear the response: "This is Anasenko. *U nas yest' problemy*, Sergei."

If it was Anasenko Sadowsky, it meant problems in Chicago too. Nothing could measure up to all that was going on in New York City.

Teplov smiled at Zhelnov and said, "We have no problems, Anasenko. We only have solutions."

Zheglov noticed he pushed the phone tighter to his ear to block him from hearing what came next.

After thirty seconds of listening and nodding, Teplov broke into a broad smile.

"Describe him, Anasenko."

He burst out laughing.

"Anasenko, someone is playing you for the fool. What you tell me is impossible. Vladimir Zheglov is sitting right in front of me at this very moment."

Zheglov didn't like that and the gun raised a couple centimeters.

Teplov raised a hand and said loudly, "Anasenko, do nothing. Think nothing. I will call you back in an hour and the mystery will be solved."

He turned to Zheglov and said, "Put down the gun, Vladimir. We have a puzzle to solve and then some work to do. Tell me if you can figure something out for me. Sadowsky tells me a man has come to him. He is a giant, as big as a bear. No hair on his face or head. He says his name is Vladimir Zheglov."

Sadowsky didn't have to wait an hour. Teplov called two minutes after they hung up.

"Kill him. Make him disappear."

❄ **42** ❄

Kristen fumbled around in the cluttered bed-room for her wallet—she hadn't started laundry yet. Where did you hide? She wanted to get to the door. Her phone chirped. What now? I have cashew chicken calling my name. Klarissa.

"Let me call you back, Sis, we need to talk."

"I know we do. So what's the rush?"

"I've got a delivery guy at the door."

"Nice try. Mom told me you're back at the condo. So I know you don't."

"Don't what?"

"Don't be difficult. I know you don't have a delivery guy at the door."

"Yes I do."

"Impossible. No deliveries are allowed to individual units."

"Then why is there a guy from Golden Palace ringing the doorbell?"

"If you say so," she says. "But they make me pick up at the lobby. Homeowner's Association is very strict on this point. So stop trying to con me."

"Never?"

"Never."

"What if Bernard likes me more than he likes you?"

"Not possible. Bernard makes all of us feel

like he loves us most. And he's strictest with the rules."

The hairs on Kristen's neck stood up.

"I'll call back, Klarissa."

"Don't hang up!"

Too late. She pulled her Sig Sauer from the lock box after turning the key with a shaking hand. She did a quick status check. Ten in the clip and one in the barrel. She released the safety. Just don't point a gun at Mr. Bernard if he's knocking because you left something in the lobby.

She crept toward the front hall.

❄ **43** ❄

Fancy car. Fancy place. She's corrupt. Too bad I had to punch the old man guarding the door. He should have just told me her number. Why do people make things so difficult? Good thing her name was on the mailbox. K. Conner.

But this is getting too complicated. I did very good, my very best with Sadowsky. But now my head is hurting from thinking too much. He hit the doorbell again.

Just come to the door skinny, little girl. Just stick your eye in the hole.

He looked at his watch. He figured he needed to be clear of the Lake Building in another two or three minutes. He parked three blocks away. After walking past the front door several times he didn't figure there was much chance the old man in the crazy purple suit would let him in without a good reason. He walked five blocks and bought a to-go pizza from Armand's. He had them put everything on it and extra sausage. It would be his dinner after this Detective Conner business was done. He knew he had said he would wait until St. Louis or Tulsa, but the deed would be done, so he would wash it down with a bottle of Stolichnaya.

Rule number one if someone potentially dangerous is knocking on your door is call the police. I am the police so I can check that off. Rule number two: don't stick your eye in the peephole. What you don't know is out there might kill you—or at least put out an eye.

The doorbell rings again, followed by five sharp raps.

Do I just wait until something happens? Do I yank the door open and point a gun in someone's face? That someone might be Bernard if he's still on duty. I don't think Klarissa lived here long enough to know anyone else in the building. Would someone stop by to ask for an egg or cup of sugar? I don't think they do things like that here.

Maybe the person on the floor below heard me doing burpees. I doubt it. The walls and floors are thick and insulated to keep sounds out. I guess I hear classical music coming from next door sometimes. But it's very low. I've never heard anything above or below.

Patience isn't my strong suit. I decide to yank it open.

❄ **44** ❄

Reynolds nodded and the three men stood abruptly. They'd been at it for three hours. He gave Pasha Boyarov a hard stare as he knocked to have the door opened from the outside. No inside handle. Boyarov met his eyes and glared back just as fiercely. Reynolds hated to be the first man to blink but one of the two guards at the door was coughing softly. Boyarov was a savage murderer with and without a weapon. Even with numbers on your side, the remanding guidelines specified not to give him room to move and attack. He was a loose cannon and very unpredictable.

As Reynolds turned, he saw the smile on Boyarov's face.

Ten minutes alone tough guy. Let's see who is standing.

This guy is going to be a tough nut to crack, he thought. We gave him too much up front and he isn't afraid. We'll have to figure out how to change that.

He exited the goldfish bowl and went up to Deputy Director Robert Willingham who was watching the interview with Dr. Leslie Van Guten, an FBI profiler and his ex-spouse, and a translator for those exchanges when Boyarov seemed to forget his English despite living in the US for more than twenty-five years. He had arrived as a young teen.

"What do you think?" he asked Willingham.

Willingham shrugged and looked at Van Guten.

"He's just playing," she answered. "He's sizing you up, Austin. And he's doing quite well. You need to curb your testosterone in the interview room."

"That I am very aware of," Reynolds said, trying to stymie the steam that was rising from him. "But what I'm asking is if you see a man who is going to be of any help to us, will he settle down and get to business?"

"If you need fast answers on this potential bioweapons threat, no," she said. "If he knows as much as you think he does about the American *bratva*, then yes, he will help you tremendously. Everyone talks eventually. But Austin, I suspect you will be on to something new before that happens."

Reynolds smiled. Van Guten liked to get her digs in any chance she got.

"Can you tell when he's lying?" Reynolds asked.

"Russian communication characteristics aren't my specialty. I've already told you that, Austin."

"Back to Reynolds' first question," Willingham interrupted. "Did you see any response from Boyarov on the key questions that might indicate he has knowledge that can help us on the bio threat, however we get him to talk?"

"I can only surmise what you two already know," she answered. "He knows a lot. But it's now out of his control. I don't think he ever really knew who his champion was against Genken. Part of the reason he's playing tough guy is there's a lot you are asking that he doesn't know. That's why he came in. That's the only reason he would turn himself in."

"Felt like bravado to me, too," Willingham said.

"There was desperation beneath it," Van Guten added. "And something else. Maybe shame."

"I know it's a guess," Reynolds continued, "but do you think he knows what he was buying from Nelson and PathoGen?"

"Yes, but with a caveat."

She paused and straightened the cat's-eye glasses she wore to look smart. Actually, she is plenty smart without the glasses as a prop, Reynolds corrected himself.

"So, shoot," Willingham said, impatient now.

"He probably knows broad parameters but I don't think he's high enough up in the hierarchy to know details."

"How are the computer techs doing?" Reynolds asked Willingham, glad to shift the focus from Van Guten.

"His transaction with Nelson was very sophisticated. And maybe impossible to crack because the program was hosted in several international locations on the deep net before it erased itself."

The deep net, home to hackers the world over. It was much more vast than what the world assumed was the extent of the worldwide web. Finding traces there, without having the originating hardware, was like looking for a needle in a haystack, no matter how many spiders the NSA had trolling.

"Did the Russians get what we think they did?" Reynolds asked.

"No way to tell at this point—and maybe never. But we do have one lead. In Switzerland to be exact. I've been told the transaction protocol matches a whisper of a fingerprint of a broker in Geneva. The problem is, if it's the man we suspect of facilitating the transfer of a biotech code in exchange for a large sum of money, he sets it up so not even he knows how to retrieve the electronic files and transfers."

"That's convenient," said Reynolds.

"Very convenient," Willingham said. "It's his way of staying out of jail and, more importantly, staying alive. If he is powerless to do anything, he has fundamentally shielded himself from dangerous clients that aren't satisfied with his services. Best of both worlds. He explains it very clearly up front and has a document signed by both parties that nothing criminal is being exchanged."

"He learned from the best," Reynolds added. "No one better than the Swiss bankers at maintaining an aura of neutrality to help bad people. They were Hitler's best friends."

"Things have changed," Willingham said. "They've had to cave to international pressure so they've lost some of their business based on losing absolute confidentiality in regard to their clients. But yes, this echoes what some of their best and brightest—and richest—did during World War II with the Nazis."

Reynolds looked through the one-way glass at Boyarov. There were ways to get him to talk. But none were legal. He doubted if the top floor of Homeland Security would change that reality without a battery of meetings that could take days or weeks—time they didn't have.

"What next?" Reynolds asked. "I'm ready to spend more quality time with Pasha."

"I wouldn't advise it right now," Van Guten answered for Willingham. "You two are in an alpha struggle of epic proportions. I know you both will hate what I have to say, but give Boyarov a day by himself. Let him think. Let his imagination click in. Let him get annoyed no one is paying attention to him. You'll get a lot more out of him next time you talk."

"Do we have time for a slow dance?" Reynolds asked Willingham. "If this guy has secured a bioweapons formula for the Russians, we need to squeeze him now."

"Every bit of Intel suggests the operation failed," Willingham answered after a pause. "Could be part of the plan to make it look that way, but I don't think so. Even if the American *bratva* is relatively independent of Moscow control, no way would Putin and the oligarchs allow this lucrative and destabilizing foothold on American soil to cannibalize itself the way it has the past week. What we're going to get from Pasha is ammo to do more damage to the Red Mafiya here, not find out who is trying to secure classified scientific secrets."

"I hope you're right," Reynolds said.

"Van Guten is right," Willingham said with a chuckle. "You are my 'shock and awe' hammer Austin. Usually works. Didn't with the Russian. At least not this first go round. No surprise there. I've got a team looking for our friend from Switzerland and there's nothing you can help with for a day. I think you've done all you can taking apart the Pathogen offices and labs in California. You work too hard. Take a day off. Go somewhere. Why don't you go to Chicago and decompress for a day?"

Van Guten knew all about Reynolds' relationship with Detective Kristen Conner and rolled her eyes.

"That's where I'm heading. Want to hitch a ride?" she asked him, with exaggerated sweetness. "I was able to snag the company jet. I can't be more difficult to talk to than Pasha Boyarov."

That set Willingham to laughing.

"I might take you up on that ride," Reynolds said to her, wondering if this was Willingham's plan all along. "Anything happening with the Cutter Shark?" he asked her politely.

"Quite a lot actually," Van Guten answered. "He's decided to stoop down from his throne on Mount Olympus and talk to me, just a mere mortal."

"Better you than me," Reynolds said. "I think we need to ignore the jack wagon and push harder on the prosecutorial schedule. But you already know what I think on that."

She didn't respond to Reynolds' barb but looked at Willingham who nodded yes.

"We have a new development, Austin," she said. "And a new approach . . . He's lawyered up. He thinks he can challenge his arrest. He's so happy plotting his escape that he's talking."

"What's his legal basis?"

"Conner broke in on him without an arrest warrant."

"Imminent Danger."

"But how did she know that there was imminent danger in that townhome?" Van Guten asked, again too innocently, arched eyebrows.

"Oh brother," Reynolds sighed in exasperation. "Don't tell me you got the wheels of this turning."

He looked at Van Guten and Willingham. Neither were answering. Bad sign. This is Leslie's doing and Willingham has okayed it.

"Let's not get too clever and let him get away with something. It is possible to outsmart yourself," Reynolds said, staring pointedly at Van Guten.

"We're on it and he's not getting away with squat," Willingham broke in brusquely. "But . . . we are going to let him think he's getting somewhere to embolden him to talk more."

"Is Conner in on this new approach?" Reynolds asked.

"Absolutely not—and she won't be," Willingham said. "That's an important element of the plan."

"I think I'm going to skip Chicago and head back to California," Reynolds said, knowing where the deputy director and his ex-wife were headed. He had enough troubles in his relationship with Kristen and didn't want to add more. She might not figure things out immediately, but when she did, something that smelled bad would hit the fan. She struggled enough with trust. He didn't think their relationship could withstand anything close to this kind of breach, whether a greater good was involved or not.

"There's nothing more you can help with in California," Willingham said, a hand raised to brook any objection. "Go to Chicago and see your friend. Just make sure she remains clueless that we're helping the Cutter Shark open up."

Reynolds loved his boss—and hated him almost as much. Willingham was a legend. No one in the bureau had more big kills under his belt. He was the agent responsible for locating the terrorists who planned the downing of Pan Am Flight 103 over Lockerbie, Scotland. Willingham was charming. But ruthless. Willingham set up a job offer for Conner in the FBI. He thought the Bureau was too dependent on technology and wasn't hiring enough hard-nosed street detectives. Willingham admired Kristen's handling of the Cutter Shark case and grew fond of her, rough edges and all. He was still plotting ways to lure her to the FBI. But that didn't mean he wouldn't use her. Or me.

Conner was hard-nosed, no doubt. He knew that too well. After she left for the airport in New York City he called Klarissa to meet with him so he could ask for advice on how to win the heart of her elusive sister—or if she thought it was even possible. He'd been content to let things float along. He wanted to see if something real was there. He knew his feelings were real but if she wouldn't or couldn't reciprocate, it was time to move on with his life. Klarissa's advice was simple.

"Give Kristen her space. Go to church with her—I think that's a non-negotiable. Fight her tooth and nail on the mat. Babysit the kids once a month without complaining. Do things her way. Then tell her how much you love her. No guarantees, but I think that might work."

They both laughed and toasted that.

✻ 45 ✻

Okay. Maybe yanking the door open isn't the smartest idea. I strain to hear any sound. Nothing. The door is thick and fits the frame a lot better than the door in my old apartment did.

I sniff. No cashew chicken in the air.

Maybe whoever was there is gone. Doesn't feel like it.

I walk on the sides of my feet from the foyer to the hall leading to the master bedroom. I still feel funny sleeping in Klarissa's bed, even before the Reynolds' fiasco. I need my space and my stuff. Now isn't the time to let my wandering mind wander though.

I rummage in my small leather makeup case and find my compact. I'll put the mirror up to the peephole to see if anyone is in line of site. If they're waiting for an eyeball to appear they can blast my compact.

Not a bad idea. Better keep my fingers low.

I wish she didn't live ten floors up. That view alone must cost a suitcase full of rubles. I need to get out of here. I can't take the elevator. I have to run down the stairs to the garage, jog out the opening around the gate, and get two more blocks to my car. Everyone knows a bear likes to run uphill better than downhill. Won't take long and the rear exit won't be covered immediately but an alarm is going to go off when someone realizes the old man is missing. I'll bet he was a fighter in his day. That was a nice jab. Slow but nice. Not much power or I'd have more than a black eye. I need to be careful.

It might be time to blast my way in. Shoot her and run. I can dump the car and get my truck. I should have packed earlier. Either way, I can be in St. Louis in five hours—unless roads are still icy. I'll stop and sleep for a week.

He looked at the Springfield in his right hand. One in the chamber and thirteen in the clip. That's why Pasha had most of them switch to the model. A second magazine with thirteen more rounds was in his pocket. The 45-caliber bullet would blow a hole the size of a Kennedy half-dollar through flesh or wood. Wouldn't take more than four or five rounds to get inside, depending on the make of the lock.

But she was a detective and would have a handgun. She might already have it locked and loaded. There was a reason she wasn't answering the door. He would have to move fast and blast anything that moved and then get to the stairwell. If any nosy neighbors poked a head out the door to get a look at him . . . well that was bad luck for them.

I could just leave. I'm leaving too big of a trail. Now others have seen me, including Sadowsky. He won't talk to police but he will report to whoever the new Pakhan is in New York. But with Pasha in custody will I matter enough to pursue?

He reached in his left pocket, pulled out the bottle of vodka, and took a big swig. One drink for courage even if it is only a skinny girl I have to kill.

He felt the warmth all over. She has no chance against me.

Just do it. He pocketed the bottle and lifted the gun from his side to the lock on the door.

❄ **46** ❄

Blackshear was about to go crazy. He had just spent the day at his in-laws for a big family gathering to celebrate his niece's christening. Nothing more important than family, he thought, but we still have leftovers from all the holiday get-togethers. He'd missed too many family occasions as a cop and knew his wife would sulk for a week. Had to go. But after getting bumped back to lieutenant after the Durham case, he needed a quick victory.

He wanted to get over to the district attorney's office with the case in the morning. He'd stay up late putting the case on paper. We have motive and means with the wife alone. We might have the weapon too. The crowbar hanging neatly on a pegboard inside the Keltto's garage door had been wiped down. Had to be the crowbar.

The kid witnessing Leslie Levin's car on the street that morning sewed things up tighter that Nancy and Leslie were in it together. He'd love to deliver the pair of them to the DA.

If Leslie had been there and lied about it, they would put the screws to him. One of the two would flip on the other. We just need to confirm Levin's car wasn't sitting in a parking space at O'Hare at the same time. I need to know if I'm giving him to the DA as a conspirator or direct accomplice.

He looked at his watch and wondered if it was too soon to call Conner. He hated that she lost her Sunday afternoon doing his work. *I've got to fire Alyson. But that would be messy and won't help me get back on the path to promotion. Maybe I just talk her up and get someone to take her off my hands in a transfer.*

His phone rang. It was dispatch. He listened for a minute and whistled before confirming he was on the way. He hoped Squires and Conner didn't want to watch TV tonight.

Nancy Keltto slit her wrists in the bathtub. Levin stopped by—contravening a written agreement he signed. *Levin probably went there to make sure they got their story straight,* he thought cynically. *Stupid move if you are a murder suspect.*

But Levin found Nancy Keltto in time to save her life. She was in ER at Advocate Christ Medical Center in Oak Lawn. *Those two are thicker than blood and guilty as hell.*

❄ **47** ❄

"Okay, I go to Chicago and kill Medved. What about the Detective?"

"Sadowsky provided the Bear with everything he needs to do the job. It might be done before you get there. That would be unfortunate. It's never good to kill cops. Much cheaper to keep them on your side. All our informants say she saw nothing. She is not a threat. We also lose our bear bait if she's dead. Anasenko just sent a crew to intercept the Bear and keep her alive."

"So why send me?"

"We're just speculating he's still after the detective. If he is, things are easier. Sadowsky's men will treat her like bear bait. When they see him coming they put him down. But maybe he's taking his time. Two of Sadowsky's men have seen the Bear once. You know him better. So that's why we want you there."

"Pasha always said Sadowsky was good," Vlad said. "How'd he lose track of Medved?"

"He didn't have him followed because they had a transmitter on the car. But the Bear found the transmitter and put it on a pickup truck heading to Indianapolis. That wasted some time."

Vladimir shook his head. "Medved surprises me. He's doing the right things. He must be sober."

"So why did Pasha use a drunk to screw up the deal?"

Vladimir would love to know more about the deal but didn't ask. Keep your mouth shut and your ears open. Most people can't handle silence. Teplov looks like a talker.

"Pasha wanted to get rid of Med for a long time. Med used to be okay, which kept him alive longer than he deserved. But he was never right in the head after Riker Island. Pasha would have killed him when he brought the man to the warehouse."

"Pasha or you?"

"No matter. Same thing."

"Good point," Teplov said. "Loyalty is everything. We are one."

"Med was okay. Riker broke him."

Teplov nodded understandingly—maybe a bit condescendingly. "The real issue is we put too much confidence in Pasha Boyarov."

Vladimir said nothing. He didn't like this guy and he didn't like him talking Pasha down. Pasha had broken the vows of the *vory v zakone*, but he had been one of the best soldiers the American *bratva* would ever know. He would kill Pasha himself for his betrayal. But the man sitting across from him had seduced Boyarov to do wrong. He was no better. He didn't have the right to speak against Pasha.

"So it's understood?" Teplov asked.

"Simple enough. I am to kill the Bear. When do I leave?"

"In the morning but not from here. Even with your remarkable change in appearance, we don't want to risk you flying from a New York airport. You and I will drive to Dulles together tonight. I've done all I can to calm things here. Everything will soon be settled here. Order restored. No more killings."

"Who will be Pakhan?"

"You might as well be one of the first to know. It's Ishutin. We need a steady hand at the helm."

"Where do I go after I've done the Bear?"

"I'll wait for you in D.C. I'll have a new name and passport ready for you and you'll fly to Switzerland to lay low. Plus there's a man in Geneva we need to talk to—you can help."

Ishutin as Pakhan? No way. Everyone knew he was too old. With Pasha out of the picture, it would have to be Luytov. And send me to Switzerland? I don't trust this guy as far as I can throw him. He's stringing me along until whoever is in charge knows what they want to do with me.

❄ 48 ❄

This is so unacceptable. Dr. Van Guten has missed two of our last three meetings. Just when I started opening up to her. It is human nature to pursue what you cannot have and then disregard it once you think it is yours. This is not about her. It's about me. I need her full attention. I won't speak to her next time she comes to see me. That will get her attention. She's confused as to who is in charge of our talks.

The attorney. What do I think of Joseph Abrams? He's full of himself. He didn't like it when I called him Joey and asked me to call him Mr. Abrams. Yet he claims to be a man for the people. Hypocrisy has no boundaries.

But he's smart. I believe he has identified the one thing that could free me. Detective Kristen Conner did not have permission to enter a private residence, no matter what I might be doing there. Not without a warrant. Not without more than a hunch of where I might be.

The law is another revealer of human nature. People love boundaries that protect their freedom but don't mind if someone else's rights are trampled.

Fortunately for me, our poorly dressed detective trampled all over mine. How inconsiderate.

It's not the right time to bring it up with Joey, but I plan to sue her for the violence she inflicted on me. I doubt she has much to lose so I will include the Chicago Police Department and the entire Chicago city government. They are broke from what I read, but as long as you can raise taxes, you can pay off your damages. I need to ask Joey about suing the FBI as well.

Leslie Van Guten is playing a game with me. She thinks she is pulling strings to make me talk to her. It's time she learns that I make the rules.

❄ **49** ❄

I creep to the side of the door and lift the compact to the level of the peephole. The trick works. Inconceivable. Somebody's there! I see his eyes lower in the direction of the doorknob.

I crouch into a shooting stance.

Boom.

The world explodes and I feel a blazing pain sear my side.

I'm hit. I fall backward and almost drop my gun. *Boom. Boom.* The door is splintering and a man as big as a mountain is pushing his way through.

I get the Sig up and fire a first shot. He jumps back and crouches to the side. I start blasting holes at the door until the clip is empty. How bad am I hurt? Is he coming in? Can I defend myself?

Boom. Boom. Two more gun blasts ring in my head and then I hear a thud of steps receding down the hallway. Neither of the last two shots was aimed at me. Did I scare him off? I pray so. I am breathing. I just might be alive.

I breathe heavily, in and out, in and out. My mind won't slow down. I have an appointment with Dr. Andrews tomorrow that I suspect I will miss. I'll bet I have to make it up. I bet they add more sessions after what just happened.

I touch my side tenderly and it feels like I've

stabbed myself with a hot poker. And then twisted it. I look at my hand. Bright red goo is dripping. I need help.

My hand jabs at the ground looking for my phone. I get it in my hand and swipe the screen to turn it on. Now the screen is a red gooey mess and isn't detecting my finger motion—or it's grossed out by what it sees.

I rub the screen against the pajama shorts I'm wearing. They will soon join the new outdoor gear I got for Christmas in an evidence bag. Years from now someone might try to donate them to Goodwill but I doubt Goodwill will accept anything stained blood red. I dry my finger on my sweatshirt. Oh man, I am going to lose my faithful friend that everyone has been telling me to throw away for years.

I feel light-headed. I've got to call 911. My phone vibrates and chirps first. Klarissa. I jab the red button to refuse the call and it chirps again. Squires. I've got to get an EMT over here soon. I pick up his call.

"Don! I've been shot. Get an ambulance over to Klarissa's ASAP."

He laughs. Do I joke around that much? No time to convince him. I hit the red button and call 911 on my own. The operator is extremely quick and helpful because he's already been dispatching police and emergency crews to my location.

I'm feeling loopy. Squires' name pops back up

on my screen. I hit green but can't say anything.

"Conner? Kristen? KC? Tell me you're joking."

"Don't sweat it, Don," I rasp out. "I got hold of 911 myself. They're sending an ambulance."

"You better not be joking! What is going on?"

I really am going to stop kidding so much. No one knows when to take me seriously and it's going to kill me. Literally.

"Kristen?" I hear Don yelling.

I want to answer but my head is reeling.

I drop the phone. The only thing I want in the world right now is to sleep and wake up alive.

❄ 50 ❄

How did Sadowsky find me? Spotting the car he loaned me would be like finding a needle in the haystack. Med scowled and smacked his head. The detective. He knew I was hitting the detective.

Medved was carefully driving the speed limit. If he got pulled over he was done. Even if an officer didn't see the bright red circle on the front of his coat, he would undoubtedly smell the alcohol. He poured some of it on his wound and some of it down his throat. Some people drink vodka because they claim no one smells it on your breath. That's more than a little exaggeration he thought. Even if the officer didn't see the blood or smell the

305

alcohol he might notice two handguns on the passenger seat and a sniper rifle on the backseat.

He had been parking Sadowsky's car in the back lot of a motel a mile from his. He didn't mind walking in the cold. He grew up north of Moscow. This was child's play. But now he had a bullet lodged in his chest.

Do I risk parking closer or do I walk?

He looked at the near empty bottle beside him. Maybe one big swallow left.

That will be enough to keep me warm. That and the memory of shooting one of Sadowsky's bulls between the eyes. One shot from fifty feet—with a bullet in my chest—that's impressive. Best shot ever.

How in the world did I let that skinny detective shoot me? It had to be the vodka.

Time to get back to the motel room and dress his wound. Unless it was within an inch of the surface, he would probably leave the bullet in to be removed later. It might not have to come out ever. He had an uncle who left a bullet lodged in his head as a souvenir of getting out of Afghanistan alive.

One small stop for supplies. He pulled into the parking lot of a Walgreens. It was impossible to be discreet at 6′ 7″ and 350 pounds. Med did the best he could, keeping his head down and making eye contact with no one. He looked at the aisle signs and headed for the first aid section. He scooped up two bottles of rubbing alcohol, a brown bottle of peroxide, a packet of rubber gloves, a disinfecting soap, antibacterial ointment, gauze, and tape. He went back for two bottles of iodine and some tweezers, just in case.

The kid working the cash register didn't even look at him—or at least pretended not to. Good thing I bought a dark coat at Dollar General. Makes it harder to see the blood.

Sadowsky took the call at Minsky's, expecting to hear that the Bear was dead. No one looked at him when he talked on a special line that had so many relays and cutouts it was next to impossible to know its actual location. If any of the men huddled in small groups, drinking and talking quietly, had been watching, never a good idea, they would have seen a first. Sadowsky's teeth clenched shut and his pasty white face turned red with rage.

The Bear was alive. One of his men was shot dead. Another was taken into custody.

What is going on in New York? Everyone kept telling him all would be settled and fine within days. So why is their smoke and fire blowing into my city?

❄ 51 ❄

Grace Conner looked up from her crossword puzzle. Who could be at the door at this time of night? She checked her memory. Yes, she turned the knob on the door handle and both deadbolts. You can never be too careful living in the big city. Murder might be down significantly in the United States, but not in Chicago. It just happened on my street.

She picked up her cell phone. They say you're not supposed to put 911 on speed dial. She put her finger on the seven button. They say a lot of things you shouldn't listen to.

She looked through the peephole. Two uniformed officers were on the front stoop. Their faces were different—somehow younger—but they looked just as solemn as they did five years ago. The night her Michael was shot. The night that changed everything.

Tears were already streaming down her face as she fumbled at the locks and pulled the door open.

No. Not Kristen. Dear God, no. Not Kristen. Not my baby. But she knew in her heart of hearts they were here because of her daughter.

Before the officer could say anything she had sunk to her knees sobbing as a wail from some part of her she didn't know existed pierced the night.

The call to Jimmy came late, even for a pastor. He got up quickly from the table where he, Kaylen, Kendra, and James were munching on pizza. The baby was asleep upstairs.

Kaylen looked up when he reentered the kitchen. His eyes were welling with tears.

"Kaylen . . . we need to call a neighbor to watch the kids."

"What . . . what's going on?" she asked as her heart sank. "Not Kristen."

"What daddy?" Kendra asked, wide-eyed. "Did something happen to Aunt Kristen?"

"Aunt Kristen is hurt, Kendra. Maybe not very bad. Mommy and daddy need to go find out."

Don't cry in front of the kids, Kaylen told herself, as she burst into sobs.

Six-year-old James just stared, frozen in place.

"Austin, I know you don't want to hear what I have to say."

"Then don't say it, Leslie. I'm just a hammer and I probably wouldn't understand it anyway. I don't have an IQ that Stanford-Binet calls very advanced."

"IQ has never been your problem, Austin."

"That's good to know even if you're reminding me of my myriad of other problems."

"Don't be so surly, Austin. I'm actually thinking of you and your good, which I admit I didn't do a good job of in our marriage."

Reynolds wanted to nail Van Guten with a quick quip but held his tongue in check. It would only get her going on explaining the deficiencies of him and everyone else who wasn't Leslie Van Guten, PhD, MD, and whatever new initials she'd acquired. They were cruising at thirty-five thousand feet in a Gulfstream the FBI kept on call for bigwigs, which in this case, despite his relationship with Willingham, was not him.

"I know you, Austin. I can see it unfolding. Things didn't work out between us so you are in a compensation mode. You are bonding with someone who is my diametric opposite."

"You mean someone with a heart? Or just not very smart?"

"There you go. Don't you see?" she said. "You are still angry with me. That's what you need to deal with. Me. Us. Until you do, I don't believe you will be capable of an authentic relationship."

The scary thing was she actually believed what she was saying. He would explain the abject narcissism of her comments to her, but she would only deflect and turn it on him. Is it possible to make a narcissist recognize that they make the world about themselves?

What was on Klarissa's list to win the heart of Kristen? Go to church? Not sure my heart is in it, but I could do it. Heck, I haven't gone to church since I was a kid. It's probably about time to get back. I basically believe in God. Babysit the kids? Sure. I like kids. Fight on the mat? Heck, yes. Tell her I love her? I might be there already. That might be the easiest part. Agree to anything she says? If it means not listening to a narcissistic egomaniac on a three-hour flight from New York to Chicago, I'm at least open.

Conner doesn't drink. Don't know how big a deal that is to her. But that wasn't on the list. I don't drink much myself but desperate times call for desperate measures. He held up his glass to the flight attendant. She brought him another Woodford Reserve. Just in the nick of time.

PART THREE

Things are not always what they seem;
the first appearance deceives many;
the intelligence of a few perceives
what has been carefully hidden.

PHAEDRUS

❄ **52** ❄

Vladimir Zheglov thought about his situation as he drove with Sergei Teplov in silence. In decent weather the drive was maybe four hours. With icy snow on the roads they had been driving that long and were only a little more than halfway there.

Chicago made sense. Send someone who knows the Bear by sight to make sure the right guy got shot. Geneva didn't make sense. Why send an American citizen on the run from the law to an unfamiliar city when Moscow could direct local talent to sweep away problems there? Local talent would be faster, cleaner, and more effective.

It was obvious. Medved was disposable to Pasha. He, Vladimir, was disposable to Teplov and whomever Teplov answered to. He was good at what he did. But so were a lot of others. It didn't help that his boss had screwed up a major operation.

He grew up with Boyarov in Moscow. He'd never had reason to doubt him before. But he was certain that Pasha knew the score on where he stood and what his options were. Pasha had doubled down on a losing hand and done the one sure thing to save his skin. He'd set up his own capture—and of his lifelong friend. Vlad replayed the arrest. No doubt. Pasha was planning to break the oath of *molchaniye*. There was no greater sin in the Russian *bratva*. Boyarov knew he would be a hunted man the rest of his life and his death would be horrific and fabulous as a warning to anyone else who thought of betraying the family. What had the Americans promised him? Immediate protection, money, and a new identity. But Pasha knew as well as him that you could never trust the Americans to keep their word. There were officials on the take—or ripe for blackmail —at every level and in every department of government.

Pasha was smart. He wasn't turning himself in just to look over his shoulder the rest of his life. He probably had a tidy sum of money and another identity squirrelled away somewhere. The first chance he got, he would escape the clutches of the Americans, no matter what their assurances and guarantees, and set up a new life on his own terms. It might take a year before they were done questioning him, but Vladimir knew that Pasha had a backup plan that would let him roam as a free citizen again.

Vladimir wanted to hate his friend for his betrayal, but was he so wrong? It would probably work. A little cosmetic surgery and he could settle anywhere in the world with a decent backstory. That kind of thinking was why Pasha had come so close to seizing the title of Pakhan from Genken.

My wagon was hitched to Pasha. Teplov and his handlers don't know me. I'll do the business in

Chicago. Nazar must die. But it might be time for me to disappear then. The problem is I've been too loyal. I haven't made disappearing plans.

He sighed.

"What?" Teplov asked him.

"Nothing. Just tired."

"Take a nap. You're going to be busy tomorrow. You need to be in top form."

"Don't worry about me. Just tell Sadowsky to do his part."

"He will, don't worry," Teplov said as his phone buzzed.

"Yes?"

Vladimir noted that he kept the phone tight to his ear. He wasn't going to let Vlad overhear any more conversations. He watched Teplov out of the corner of his eye. He didn't trust him. But what choice did he have at the moment?

There were always choices . . .

❄ **53** ❄

Between the tag team of ice and salt, Chicago roads take a beating during the winter. Most of the potholes are filled in by the time the next winter rolls around.

I'm on a gurney in the back of a rectangular ambulance that looks like a meat wagon, bouncing my way to the ER at Advocate Christ Medical Center.

They have wrapped my waist so tight in compression bandages that I feel sorry not only for those Victorian or Edwardian or Elizabethan or whatever-era-it-was ladies that had lace corsets tied tighter than a boa constrictor on a fat pig—but for the actresses that play them as well. If this is what a Spanx waist cincher feels like, no thank you, no matter what the years do to my waistline.

No one will tell me how bad I'm hurt. My current state of mind tells me this is going to end up being much ado about nothing.

Apparently my EMT, his name card says Thad, has enough certificates to allow him to administer a sedative. He has let me know this several times. I think he is disappointed I won't let him inject me with a syringe full of Ativan that he has prepped—"just in case."

I need to be alert. Scratch that. I need to at least be awake. Too much is going on with the Keltto case—I didn't get a chance to let Blackshear know that Levin's car and Levin's face can be seen on security cameras at a time that makes it possible but not likely he was in my mom's neighborhood at the time of the murder.

Why am I even worrying about the Keltto case? I just got shot by a Russian hit man. I guess Reynolds was wrong when he said we should be concerned but not overly. I'm guessing he's going to feel quite guilty about misdiagnosing the situation. I shouldn't feel so happy about that. I wonder if Deputy Director Robert Willingham will personally apologize to me that the FBI was wrong about there being a contract to kill me. He's good at that stuff. I'll probably accept the apology and thank him for it.

It feels like we go airborne before landing on pitted, ice-crusted asphalt with a bam. I can feel the jarring from hitting another pothole deep in my core.

I look over at Thad. He is watching me with a hopeful gleam in his eyes. He wants to stick that needle in me. People like to say some people become cops because they get to carry a gun. I'm sure we have a few nut jobs in CPD. But I think I've just discovered why some guys become ETs.

❄ **54** ❄

Zheglov knew Teplov had something to say. He decided to wait him out instead of asking. He sat up straight in the passenger seat of the Cadillac CTS they were driving down to Dulles. He wouldn't speak first but at least he'd let Sergei know he was awake.

"We've got a problem my friend," Teplov finally said fifteen minutes later.

"Chicago?"

He just nodded. The two men nursed their thoughts another slow twenty miles. It was snowing hard and the wind was whipping it around in a white mist to limit visibility to maybe fifty feet. Teplov had slowed down. He probably realized it would not be a good thing to end up in a ditch with me.

"Just when I think we have New York under control, the man who set the city on fire decides to light another torch. Chicago is now officially in flames."

"Med?" Vladimir asked.

Teplov just nodded again.

"It's funny how things happen," Teplov said reflectively. "You do everything in your power to shield yourself from outside enemies. Even with RICO, the NSA eavesdropping on American citizens, and all the technology in the world to stamp us out, the US government can't do much to curtail our activities. We've made sure of that with our generous gifts. We've never been stronger. So what happens? We destroy our work from the inside. We go to war with ourselves."

"No problems, only solutions, right comrade?" Zheglov asked with a half-smile.

"You are right," Teplov said with force, not picking up the irony in Zheglov's question.

"Okay, Vladimir. Your job has gotten harder. Sadowsky sent three men to the detective's apartment to set a trap. But the Bear got there first. He shot the detective and killed one of Sadowsky's best men."

"Is she dead?" Vladimir asked.

"She's alive for now. No one knows how bad she's hurt. But Med got away."

"And the Bear killed one of Sadowsky's best men," Vlad added with a chuckle.

"It's not so funny, my friend," Teplov said. "Another soldier was arrested. Apparently the Bear beat up the doorman where the detective lives and someone found him and called the police. The police showed up as Sadowsky's man was getting out of the building. He walked right into their hands. The third *torpedo* escaped."

"But the Bear is on the loose again," Zheglov said, laughing harder now.

"You find this funny?"

"Not at all. But I am amazed at the Bear. We all underestimated him."

They plodded along in silence. This time Vladimir spoke first.

"So why am I going to Chicago? You said it is on fire."

"The Bear."

"Sadowsky's men can handle it."

"I still want you there. I'm losing confidence in Sadowsky by the minute. I want to make sure the Bear is dead. I'll feel better with you there."

"The police are going to be all over this and all over Sadowsky. I still need a weapon and some wheels and some Intel. How does that all happen now?"

"I told you before, I can't call Sadowsky back to change plans now. You won't be going anywhere near him. He's got a guy for you to meet. You need to work with what we've got and be extra careful. Speaking of careful, we'll throw our phones away before we get to Dulles. I've got a couple prepaids we can use to stay in touch. No more names."

Zheglov nodded in agreement. He looked at the bleak winter nightscape and smiled. No way was he going to trust Sadowsky . . . nor Teplov. If Teplov was losing confidence in his men right and left, then undoubtedly, whoever he worked for had lost confidence in him as well.

Who was Teplov anyway? Who did he work for? If he was a real player, Vladimir figured he had cost his masters millions of dollars on the PathoGen fiasco with Frank Nelson. There were twenty-one billionaire oligarchs that controlled a third of Russia's wealth. The money was a drop in the ocean, but rich people got rich and stayed rich because every ruble and dollar mattered to them, including the interest.

The richest oligarch was Putin. That made him both president and Pakhan of Russia. Surely he wouldn't be involved in a bioterrorism plot. He might approve of someone else's initiative or he might not. Probably not. He needed American money.

The real point was you never knew who you

were really working for or how stable their hold on power. Teplov was nervous. He was in trouble. This was Pasha all over again.

Zheglov decided he'd land in Chicago, meet with whoever Sadowsky had set up for him. If nothing else, it got him away from the heat in New York. Maybe he'd stay in Chicago until the fires burned down—or he ran out of money.

He had squirrelled enough money away in a safety deposit box to live on for maybe a year. He had been a loyal soldier in the *bratva* and hadn't thought enough about himself and his future. Those days were over. Time to think like Pasha.

What about Medved?

Leave him alone? Find him and kill him?

That would be one way to raise money if he could bypass Teplov and talk to the right guy. Had to be Luytov.

Killing the Bear could be worth another year of cash.

❄ 55 ❄

This is the second time in a year I've established a police command center in a hospital room. It worked out okay last time. We caught a serial killer a week later.

Frank Nelson is in charge. Hard to believe that only a week ago I was trying to save the life of another Frank Nelson. I wonder how his wife is doing? Maybe Austin knows. Where is Austin anyway? He usually shows up where the action is. I think I want to see him. I have no clue how to talk to my sister about what I saw, but I'll happily punch him in the nose and let him figure out how to get this mess resolved so I can still be friends with Klarissa. I'm the one who was done wrong. Why should I be responsible for fixing things? I'm delegating this to him.

I'm not happy with Klarissa, but she's blood. My family drives me crazy—though probably not as much as I drive them crazy—but I'm glad we're close. I'll do my part to keep it that way. I don't believe in forgive and forget. Forgive yes, but how do you forget? The harder you try the more you remember. But yes, I tell myself, I do believe in forgiving and moving on. Life's not perfect but that's the point of forgiveness. Maybe I'll tell that to Jimmy and he can work it into a sermon. I laugh at that thought.

Zaworski doesn't look good. He's always been pale-faced. But it is Casper the Friendly Ghost-white tonight. He's got to be wondering why he agreed to come back. If he has to deal with me much more he's going to end up back in the hospital. Actually he already is back in the hospital—to see me.

Czaka showed up with the head of the organized crime division, Spencer Doyle, who is the nephew of our recently departed but long serving mayor,

Michael T. Doyle, Jr., and great nephew of Michael T. Doyle, Sr., another longtime mayor of Chicago. I'm a little surprised the big guns showed up. Squires and Blackshear pull chairs in from the waiting room, despite the head nurse's protestations.

"I'm fine, I'm awake," I say to speed up the process. I'm going to conk out soon, so I want to get things going. I don't want to wake up in the middle of the night with a bunch of questions and no one to answer them.

FBI agent and fellow workout warrior, Heather Torgenson, is present and so is Martinez. I know why she's here, but not Antonio. Last time he visited me in a hospital room he ended up with an ice pack and walked funny for a week. I intend to remind him of that.

Nelson drones on about how we are going to keep me alive. He's thorough and his ideas are right on but I don't sense he's a visionary. I can't stay hunted long-term. We're going to have to catch the hunter.

"Thanks Frank, good work," Doyle breaks in. He looks at me kindly. "We'll take care of you Detective Conner. No disrespect to the FBI, but you are one of our own."

He's smooth. He can follow his uncle and great uncle's footsteps if he wants to be mayor. Busting a Russian mafia chief in Chicago would be a good springboard to higher office.

"What I say next stays in this room. If I hear even a hint of a whisper I'll be going through everyone's emails and phone logs with a fine-tooth comb."

I don't know anything about him but he sounds tough enough to be a politician.

"I've been on the phone with the Director of the FBI. Honestly, no one knows how this Red Mafiya war is going to shake down. The FBI doesn't even know who is behind it but is certain Moscow's fingerprints are all over it. No murders in New York for the past twenty-four hours. We'll soon have confirmation if the deal to get the blueprints for a bioweapon from PathoGen was killed before it happened. We can pray that is the case, even if it only delays what someone in Moscow has in mind.

"We think the man who shot Conner is rogue and not acting under anyone's orders. That's the good news. The bad news is he is still at large—and we're afraid the open warfare that hit New York could erupt here. Everyone in this room is going to get a dossier with pictures and information on Anasenko Sadowsky and his key soldiers. You'll sign for your copy and be responsible to turn it in when this is wrapped up. No copies. No one peeks over your shoulder while you're reading."

Good thing I'm forgotten. I can barely keep my eyes open. If I fall asleep I hope I don't snore.

❄ **56** ❄

Ilsa always told me to lose weight. But she's dead and I'm alive. That detective must be a bad shot. She fired more than ten times. Only one round hit me. The door slowed the bullet down. I've got enough meat it didn't make it to my organs. I'll dig it out later or maybe never, just like my uncle.

Medved sat in the bathtub, a hot shower running over him. His uncle told him heat and maggots were your best friends for cleaning a bullet wound. If you couldn't find maggots, flies would do. They itch but let them do their work. There were no flies in ten degree Chicago weather. His uncle got shot in an ambush by Mujahideen rebels on the Salang Pass. Abandoned by his comrades, he trekked down the mountain, skirted Baghlan, Alkh, Kheyrabad, and other areas back under the control of the Tehran Seven, and walked into Uzbekistan, fifty pounds under weight, but none the worse for the bullet next to his brain. He claimed he never had another headache in his life.

The bullet stays. I will name it Kristen Conner. That way I never forget her, even after I kill her.

Warmed up, he lifted his three hundred and fifty pounds from the tub and reached for the rubbing alcohol. He put a washcloth in his mouth and poured half the bottle over his upper chest. He clenched his teeth hard enough to break teeth but remained silent. The TV was blaring a war movie in the other room to disguise any sound of pain that might escape his lips through the paper-thin walls.

Next came the hydrogen peroxide. His mom told him that the white foam and bubbling meant germs were being killed. He poured it on the wound and watched the clear solution turn white and bubble. He was killing germs all right. Lots of them. Next he doused his chest with the red iodine. He didn't worry about drying off. He sat on the end of the bed and applied a thick coat of Neosporin, covered the glop with gauze, and ran half a roll of tape around his upper torso.

He grabbed five Excedrin P.M. tablets and downed them with a swig from a fresh bottle of vodka.

No question I'll sleep. We'll see how it looks in the morning. I can decide what to do then. One more shot at her or get out of town.

I wish my uncle was alive to tell him about this. My family is all dead. Ilsa is dead. I am alone. That's okay, I'm alive and I have a truck.

He was snoring almost as soon as his head hit the pillow.

"Let's get out of here, Squires. Unless he has a twin brother, no doubt Conner is right, that's Levin."

Before she fell asleep in her hospital room,

Kristen was able to let Blackshear know what she'd found on the O'Hare surveillance tapes. She told him her time stamp notes were on a notepad on the kitchen table.

Blackshear and Squires watched together, running the footage backward and forward. Levin's car pulling into the long-term parking lot at O'Hare and Levin pulling a roller board suitcase in the door of the main terminal.

"So who does what tomorrow?" Squires asked. He had a sinking feeling he already knew the answer.

"Since I've been to the house a couple times and questioned Bradley Starks first time around, I think I better follow up there."

Squires scowled.

"Listen, Don, I know you live further away and got to get up a little earlier to drive the route from the Keltto's house to O'Hare to see if he had time to whack Ed Keltto in the head and still make his flight. But I got to get there before the kid goes to school. I'll be pulling up only fifteen or thirty minutes later than you. Just thinking about how his mom is going to respond when I knock on the door, I'd be happy to switch."

"No problem, Bob. Makes sense," Squires said, accepting Vanessa would not be happy with him getting home so late and leaving so early. It just added fuel to the fire of a long running argument about his job.

He wanted to apologize to Conner for not taking her call seriously but she was asleep before the meeting in her room ended.

Why would she try to kill herself? Did she actually love her husband—after all the other men in her life? She isn't my problem. Stop worrying about her.

❄ **57** ❄

I am being chased by a bear in the woods. Everyone knows you can't outrun a bear. I can hear him crash through leaves, twigs, and branches on the path behind me. I can hear his ragged breath and a snarl. I am sprinting with all my might—my feet are barely touching the ground. But he's relentless. The bear draws closer, before falling back, but then gains ground and gets close enough that I not only hear his breath but feel it on the backs of my thighs and calves. I don't know what's sweat and what's the foam spraying from ferocious jaws, yearning and poised to take a chunk out of my backside.

Time and distance are fluid and the topography changes so often I'm not sure where I am anymore. Isn't that something Einstein wrote in his Theory of Relativity?

Is that what Einstein was trying to explain? Am

I awake or asleep? My mind is somewhere between hyper-drive in deep space, a forest trail in Wisconsin my family hiked when I was a kid, sheer terror, and a strange serenity. The question of Einstein jars me awake. I'm breathing heavy even though I'm flat on my back in bed. I feel a hand touch my cheek and I open my eyes. Kaylen's face is the first thing I see, with her beautiful hazel eyes pooled with tears. She looks angelic. She definitely got the angel DNA between us three sisters.

"Are you okay, Kristen? You were calling out in your sleep."

Uh oh, what did I say?

"What did I say?"

"I think you were saying there's a bear chasing you."

Whew. Nothing too psycho. We all need to keep a few secrets safely buried in our subconscious. Unless Dr. Andrews tells me bear dreams indicate a deep pathology. I'll tell her about this one even though I think I already know what it means. Someone's trying to kill me. Duh. If it's the same mountain man I saw in Central Park, he might have a bear for his mother.

I think I read a long time ago that Andre the Giant died of a heart attack. His lookalike is still alive and well—and trying to kill me. Inconceivable.

"What time is it, Kaylen?"

"Just after midnight."

"What are you doing here? It's late."

"That's a dumb question even for you, Kristen."

"Are you calling me dumb? I've been shot. Everyone is supposed to be nice."

She laughs, bursts into tears, and then presses the side of her face next to mine, draping an arm gently around my shoulder. It feels wonderful. Even the tears. How come everybody else knows how to express their emotions but me?

"Does Mom know?" I whisper.

"She's here. She's been sitting by your side for the last two hours. She just got up for a potty break."

Do people still say potty break?

"She okay?" I ask.

Kaylen sits up and looks at me with haggard eyes.

"None of us are okay, Kristen. Especially not Mom. Two uniforms knocked on her front door. Again. It wasn't that long ago it was for Dad."

No it wasn't. Four years, five months, and sixteen days since my dad was shot. Two years, one week, and thirteen days since he passed, with yours truly finding him.

"Does she know I'm okay?"

"The doctor says you are lucky to be alive. Mom set him straight and told him it was her prayers. You do have an angel looking out for you, Kristen."

"I was just grazed. The bullet passed right

through my side. No bone, a little muscle, and two nice new scars, front and back."

"I'd yell at you for being too skinny, little sis, but maybe that makes you a smaller target."

We both laugh, which cuts off quickly for me as I feel a stab of pain and give a little yelp.

The door opens and Jimmy and Mom walk in. She rushes to the bed and bends over to give me a big hug.

"Careful, Mom," Kaylen says.

Mom bursts out in sobs. I wanted to tell her I love her and I'm fine—and I want to ask who was watching the kids. Problem is I hit the painkiller button and I'm drowning back to sleep before I can get the words out.

"No, Donald! This is not a reason to hold your letter. First you were supposed to turn it in last Monday, but you just had to tell Kristen first. Then you promised it would be Friday—but things got too busy. What happened to Kristen is exactly the reason you turn your letter in now. Tomorrow."

"Vanessa, it's not right to bail when your partner has been shot."

"Oh, is this bailing? I thought this was about your kids growing up with a father that wasn't always in harm's way. I thought this was about you thinking about your wife so she doesn't worry to death every night you are out working on a murder case. I thought this was about you following your dream of being a lawyer. But I guess I was wrong on all counts. This is about me forcing you to bail. Thanks a lot, Donald. Thanks a lot. I guess I know where I rate in your life; definitely below your real partner."

"Vanessa, you are taking this all wrong."

"Am I? Am I?"

"Yes. This is about me finishing the job."

"No, this is about your work being more important than your family. Look at your partner. She's in the hospital—again. Her dad got killed on the job."

"Not exactly on the job. He died a couple years later."

"Well that's great. Now we get to take care of you in a wheelchair. That'll be great for me and the kids."

"Now you're being unreasonable."

"I'm not listening to what you're saying. I seem to remember you telling Devon you would coach his basketball team. You've missed more practices and games than you've been there."

Vanessa stormed out of Donald's man cave office and slammed the door shut.

Man, oh man. Why isn't life simple? You try to do the right thing and it's still all wrong.

What in the world did KC get mixed up in? What has she got all of us mixed up in?

He'd had an internal argument as to what his next career move would be for a couple years.

When Blackshear got promoted it sealed the deal in his mind. He wasn't on the radar screen of the brass for promotion. It hadn't worked out well for Blackshear but it didn't undo the sting of not even being interviewed.

He didn't want anything given to him because he was black. He wanted to move up because he was good. And he was good.

Partnering with Kristen Conner was great. They worked well together. But she was a force of nature. She burned so brightly everyone else ended up in the shadows.

No excuse missing all of Devon's practices. I'd like to tell him I'm sorry but I'll be on the road before he's awake.

He looked at the business envelope with his neatly typed resignation nested inside of it.

I'm too shot to think tonight. I'll figure out whether to hold it or turn it in tomorrow morning on the drive back from O'Hare.

I wonder if Vanessa locked the door to the room.

❄ **58** ❄

Vladimir Zheglov had taken over driving duties.

Dulles was only forty-five miles away, but with the road conditions, it would still take another ninety minutes to drive it. In good weather they would have been there three hours ago and fast

335

asleep in a Marriott or Hyatt or Sheraton or some other nice hotel near the airport. He didn't think Teplov stayed at Budget 8 or Motel 6. An exit ramp for a rest stop was ahead. The red tail-lights of countless semis lined the shoulder of the road. Not even the truckers want to mess with these roads.

"Pull off here," Teplov said. "I got to use the head. We can get rid of phones here."

"Sounds good," Zheglov mumbled.

Vlad parked the car. The two men stretched and shuffled to the drab concrete structure with a small hall of vending machines and men's and women's facilities on either side.

"This might take a second," Teplov said, opening the door to a toilet stall, pulling it shut, and sliding the lock in place.

Longer than you think, Zheglov said to himself. He crouched down and looked under the opening beneath all the stalls. Teplov's were the only set of legs he saw, his pants gathered in a heap at his ankles.

Move fast. If someone else comes in, deal with it then.

He pulled the switchblade from his coat pocket and flicked open the blade. He crept to the front of the stall door, took a deep breath, coiled himself, and kicked the door in. Teplov's jaw dropped open. He was sitting on the toilet and screwing a silencer on his Makarov. He jumped to his feet and tried to jerk the handgun up into firing position. Zheglov knew the moment was coming when Teplov would try to tie him up as a loose end and was ready. Vladimir lunged and slashed too quickly for Teplov to get his finger on the trigger. The only sound he made was a gurgle from his slit throat.

Keep moving fast. Zheglov checked and emptied Teplov's pockets calmly and thoroughly. He needed to make the police work to identify the Russian on a business visa. He also needed any weapons, IDs, and money the man had.

He walked calmly to the CTS sedan and was back on the road in five minutes.

Thirty miles from Dulles he checked into a non-chain motel called the Satellite. The man working registration checked him in from an outside security window and was happy to take cash and fill in any name he wanted on the registration sheet.

Time to take inventory.

❄ 59 ❄

I slept until eight-thirty and ate breakfast with Mom, Kaylen, and Heather Torgerson. I told Mom and Kaylen to go home and get a shower and some rest. They put up a fight but relented. Don called at ten.

"You okay, KC?"

"Slept like a baby. I feel great. I'm planning to bust out of here by noon."

He snorted but didn't argue. He must be busy because there's no time for the inane small talk I have mastered.

"How certain was the ME about time of death?" he asks.

"We're talking Keltto?"

"Yes."

"Technically not very—it was close to zero degrees so it was a lot colder than a meat locker. No noticeable body deterioration."

Meat locker? Body deterioration? I think of nice Mr. Keltto and wish I hadn't said that.

"But not sure it matters," I continue. "Reports say Mrs. DeGenares heard him shoveling her walk between five-fifteen and maybe five-thirty-five. Nancy called 911 at five-forty-five."

"I've been on the road all morning from my place to the Kelttos and then to O'Hare. How do people get up so early?"

"Some of us have to work, Don," I say. "We don't all have a rich wife to keep us in style."

I wish I hadn't joked as soon as the words come out.

"Not now, Conner. This is definitely not a good morning for that."

"Sorry, Don."

He takes a breath and asks, "What time did Levin pull in to O'Hare?"

"You already know. Just tell me what you found."

"Humor me."

"Right about six-thirty."

About two hours to the second as I was crawling into the back of a squad car on Columbus Circle to talk to Tommy Barnes.

"Roads were lousy on the day of the murder but I've gone through all the reports and traffic was still fairly heavy on all routes to O'Hare from your old neighborhood. Just call it Chicago pride. Nobody's gonna let a blizzard keep them from proving they can drive on ice. I-280 had major slowdowns due to an accident on the day of the murder. But we don't know for sure he took that route."

"So what are you saying Don? Could he have made it to O'Hare at six-thirty?"

"I'd hate to base a case on that fact, but technically yes. Doesn't prove he did it and definitely doesn't prove Nancy didn't do it—or at least wasn't an accomplice."

"So what's Blackshear gonna do?"

"He's going to meet at the DA's office to update her on Leslie Levin. Some of us have to work so we've been busy while you sleep in."

Good. Don's joking so he's not mad. *Touché.*

Murder is an awful thing. But I'm still relieved

to be talking about something other than Russian mobsters trying to kill me.

"Anyone talk to Nancy?" I ask.

"Nancy was your neighbor. Mrs. Keltto is a murder suspect. You need to keep that straight. And no, no one has talked to her. She is still in ICU under suicide watch and police guard. She's right down the hall from you."

"I could—"

"Don't get any ideas, KC. She's off limits. Don't do anything to hurt our case."

Ouch. That makes me think of the Cutter Shark working on an appeal because I busted in on him in a place he wasn't supposed to be while he was in the act of attempted murder. I'd rather think about the Red Mafiya.

"Listen, KC. Don't worry about anything. Get some sleep. Get better. We have it under control."

"Keep me posted."

"Will do."

I don't think he said that sincerely.

"And I want to apologize for not taking your call seriously last night."

"Not necessary, Squires. I'm not even listening. I'm going back to sleep."

We sign off. I just don't handle emotional exchanges well do I?

❆ **60** ❆

Vladimir walked calmly beside a moving sidewalk through a long tunnel filled with neon lights and space age music. Strange ambience for an airport he thought. He travelled under Teplov's name. They didn't look much like each other but at least they were the same height and both had black hair now that his was dyed. The TSA agent at the Dulles security checkpoint took a quick look at him and the driver's license and quickly scribbled the magic initials that got him through security. Teplov had lied to him on every point. He was a US citizen, not a Russian citizen traveling on a business visa. Whatever was happening between Moscow and New York for control of the US *bratva* was too confusing to worry about. Thirty comrades killed already. He doubted that things were about to settle down, no matter how much Sergei wished it to be.

There were two more IDs in an attaché he would save for later. How could he find out how good they were? It was a moot point. Using them in the future would let the *bratva* know he, the man who murdered Aleksei Genken, was not dead.

He hit the pay dirt on cash. The trunk had a suitcase with more than fifty thousand in hundreds. Now he was getting somewhere.

He wished he could have disposed of the body. But there were too many diesel engines idling in the rest stop area. Someone would be awake watching TV in their sleeper cab who heard a sudden call from nature and saw him dragging a body to the trunk of the Caddy.

He studied the major Chicago roads and high-ways using the in-air Internet system. He'd never been to the Windy City. No way could he move around smoothly.

No way am I going to let Sadowsky's man know I'm in town. So how do I find Med?

He looked at his phone thoughtfully. It was worth a try.

Der'mo! That hurt. Medved put too much oint-ment on his wound, causing the gauze to stick like glue to the red, purple, gray, yellow, and white mess on his chest.

His momma always told him it was worse to pull bandaging off slowly than just ripping it off. She was wrong this time, he thought.

What little scabbing had formed came off with the gauze, along with sticky yellow pus and clear fluids, and a stench that reeked of raw sewage. The wound was a mess of white tissue, purple bruising, and cherry red welting. Med felt his forehead. He was burning up.

I must drink water. No more vodka.

He stumbled to the sink, turned on the faucet,

ripped the wrap off a cheap plastic cup, filled it with water, and guzzled the whole glass in a single swallow. He did this two more times, then crushed the plastic cup and stuck his mouth directly on the pipe, sucking in the water in a mad attempt to put out the fire that consumed him from within.

He turned on the shower and sat under it, letting the spray wash away pus and dark red clots of blood.

He didn't know if he had the energy to move but forced himself to act. He repeated the process of pouring alcohol, hydrogen peroxide, and iodine over the wound. He took a small piece of cloth and dabbed ointment in a thin coat, then wrapped himself up tight.

Forget the detective. Save her for another day and time. Sleep for another day and then drive to St. Louis.

He fell on the bed with a groan.

Don't leave me now, Lady Udacha. Be kind to the Bear.

His phone rang. He had almost forgot he had it.

He wasn't sure he had the strength to answer.

❄ **61** ❄

I run a brush through my hair. It feels great to be clean again. The doctor has been adamant I can't leave this morning, but I've pushed, cajoled, and begged until I wear him down about maybe leaving in the afternoon.

"I'll let you know in a couple hours."

"By noon?"

"One at the earliest."

Sounds almost like a yes to me.

I sense a presence and look up. How long has Reynolds been watching me? He walks to my bedside, takes my face in both hands, just looking in my eyes. I want to look away but can't.

He kisses me on the forehead. Then on both cheeks. Slowly. Slowly. It feels like he is breathing me in.

I try to remember if I brushed my teeth after breakfast, almost breaking the spell he's got on me. But then he kisses me on the lips. I don't want to respond. I can't respond. But then I do. It feels so . . . good. But isn't this all wrong?

"Kristen . . . there's something I've been wanting to say to you."

"No. Don't. Austin you can't."

"I know you keep the world at arms-length,

Kristen. I respect that. I do, too. But something's changed."

"Austin . . . this isn't the time or place."

"You can fight with me all you want. You can push me away. It's not going to change how I feel."

"But you . . ."

"I know I've been distant. I haven't known what to think or do. After my . . . my . . . after my divorce I haven't wanted to be close to anyone. I don't trust myself. I can't believe I'm about to say this but—"

The door bangs open and Klarissa and Kaylen enter arm-in-arm.

Klarissa lets out a squeal and rushes over. She gives Austin a playful push.

"Get in line, Romeo. Kristen needs her baby sister."

Was I just saved by the cavalry or put back into love limbo? What is Klarissa doing here from New York?

Austin stands and Kaylen gives him the chaste half-hug she reserves for members of the opposite sex not named Jimmy.

Klarissa, never shy, kicks off her shoes and lays down beside me. I'm at a loss for words. Nothing new.

"Kristen," she says. "I've been worried out of mind since Jimmy called. I booked the earliest flight I could to get here."

"But you're on-air tonight."

"No, I'm not. Not with my sister in the hospital."

"You didn't have to—"

"Kristen, just shut up and let me talk." She pauses, wrinkling her forehead. "I don't know why we fight. I love you. I know you love me. I don't know what I did in New York to get your panties in a bunch. But don't be mad at me. I couldn't sleep last night. All I could think about was not wanting there to be anything between us. I was worried sick all night."

"You were?"

"Duh!"

I look over at Austin and Kaylen yammering away. What am I missing? Is Klarissa about to confess what happened between her and Austin? I decided to let Austin handle this mess with the two of them in the lobby of the Sheraton and not ever bring it up with her. But here she is, snuggled against me. Tough and savvy. Vulnerable and brittle.

When Kaylen went off to college and we each had our own room, Klarissa had terrible problems sleeping. She was afraid of the dark. She ended up in my bed for most of the first couple years until I hit high school and wouldn't allow it anymore. Was that the source of our struggles? I want this thing with Reynolds and her out of the way or I'm going to go crazy.

"Klarissa . . ."

"Yeah?"

"You know how I was supposed to get the last flight out of New York last week? After the murder in Central Park?"

"Yeah?"

"My flight got cancelled."

"Yeah? Why are you telling me this now?"

"I came back to the hotel."

"Yeah? Why didn't you stay with me?"

"I was planning to."

Curious, she props herself up on an elbow and looks me in the eyes. "So what happened?"

"I came in the lobby and I . . . I . . ."

Now she's sitting up at an awkward side angle. "What?"

"I saw you . . ."

"Saw me what?"

I lower my voice to a whisper and say it. "I saw you and Austin together in the bar."

"Yeah? You were there? Why the heck didn't you join us? Where did you spend the night?"

Realization of what I'm saying dawns on her and she opens her mouth in disbelief. I see a tear drop from her eyes. Then I see that hard stubborn look she gets. Then it disappears and she cuddles next to me.

I'm not sure if she is whispering or hissing when she says, "Kristen, you are the most wonderful, beautiful, absolute idiot in the world. I meant what I said. I love you. But I could kill you right now. I know we're in a hospital but I know you know I don't mean that the way it sounds."

Hey, even if I feel good enough to leave, I've been shot. People are supposed to be nice to me and not call me an idiot. Even if I am.

"You indeed saw Austin and me together in the lobby bar. He asked me to meet him there. For one reason and one reason only. He's crazy about you. He's in love with you. You are stupid and blind. I can't compete with you. Nobody can. He called your baby sis to ask for advice on scaling the walls of Fort Kristen."

I can feel her start to get up, mad and hurt again, but I get hold of her around the waist and don't let her leave, even though it hurts like crazy to keep her close. Now she's the one who is stiff and cold.

Words cannot describe how stupid I feel. But I don't know what to say, so I just hold on. Kaylen looks over, takes Austin by the arm, and they exit the room. She always knows the right thing to do. She's good at that.

I try to roll on my side to look at Klarissa but the effort hurts. Neither of us moves. We stare at the ceiling. I finally force myself to say the only thing I can think of.

"I love you, Baby Sis. I'm so sorry. Forgive me."

Okay. How's that for a role reversal. I've gone from being done wrong to being a heel in about thirty seconds. I liked being a martyr better.

At least I don't always have to be right.

❄ **62** ❄

The winter getaway was all that Heinrich Hiller had hoped for and more. He had gone on the Internet and picked the Seychelles Islands. He called his wife and told her to pack. He gave his secretary instructions on what to say if anyone called needing his services. It was simple. Herr Hiller will be out of the country for the next month and will not be able to get back to you until then. She asked where she could reach him if an emergency came up.

"You can't," he said.

The Russians knew the rules when they hired him. He held nothing back. No sugar coating any-thing. It wasn't a matter of him not being willing to undo the transfer protocol, including the immediate recovery of funds or files. Eventually the initial sum would be returned to the sending account—minus an additional two percent servicing fee—but he stressed it could take up to a month. It needed to pass through numerous accounts and company shells to eliminate any tax burden and connection to Herr Hiller. He couldn't make things clearer. You don't use my service if you think you might want to change your mind or any details. Once we push the button, don't even ask me to do anything. I can't. That was the beauty of what he did. Once he punched in the code all was in the hands of God. But Russians were bullies. They thought anything could be fixed with enough threats. He didn't want to hear them.

Anse Lazio was rated as the top beach in the Seychelles and maybe the Indian Ocean and maybe the entire world. It was costly but he couldn't imagine a more idyllic spot. Snorkeling in the morning, but not too early. Lie on the beach and read a magazine or people watch in the afternoon. Order drinks with umbrellas. Take a walk and splash in the water with his wife. A late afternoon nap, a shower, and then out for dinner and maybe one of the clubs if they weren't too tired. He didn't dance, gamble, or take illegal drugs, but the sights of young people with no inhibitions was energizing.

He looked at his wife and said, "One more dip, then let's go back to the room."

She smiled and raced ahead of him. She looks ten years younger and we've only been here for four days.

When they entered their luxury suite with an ocean view, his mouth dropped open. Two men were sitting on the couch in the sitting room.

"We must talk, Herr Hiller."

"What is this, Henry?" his wife asked him, fear in her eyes.

"Just a moment of business. Go back to the bedroom. I'll join you soon."

❄ **63** ❄

I want to tell the doctor what he can do with his stethoscope. He was too big of a pinhead to tell me himself so he sent an intern to give me the news I had to say another night. Ugh.

They moved me out of ICU to the seventh floor. Austin was already gone almost as soon as he got here. He called to tell me he would be back after a phone conference with Willingham. "At Van Guten's office," he added. I guess that's his stab at transparency. He never got a chance to finish telling me what he had to say. I still haven't heard anything more from him. Must be one heck of a conference call.

Jimmy brought James and Kendra to see me. James' eyes darted everywhere. I am pretty certain he wanted to tug on some tubes running from a machine to my arm or push a few buttons. I've heard hospitals are dangerous for your health. With James present, I agree.

Blackshear, Squires, Martinez, and Green came back by before dinner to update me on the Keltto murder.

"Jones and Mangold just arrested Levin at his house," Blackshear said. "It was in front of his wife."

Martinez whistled and made the sign of the cross.

"I don't know Jones and Mangold," I said.

"They work with me in the Fourth," Blackshear answered. "With you in the hospital and the rest of us in meetings, no one from the Second was available. Mangold told me the arrest was quite the scene with lots of tears and screaming. And that was just Leslie."

"The guy is a creep," I said, "but I'm almost glad I wasn't there."

"You got that right," Squires added.

"So what now?" I asked.

"We've hit a standstill for the moment," Blackshear said. "Levin has lawyered up. It'll be a while before we can talk to him on the record. Even if Nancy Keltto is in any shape to answer questions, her lawyer says no and her doctor is in 100 percent agreement. So we hurry up and wait."

"Between a failed suicide attempt and pain meds, I don't think it would be good to interview her anyway," I said. "That oxycodone will make you think and say crazy things."

Like bears chasing you in the woods.

"You were ready to pay her a visit last night," Squires said.

"Like I said, the pain meds will make you think crazy things."

I think they took that as their cue to leave.

Mom said she wanted to stay and sleep in the chair that pulls out into a bed next to me. I wouldn't wish that on anyone's back. I told her to go home. She ate hospital food with me for dinner. That's real love.

Then Tony Scalia stopped by. He was my dad's long-time partner. When Doyle was mayor he was CPD liaison to his office. The new mayor wanted someone else. I'm not sure what Tony does anymore. He's a big guy with a barrel chest and a thick head of black wavy hair. He's got to be over sixty. I've always wanted to ask if he uses Just for Men or if he hit the genetic jackpot on men's hair. If he wasn't a cop, he could have played a Mafioso in a show like *The Sopranos*. He's never said it, but I think my dad getting shot knocked some of the fight out of him. He never went back on the streets.

My dad was a big guy too. He boxed Golden Gloves in his teens and was apparently a bad boy until he met my mom. She gave him a take-it-or-leave-it deal he couldn't refuse. "If we get married we go to church and raise our kids Baptist." He had his mom's rosary in his hands when I found him dead. I think he was covering his bases. Barry Soto trained both men and said the two of them were legends in and out of CPD. "You wanted them on your side in a bar brawl."

"Okay you snot-nosed brat, what have you got yourself mixed up in this time?" Scalia asks before giving me a big hug.

Baptists don't have godparents, but Big Tony always played the role with me.

"Must have been bad parenting . . . someone always wants to kill me."

"Especially your parents. Your momma did her best to get you to play with dolls but they always ended up in a fight so she let you do what you liked."

Was I James as a kid? Oh man . . . my respect for mom and dad might have just gone up a couple notches. I see James once or twice a week—they had to live with me.

"Klarissa played with Barbies enough for both of us."

"It takes all kinds to make the world go round doesn't it? How you feeling kiddo?"

"Way too good to be stuck in here."

"You'd say that if you had a bullet in your head. Why don't you just relax and let the world take care of you for a while?"

"Even if I wanted to, I can't drink the coffee here."

He smiles, reaches into a bag he carried in and lifts out a ceramic travel mug from JavaStar.

"I got it around the corner. Might still be hot."

"You are an angel, Big Tony."

"I'm not so sure. I think I lost my wings. I told your pops I would keep an eye on you. I'm not doing so hot."

"Aww, you're doing just fine. I'm grown up. I can take care of myself."

"And yet here you are. Again."

"Hey, I've been shot. You're supposed to be nice."

"That reminds me, after telling me I need to lose eighty pounds, crazy Barry Soto told me to give you a message."

"Let me guess. If I trained harder I could block bullets with my bare hands?"

"Nah. He was off his game. He said to tell you it's not smart to bring a knife to a gun fight and you did good."

"I did good? He said that?"

"Yeah. I didn't tell him you fired an entire ten round clip and the guy still walked away in one piece."

"There was a door in the way."

"But he was a big guy."

"I gotta get back to the range."

"I'm just tugging your chain, Kristen. Take your time getting back to the range or anything else. You've had a tough year physically. You should have taken time off after the Durham case."

"I already took time off after the Cutter Shark."

"Probably not long enough. And you spent your time trying to prove how tough you are at Quantico with the FBI. Take it from someone who's been at this a long time. You'se got to slow down or you'll burn out."

"I've got plenty of energy. I don't like slowing down. I'm happy when I'm active. That's not a sin is it?"

He shrugs his shoulders and says, "I'm just saying."

"Not sure I know how anyway."

"Like I said, it takes all kinds to make the world work. I get that. By the way, how's that FBI agent of yours? Any romancing I need to know about? I can check him out you know. Heck, I can give him the talk your dad would have given."

"While cleaning your gun?"

"Doubt that would be the right angle with him. He's ex-Ranger or something isn't he?"

"Reynolds is a good guy . . . I think. But he plays his cards close to his chest. He might have let it slip he was Delta Force."

Scalia whistles. "Nah, I won't clean the gun in front of him. I'll just give him the score on what we think of you and that he better appreciate who you are and how many people love you."

"Which is why people keep trying to kill me. Listen, Big Tony . . . you can think through your speech but I'm not sure it will be needed anytime soon. Romance doesn't come easy for me."

"No problem with that. Time is God's way of keeping everything from happening at once. You'll know when you know."

We talk another fifteen minutes. I see him steal a look at his watch.

"You got a date with that hot wife of yours, Big Tony?"

"Every night. But since I was over here I thought

I'd stop by the basement of Fourth Presbyterian for a meeting."

He's carried his chip for fifteen, maybe twenty years. He says my dad was the one that got him in AA and saved his job—and life.

"Go give your speech. It's a good one."

"I usually just listen but maybe tonight I will."

"Somebody probably needs to hear it. I know I did."

"I might."

I probably should have let my mom stay. I somehow keep forgetting I wasn't the only one traumatized by what happened to dad.

You'll know when you know. Earlier today I knew. No question in my mind Reynolds and I were through. He had cheated with Klarissa and we were done. I screwed that up royally by not being a very good detective.

Unless they hatched a plan to cover up what was going on. See, it's this kind of thinking that gets me in trouble. I do better when I'm active.

Three hours later Heather Torgerson checks in with me when she arrives for her shift. I've got two CPD officers guarding me on the floor and two more cruising the area. That should keep the wolves at bay, though I do wish I had my Sig Sauer under my pillow. I wonder when I will get it back from the ballistics lab.

The FBI insisted they place an additional

resource on the floor because the case falls in their jurisdiction. I think Heather wants to chat but my head is buried in the casebooks for the Keltto murder. I may be stuck on the sidelines but Big Tony brought me enough caffeine to last me until midnight. I might as well put the time to good use.

❄ **64** ❄

The Bear is in bad shape, Zheglov thought. The room reeked of infection. The giant was delirious. He should just put him out of his misery. But oh what a tale he had to tell. I can't believe he was asleep in the room over the garage when we hit Genken. Stealing the truck was pure genius. Then he sold Sadowsky that he was me. He did good. Very good. His business idea isn't bad either. I wish I could drive a truck. He should have gone straight to Dallas or Phoenix or wherever else he was thinking about. He didn't need to kill the cop. She didn't see anything. Coming after her only let the *bratva* and now probably the Feds know he's not dead. Much better to be presumed dead.

So what does this mean for me? What do I do next? If I could drive a truck I'd follow his plans. If I was a miracle worker and could save him I'd go into business with him. That would be so inconceivable that no one would find us.

He looked down at the giant of a man. His chest was heaving as he gulped for air. He alternated between laughing and crying. Vlad sat next to him on the bed, doing his best to block out the stench of dying flesh.

"Med. Med. Nazar, can you hear me?"

"I can hear you, Mommy."

"I'm not your mommy. It's me, Vladimir."

"Are you an angel?"

Vlad almost laughed and said, "I'm not your angel, Med."

The Bear just smiled and nodded, no clue who was in the room with him. Maybe he sees an angel.

"Nazar. Tell me about your new business again. Tell me what you are going to do with the truck. Tell me about your new life."

The Bear smiled and babbled in his native Russian and then switched to English and then just slurred. Didn't matter what language he spoke in. The words made no sense anymore. I've lived a bad life, Vlad thought. I've seen many men die. Better to die happy. What better way to go? He reached for the pillow and pushed it over Med's face. The giant was too weak to fight. He might not even know it was happening. He pressed down and put his weight into it. After sixty seconds he felt no movement. He kept the pillow pushed tightly for another two minutes to be sure.

He'd already gone through Medved's belongings and picked out what he could use, namely cash and weapons. He had the keys to the Malibu in his pocket. It would be nice if he could drive a truck.

As Med's body relaxed a silver crucifix fell from his hand. Vlad picked it up and looked at it closely. He crossed himself and repeated the motion over Nazar—Medved, the Bear—Kublanov. I think that's what the priests do. Maybe he is in a better place. I think he is probably nothing in nothingness, but why not hope?

"This is a ridiculous plan, Bob," Reynolds stormed.

"Not your call," Van Guten interjected.

"I think Bob can answer for himself," Reynolds snapped at her.

"Don't fight, kids," Willingham broke in. "Since when has a ridiculous plan bothered you Austin? We've done many ridiculous things as a team and a lot of them have worked. I hope you're not letting your personal life bleed into work."

"Bob, I'm not going to even address that last sentence. Let me say this. First, we've done some ridiculous, outrageous plans, but they haven't included the abuse of a fellow law enforcement official, at least not one of the good ones."

"I resent your use of the word abuse, Austin," Van Guten interrupts.

"I'm not going to get into a war of semantics with you Leslie," Reynolds says back. "Pushing an appeal forward to question everything some-one—a hero in this case and the one that brought you the Shark, I might add—did in a near fatal encounter with a serial killer, without her knowledge, is dirty pool. Plain and simple. Which brings me to number two. Bob, when we've gone with outrageous plans there's been a clear outcome. What's all this for? To get a sociopathic or psychopathic serial killer to maybe talk about his delusions of grandeur? Van Guten said it herself. He's living on Mount Olympus. So all this for what?"

"Austin, you know there are forty-seven active cases we can definitively identify according to our Elite Serial Crime Unit," Van Guten says, breaking in. "And we all know that is a very conservative estimate. Some seemingly random murders have a common denominator and pattern that not even our best effort with Operation Vigilance has identified yet. By the time we catch most serial killers they are dead. Or they lawyer up or clam up. I thought that was what the Cutter would do and he didn't disappoint the first eight months. But now we've finally got a live one who wants to communicate. We can't let this get past us. Getting him to talk will save lives. I think that's a very clear outcome."

"Then let Conner know."

"If we did that, we'd have to let the whole Chicago Police Department know," Willingham said. "No matter how small the circle, someone will tell someone else."

"If CPD brass finds out about this they'll never help us on a case again."

"They won't find out," Willingham persisted.

"What if the judge agrees with Abrams?"

"He won't," Willingham said.

"You know that for sure? It's already fixed?" Reynolds asked.

"That would be something you learn strictly on need to know basis, soldier. I wouldn't tell you either way."

"Is this even legal?" Reynolds asked.

"Of course an appeal before trial is legal," Van Guten said.

"I hope we're not crazy enough to tamper with a judge on a case this important," Reynolds said. "But I might be even more afraid of what we're trying to do if we haven't."

"You're pushing it, Austin," Willingham said.

"Okay, Bob," Reynolds said, matching his glare. "Do your thing. But don't ask for my help if you and Leslie screw the pooch. I work for you but I have nothing to do with this."

"Is that for you to say?" Willingham asked.

"Of course it is," Reynolds said.

"Austin, you are not thinking clearly on this," Van Guten said, stepping in to interrupt an escalation of words.

"You'd be surprised how clear my mind is these

days," Reynolds said. "I'm heading back to New York. Time to bear down on Pasha Boyarov."

Reynolds looked at his watch. No time to get back to the hospital.

He texted a quick message: *Back in a few days. Be safe.*

❄ **65** ❄

After reading through the Keltto murder case notes twice—and finding nothing new to help us—I go through the Chicago *bratva* pictures and notes that Spencer Doyle gave us. I need to stay in touch with him. I suspect he will be mayor some day.

The Red Mafiya. The American *bratva*. The Moscow oligarchs. This has nothing to do with me. My involvement with them is absolutely accidental. I heard a preacher say that there are no accidents, only Providence. I pray every day. I ask for God's help. I ask Him to use me. But I'm not real sure I'm on His go-to list. Feels for sure like a coincidence to me. But there were some pretty amazing coincidences that helped me catch a serial killer. I did some things right as a detective but at the end of the day, my encounter with the Shark seemed meant to be. I got a few breaks and worked them hard—but at times, most of the time—I was blind. Providence? Okay, it's too hard to follow this line of thought. I'll go with what my dad said. God works in mysterious ways. I hope so.

I hit my walkie-talkie call button and Heather comes in. She's faster than room service.

"I'm going to lock up my files and need a witness," I say.

CPD has to approve any secured locations outside the premises for classified documents—or they don't leave the building. Zaworski and Nelson worked out a special dispensation that consists of a metal attaché handcuffed to a radiator. Torgerson is on the short list of approved witnesses.

We check in the files and she asks, "You have enough energy to talk?"

"I don't know, Heather. The caffeine is finally wearing off and I'm about ready to zonk out. Can we talk another time?"

"Not with me," she says, almost smiling. "There's a patient in ICU. Says she knows you. Just so happens she's under police watch as well. Want to guess who?"

Oh man. No way can I talk to Nancy. I've been told to stay away.

"Here or there?" I ask.

"Has to be there."

"I think I just woke up, Heather."

"You've done so good Kristen. I know it sounds weird but I'm proud of you. I remember when

364

you were just a little girl at the bus stop. Eddy and I could never have kids. I didn't think it mattered. But then I'd watch you guys messing around before the bus came and went. Sometimes I'd wish."

Nancy pauses, her thoughts miles and years away. She was always a pretty lady. She looks old all of a sudden. I shouldn't be here.

"Do you remember when you and that kid . . . I can't remember his name . . . got in a fight?"

Paul McIlwain. A bully. He was picking on another kid. Can't remember the kid's name. McIlwain was bigger than me and had me flat on my back with his fist raised to punch my lights out. He would have won if he had. But he had to be a big shot and lower his face to my face to tell me girls couldn't fight. I head-butted him and broke his nose. A punch or head-butt in the nose ends most fights. His mom came down to my house to complain. My mom was shocked and horrified. My dad did his best not to smile.

"Your family was always very nice, Kristen. Wish we'd spent more time with you guys."

"So what's going on, Nancy? I don't think you want to talk to me for a walk down memory lane."

A tear runs down her cheek.

"I've messed my life up, Kristen. Eddy deserved better. I was never a very good wife. He was always such a good guy. He'd give the shirt off his back to help anyone in need. I never did anything. I was difficult to live with. I think that's why he got involved in so many outside activities. It was a lot easier than listening to me complain."

"Is that really the way it was or are you trying to get me to feel sorry for you?"

"I wish I could say it was the latter. But no, I wasn't great to live with. I'm ashamed to say, but Leslie wasn't my first affair. Does that shock you?"

"Honestly? I know it shouldn't with all I've seen in police work, but it does."

"You're probably judging me right now aren't you?"

"Do you want me to be honest?"

"Nah, don't answer," she says with a half laugh and half grimace.

We sit in silence for a long moment. I can't ask her anything. I shouldn't be here. I've got Torgerson to back me up that this conversation is at Nancy's insistence. But with the Cutter working on an appeal and Don warning me to stay away from her, I really want to get out of here. I don't want to hear anything that will hurt our case—we have enough ammunition already. I don't want the slightest taint on what we have on her.

"Kristen, I deserve anything I get on this. I don't want to screw up things for anyone else. I know you want out of here. But I'm going to tell you three things you need to hear if you want to find who killed Eddy. Have your FBI friend come in if you want a witness that I'm in my right mind."

You don't want to slow down the flow when a suspect starts talking. But I realize she's right.

"Give me a second."

I get up, go to the door, and tell Heather what's going on. She returns to Nancy's bedside with me and pulls up the second visitor's chair.

I have her give her name, the date, and that she is not being coerced. She says the words as I write them. I hand it to her with a pen and she signs it.

"Okay Nancy, tell me," I say.

She takes a couple of deep breaths and says, "First, I didn't kill Eddy. Second, Leslie had nothing to do with this. He said some crazy things about us getting married and him moving in with me or us starting over on the West Coast. But he never said anything about getting rid of Eddy other than pushing me to file divorce papers on him so we could be together."

And? That's it? I think Heather and I are holding our breath.

"Third . . . you need to take a hard look at Bradley."

Where is this coming from? Bradley's only fourteen. Sure there are juveniles who commit murder. It's not common, but it happens.

"Why Bradley?" I ask.

"Eddy tried to help him some. He told me he didn't trust him. For Ed to say that is a big deal. Eddy also said that Bradley had a temper and gave him a push one day."

"Where did that happen?"

"In the garage. Eddy was teaching him how to do woodwork."

"Did Ed report it?"

"No. He just told me. So I'm sure that doesn't hold much weight with you. I know for a fact Bradley's had some troubles with the law that include violence. I'm pretty sure his records are sealed. His mom told me."

Okay. This is big. Why are we just learning about Bradley possibly having some violence in his past now?

"Anything else, Nancy?" I ask.

"Well . . . this is kind of embarrassing . . . but I caught him trying to spy on me some. I didn't think anything at first. Teen boys can get a crush on an older woman or anything that walks on two legs easy enough. But he was sneaky about it. I started pulling the shades. He really started giving me the creeps."

Okay.

"I'm not saying he had anything to do with Ed's murder . . . and I don't what to see a kid get in trouble any more than he already has . . . I hope I'm wrong, but I'd just take a look if I was you."

I feel sick to my stomach. Was Leslie Levin set up by a fourteen-year-old? Have we been set up?

Back in the room, Heather helps me go through the case files one more time. It's tiny but there is definitely a notation on Bradley's information sheet that a juvenile court has sealed files on young Mr. Starks. Heather caught it. I'm mad. I shouldn't have missed it. It is way too late to call Squires or Blackshear. I ping them with a text and set my alarm for seven to call them early. I drift into a troubled sleep, my thoughts darting back and forth between the Cutter, Nancy, Bradley, even Reynolds. For having something he just had to tell me, he sure has gone silent.

❄ **66** ❄

Vladimir Zheglov drove the Malibu due east on I-80 and stopped in South Bend, Indiana, to check into a motel and catch some sleep. South Bend. The only reason he knew the name of the town was the Notre Dame football team. He watched a little pro football but didn't really care enough to understand it. At least there was real football to watch on TV now. The only time he got to see Dynamo Moscow was during Euro Cup match play. But he'd taken a liking to Arsenal in the British Premiere League, which was on TV a lot in the US. The Arsenal was owned by a Russian oligarch.

Who is in charge? Vlad asked himself.

Genken held on too long and didn't have a succession plan in place. It would probably be

Luytov now. Ishutin was too old. Teplov didn't know what he was talking about. Genken should have set it up a couple years ago, but naming your successor was dangerous. And everyone knew Pasha was his favorite. Maybe that's what emboldened Pasha to say yes when Moscow came calling with a lousy idea.

You didn't have to be a genius to know someone wanted to create bioweapons to use against the US. But that was stupid, he thought. The US was where the action and money was. Why would Putin kill the goose that laid the golden eggs?

He slept eight hours. Vladimir wasn't sure he moved the entire night. He was up at seven and looked at the four phones on the small desk in his room. His, Teplov's, and the two untraceable prepaid phones Teplov had got for the two of them to stay in touch with. Risk turning them on? He needed to know what was going on. He could turn them on and put them in airplane mode except for a minute or two at a time. But still, no more than three or four minutes of power per phone in case there was some other signal going out. He would be on the road shortly. East? West?

He turned on his own phone first. He put it in airplane mode as soon as it powered up. Hopefully it hadn't connected with a cell tower letting someone know he was alive and where he was. He had thirty missed calls with no voice messages. Everyone in Pasha's gang was running scared and didn't dare put their name into the digital ether world—but they wanted to know what was going on. He scanned the list and saw two calls from Luytov. He wrote down the number. He checked for text messages and had more than fifty. He scanned them quickly. Most were from men that reported to him and all basically asked the same thing, Vlad, what is going on?

Wish I could tell you.

Two texts from Luytov. Gleb Lutyov. The first said, "Call!" The second said, "We need to talk."

Do we?

He turned the phone off and followed the same process on Sergei Teplov's phone. He didn't recognize most numbers. There were a couple from Luytov and a bunch from Sadowsky. He wrote down Sadowsky's number and turned off the phone.

He powered on Teplov's cheap prepaid Nokia. The model had been around so long the call time probably cost more than the phone itself.

He called Luytov. Gleb picked up on the fourth ring.

"Yeah?"

"You know who this is," Vlad said.

The man would know it was him or he wouldn't. No way was he giving his name to be heard by the NSA listeners.

"Where are you?"

"I don't have long to talk."

"We need to meet. Now."

"That's not possible."

"Are you in Chicago?"

"I don't have long to talk. You asked me to call."

"You know your friend is singing, right?"

"Not for sure, but I figured he was."

"We love his music so much we have plans to send him a special package."

"He will appreciate that."

"Yes he will. Why don't you keep doing what you are doing until he gets that. Then come home and you and I will have a nice coulibiac together. My wife makes the best. With sturgeon. We might have a nice position for you at the store. Are you interested?"

"I like coulibiac."

"Good. We're losing customers and need some-one who can help tidy up the shop."

"I'll think."

"Think hard, my friend. The window for being welcomed back into the family as a son won't stay open long. If you see Sandy, tell him hi for me. He has a little work for you to do."

"Why me? He can handle his city just fine."

"With all the storms that have blown through, his major power lines are down. No real electricity until the power company gets things fixed."

"I'd hate to get electrocuted because the power company is having serious quality control issues."

"Is there a problem?"

"Let's just say I've been underwhelmed by the quality of the product and the customer service."

There was a pause and Luytov said, "Okay. I can understand your concerns. How about if you work outside the company?"

"I don't know."

"Think of yourself as an outside consultant. I'll text you a number."

Vlad hung up and I turned off the phone. He powered on the matching Nokia. Who to call? No one. His gang was dead, in prison, or already worked for a different brigadier. Touch bases with Sadowsky? Nah. Too big of a risk. He powered the phone off.

East or West?

Zheglov loaded the trunk. He pulled into a gas station and filled up the tank. Return to the family or go his own way? What was his own way? What could he do? Medved was the smart one. At least he knew how to drive a truck. My skills are more specialized. I can't think of anything else I could do to make a living.

He turned west toward Chicago. If Luytov was truly the Pakhan this would be the only route home to the *bratva*.

❄ **67** ❄

No one is happy. Blackshear had written up a neat and tidy—and winnable—murder-one case against Nancy Keltto for the District Attorney's office. Not as an accomplice but as the one who wielded the weapon. Now there is a witness who says her boyfriend was there. She says the witness needs to be looked at. It's getting messy.

I don't know whether Zaworski or Don is madder at me for speaking to Nancy Keltto at the hospital, but Don is walking the request to break the seal on Bradley Starks' files to the Cook County courthouse at this very moment.

I'm unhappy because I'm twiddling my thumbs waiting for the doctor to make his rounds and release me. He's late again.

Zaworski said I can't come into the office today, not even to review my case files on the Cutter Shark. However, he didn't specifically say I couldn't do anything office-related. I called Dr. Jeana Andrews' office and rescheduled a therapy session for mid-afternoon. I'd better be out of here by then.

It was still hovering around ten degrees but the roads were clear all the way back to Chicago. The heat was on Sadowsky with the CPD and FBI so

Luytov sent Zheglov to a *shestyorka*—a volunteer who wasn't actually a member of the *bratva*—to meet with him at George's Diner on South Pulaski in Alsip.

Vladimir arrived thirty minutes early, which wasn't enough time for his liking. But it gave him just enough time to survey the area and do a quick tour through the restaurant, including the men's and women's bathrooms. When his contact drove into the parking lot in a gleaming black S-Class Mercedes and walked into the restaurant, Vlad nodded to the bathroom. He locked the door and gave the man a rough and thorough body search.

Satisfied, Vladimir led the unnamed man into the dining space and the two sat across from each other. Vlad was hungry and ordered a big breakfast with coffee. The man ordered a bagel and coffee, probably for appearances, as he never touched either.

The man finally slid a single sheet of paper across the table to Zheglov.

"You may ask any questions you like and I will tell you anything I know," the man said.

"First. Are you connected to Sadowsky?"

"Yes and no," the man answered.

"Explain."

"I do work for Sandy from time to time. But not on this one. He doesn't know I'm meeting you."

Zheglov nodded.

"If I eventually need help, will he?"

"He won't be happy he's been left out. But if Luytov gives the order, he will obey."

Vlad looked down. There were three pictures from different angles and outfits. She was a pretty girl. Dark brown hair—maybe a touch of red that might be real—big intense eyes, tallish, and very fit based on a shot of her punching a large boxing bag. There was a list of places she could be found, including her office address at the Chicago Police Department's Second Precinct, her condo, a health club, an indoor soccer facility, a church, a couple coffee shops, and her mother's and her sister's homes. He folded it twice and slipped it into a pocket.

"Second question."

"Anything I can answer I will."

"Why?"

"Why what?"

"Why does she matter to us?"

"That's the first question I was told you would ask. Here's what I know to tell you. Not my words—I am only repeating what I have been told by Luytov's *sovietnik*. First Gleb believed the information coming from the NYPD. The detective didn't witness the murder. She just showed up while Kublanov was supposed to be securing Frank Nelson. Gleb had his people take a closer look. The cops were putting the *bratva* off her scent. She is definitely FBI. She spent time at Quantico last fall. She's connected to the deputy director of counterterrorism. No way was she in Central Park by accident. She was part of an operation against the *bratva*."

"A bad operation that has led to many deaths. Even if she is FBI, does it matter? Why rattle our saber against the Feds for something that is already dead? I see only troubles for us."

"I was told you might see it this way. What I can say is we have been wounded but need to show we can fight back if we are to get back to business as usual. Our biggest weapon against US law enforcement is money, but close behind is fear. We must maintain that."

Vladimir shrugged.

"I am only reporting what I was told. I am not savvy to such matters. Gleb Luytov sent a personal message for you. If you want out, go. Leave now. Just don't come back."

Vlad poured more sugar in the coffee and stirred it, pondering as he watched the black liquid circle in slow patterns. Just go? He doubted it. There was a chance a backup team was close. But even if he could, where?

"Is there anything else?" the man asked.

"Yes. Give me your car."

"Certainly," he said, sliding his car keys across the table.

The two men went to the parking lot and shifted contents between the trunks.

A ninety thousand dollar automobile. That was

too easy Vlad thought. Maybe I don't have more because I haven't asked for more. I'll call Luytov when I'm done and tell him to wire money somewhere while I lay low.

❄ **68** ❄

Willingham hung up the phone and looked at Reynolds. It was seven in the morning, noon in Geneva. Herr Hiller was flown in a military jet home to confirm what he was happy to share with a joint team of officers from the CIA, FBI, US Military Intelligence, and Informationsdienst des Bundes—the Swiss secret service.

"The deal didn't go through. The Russians didn't get the PathoGen research."

"We're sure?" Reynolds asked.

"Heinrich Hiller is a very frightened and subsequently forthcoming man. Henry opened his computer and showed how his system works. He provided every scrap of information and password. The deal didn't happen and the money is moving in small chunks through a random network he has no access to. He doesn't even know the account the money came from nor where it will end up. His services are dirty but brilliant."

"Can we walk the cat back and identify who sent the money?"

"Maybe, maybe not. We've got a team of techies

on it. What we do know for sure right now is both parties failed to enter the codes that would initiate the transaction. Francis Nelson didn't because Nazar Kublanov panicked and killed him. Pasha Boyarov missed his deadline because he knew Nelson was dead."

"So mission accomplished, sir?"

"Doesn't feel like it, Austin, but yes, we blocked the first stage of a bioterrorism threat that may have been aimed at US soil. All Boyarov can give us now is details on the US *bratva*. Not a bad haul even if it does feel a little hollow."

"You really think we got enough? Do you believe what you're saying?"

Willingham sighed and said, "We'll make some arrests and shut down some operations. But they'll all be replaced over time. We don't have the resolve to do what it takes. The lines are blurred between crime and legitimate business. Too many of our best and brightest feather their nests by looking the other way and letting things go. When we do get serious, the legal process is stacked against timely justice. So do I believe we did good? Sure. Why not? Did we get enough to offer him Witness Protection? Nah. I may be getting too old for this."

"You've been telling me that for five years, Bob."

"But this time I think I mean it."

"Can I ask a favor?"

"Sure. What do you need?"

"Quash this plan with the Cutter Shark that Van Guten is working. It has disaster written all over it."

"I'm not sure I can, now, Austin. It's already in the works—Herr Hiller would be proud of it."

"I'm not letting this go," Reynolds said.

"I know you won't."

"I want one other thing right now, Bob."

"Name it."

"Let me rock Boyarov's world today—and back me up."

Reynolds and his team barged into Boyarov's cell at 7:30 a.m. and manhandled him to the interrogation room. No food or beverage, just an assault of questions for five hours.

"Pasha, I need to leave town a few days," Reynolds finally said, standing up. "One of my stops will be to the Hoover Building in D.C. I'm not sure you're upholding your end of the deal. Not for me to decide. But I'm going to suggest you be moved to the general prison population."

"You can't do that, Special Agent Reynolds," Pasha sneered. "We signed papers. But nice bluff."

"Actually Pasha, even if you're right and I'm bluffing, you already know we can do whatever we want . . . if you don't cooperate . . . and really, even if you do cooperate. But like I said, it won't be my call. I'll just make my personal recommendation. If you're still in this area of New York Metro in three or four days, I'll see you then. If not, I'm not sure who your case worker will be."

"My deal was with Deputy Director Robert Willingham. He'll set you straight."

"I'm sure he will. Bob and I are having dinner tonight. I'll let him know you don't like the way I'm thinking. Or you can just smile, look at the mirror or one of the cameras, and tell him yourself right now."

"You won't put me in the yard."

"Why not? You're a tough guy. You should be fine."

Pasha snorted. "You wouldn't do it. I can't fight everyone the brigadiers would send at me. But then you'd get nothing for all the time and effort you've put into me. You wouldn't get what I know up here," he said, pointing a finger at the side of his head.

"Bringing you in hasn't cost us that much. You were desperate. That made you a cheap date. So no big loss for us if something unfortunate were to befall you. In terms of what you have up there"—Reynolds jabbed a finger in the direction of Pasha's head—"you haven't told us much of anything and frankly, we're not convinced you know as much as you think you do."

"I know plenty. I would have been Pakhan."

"Then why was Moscow setting you up to

take the fall after you delivered them their bio goodies?"

"Wouldn't have happened."

"We've got a Sergei Teplov in custody who says differently. We're thinking about giving him the deal we offered you."

Pasha turned white. Throwing Teplov's name in the conversation was Reynolds' first bluff—but Boyarov fell for it and started talking. This actually worked a lot better than I thought it would, Reynolds thought.

❄ **69** ❄

"Where you at, KC?" Don asks.

"Driving up to Wrigleyville for an appointment with my doctor."

"Why aren't you meeting him at the hospital?"

"I was released."

Is it a lie that I'm not telling Don that the doctor I'm meeting is Dr. Andrews, my therapist? How far does the sin of omission go?

He's not interested and plows in, "Three things you need to know. Do you have a second?"

"Shoot."

"First, the judge broke the seal on Bradley Starks' juvenile record. Man oh man. This is a troubled youth with a long list of crimes, including some serious violence. He put a vice principal at his middle school in the hospital. The guy turned around in his office and Bradley hit him in the back of the head with a bronze bookend that was sitting on the guy's desk."

"How is he even in public school?" I ask. "Shouldn't he be in a juvenile detention center?"

"That's the second thing you need to know. Get this. Ed Keltto showed up in court to volunteer to be Bradley Starks' mentor. If I'm reading the transcripts right, that swayed the judge to let him serve an in-school suspension and go on probation until he graduates from high school, if and when that happens. Did Nancy tell you that when she talked to you?"

"No. But she pointed us in that direction."

"She probably felt too guilty to tell you one more time what a good guy her husband was."

"So what happens next?"

"Blackshear and I are meeting up in your old neighborhood along with a couple of uniforms. The uniforms will take Bradley to Cook County juvenile. We'll question him there."

"Does that change anything for Nancy or Levin?"

"Not until we talk to the kid. But it might."

"How's Blackshear taking it with his righteous arrests up in the air?"

"He's not happy but he's got his head on straight."

"Wow. Nancy wasn't lying about Bradley being

in trouble. Why does this make me feel so lousy?" I ask him.

"Because it is. You ever get the feeling society is falling apart?"

I can't answer. When I'm with my family, life feels pretty normal. Maybe even sweet some-times—except when I think my baby sis is cheating on me. But this is so messed up that I wonder what in the world is going on that so many people are on the edge or over the edge of self-destruction and taking others with them.

"Third," he announces.

There's a dramatic pause.

"I gave Zaworski my letter and signed the papers before I hit the road tonight. It's official. In two weeks I'm a civilian."

No question this was coming. It still feels like a punch in the gut. I'm slow on relationships and don't want a new partner. I'll miss him and his expensive shoes, suits, and ties. He dressed our little team up. I'll even miss his disapproving comments on my wardrobe and attempts at humor. If he hadn't resigned, it was only a matter of time before he got promoted. But he'd still be around. It's good to have a few friends who understand you.

Martinez. Blackshear. Zaworski. I have other friends—but I guess what Barnes said was right. I'm not always a team player. I'm not a free spirit as anyone can tell you—but I do hold the world at bay. I'll still have old timers like Scalia and Soto watching my back, though I'm not sure Soto understands anything about me except my need to keep my hands up when I fight.

"You're not saying anything, KC."

"Sorry. I was just trying to figure out what turn to make. Congratulations, Don. I'm happy for you. And I mean that."

I think I am. But I'm sad too. Does that make it a lie?

I think Dr. Andrews is in shell shock. There was no pushing and prodding to get me to open up this session. I hit her with everything right out of the gate. I started with Squires' resignation and moved straight into my dad's death. I wove in Ed and Nancy Keltto and unfinished business with the Cutter Shark case. I told her about getting caught up in internecine warfare with the Red Mafiya—and about the Bear's attack and my subsequent dream. I can't believe I remembered the word internecine. Inconceivable. I moved on to Reynolds and what happened between Reynolds and my sister but didn't. I left out my feelings on a man getting killed before my eyes during the Durham case but brought up that maybe I should have accepted the job offer with the FBI that Willingham put together. By the time I told her how much I like coaching my niece's soccer team, even if our team name is the Snowflakes and our jerseys are yellow, she had put her iPad down and given up taking notes.

"You have a lot on your mind," she said.

I wanted to ask her how that made her feel but bit my tongue and just nodded.

"So how do you cope?" she asked. "What is your secret?"

"Do you believe in God?" I asked back.

"What I believe is not relevant," she said.

"It is if you really want to know how I cope," I said.

She didn't answer but picked up the iPad and wrote a note with a fancy stylus.

I covered everything on my mind in fifty-five minutes.

"I think our time is up today," she said.

Today sounds ominous. What will we talk about next time, I wonder? That was everything. I guess I could have talked about how my family has handled—and not handled—my father's death.

"I have some questions I want to ask you next week," she said. "I want to just say how proud I am of you for opening up."

That takes me by surprise. I assumed she was writing "religious nut job" after I asked if she believed in God.

"What you did today, Kristen, is very important. Authentic relationships require authentic transparency. As humans we erect walls between ourselves and others, even people we love, because we are afraid what they will think if they see the real person we are. We grow closer as we take down the wall, sometimes one brick at a time, to be seen for who we really are. It is scary and takes trust to remove those bricks that we've carefully erected to protect ourselves. I think you did that just a little bit today and I applaud you. This is something we can build on."

Build on. Yep, I'm going to be seeing Dr. Andrews for a while.

I like what she said, but put another way, I'm building an authentic relationship with someone who can't have an authentic relationship with me because we are in a therapeutic relationship and it would go against her professional code to interact with me in any other setting.

I took down a few bricks and started an authentic relationship with someone I can't have a relationship with—par for the course for me.

On my drive home I wonder how I can tell her I took the whole wall down and what she saw was probably all she was going to get. I am all for an appropriate amount of transparency. But I've somehow come to this notion that we aren't an inside person and an outside person. We are what we do and do what we are.

I don't know if that's good theology or psychology. I might ask Jimmy what he thinks. He's a very nice man. People love him. He listens and cares and helps. He'd be that way even if he wasn't a pastor. But I'm not sure he knows how to respond to me. I've tried to broach a question I have about my dad's death but we haven't gotten anywhere.

He's not the only one that isn't sure how to deal with me. I've been told on more than a few occasions that dealing with me is like dealing with a brick wall. Andrews is right about me putting bricks up.

I don't stay too introspective very long. Maybe I have undiagnosed ADHD. Next thing I know I'm humming the Pink Floyd song, "Just Another Brick in the Wall." That might not be the actual name of the song. But that's the phrase I remember along with "teacher leave those kids alone." That gets me thinking about Bradley. Oh man.

❄ 70 ❄

I call Blackshear.

"Yeah Conner?"

Maybe I should tell him he needs to take a few bricks down.

"What's the status of the crime scene?"

"The Kelttos?"

"Yeah."

"Still sealed."

"I want to walk through it. Any chance we can meet in the morning?"

"You out of the hospital?"

"Yep."

"My team has gone through it with a fine-toothed comb."

Like their work on the O'Hare surveillance videos I want to point out, but stop myself.

"But I haven't," I say nice and firm.

"You're not going to find anything we haven't already put in evidence boxes."

"I just need to feel the vibe."

He sighs. "You got it. What time?"

"What works for you?"

"Eight in the morning too early?"

"Perfect."

"Scratch that. We see Bradley early tomorrow. Has to be tonight."

I'm tired, but beggars don't make the rules.

"Even better," I say.

"I can get there at sevenish."

"Knock on my mom's door when you're in the neighborhood, Bob. I'll stop by and see her. And thanks a ton."

I stopped by Mom's for dinner. I didn't even have to explain that I am being shadowed everywhere I go by two CPD officers and one FBI agent. She now makes extra food as the rule of thumb. That meant the FBI agent, a guy I hadn't met, John Turvy, ate with us. Mom made a mean pot of fiery chili and insisted I take bowls out to the guys in the squad car. As long as neither has my nephew James' genetic propensity toward flatulence, that should help make a bitterly cold night go easier.

Blackshear called a couple times to say he was running late and didn't show up until a little before nine. My eyes were heavy and my head was bobbing while we waited. Mom immediately talked him into a bowl of chili. She sent me outside in dropping temperatures to deliver warm blackberry cobbler and melting ice cream to the guys in the squad car—the ice cream wasn't melting for long. Blackshear may have had his nose bent out of shape with me for making him work late, but he wasn't turning down dessert. It's a little before ten and we are finally ready to head to the Kelttos.

"So what are you looking for, Kristen?" he asks.

"Nothing in particular, Bob. I just sometimes get feelings. It happened on the fourth murder with the Cutter Shark. Gigi. Remember her?"

"Don't even ask me that, Kristen. I've spent the last year trying to forget everything about that sick case."

"I should do the same but you've heard what I'm dealing with?"

"No. What's up?"

"That's for another day. I just know that my dad and Big Tony told me you have to feel the crime scene. Scalia said he'd pray even though he wasn't a particularly praying Catholic outside of

Mass. We were so stuck on that case that I did it. All I could think of was a Bible verse when I went through her house. I don't know the whole thing, but the point was basically, 'watch and pray.' So I did. And I felt something."

"Like a ghost?" he asks as he unlocks the back door to the Keltto residence.

"No, you goof. Not a ghost. Just a feeling that helped me later on."

"How?"

"I don't know. It just did."

We walk through the first floor slowly. Blackshear is watching me the whole time. That's distracting. Then we cover the upstairs. I stand in a bedroom that is probably less than fifty feet from Bradley's room next door. He was picked up three hours or so ago. I feel no vibe. Blackshear keeps peeking over at me.

"Bob, stop looking at me. I told you, I don't see ghosts."

"Sorry. Sorry. You have me curious."

"Good. Then just do what I do. Watch and pray."

"I don't really pray, Kristen. That's my wife's department."

"You either keep your eyes to yourself and start praying or I'm going to punch you in the nose."

"I've always thought I should pray," he answers, stifling a smile.

Okay. This is forcing things with him looking over my shoulder. I wasn't expecting words to appear in a mist before my eyes with the name of the murderer, but I was expecting something. Just a better feeling for Ed and Nancy and what happened. I feel nothing.

"Done?" Blackshear asks, looking at his watch.

"The garage," I say.

He purses and then puckers his lips. His mouth opens to speak the words he wants to say. But it closes. Blackshear nods and we bundle up in our coats to brace against the lake wind that has worked its ways between houses, alleys, businesses, and walls to lash into us in the fifteen short steps between the back stoop and the side door of the one-car garage.

Blackshear flicks on the light. Even with everything organized and placed on shelves and hooks and in cubbies that wrap around three walls, there is nothing but a small path around the Malibu.

I look at a bucket with rock salt on my right. I shut the world out, including Blackshear. I pass the automotive section. A case of oil. Four one-gallon containers of windshield wiper fluid. Radiator fluid. Car wash and waxes. Leather care for car seats.

The next two steps take me into home maintenance, with tubes of caulk, cans of paint, half-used rolls of shelf paper, concrete sealer on the bottom shelf, and more. I can see around the car. The other wall is yard and garden supplies and tools. A lot of stuff for such a tiny yard.

I'm beginning to feel like I'm at a Home Depot or Lowes.

I stop at the back of the garage. There is a long tool bench that reaches from wall to wall. Above are cupboards. On top of the bench is an impressive array of power and hand tools. Beneath are portioned slots with different kinds and sizes of lumber.

I stop and look at the unpainted cupboards. We might be in an enclosed structure but it is freezing. I blow out and see my breath. I look over at Blackshear. He avoids eye contact. He wants to go home. I do, too.

I look at the last cupboard along the back wall. I reach in my pocket, pull out a small but powerful black flashlight and play the beam over the wood-work. If it was daylight and the garage door was open it would be easy to see, but Chicago is shrouded in gray during the winter, and the light bulb flickering on the ceiling of the garage is weak. But there it is, clear as day. A name has been scratched in the wood by an inexperienced juvenile hand.

Bradley.

Blackshear sees it and shrugs.

I walk back to the side door and get a step-ladder. I prop it in front of the bench, two legs on a raised concrete slab, two on the floor of the garage. The bottom shelf is filled with magazines and stapled paper documents. I hand them down to Blackshear and we take a quick look-see. Do-It-Yourself woodworking magazines and plans. Handwritten scribbling in pencil.

Next shelf up I pull out a partially completed project. It is a box made out of mahogany or hickory or some other dark wood. Next to it are materials, including a roll of felt, to finish what looks like will become a jewelry box. I assume Bradley has started a project for his mom. Nice. Too bad he might not ever get a chance to finish it.

On the top shelf is a simple leather tool belt on top of a neatly folded apron. I look at the tan leather belt. The name Bradley has been burnished on the inside.

Looks to me like Bradley did more with Ed than he indicated to me at the bus stop.

Bradley. What did you do, Bradley? Did you kill the guy that was trying to help you?

"You getting a vibe Conner?" Blackshear asks, his voice hoarse.

"Yeah . . . just not sure what it means. How about you?"

"I'm praying but I'm getting a little weirded out, Conner."

❄ 71 ❄

"Vanessa, you don't owe me any explanation. This is between you and Don. It's a family decision. I'm all for whatever you feel is right for you."

I got back to the condo and thought of Mr. Bernard. I need to check on him. Amazingly, the Bear didn't kill him. Knocked him out and slid him under the greeting desk but apparently Mr. Bernard is one tough old bird. The kid working the lobby says he is going to be okay and come back to work. I notice he is nervous talking to me and looking around. He is probably wondering who else is after me.

"Did they do a good job on the new door?" he asked.

Admittedly—and I'm embarrassed to say—I hadn't looked close, but answered, "It looks great."

Klarissa's bathroom in the master bedroom has a huge Jacuzzi tub. I soaked away the last nine days, starting in Central Park with a dying man. I wonder again how his wife is doing. Justine. I saw another picture of her with a news story. She is stunning.

I haven't done a crossword in forever and planned to sit in bed and veg out doing a puzzle or two before falling asleep.

There's an FBI agent in the living room. Torgerson takes his place at eleven. I had planned to be asleep already. Then Vanessa called. She is feeling bad for pushing Don to finalize a decision.

"Don's a wonderful husband. I don't care how much he makes. Money has never been an issue."

She's made sure of that with her career. Must be nice.

"But I don't know how you guys do this work, Kristen. I really don't. It's an awful job. You work insane hours trying to keep the city safe, then you have to hear the media blast you for all the things you do wrong."

The cleansing I felt after the soak is wearing off quickly.

"He's a great father. Devon and Veronika adore him. But they're getting older. The world changes when you go to middle school. They're going to need more time from him."

I think of Kendra. Does she go to middle school next year or the year after? Oh man. Time flies.

"I hear you, Vanessa, and agree."

"But I want Don to be happy. And he's miserable right now."

"Maybe that's because of the job, Vanessa. Maybe you're making your own point. We've got some crazy stuff we're working on. That won't change."

"I know, Kristen. I know. But part of it right now is you. You got shot for heaven's sake.

He feels like he can't leave you in harm's way."

"He knows me well enough, Vanessa, and he knows I'm not his job. This has nothing to do with me."

"His head knows but his heart doesn't. He grew up being a star football player but his daddy was coach and made sure he knew it was a team game."

"I know he was a star. My Huskies still remember him putting up two hundred yards against us for Ball State."

I don't know if Don could have made the NFL. I know he would have gotten a look if he hadn't blown out his ACL his senior year. Part of the reason we are a good team is we have some things in common. I got a torn ACL playing soccer for Northern Illinois. Same conference as Ball State. I can fantasize about being the next Mia Hamm but I do know in my real world mind that I had no chance at the NFL or Team USA.

"Maybe if he moved up in management and wasn't on the street, it'd be okay," she continued, not sounding very happy or convinced.

"If he stays on the force that will happen sooner or later, Vanessa. He'll be a captain and then commander is next. He's a smart guy. Everyone respects him. The sky is the limit."

I don't think that's what she wanted to hear. She wants a new start in California. She can feel the sun already. I bite my tongue and don't mention they are running out of water out there in addition to their own problems with crime.

"Can I ask you one small favor, Kristen?"

"Anything, Vanessa. Name it."

"It's actually two things."

"No big biggie, even if it's three things. Anything for you and your family."

"Just . . . I'm not sure how to say this . . . just do your best to let him know you support his decision."

That stings a little. Did she think I was going to work against her?

"You got it, Vanessa," I say with as much enthusiasm as I can put in my voice. "That's easy. I do support his decision. What else?"

"He's worried about Debbie. He doesn't want to leave Chicago with her the way she is. He feels responsible."

That's got to be tough. Don's sister is a crack-head who has been in and out of jail for drugs and prostitution. He and Rodney try to get her into rehab at least once a year. She agrees and then bolts. I was there when she stood them up last Thanksgiving.

"I know this is too much to ask. But if you can let him know you'll check on her from time to time, he might feel better."

"Vanessa, you didn't even have to ask. I'll do it. I want to do it. I'm happy to do it. I know he'd do the same for me if our positions were switched."

"Let him know, Kristen. It will help."

I really like Vanessa. She and Don are wonderful together. She's perfect for him—she understands his need for Italian silk ties. I don't want to get into judging. I guess I'll just say, Don may be the head of the family, but she is the neck that turns the head.

"This is Squires."

No one spoke.

"This is Squires. Can I help you?"

"Donny . . ."

The broken voice was barely a whisper.

"I'm sorry, Donny. I'se got myself in troubles again."

"Where you at, Debbie?"

"Cook County Sherriff's."

"I'll come get you."

"You're gonna have to talk to them. They might not let me come with you."

"What'd they pick you up for, Debbie?"

"Some things I don't like to say out loud. Just come down if you can and if Vanessa'll let you'se."

Squires decided to ignore the last jab, even if there was a hint of truth to it.

"Donny."

"Yeah, Deb."

"Don't bring that skinny partner of yours. She's crazy. I don't like her. She gonna get you killed one day."

"Sit tight, Deb. I'm on my way."

"I ain't going nowhere. They got me locked up again, Donny."

Squires felt sick to his stomach. What in the world had happened to his smart, witty, and beautiful little sister? Problem is he knew what happened to her, but how? She might have been smartest of the three kids. Deb was definitely smarter than him. About the time he was off at college and Rodney was finishing law school, their dad got sick. Cancer. Their mom was so busy taking care of him that Deb was left to her own devices. She got in with the wrong crowd, hooked up with a bad guy—now deceased—and spiraled into drugs and the crimes required to support the habit, robbery and prostitution.

He would call Rodney on the way over. It was two hours earlier there.

Deb sounded bad. Vanessa would put up a stink if he even considered bringing her back to the house. She had never let Devon and Veronika see their aunt, not that Debbie had ever made an effort. He needed to take her somewhere else tonight. After her disappearance at Thanksgiving, Rodney put a couple top-notch rehab centers on retainer, ready to take her 24/7, no advance notice.

Debbie would squawk and cuss Vanessa up and down the whole way over, blaming Vanessa for not welcoming her into the home. The more Don defended Vanessa, the louder Debbie would get.

The truth was, he didn't want her around the kids either.

She hates Conner—since the first day she set eyes on her—and KC is my one go-to when we move to LA.

❄ 72 ❄

"So you are saying no one else in New York was involved with PathoGen?"

Reynolds was still in the room, but now as a spectator and maybe a prop, not the lead questioner. A senior interrogator was working Boyarov.

"No one," Pasha answered. "I've told you that twenty times—at least twenty times. Ask twenty more if you wish, but I'll answer the same each time. The messenger boy, Teplov, brought the deal to me."

"Directly?"

"No. I told you already. He had his own messenger boy. Ruchkin.

"Why you? Why did Teplov and whoever he worked for pick you, Pasha Boyarov?"

"He said that Genken had turned it down. The Pakhan had a lot of power and freedom, but not that much power anymore. He couldn't say no to Moscow—that simple."

"When did the New York *bratva* start answering to Moscow?"

"Always. Never. I don't know."

"I thought you were Genken's right-hand man?"

Pasha smiled. Did they think they could work him so easily?

"I was a brigadier, nothing more. I was never sovietnik. I didn't have enough gray hair. I knew next to nothing about Moscow. Really, I knew nothing. That's the way Genken wanted it."

"But you think he worked with Moscow."

"Things changed after the breakup of the USSR. Relationships were reconnected. But everyone in Moscow was still weak and poor. No one could order Genken to do anything. Ten years later, the oligarchs got half the country's rubles and weren't so weak and poor any-more."

"Do you think this goes all the way up to the president?"

"Can I give you some advice?"

The interrogator didn't answer.

"There is only one real Pakhan and one real *bratva* now. So sure. It goes all the up to the man himself. Putin. But here is my advice. You should ask me about New York. I moved from Russia when I was thirteen. I've never been back. All I know is New York and the way we are here. Now I know that will make you think I'm tricking you so I don't have to tell you who is in charge in Russia. So ask all you want. I'll make some things up for you if it will make Willingham happy. But I think you know more about Russia than I do. I know New York."

Reynolds frowned to keep himself from smiling. Maybe Boyarov was going to work out better than he first thought.

"So the deal with PathoGen was all you?"

"Yes. I told no one else anything. Genken taught me that the fewer who know the better."

"Not even Vladimir Zheglov?"

"No, not even Vlad. But you can ask him yourself."

"Why do you think that, Pasha?" Reynolds interrupted.

"Because I handed him to you on a silver platter when I made the deal with you. He's probably next door right now."

The room was silent.

Boyarov began to smile and chuckle softly.

"Is something funny?" Reynolds asked.

"You didn't get Vlad, did you?"

"Maybe we'll let you ask him yourself," Reynolds said.

"Tsk, tsk," Pasha said. "Agent Reynolds, you need to let the real interrogators do the talking. You are much too obvious. But I like you, even though if it was only the two of us in this room, only one would walk out alive. Two trained killers? It would be interesting. Who would win Agent Reynolds?"

The two men stared at each other. This time Pasha broke it with a laugh.

"Here is more free advice from me," he said, looking at the interrogator. "You need to tell Willingham to put his torpedo back in the field. If Vladimir Zheglov is loose, we all have problems. He is very good, you know? I would claim I taught him everything he knows—but he's got some special tricks I don't know. He'll know how to stay alive and free—that's obvious. And he'll know how to reconnect with whoever the puppet masters are in all this. When he does, he will become the triggerman to solve any problems. I think I might be their number one problem."

That's one mystery solved, Reynolds thought. I think we have a pretty good idea who killed Teplov.

So where is Vlad now? Figuring out how to get to Boyarov? Teplov was dead. It had to be Zheglov who killed him. If so, the two men were together close to Dulles. Better have them run passenger manifests there and Reagan International.

I was going to save Nancy. She obviously doesn't know what I am capable of. If I get out of this mess, I might kill her myself.

❄ **73** ❄

Zaworski looked like he was going to ask me what the heck I was doing in the office but I think he did the math and figured he couldn't run the department one man down—even if that one man is me, a mere woman—especially with new developments in the Keltto murder. It's just five of us. Blackshear, Squires, and Sergeant Konkade round out the small group meeting.

The meeting started with Squires and Blackshear updating Zaworski that Leslie Levin's alibi didn't quite check out. Doesn't mean he swung the shovel or crow bar or baseball bat or whatever. But it might mean Nancy didn't. Then we hit my hospital conversation with Nancy Keltto. Zaworski and Konkade give each other a look of dread.

I quickly explain that she initiated the conversation and gave full permission for the interview and that I had it in writing, signed by her, me, and Agent Heather Torgerson as a witness. I provide a copy of the agreement. The original is safely locked in my case file.

"What do you think, Konkade?" Zaworski asks him, handing him the copy.

I don't know if Konkade always moves his lips when he reads but I do know that the Sergeant smooths the hair on his bald dome when he is agitated.

"It'll get challenged for not being done in legalese. It won't help that Conner wrote it up on a yellow ruled sheet of paper. But my guess is it will hold. I'll send it over to legal and the DA's office so they can get it to her attorney. He'll throw a tantrum but I think it will hold."

"Okay, let's assume it does," Zaworski says. "What does it mean?"

Blackshear, now on loan to the Second until this case is done, runs through the new scenario we might be looking at: fourteen-year-old Bradley Starks killed Ed Keltto.

"The kid is anti-social and has shown violent tendencies—he put his principal in the hospital."

"Assistant principal," I correct.

Everyone gives me a funny look. I guess it wasn't that big of a point.

"He's also been treated for depression." Blackshear continues. New information for me. "From everything we have seen he's neglected by his mom. Mom and dad divorced when he was two and his dad moved to Florida a couple years later. It was noted in the juvie file that there is no relationship between them. So yeah, he has a lot going for him as a suspect. He is a viable option."

A lot going for him? We get jaded in how we see and say things in this line of work.

"He's a peeper?" Zaworski asks.

"That's what Nancy said," I add.

"Does that show up on the profiles for young killers?" Konkade asks.

"I think it fits within anti-social behavior," Blackshear says. "We have a call in to our juvenile expert. I've got everything we got on the way over to her and we should get her evaluation back soon."

"The sooner the better," Zaworski snarls. "Put an expedite on it." He looks at Konkade, "Get involved if that will help. I don't want to leave an innocent kid in lockup. That has lawsuit written all over it. What's next?"

"We're working to get our next formal interview with Nancy Keltto today or tomorrow," Squires says.

"Don't count on it," Zaworski harrumphs. "Not after that chat she had with Conner. The attorney will be able to delay it a couple days. What about the kid?"

"We're working on that, too," Blackshear answers.

"The mom has said no," Konkade interjects. "We're going slow. Problem is the clock is ticking on the forty-eight hours we can hold him without any formal charges."

"What's the risk of cutting him loose until this is settled?" Zaworski asks.

Blackshear is quick to answer, "Big risk. If he's a depressed, angry, anti-social killer, he might decide to do something dramatic, like shoot up his school. Heck, he whacked the one guy in the world trying to help him."

"We don't know that," I jump in.

The conference room phone buzzes, interrupting us.

"That'll be the commissioner," Zaworski says. He hits the intercom button.

"Commissoner?"

"Yeah, this is Fergosi."

"This is Zaworski. I've got Conner, Squires, Blackshear, and Konkade in the room with me."

Police Commissioner Fergosi had called him on the way to work to say he wanted to talk to the team. He couldn't be here in person but wanted everyone on the conference line.

"Okay, let me connect Doyle and Nelson."

A couple of clicks and one false start later the two men acknowledge their presence. Paul Fergosi hits it fast.

"You all can appreciate what's at stake with this Russian gang war in New York and maybe here." He pauses. "Conner, you okay to be in the office?"

"Yes sir. Feeling great."

That is eighty to ninety percent true. I fight the urge to scratch at my bandaged side. The itch is suddenly driving me crazy.

"Good. Don't push it. We're going to get through this."

"Thank you, sir."

"I was on the phone with New York's police commissioner, Gerald Kranich, last night and this morning. Looks like the worst of what they've been dealing with is over. Hopefully. No shootings for two days. Between the thirty who are dead and the two hundred arrested—plus those unaccounted for—there might not be anyone left on the street to shoot at each other. But they are quite confident a lot of guys have slipped through the nets. Some are just hiding under a rock. But others, we believe, have swum their way to safer waters in Miami, Los Angeles, Las Vegas, and of course, Chicago. And other places. Doyle is working with the FBI and together they are pushing to hound Sadowsky's gang here in the city as hard as they can legally. The hit attempt on Conner has given us some latitude with the court to be aggressive. But that's never enough. Plus our new mayor keeps tugging on our leash to make sure we are protecting the rights of our upstanding criminals. If anyone repeats what I'm about to say, I'll fire you. I don't care what the mayor thinks. I need to know if there's more we can do to keep New York's problems there and not here.

"Nelson, you feel good about protecting Conner?"

"I'd feel better if she was on the sideline and under static protective care, sir. It's hard to move security fast enough to keep up with her."

Thanks, Frank.

"What is she working, Zaworski?"

I hold my breath waiting for what he has to say.

"She's eyeball deep in a murder that happened in her old neighborhood, Paulie. It happened down the street from Mikey Conner's place."

Paulie? Mikey?

"Is Gracie okay?" Fergosi asks.

I've never heard my mom called that. Fergosi knew my dad. It warms my heart that he remembers my mom's name. Of course he was at the funeral and handed her the flag.

"She's doing good, sir," I say.

"Give her my regards."

"I will."

"Doyle, you there?" Fergosi asks.

"Yes sir."

"What do you think?"

"I wanted to call you directly before this conference call. I've been on the phone with Frank. We had a new development overnight that we're just getting a handle on."

Spencer Doyle has gone a different route than his uncle and great uncle, but he's got the politician's sense of timing. It was assumed his brother, Doyle the Third is how the press refers to him, would be next, but he got himself in trouble on an insider trading bust—it's hard to get elected from a prison, even if it is of the country club minimum security variety. Spencer knows the power of a pause. I could learn from that. I too

410

often fill in the empty space that gets others to open up a little bit more.

"Doyle, you going to enlighten us?" Fergosi asks.

"The Third Precinct got a call from a motel manager about four in the morning. It's a little hole in the wall in Humboldt Park. A lot of the customers rent by the hour. A couple of them started complaining about a foul odor. That must be a regular occurrence there because the manager didn't check on things right away. He finally opened the door on a guy who's been staying there about a week and who had specifically asked not to be disturbed, not even by the cleaners. He got in the room and there was a body in a nasty state of decomposition. No ID, no nothing. The medical examiner got in there and found a bullet in the man's chest—he doesn't think that was cause of death by the way. There was enough skin left on him that he identified a tattoo. He thought it might be Russian lettering. He's seen enough going on in national media with New York that he thought we should see it in the organized crime division. So he sent a picture over.

"No question on the tattoo. It's Red Mafiya. One of our researchers thinks it is authentic to a Russian prison. We just got the slug sent to forensics. Conner, we've got someone on the way over to pick up your gun and ammo to test for a match. Body size and mass matches Nazar

Kublanov. He did prison time in Moscow at Butryka—and the tattoo matches what was being done there. Once we positively ID him with prints, the threat to Conner might be over."

"With all due respect," Nelson breaks in, "last time we heard that we let our guard down."

"I'm not saying to remove security from Conner," Doyle shoots back. "I'm just saying we might be out of the woods."

"Okay," Fergosi jumps in. "Nothing changes on Conner for the time being. What about Sadowsky? You talked to him yet?"

"No one seemed to know where he was the last few days," Doyle says. "Frankly, we began to wonder if he got taken out by whoever got Genken. But lo and behold, it seems that he decided it was time to visit his compound in Phoenix and get in a little golf. The weather was too cold here. That's what his secretary told us this morning."

"More like too hot," Fergosi says. "What can we do to talk to him?"

"Nothing," Doyle says, "but the FBI can. We notified Chicago and Phoenix offices right away. Phoenix is sending agents over as soon as they can get them briefed. Chicago might fly in a second wave. They might be on their way already."

"We'll get a full report?" Fergosi asks. "And soon?"

"They promised yes on both counts, but it

doesn't mean keeping us in the loop is at the top of their priority list."

"Same old same old. Are your relations with local FBI good these days, Spencer?" Fergosi asks.

"Not always, Commish. But we're all playing nice on this case. We have to. Everyone is desperate for information on the gang war so everyone is cooperating. Even the FBI."

"Good. Let's all stay on top of this and keep it from going anywhere."

I think we're done.

"Conner," Fergosi says before we can hang up.

"Yes sir?"

"How is your relationship with the FBI these days?"

Is he talking about Reynolds and me or the whole bureau? Oh man.

"Not much contact, sir."

"Glad you decided to stay with our happy family and not go Fed on us," he says. I'm surprised he knows about the offer. "Listen Conner, if you do hear anything from our friends in the FBI— anything big or small—make sure you pass word to Doyle right away."

"I doubt I'll hear anything but if I do, I'll get it to Doyle."

"Thanks, Kristen," Doyle interjects.

Now we're done.

"What about Conner?" Nelson blurts out quickly. "I think we need her out of circulation."

"I don't think that's necessary, sir," I respond. "Sounds like the Bear has been put down."

"What bear?" Fergosi asks.

"The Russian. Nazar. His nickname is Medved, the Bear. Plus, even if there is any more mistaken interest in me, it's harder to hit a moving target."

I look over at Don who is rolling his eyes. Maybe that wasn't the right way to put it.

After a pause Fergosi says, "Keep working for now Conner. But be careful. If Doyle finds out anything new that says your part in all this isn't over, we'll pull you in like Frank wants. Everyone communicate. Let's put this thing behind us. We got enough troubles with the local natives. You guys probably saw the stat sheet this morning. It's too cold to go outside and domestic violence reports are spiking through the roof. We don't need a Red Mafiya gang war in Chicago."

The first murder in recorded history was Cain killing his brother Abel. Nothing much has changed. Random murder gets the headlines, but most murder comes at the hands of someone the victim knew. We maim and murder the ones we love.

I think of Bradley. Did Ed Keltto getting involved and trying to help the kid put him at risk?

I'm no social scientist, though I took my share of classes in my criminal justice undergrad degree at Northern Illinois. I know enough to know that

414

when marriages fall apart the kids pay the price. Bradley's parents split up. His dad headed for Florida. His mom is too busy to keep an eye on him. He and everyone around him seem to be suffering the consequences.

Maybe Vanessa is right about a career change for Don. If it's good for the marriage it's good for Devon and Veronika.

I think of my family. Klarissa went her way for a while. I was in my first years with a badge and working insane hours. Dad got shot. We could have fallen apart but we didn't. I need to better appreciate what Mom—Gracie—and Kaylen did and do to hold us together. Of course Dad asked a lot from me, too.

❄ **74** ❄

"So when were you going to tell me Zheglov is at large, Robert?"

"For all we knew, he was already dead, Austin. It would be just like Boyarov to kill his best friend so he didn't have to betray him. In his warped sense of truth and justice he would see that as an honorable thing."

"You're getting off topic and not answering my question."

"Austin, you want the truth?"

"I do."

"I didn't want you to worry."

"I like to worry, Robert."

"That's a good thing, Austin. It means you care about my favorite detective. Time for you to move on and make a move, Austin. How long have you and Leslie been divorced?"

"I think since the first day of our honeymoon. And I always appreciate your advice into my personal life."

"You're like a son to me."

"Thank you, Dad. Since we're making this personal, I'm telling you again, you have to squash this Cutter appeal ploy. It's a bad idea. It's a joke."

"You may be right, Austin. It was probably a bad idea. But I wanted to get more out of our investment in him. You have a business degree. You understand we have to justify our budget expenditures on the basis of ROI these days. Return On Investment. That seems to be the first agenda item in every meeting now. We used to talk about putting away bad guys. I told Van Guten yes because we haven't got enough out of him to keep a high-priced independent contractor like her on it."

"Convenient for her to come up with an idea that keeps her in Chicago studying a world-renowned sociopath or psychopath or just plain freak while cashing our generous checks. No conflict of interest there."

"Of course there is, Austin. I understand the irony. But Leslie's right. We don't know enough about the mind of serial killers."

"Even if we did, they compartmentalize and isolate. Almost by definition, we'll never know they're coming until they do. It won't help us in prevention."

"But it might help interdiction and that might save a few lives."

"And kill a forest publishing Van Guten's reports in order to prove how smart we are."

"Now you're being cynical, Austin."

"Bob, the only reason we caught the Cutter Shark was we got a lead on one of his hunting grounds. We followed that up with good old fashioned investigative work."

"True."

"So you'll quash it?"

"I'm not sure you heard me before. I can't. It's an organic operation. It's already in play. I couldn't stop it if I wanted to. Conner is going to have to stand and deliver in front of a judge."

Reynolds blew out his breath to vent the anger welling up in him.

"She's a tough girl, Austin. She'll be fine. If you two make a go of it, it won't be because she needs you to protect her. She's got plenty of fight in her."

"Don't I know it," Reynolds said under his breath, standing to leave.

He had no clue where to head next. His phone buzzed. He saw the number and answered. Willingham already had his head buried in a report anyway.

"What you got?"

Reynolds stopped in the doorway as he listened. He stepped back into Willingham's makeshift office across the street from where Boyarov was being kept at New York's Metro Correctional Center in Brooklyn.

"Are you sure?" Reynolds asked.

Willingham looked up, curious. He knew Reynolds. Something big was happening.

"Okay, get the word to the office—this is a red alert," Reynolds said, ending the call.

He stood speechless in front of Willingham.

"What?"

"Nazar Kublanov is dead. Conner must have got him through the door with one of her rounds."

"Good. That's one problem out of the way."

"But we now have a bigger one. Zheglov definitely flew to Chicago. He used Teplov's name out of Dulles."

Vladimir Zheglov took another pass through the neighborhood. Too many cars on the street. Too many stop signs. Not a good place for a shoot and run. Not a good place to watch either. But watching wasn't necessary. Once she and her

418

police escort turned south on Ashland or Western this is where she always was headed. Her mom's house.

One patrol car. An agent inside. Her mom. Her. Five people. Four of them with guns. Probably only one with a significant level of combat training—the FBI agent. But none with his level and none with his tactical training for situations like this. When the moment came, that's what he'd be dealing with. Solving the math wasn't easy but it wasn't overwhelming. He had fought through worse. Much worse. He had planned, organized, and led the assault on Genken after all.

Instructions were clear to limit collateral damage. Four others weren't that many. That should fall within the range of his instructions.

❄ **75** ❄

"What's up Barnes?"

"I'm glad you've kept me in your phone directory, Kristen. Call me Tommy."

If I don't call him Tommy he will make me play twenty questions to find out what he's calling for.

"To what do I owe the pleasure of this call, Tommy?"

He doesn't answer as quick as usual. I think he's disappointed that I'm not fighting.

"You have a sec?"

419

"I do. But just a sec. We're a few minutes from interviewing a murder suspect."

"Got a call from a little birdy today. A couple names came up that might matter to you."

He's stopped so I guess I'm supposed to express how impressed and excited I am.

"Tommy, you definitely have the contacts. I'm impressed. So what have you got?"

"First is Nazar Kublanov."

"I just heard the Bear is dead."

Not smart showing him up. Now I'll have to work for the second name.

"News travels fast."

He's going to pout.

"But I'll bet you saved the best for last didn't you, Tommy?"

Good question.

"As a matter of fact, I did," he says. "Vladimir Zheglov. Know him?"

"I don't think so," I answer. "The Russian names have me confused. Nothing new there. I never had anything to do with the Nelson murder and the Russian mafiya anyway so I've let some of this blow past me. Who is he?"

"Zheglov is Pasha Boyarov's right-hand man. He's got a bad combination to him."

"What's that?"

"He's smart and he's dangerous."

"What does that have to do with me?"

"Hopefully nothing. But it has been confirmed

he flew to Chicago and no one knows exactly why. With Genken dead, the head has been cut off the beast, but the beast is still alive and out of control. So who knows, it might be you he's after. He might be laying low. He might be there to shoot the Chicago Pakhan, Anasenko Sadowsky. But I got a bad feeling it might be you. I don't think they every really bought in that you showed up at the Nelson crime scene by accident. I sometimes wonder that myself. I know you aren't going to admit if you were doing something for the FBI so I won't ask. Just know, you need to keep your eyes open."

"I've still got a protective detail."

"Tell them you want more. I'm being serious on this guy. He's the real deal. He's a nasty piece of work."

"I appreciate that, Tommy. I really do. I've got to go into the interrogation room so I gotta cut loose."

"Give me a call if you have any questions."

"I will. And let me know if you hear anything else. And Tommy?"

"Yeah?"

"Thanks again. I appreciate it."

Dang. I forgot to ask him if there is a prayer in the world that the NYPD will replace my cold weather running gear.

I'm behind the glass today. Squires and Blackshear are the grinders. First up is Leslie

Levin. Nancy Keltto is on deck. She's out of the hospital and for some reason her lawyer insisted she come down for questioning immediately, with him present of course. No word on when we can talk to Bradley.

My stomach is roiling. If I send a note to Doyle and Zaworski on the call from Barnes, they'll pull me from the Keltto case. We're so close. I want to be part of it, no matter what the outcome.

Fergosi did order me to pass on anything I heard from the FBI. Barnes isn't FBI. Now I'm nitpicking on the letter of the law. I'll send an email when the interviews are done. Crud.

I look at my watch. Just a little after one. I should get out of here on time for once. I'll head to my mom's house for dinner.

Reynolds looked at the picture closely, studying the eyes, lips, ears, and jawline. Vladimir Zheglov. He needed to memorize every detail—it was too easy to change appearances with simple cosmetic fixes like a new hair color or a pair of glasses.

"Would you like anything else, sir?" the flight attendant asked him.

"Anyway the inflight internet is back up?"

"I'm sorry, sir. It looks like it is down for the duration of the flight."

Reynolds gave himself another punch inside. I should have called Conner before I took off. The

Chicago FBI office will undoubtedly connect with the CPD and give her and everyone else minding her a heads up.

Stop worrying. Nothing is going to happen in the next few hours.

But he was worried. Zheglov was in Chicago.

What a lousy time for the inflight internet service to be out. I can't send Kristen a message and I can't get an update from the office.

I'm sure the information has worked its way into the system.

"You guys have ruined my life with this. My wife knows . . . my boss knows . . . even my kids know after hearing their mom scream at me all night."

I feel bad for the wife and kids. I don't feel bad for Leslie.

"I should never have been included in this investigation. I told you I was on the West Coast on a business trip. If you had just asked me I could have given you my receipts from the trip. I think I have pictures of a group of us on the golf course."

"Doesn't mean you weren't there when the murder happened," Don says.

"No way could I have been there and at O'Hare at the same time."

"That's true," Don deadpans. "But your car was there. Interesting you didn't feel the need to tell us."

"Says who?" Leslie demands.

"Doesn't matter," Blackshear says. "We know your car was in the neighborhood the morning of the murder."

"You got proof or are you listening to a juvenile delinquent and peeping tom?"

"No one said who told us," Don says.

"Yeah, but we all know, so you can stop playing games with me," Levin says. "Why would you even listen to a kid like that? I went straight from my house to the airport."

"That's your story?" Don asks.

"Yeah," he sputters. "That's my story because it's true. No judge or jury is going to believe a teenage criminal over a guy with no record. So why don't you focus on the kid so I can get back to rebuilding my life? I shouldn't be in here."

His righteous indignation is breathtaking—and hollow. He has no right to point fingers at anyone.

"I told you I'd make myself available whenever you needed. That was to shield my family. Well it's obviously too late for that. But I thought I'd try one more time to clear this up directly, man-to-man. But I'm still in jail because you're obviously not listening, even after Nancy and I gave you everything you need to know on the kid."

"You signed an agreement with me that you wouldn't talk to Nancy," Blackshear says.

"Are you kidding me? She tried to kill herself. I wasn't supposed to help her?"

"You could have called 911," Don says.

"You guys won't give it up, will you? This interview is finished. Next time you want to talk to me, work through my lawyer."

It's a good thing I'm not in there with Blackshear and Squires for the interview. I would love to set Mr. Levin straight on who has ruined his life.

I check email between interviews. Got a note from Tom Gray in Internal Affairs. Investigating other cops for criminal activity is not all IA does—but most of it. Their investigators are rarely popular outside IA. But the joke is they don't have depart-mental friends either—they're too busy spying on each other. Gray knows how defensive I can get and makes sure I know I'm not being investigated first thing in the email. He is letting me know he has been assigned my case for the Cutter appeal. He will work with me and legal counsel to prepare for questioning.

Thanks, Tom, I text him.

I feel sick to my stomach again.

Nothing from Reynolds. It's been three days since he had something he just had to say to me. Maybe we're too much alike to ever go anywhere in our relationship. Both of us get consumed with the job.

I think about the kiss in the hospital again. Best ever. But is now the time to think about that? That starts me thinking about it even more. I force my mind elsewhere.

I need to call Klarissa tonight. I can do that from Mom's house. She had to fly back to be on-air the next morning. I know she feels hurt that I suspected her of fooling around with my sort-of boyfriend. But if the roles were reversed and she had seen what I did, she would have thought the same thing.

I replay the scene in my mind. It's getting fuzzy. I sure seem to remember the two of them being a lot cozier than necessary to talk about me behind my back. My mind is playing tricks on me again.

Who told Levin about Bradley?

❄ 76 ❄

"You have been most helpful."

"It's my pleasure. What else can I show you?"

"Nothing right now. This one caught my attention. Now I need to think about it for a day or two."

"Why don't we sit down for a cup of coffee and let me work through numbers with you. I have an idea they may accept a little less than they're asking."

"That would be good but I need a little more time to think about if I'm really ready to buy a house."

"Of course there's not as many offerings on the market in January, so they won't come down a lot. But I'm just saying."

Zehglov was getting impatient but trying hard not to show it. He saw a for sale sign on a house a couple blocks from where Conner's mom lived. They all looked the same to him, but he drove by Conner's old neighborhood one more time and confirmed that the two row houses had the same number of doors on the front and sides, the same number of windows, and were pretty close on size.

He called the number on the sign to have the realtor show him the house. He studied doors, windows, stairs, and halls. He was surprised that there was a basement too. He asked about the out-side entrance, which was a steep flight of concrete steps with a rail on the left and a retaining wall on the right. The stairs dead-ended into a small square slab of concrete that provided just enough room for the basement door to swing open.

He asked about the history of the neighborhood and got the feeling most of the floor plans were pretty similar. Still, there was no way to know with absolute certainty what he'd walked through was the same as Conner's house. He also couldn't remember if Conner's mom had a basement but he didn't intend to drive by for a fourth time. He should have kept the Malibu. Less conspicuous in a working class neighborhood than the Mercedes.

"You've got my number, I've got your number," Zheglov said. "I'll call you back on Saturday when I'm done with a project. No need to call me because I'll be too busy to pick up."

She smiled and nodded and gushed about the solid oak flooring and marble countertop in the refurbished kitchen one more time. If she had kept going I would have to kill her for being obnoxious, he thought to himself. Need to get back to Conner's workplace. Let's see where she's going tonight.

When he got in the car he called the *shestyorka* who answered on the first ring.

"I need men and guns."

"That I can help you with."

❄ **77** ❄

"I just want to be clear on this point. I'm not saying Bradley Starks did it. I always liked him. I thought he was a sweet boy until I caught him . . . uh . . . looking at me."

"You don't have to defend Bradley Starks," her lawyer says, interrupting and putting a comforting hand on her arm.

Gag me.

We get to talk to Starks tomorrow morning. We no longer have to worry about the twenty-four-hour rule for holding someone who hasn't been charged in a crime. Apparently he's been busy over at the juvenile wing of the Cook County Jail.

He's started a couple fights and about set off a riot in the cafeteria. He may have a number of assault and battery charges to face before he gets home. That will be least of his worries next to murder.

"Tell us again how much time your deceased husband and the boy spent together?" Blackshear asks.

"Eddy used to be his scout leader. But really not much in the last two years. Things change when kids become teenagers. Eddy teaches fifth grade and is very good with children. I'm not sure he relates well to teens. And vice-versa."

"The two didn't spend time together even though Mr. Keltto was his court-appointed mentor?"

"Not really. I'm sure Ed tried . . ."

She pauses and lowers her head. She begins to cry.

"We may be done here," her lawyer says.

"No, that's alright, I can keep going," she says through sniffles and tears.

"This is what I didn't want to say. But about a month ago Ed said something that I didn't think about at the time."

She stops to gather her thoughts, taking deep breaths. Blackshear waits. Don is in there with arms folded. He hasn't said a thing the entire time. I did see him smooth his suit jacket lapels and check for dandruff on his shoulders.

"Ed said that Bradley wasn't cooperating and

had missed almost every weekly meeting they were supposed to have. He said he should contact the caseworker but didn't want to do anything to send the kid to prison. Then he told me about Bradley pushing him . . . and threatening him."

She told me Bradley lost his temper and pushed Ed. She didn't say anything about him threatening her husband.

"And you didn't think to tell us what your husband had said after he was killed?" Blackshear asks.

She begins to cry again. "Ed had so many projects he's working on . . . so many people he helped. It all blurred at times. He told me a lot of things. It just didn't click in my mind at the time. I'm sorry; I know I should have thought about what Bradley did after Edward was killed . . . but I was so confused. I'm sorry. I'm sorry."

"You don't have to apologize," her attorney says gently.

Gag me again.

"Was Leslie Levin at your home the morning your husband was killed?" Don asks.

She looks up quickly, surprised and puzzled.

"You don't have to answer," her attorney repeats.

"No," she says emphatically. "Of course not. Where would you get that idea? He was on his way to California."

"Before going to the airport," Don says.

"No."

"You sure?" Blackshear asks.

"I think I would know if he was at the house," she says firmly. "Of course not. Ed was home. Why would he be at the house?"

There is a long, pregnant silence as everyone mulls the answer to that. I stare at her closely. I see doubt in her eyes. She lowers her head and begins to sob again. Why do I get the feeling she is trying to buy time so she can recover from a broadside with this round of tears? Is it because I'm a detective?

"This interview is done," the lawyer says, standing.

Blackshear and Squires don't look too bothered by that. In fact, they look pretty pleased with themselves.

Nice work, guys.

"What do we do?" Blackshear asks.

The three of us are sitting at a table reviewing the two interviews.

"Nothing until we talk to the kid," Don says.

"Her attorney wants her re-released on original bond," Blackshear says.

"Last time we let her go home she tried to off herself," Don says.

"She looked like she's feeling better to me," I say. "Until you brought up Leslie's car being there the morning of the murder. I wouldn't cut her loose."

They both look at me.

"So you deliver Bradley to us as a suspect and now you think she did it?" Blackshear asks.

"I'm not saying anything," I answer. "But after seeing her and Leslie in action, I don't trust either of them—even if the kid did it."

"What you want to do, Bob?" Don asks.

"Captain is gone for the day," he says. "I may wait until morning. Nothing is going to happen tonight anyway."

"What's the status on her house?" I ask.

"Now I know why you don't want her cut loose," Blackshear says with a toothy grin I've never seen. "You getting one of your vibes, Kristen?"

"What are you two talking about?" Don asks.

Bob tells him about our walk through the Keltto's house and garage in the dark. He's making it sound like our tour of the crime scene was a Halloween ghost walk. Thanks, Bob.

"What do you need, Conner?" he asks.

"I don't know. I'm having supper at my mom's house tonight. I figured I might take one more walk through."

"Was it something Nancy said?" Don asks.

"No . . . maybe . . . I just know something's bothering me."

"Something's bothering me, too," Blackshear says. "Actually a couple things. I was convinced Nancy Keltto did the deed and that Leslie Levin was involved. Now I'm almost positive I was wrong. I'm convinced it was the kid."

"What do think, Don?" I ask.

"Unfortunately, I think it was the kid after hearing about his reign of terror at Cook County. You?"

"Probably I lean toward Bradley but not by much. It doesn't feel right."

"Nothing feels right on murder most of the time," Don says with a shrug.

"Squires, tell me the rumor I heard isn't true," Blackshear says.

"Can't believe everything you hear," Don says, popping out of his seat. "I'm out of here guys. I'm coaching Devon's practice tonight."

Good for him. Coaching. Moving on to another stage of life. But I'm going to miss him and his threads.

"Can you clear a walkthrough for me, Bob?"

"Yeah. Make sure you log it in the morning."

This job can be sobering. I don't go out and drink to get my mind off the situations and people we deal with. My escape is to work out. I think I'll hit the health club on the way to Mom's. I can't lift anything or move my upper body but at least I can do a spin class or something.

I head back for my cubicle and check emails and phone messages for five minutes. Two missed calls from Reynolds. No message. But there is also a text from him: *Call ASAP! This is important.*

I hit his number. It goes straight to voice mail. He's in the air or turned off his phone. Whatever has his hair on fire will keep.

I input my report on Tommy Barnes' call, then add Doyle, Zaworski, Nelson, Blackshear, and Squires in the TO: box. I blind copy myself so I can add it to case file. At the last minute I blind copy Reynolds so he knows what's up. I hate to hit send. I know this is going to boot me off the Keltto case. I don't want to be left out of the action. Nothing to be done about it. At least I'll get my final walkthrough of the murder site. I hit the envelope icon.

I look at my watch. Twenty till five. I can leave early. Then it hits me. I haven't picked up a replacement handgun. I have to get down to the weapons locker clerk on the second floor or I've got nothing. Okay, I know I'm being dramatic, but there might be someone who wants to kill me out there. Not just the usual suspects who aren't really being literal with the word murder.

"What's up tonight?" Heather Torgerson asks. "You are stuck with me."

"The health club, Mom's for dinner, and then home. That's an exciting night for me. Want to drive with me and work out?"

"To think, I was going to see if you wanted to go clubbing down on Rush Street—knowing full well we wouldn't get approved for it, but hoping anyway."

"I guarantee I would cramp your style even in spots where the music is too loud to talk. But you're welcome to join me."

"I think I will."

"Meet me downstairs at the door to the parking lot," I say. "I gotta pick something up on my way down."

"Great car," she says as I turn the wheel and head the GTR north.

"You know it's my sister's."

"You told me about ten times. Don't worry; I won't think you're a crooked cop who can afford a car that costs more than a hundred grand. Is it yours to use all the time?"

"I guess. I hadn't planned on it though. I figured I'd drive it once a week to keep the oil good. I'm driving it all the time lately because I haven't had a spare two hours to pick up my car from the garage. I think I better do that Saturday or they start charging me a storage fee."

"What do you drive?"

"You don't want to know."

I miss my little Miata convertible, no matter how unkind it has been to me through the years. But I'm going to miss the GTR more I'm afraid.

435

❄ **78** ❄

At first Vladimir Zheglov thought she was heading home. Then he realized she was stopping at the health club, which was one of the eight regular spots on his list of where best to find her. It was on the east side of Western Avenue, the road she would take south if going to her mom's or north if she was going to her condo.

Zheglov wanted this done with. It wasn't a priority in his mind but if she was FBI and had cost them millions of dollars, she had to pay the price. As a lesson—and as part of his path back into the *bratva*.

Gleb Luytov. Could he trust him on the offer to try his wife's homemade coulibiac in his home? Or would he have him killed? He couldn't drive a truck but he was very good at killing people. What choice did he have?

I let Torgerson out at the door. No point both of us freezing to death before working out. I park and check my phone. I got a missed call from Mom. I call her to let her know I'll be home for dinner.

"I can't believe it, my daughter has called back," she says as greeting.

"Very funny, Mom. Just letting you know I've stopped at the club for a workout."

"Did the doctor say you can do that?"

"Just riding the bike is okay."

"Did the doctor say that or did you say that?"

"Mom, if your offer to feed me is still there, I'll be home in ninety minutes tops. Six-thirty, maybe six-forty-five."

"That's perfect. Jimmy and Kaylen are coming over and bringing the kids. We'll have a real family meal."

"I've got Heather with me, the FBI agent. Sure you have enough food?"

"Plenty. I shopped the other day after I left the hospital with you. Bring her. I'll make something for the boys in the car, too. I was going to make something to take to Kaylen's for Sunday dinner. We'll have it tonight."

I've got to hand it to her and her generation. They can have an army show up an hour before dinner and feed everyone with leftovers. I don't usually have enough stuff that is still edible in my refrigerator to feed myself at any given moment.

She is going to kill us. We're climbing hills and sprinting on the flats like a team in the Tour de France. Sweat is pouring off me and I'm panting like a chain-smoker on a walk to the mailbox—at the end of a five-mile driveway.

My side is on fire. I feel the throbbing pain of the bruising to my flesh and the needle pricks where the wound is itching. Should have done one

437

of the recumbent bikes and stayed away from an advanced spin class.

I want to quit but I hate quitting. I look at my phone and see it is ringing. Reynolds. I have the excuse I need. I hit the answer button but can't quite answer because of my ragged breathing and the exertion of slowing the spin bike down and dismounting.

"Kristen, you there? You okay?" I hear as I press the phone to my ear. He sounds worried. That's sweet.

"I'm here, give me a second," I puff out through gasps for air.

"What's going on Kristen? You okay? You there?"

"Just finishing a spin class."

"There are a few things I want to say about you doing a spin class the day after you leave the hospital, but you are hard to reach and I'm going to hold comment until later."

"And you know it won't do much good anyway."

"That too. But time to get down to business. There are new developments happening right now that you and the CPD and the Chicago FBI need to be aware of."

"Zheglov?"

"How'd you know?"

"I have my sources."

"So your team has already amped up guard

duty and everybody in law enforcement in a three-state area has his picture?

"Not exactly."

"Kristen, this is not a guy to take lightly. He's just old enough to have been sent to fight the Chechens. He's a trained killer and a survivor."

"I just sent a note to our organized crime guy about an hour ago. Spencer Doyle. He's in tight with local FBI. The wheels should be turning."

"Okay, good. I'll check in with the local office. Willingham is on it too. I'll head to wherever you are."

"You going to be my bodyguard?"

"Actually I am, whether you like it or not. I hope you're taking this seriously, Kristen."

Lighten up. I was just joking.

"You on your way home next?" he asks.

"No, I'm going to Mom's for dinner. An army is converging there, including Kaylen and her family. So you're welcome to join us."

"I'll be there in less than an hour if I can get through traffic."

"That's about the same time as me. I'm done working out but I have to get a shower and blow-dry my hair."

"Eyes open, Conner."

Eyes open, Conner. He is a romantic dog.

❄ **79** ❄

"When are you hitting her?"

The *shestyorka* called Zheglov on the throw-away phone.

"As soon as tonight."

"When you called for reinforcements, I didn't know we were this pressed for time."

"An opportunity has presented itself. Can you get me the men or not?"

"Yes. It is done. They are gathering now. But I'm not sure they are ready to go out tonight."

"Then they are the wrong men."

"Not these guys. They're good. The best. I just thought you would want more preparation time."

"Not for what I have planned. It's not complex. Better to move fast. Plus I will know that no one is talking in his sleep."

"Just so you know, Sadowsky knows. He wants to talk to you."

"I don't want to talk to him. I already made that clear."

"Okay. I understand. I was just thinking he might have some ideas that would help."

Zheglov had served in the army in the mountains of Chechnya. Some officers wanted to tell you exactly how to do things. They usually ended up dead by a suspicious gunshot wound, which would be attributed to the guerillas but that everyone knew was delivered by one of the guy's own men. The smart officers let the soldiers in the field do what worked.

"Are you there, Vladimir?"

"No names."

"Right. I apologize."

The death of the American *bratva* wouldn't come at the hands of the FBI and local police. With the guys we're using, we'll do it ourselves. Why are these young guys coming to work for us anyway? They've got college degrees and can get good office jobs. They need to go work in big companies. Ruchkin was bad. Teplov wasn't much better. Now this contact in Chicago who makes sure I get what I need from Luytov and Sadowsky is going to drive me crazy.

"Where are they?"

"I'm going to text you a phone number but there is something you must hear first."

Vlad sighed. "Tell me."

"The plan has changed. You're not to kill her."

"Good. I'll go home."

"No. The new plan is to capture her."

Vladimir mulled this. He started to ask a question but then realized he already knew the answer. It might not work but it was gutsy. Maybe brilliant.

Even trade. Take Conner as a prisoner and then offer her straight up in an exchange for Boyarov.

He smiled. Maybe Luytov knew what he was doing.

"You say they are ready?"

"No—you said that. I said they have been called together. Five of them. They will come to wherever you say, the second you call the number."

"Send two home. I just need three."

"Are you sure?"

Vlad seethed at being questioned.

"I apologize," the man answered.

"What part of the city are they in?" Vlad asked.

"They're at a hotel just west of the Loop."

"Can they shut their mouths, take orders and move fast?"

"They're the best we have. Three of the five are ex-military."

"Chechnya?"

"Two of them. One goes all the way back to Afghanistan. He's older but he might be the best."

"Keep the three military members. Send the two others home. Give me the number."

❄ 80 ❄

Reynolds hit the touchscreen on the dashboard to exit the call with Robert Willingham, Spencer Doyle, and the Chicago FBI station director, Beverly Mundee, who was new on the job. She was promoted to Chicago from New York City and moved to the Windy City the weekend before the missiles started flying in the City. Two ways to look at that. Her timing couldn't have been better—or she was missing the action.

Reynolds continued an inner dialog. He had told himself that if Willingham wouldn't pull the plug on the plan that Van Guten had hatched to get the Cutter Shark talking, he would quit. The fact that Willingham couldn't pull the plug—if he could be believed—changed the construct, forcing him to look at it from at least two angles. If he just quit, it would let Willingham know the depths of his displeasure that he would allow a profiler to concoct a tactical operation. There were plenty more where he came from, so he doubted Willingham would miss a beat. On the other hand, he could stick around if the hearing didn't go the way Willingham and Van Guten assumed it would and help deal with the aftermath.

Reynolds had looked into the appeal and the judge was definitely anti-law enforcement. He'd gone on record in a national interview that he believed America had become a Nazi police state.

He looked at his watch. He should be at Mrs. Conner's house in about fifteen minutes. It would be good to see everyone and, who knows, he might get to see Kristen alone for five minutes to lay it all out there for her. He didn't want to give her a take it or leave it proposition, but what he had to say would definitely force some response from the elusive Detective Conner.

Suddenly Reynolds was struck with a thought. His face froze. What the heck am I thinking? Zheglov is here. We can't have those kids in the same house as Kristen.

He hit speed dial. It went straight into Kristen's voice mail.

He looked at recent calls while accelerating on black, cold, sometimes icy, city streets. Mundee hosted the conference call. He hit her number, hoping she would pick up. She did.

"This is Reynolds. I don't know if we have a situation. But we might need to move quicker to surround Conner than what we discussed."

❄ 81 ❄

My phone died and I still haven't put a battery charger in Klarrisa's car. I hadn't planned on driving it more than the first day or two. Klarissa's going on-air in a few minutes anyway and couldn't have picked up so we could set up a time to talk tonight or tomorrow. I need to start watching her on TV more. It hurts her feelings when she can tell I haven't watched her.

"You're getting to be a regular member of the family, Heather."

"Your mom's very nice, Kristen. If I hadn't

worked out with you a couple times I would have said there was no way you could stay thin with the way she feeds you."

"Food has always been one of her favorite ways to solve family problems. Usually works."

"Food is an opiate for a lot of us," Torgerson says with a laugh.

"You haven't met my sister and her husband and the kids. You are in for a treat. When James, the six-year-old, is around, keep your eyes open or you might lose one of them."

"And I get to meet the legendary Austin Reynolds in the flesh."

"He says he'll be there."

"He looks pretty good in high definition too—but I promise I'm not trying to steal your beau," she says with a wink.

"I have no claim on him."

"So he's a free agent?"

She's playing but I need to give that question some thought.

"Ask me next week," I say.

"You know what he's called by the SWAT members?"

"I'm afraid to ask."

"Since he's Willingham's right-hand-man they call him The Hammer of Bob."

"Seriously?"

"He's been called a lot of things, including hunk—not by me, of course—but yeah. Everyone knows he's Willingham's shock and awe enforcer."

Hmm.

"I think he's very smart, too," I say, "but that's coming from my level. I may not have as high a standard."

"You're funny, Kristen. You love to play that you are clueless what's going on and everyone is smarter. You're plenty smart and everyone knows Reynolds is too. He just has a different background than most with his time in Delta Force. He's been on the sharp edge of the sword."

The Hammer of Bob. How well do I know Reynolds?

I'm not sure if I should tell her that I'm not always playing that I'm clueless. Sometimes I just am.

He could feel it. Tonight would be the night. Almost didn't seem fair, Vlad thought. This would be a quick and easy grab. The *shestyorka* said that Sadowsky had five men available. He just wanted three. Any more and they would be shooting each other.

He had them meet him at a grocery store parking lot across from the health club where Conner was working out. He quickly brought them up to speed on the operation. He gave each man an assignment and asked if there were any questions. There weren't. Good. He liked the team already.

If the detective headed to her mom's house

from the health club the smash and grab would happen tonight. It was a fast but solid plan. Only five people to deal with. One, the mother, would not be able to fight. Only four to take down and his team had the element of surprise. It was almost failproof.

One of the men would position himself where he couldn't be seen between the house and wherever the cop car parked. He had one job only. Shoot anyone that got out of the car. Both officers would undoubtedly get out and come running with what Zheglov had planned. They would be easy targets.

He thought about having his outside man just shoot the two cops through the window, but every now and then, auto glass would cause crazy trajectories with bullets. He didn't want one of the cops to get missed and have time to shoot back. He wanted them out of the car and running toward the front door so his man could pick them off nice and easy. No prolonged battle.

Zheglov's second man would head down the outside steps to the basement door. On cue— namely a brick through the front window—he was to wedge the door open with a crow bar and hustle up the steps, ready to fire. The third man would shoot in the front door immediately after throwing the brick through the window and shoot anyone in the front room except Conner. He could wound her with a non-fatal shot if necessary. She should be weak from the Bear shooting her anyway.

Vlad would be coming inside through the back door at the same time. The window being smashed was his cue. He expected everyone—Conner, the agent, and the mother—to have their eyes up front. With the third man coming up through the basement, no way could they handle all the angles of defense. The FBI agent was primary target. She would be armed and might know how to use her gun. Whoever got to her first was to shoot her dead. No need to kill the mom unless necessary. Whoever was closest would head for her and put a gun to her head. That should be all the inducement the detective needed to put down her weapon.

The order of events was designed to create disorientation. What is happening and where is it coming from? No matter how good your vision and nerve, you couldn't cover every angle. Vladimir figured it would be over within seconds. Securing the mom was key. It would keep them from having to hurt the detective. Not immediately anyway. If the Feds didn't give them Boyarov, they would hurt her real bad.

Pasha had probably already spilled his guts. Significant damage to the *bratva* was undoubtedly done. But with him gone as a live witness, the repercussions would at least be limited.

Vlad parked the Mercedes in the Planet Fitness parking lot. If tonight was the night, he wouldn't need it again. The *shestyorka* could pick his car up later tonight. There was nothing suspicious about it. To be ready to make the hit and escape, he moved all his stuff to the back of the Escalade. It was a lot nicer than the other cars in the mom's neighborhood, which made it too noticeable. But it was the right size for what they had to do and this was going to happen soon and quick.

He kept his eye on the door. Conner exited alone. Maybe he should have made this the place. They could take her right now. But the parking lot was lit up bright, which would have made it harder to hit the cops in the idling car across the street.

She started her sports car and pulled up front. The FBI agent got in. Two pretty girls he thought as he saw their faces illuminated for just a second by the interior light.

Which direction?

She turned south on Western. Tonight it was.

The driver put his hand on the gearshift.

"No hurry," Vladimir said. "We know where she's going. Let the police car go on ahead and set up. We'll just take it nice and slow and park a block over as planned."

❄ **82** ❄

"This is Squires."

"Don, you heard from Conner?" Zaworski asked.

"Not since we interviewed Keltto and Levin,"

he answered. "Hold on," he said into the phone and then covered the mouthpiece and yelled, "Okay boys, get a quick drink of water. Two minutes."

He looked over at the stands where parents were chatting. Vanessa was giving him the stare.

Why'd you pick it up, you idiot?

"Yeah boss, what's up?"

"You sound busy."

"Coaching my son's basketball team. We're halfway through practice."

"Get back to it."

"Something happening with Conner?"

"Some Russian guy involved in that mess she got into in Central Park has been confirmed in Chicago. We're dealing with it. Problem is no one can reach her. She's either turned off her phone or let the battery die."

"Dead battery, if I know her," Squires said. "Need me to drive by to check on her after practice?"

"Nah. We're sending a squad car over to her place right now."

"She said she's eating at her mom's house. Have them check with Nelson's security detail. They might be heading to the wrong place."

"Stupid of me. I should have done that first. I'm not sure how much longer I can do this, Squires. They say retiring is dangerous for your health and it's good to keep working. After being through cancer I think not working might be better for my health. Especially since Conner got back in town."

"She stirs the pot, no doubt about that, Captain."

"I'm going to get back to finding KC. Someone needs to buy her a portable battery charger. But before I get off . . . let me plant a thought in your mind. Don't answer now, just think about it. If I re-retired and you were named captain, would you consider pulling your resignation letter? Just think about it."

"I will."

"The squad car is going to have a tough time finding a parking spot," I say to Heather as I back into a small opening a couple doors away from Mom's.

"It's a full house tonight," she says. "Ready to make a run for it? I think it's getting colder again. I about froze walking ten feet from the front door of Planet Fitness."

"Listen Heather, go on in. Just open the door. Looks like Kaylen and the family are already here. They got the last spot on the driveway. I need a sec."

"To call Austin?" she asks, a twinkle in her eye.

"Nah. My phone is dead. I need to look at something across the street. It'll just take a minute or two."

"Not sure I can leave you out here on your own."

"I somehow suspect I'll be safe for five minutes. Just go in." I give her a light punch to the shoulder.

"Okay. Don't be long."

Bradley Starks stared at the ceiling in the infirmary. The bed was bolted to the floor and he was cuffed to the bed. The cut beneath his eye was stitched up. It didn't hurt and he was glad to be away from the other adolescent inmates.

His mom stopped by and yelled at him for fighting. She wanted to know why he was starting fights. He couldn't give her the real answer. He'd been in trouble and around guys like this before. You either threw the first punch or you got hit by the first punch. Better to come out swinging.

I thought life was going to be different. Mr. Ed was helping me learn woodworking. He was helping me think about ways to make money even while I was in high school. He was helping me think about college or technical school. He was a good guy. He was weird but good.

Why wouldn't he listen to me when I told him that his lousy wife was cheating on him with that loser? He just looked sad and wouldn't say anything. I guess he already knew.

I can't believe I tell the police about her boyfriend's car on our street the morning of the murder and they end up arresting me. I guess they were going to find out about my troubles at some point. I wonder if Nancy told them.

If I'd kept my stupid mouth shut, Nancy would be the only suspect, not me. But then the creep would have gotten off.

Police come by to talk tomorrow. I hope the lady detective who used to live down the street is there. She might be the only one who will listen to me.

Man, this sucks. One minute I think my life is getting better. I'm measuring and sawing and sanding and nailing some cool stuff. I was going to make Mom a jewelry chest for mother's day—even if she doesn't have much jewelry.

Then the next second I'm sitting in jail. It would have been better if Mr. Ed never tried to help me.

❄ **83** ❄

"You sure it's only five we're dealing with Vlad?"

"You know as well as I do you never know what you're dealing with until you get there. Be ready for anything."

The number of real players hadn't changed. But with kids there, things had gotten messier. There would be collateral damage. No one liked that. But sometimes it couldn't be helped.

I need to get phone numbers for everyone in Kristen's family, Reynolds thought. It's impossible to reach her at times. Looks like everyone is here, including Kristen. So she's still driving Klarissa's wheels. She swore she couldn't wait to get back in the Miata. We'll see if she still feels that way once she gets it back. With her, who knows? She might. She thinks pizza and hot dogs are fine dining.

I'm probably worrying about nothing. At least tonight. I still don't like this set up. If someone is coming after Kristen we don't need innocent bystanders around. We need clean sight lines.

It would be good to have the second squad car here, though that probably doesn't matter with Zheglov if he has any help. And maybe he's not here for Conner. Maybe he's just in town to lay low.

Reynolds blew steam into the air, shut the car door, and walked briskly but warily toward Mrs. Conner's house. He drew even with the squad car and rapped on the window. The window came down on the driver's side as the passenger door opened with an officer holding his gun in the ready position.

"I'm FBI" Reynolds said. "My badge in my top left pocket. I can take it out or you can take it out. I was just checking to see if you all received word that there is a credible threat to Detective Conner. Looks like you have."

"Pull your badge out slowly."

Reynolds pulled off his gloves, kept one hand up, reached inside his winter coat, pulled the badge out deliberately, and handed it over, careful to keep his hands in sight. His fingers were turning to ice quickly.

"I've been invited to dinner at the Conner home. What would you have done if I had just gone to the front door."

The officer from the passenger seat handed him his badge back.

"That's the problem. We've been told as of ten minutes ago that this detail is now on high alert and that backup is en route. But we have no clear-cut directions on who can come and go. And there's a full house in there. We've been promised new protocols in the next few minutes. Doesn't help us now, even though it looks too quiet for anything to be coming down tonight."

This is what Reynolds was afraid of. No one protecting Kristen knew what they were doing. Conner needed to be yanked out of her happy home now. Zheglov, for one, would know what he was doing.

I hate to break up the party but I think I need to get everyone out of here. Kristen will argue but that's a given. I outrank her.

He walked back to the short walk that split Mrs. Conner's postage-sized front yard.

In the bitterly cold winter air he was sure he heard a tiny but distinct crackle of static. And a whisper. He felt a tingle from the base of his spine rise to the back of his head.

He's here.

If my lawyer's right, the kid is in big trouble. Things might work out after all.

What do I do about Nancy?

Does she not understand how much I really love her? I killed for her. If I didn't, she was never going to leave Ed, no matter how much she complained about her marriage.

She doesn't know I did it but she has to suspect me now.

Who knows? Maybe she'll finally realize this was never an affair for me. We are meant to be together.

The outside man wasn't sure what to do. He had been told to shoot anyone that left the car and headed inside. But that wasn't supposed to happen until after the fireworks began. He wasn't sure if that meant to shoot the guy in civilian clothes.

"Calling Alpha."

"Speak to me, Beta."

"Got a guy who just stopped to talk to the police officers in the squad car. He's heading up to the front door. Should I do him?"

"No! We can't have a gunfight in the street and alert everyone inside."

"Then there's an extra man inside to deal with, Alpha."

"Police?"

"No uniform on him but he's a big guy. Might be law enforcement."

Not what he wanted to hear, but the math was still okay, Zheglov thought, especially since his team had the element of surprise.

"Probably the next shift of FBI babysitter. The woman has been with our target all day," he said to the man.

Another voice crackled over the short wave, "This is Delta. We still on, Alpha?"

"Nothing's changed, Delta. This is the best time and place. Beta stays outside. The three of us just need to be prepared for a second active and armed target. Consider him very dangerous. The two agents are now equal first priority. Confirm you got this."

"Delta confirmed."

"Gamma confirmed."

"Beta, those two cops are going to move fast. You ready?"

"Beta confirmed."

Zheglov was confident the two men in the squad car didn't have the tactical training or experience to handle an event like this. If they did, one would go fast and low, the other covering him. The one covering wouldn't follow the first until the coast was clear. They didn't know he was here. They were hoping the threat to Conner was finished. They had messed up royally.

"Time to move. Everyone look at your watch. We go in sixty seconds. And counting . . . starting now."

●●●

Reynolds focused hard to gather more Intel. He was suddenly making his way toward an Al Qaeda stronghold in the hills of Afghanistan, not the front door of a Chicago row house. Every nerve, every sense was straining to locate the enemy. He knew they were there.

He turned the doorknob. It was unlocked. He wanted to scream, *Kristen, you aren't taking this seriously!*

Jimmy King, Kristen's brother-in-law, his face beaming a warm smile, made a beeline across the small room to shake his hand. He saw Reynolds' expression and stopped a couple steps away, the smile melting to concern.

"Jimmy. We have to move."

"What is it, Austin? Is something wrong?"

"Yes. Don't ask questions. Get Kaylen and the kids. Go in the back bedroom. Take Grace. Now. Move it. Tell the kids it's a game and to be quiet." Jimmy seemed frozen in place. "Now!" Reynolds hissed.

Torgerson looked at him, asking him with her eyes what was going on.

James started to yell when his dad picked him up to go into the back bedroom.

"James!" Reynolds said, no longer the nice guy who played Thomas the Tank Engine with the kid at Christmas. The boy looked in Reynolds' eyes with fear. "You're going to go in the back room and take care of your grandmother and baby sister. With no sound. Not a sound. Do you hear me?"

He nodded wide-eyed.

"What is it?" Grace Conner asked.

"I hope I'm wrong . . . but we've got a situation. You need to get back there now. Do you have a handgun?"

She nodded yes. She had never admitted to the girls she kept one locked in the bottom drawer of her nightstand.

"Get it and get in the closet with everyone. If this doesn't go well, somebody bad is going to come back there. No matter what you think is right and wrong, just know, it's right to pull the trigger."

This was taking too much time. He couldn't hear them coming but he knew they were poised to strike. He had to mount a defense. It was life or death time.

Reynolds looked at Torgerson and pointed to the front door, the back door, and at the floor. He suddenly realized Kristen was nowhere to be seen.

"Where's Conner?"

Torgerson felt sick to her stomach as a wave of fear and guilt gripped her.

"She said she'd be in in just a sec. She had to do something outside."

Reynolds wanted to scream but kept a stone face. It was what it was.

He would have stationed Kristen on the

basement door, the safest spot. Now he would have two points of egress to monitor.

No time to think, just act and improvise, he told himself. It's kept you alive before.

"You got front door," Reynolds said, low and soft to Torgerson. "Safety off. Shoot to kill."

"What if it's one of ours?"

He looked at her and couldn't help but think how young and inexperienced she was.

"It won't be. They're going to come in fast and loud. Any second. I've got the back two doors. Just hold your position."

He wanted to ask her if she knew how to use that pretty little Glock 23 she had in hand and if she'd experienced live fire. No time to ask and he didn't want to hear the answer.

Don had already told Vanessa he was leaving right after practice to see Debbie. Rodney pulled some strings and got her in a nice place in Oak Lawn. It was Don's job to get her to sign the papers that basically waived her legal rights to leave the premises. She was in a comfortable but secure wing for patients that had the habit of running off.

The thing was, you can't leave your partner in harm's way. Paperwork would have to wait for morning. He kissed Vanessa and the kids. He didn't want to say anything. They'd had a tough stretch the last few months of their marriage.

"I'm going to be later than planned."

"What's up?" Vanessa asked.

Better to just be upfront.

"Conner is not answering her phone and we're having to amp up security. I'm checking in at her mom's."

He could tell she wanted to argue. Instead she gave him a hug.

"I don't care how late you are. Just be careful and give me a call when you know what's going on."

"I will. Love you baby."

"I love you, too, Donald."

Now the wind was howling and blew his SUV from side to side as he slid in the direction of Mrs. Conner's home.

LA sounds good about right now. Maybe we can get Debbie transferred to a place out there. She needs a fresh start. We all do.

Conner, how do you get yourself in so much trouble?

Delta stole to the front of the house from the opposite direction of the squad car. He liked Vladimir. They had a lot in common. Both had combat experience. The man kept it bold and simple. He gave clear orders and expected them to be followed. He didn't shy away from the action. A good combination of traits. A good man.

He looked at his watch. Five seconds until show

time. He took two deep breaths, stood, threw the brick as hard as he could through the front plate window. It shattered immediately. He was already moving up the steps with his gun aimed at the doorjamb. He didn't want to switch out clips unless necessary. He unloaded three rounds and kicked the door open effortlessly.

The female FBI agent had a gun pointed at his chest but seemed frozen. Their surprise attack was apparently not a surprise. Nothing to do but move forward. He raised his gun and pulled the trigger as she fired back. He felt a fireball erupt in his stomach. He staggered back to the threshold. This was bad. But she was down and he was up, so he forced his feet to move forward.

A man looked around the corner of the hall and shot him between the eyes.

❄ **84** ❄

Was it something Bradley said in our first interview? Was it something Leslie Levin or Nancy Keltto said? What's bothering me? Maybe I'm just bothered by the thought of a fourteen-year-old killing his volunteer mentor. Except Nancy told us Ed wasn't actively serving as mentor because Bradley didn't like him. I'm beginning to feel tingles. I walk into the Keltto's backyard. I look at the back windows. I walk back out front and look at the windows there too. I circle back to the back-yard and over to where the Keltto and Starks yards meet at the fence. I look between the two houses.

Despite some drama and tears, Nancy was feeling better today . . . until Don asked her about Levin being there the morning of the murder. That threw her for a loop. What does that mean?

I think of the garage and what Nancy said. I look at the two houses side by side. Another click registers in my brain. I think I know what's . . . no . . . I *know* what's bothering me about her story. It's all suddenly clear.

Then I hear a crash. Maybe a window being broken in. I move toward the side of the house and hear a gun blast, followed by another at almost the same instant. Then a third, fourth, and fifth gunshot shatters the thin, wintery night air—I stop counting.

Everything is coming from my mom's house. I pull out the Glock 9mm I was issued earlier today. I was given two full clips. I pop one in and start sprinting. I start to slip at the corner of the house but I keep my footing and pound forward. I don't know how the mind processes things so quickly, but I remember a Bible verse from when I was a kid. "He will not let your foot slip." No idea where that is in the Bible. But I know what it means now. Dear God, you are going to have to keep me on my feet. I run as fast as I can on snow and ice. I can't slip. I can't slip.

• • •

The two uniforms leaped from the car, slammed the doors shut, and headed for the front door, weapons up.

Beta smiled. Just like Alpha said. He shot for the center of the body with both shots, using a Desert Eagle 50-caliber handgun that hit the targets like a bazooka.

He stepped from the shrubbery. If they were wearing body armor they might conceivably be alive but would probably still be out of commission. Alpha said to play it safe and verify. If necessary finish them off. Then go back for the car.

Forget what you saw in the living room. Nothing more you can do to help. She's dead or alive. Reynolds' head was on a swivel, eyes to back door, basement door, back door, basement door continuously. Thankfully they were lined up in the hall that ran the length of the house.

He heard crying from the bedroom. Keep focused and maybe you'll keep them alive—and get out of this with your own life.

He heard pounding coming up the basement steps at the same time he heard shots splinter the back door. This is going to be close.

Conner almost fell as she slid to a stop. She watched in horror as her two body guards from CPD were gunned down. She saw the shooter emerge from the bushes. He didn't see her . . . yet.

I don't care what your range scores are. You gotta drop him and get to the house.

She crept forward. Suddenly his head snapped up and his eyes found her. He raised a huge gun as he pivoted her direction.

The basement door to the ground floor slammed open at the same time as the back door. Reynolds shot the man coming up the steps between the eyes and grabbed him before he could fall. The door had blocked the vision of whoever was charging down the hall from the back door, firing five rapid rounds through the two-inch wood shield he had ducked behind. All hits were too close for comfort.

Reynolds grabbed the dead man in a bear hug, face to face, with blood gurgling between the man's lips. Reynolds turned him into the hall and rushed forward, slamming the door into the wall and throwing the man into the attacker. All three men hit the floor in a heap, guns skittering across the oak planks. Reynolds was halfway to his feet as a snarling Vladimir Zheglov lunged at him, launching a lightning fast judo punch for his trachea.

I dive sideways at the same instant a fireball bursts from the muzzle of the shooter's gun. I feel a concussion of air pass by. Despite a flood of pain coursing to my bandaged side, I roll to my knee and get the Glock up in firing position.

Reynolds ducked his head forward and to the side while firing a flat palm at the man's wide-open torso. Vladimir's punch landed hard enough on his jaw to maybe break it, sending waves of pain that threatened to blind him. But Reynolds' counter move kept it from being a disabling blow. His shot to the solar plexus took the air from Zheglov's lungs.

Austin pounced on top of him like a puma, one hand going for the Russian's eyes, the other for his throat. But Zheglov was an expert grappler— and a survivor. He pried at Austin's hands as he arched his back and twisted his head free. He quickly let go and maneuvered his hands to Reynolds' throat.

The man was drawing a bead on her as Kristen pulled the trigger and rolled before another explosion sounded from the Desert Eagle. She made it to one knee, her gun back in the ready position. Her shot had hit him and he stumbled backwards and fell, but he turned over, popped to his knees, and dove for the shrubbery. If he got there, Kristen realized he would have cover and she would be a sitting duck. She fired another shot and saw his body spasm. She leaped forward to finish him.

Two men trying to protect her were dead or dying. Her family was trapped inside a war zone. She had to get inside the house.

Reynolds knew not to give him space and pressed his shoulder into Zheglov's face while grasping his wrists and pulling apart with every ounce of strength he had.

Zheglov used the momentum of Reynolds' hands pulling sideways and flung his own hands to the side while twisting his body hard, flipping Reynolds on his back, and gaining the upper hand. Without a nanosecond of hesitation, Vlad began pounding at Reynolds' head with a furious rage and strength.

This guy was good but not good enough, Vladimir thought. But this has taken way too much time and we don't have the detective. Finish him fast and get out of here.

He was hurt bad but didn't stop moving. Kristen could see him clambering through a hole in the bushes as she rushed forward.

No hesitation. Get him.

When she broke through the gap of evergreens, he had got his back to the house and was raising the Desert Eagle to shoot her from a sitting position.

Now or never.

She held the trigger down, letting seven rounds

explode from the barrel at near point-blank range.

No question he was dead, but she still moved cautiously, her gun never lowering.

Do I have another round in the barrel?

She kicked him and he slid from the side of the house, splay-legged, flat on his back, the gun a foot beyond his outstretched hand, his eyes staring lifelessly into the night sky.

Her fingers were nearly frozen from throwing her gloves down on the Keltto's driveway, but she managed to get her hands on the extra clip in her outside pocket while sprinting for the front door. She pulled the spent clip and popped the new one in.

Reynolds curved his spine forward and then backward in a desperate movement, giving him the space to drive his knee into Zheglov's groin, loosening the vise-like grip of Vlad's hands just enough for him to jerk his head forward and head-butt the Russian mobster in the mouth. Blood spurted everywhere, but he hadn't caught him in the nose, which would have immobilized him.

The fight was still on and the man was still on top of him.

Vlad's mouth was a bloody maw with gaps where teeth were broken off, but he ignored the pain, throwing more tight, controlled, downhill punches. Reynolds jerked his head right and left but some were catching him. He knew the second one well-timed punch broke his jaw, probably finishing what the opening judo punch started. The pounding was taking a toll. Zheglov was sliding his knees up Reynolds' torso to keep a grip on his body and keep him beneath him.

I should have told Conner what I had to say, Reynolds thought as he jabbed his fingers at Vladimir's throat, giving him a temporary respite from the onslaught of punches.

I've got to get him off me or I'm a dead man.

As Don turned on Mrs. Conner's street he laughed at himself. Everything's so quiet. You should have just gone to see Debbie and sign the papers. It might be too late after stopping here. Then he heard a series of booming gunshots. He hit the accelerator, fishtailing left and right, but heading in the right direction.

The last thing his sister said to him was that his skinny partner was going to get him killed. She might be right.

As he braked to a sliding stop in front of the Conner home, he saw that the front door was blown off the hinges. Two uniformed bodies were sprawled on the ground. Conner burst through the front hedge and was racing for the gaping doorway.

Am I too late? I crash through the splintered opening, nearly tripping on the two bodies lying on the tiny living room floor. The bad guy is down but so is Torgerson. I can see her gasping for air like a fish out of water. Then I hear baby Kelsey cry from my mom's bedroom.

I hear a feral roar and take two jump skips to the hallway.

Vladimir Zheglov was a disciplined fighter. He threw no long, wide-open punches like they show in police dramas. He tightened his elbows even more, protecting his throat and face and helping him keep his balance, no matter what Reynolds did to move him.

Reynolds anticipated Vladimir's next punch perfectly and sunk his teeth into Zheglov's wrist, clenching hard enough to loosen teeth in the effort to try to hold it.

Vlad bellowed in pain and yanked it away, losing some skin and tissue. But he didn't stop punching. His violent world taught him the simple lesson that you punch until the other guy can't fight back and then you keep punching until he is dead.

Reynolds knew he was out of options—and strength. Adrenaline could only carry you so far. He lost the fight when he lost top position, he thought ruefully.

Zheglov felt Reynolds' muscles relax and immediately stopped punching, bringing both hands to Reynolds' throat for the kill. Amazingly,

Reynolds' hands met them there, stealing precious seconds from Vlad—maybe enough to save Conner's life, Reynolds thought. When do the reinforcements arrive?

Vlad pressed down as Austin pushed back, fighting every centimeter of the inevitable. His larynx would be crushed and he would be strangled to death. Zheglov's strength, gravity, and his quickly flagging energy combined to spell his doom.

You don't quit until it's over he yelled at himself as he pushed back with a hidden reserve of strength. But Vlad barely budged. His hands were now on Reynolds' throat. He felt the flow of air being squeezed shut a millimeter at a time by a vice-like grip.

Bam! With the explosion, Zheglov's fingers were no longer crushing the life from him. *Bam.* With a second explosion, the Russian mobster slumped forward and rolled on his side next to Reynolds, his mouth and eyes wide open in shocked amazement.

Reynolds looked up. Grace Conner was frozen in place, still in a shooter's stance, her .38 special pointing at the body.

Kristen and Squires crashed into the hallway a second later, weapons up.

Is it possible to scream with a question mark behind it? If so, I just did. Don and I got to

Reynolds as my mom shot Vladimir Zheglov in the back.

Bam. Bam.

"Mommmm!?" was all that came out of my mouth.

❄ 85 ❄

"Mom, go make sure Jimmy and Kaylen and the kids are okay. Keep the kids back there, especially James. They can't see this."

I am nearly in shock from seeing my mom holding a smoking revolver.

She nods and turns toward the bedroom calm as a lazy summer day.

"Mom."

She turns back.

I hug her hard and say, "Thanks . . . and good shot."

I feel her shake as she pulls away to head back and take care of family. Okay, maybe she's not calm. She might be in shock. But we've got a triage center here and there are critical needs to care for.

"Don, you get Torgerson," I say.

He is calling the situation in and nods. He has a dazed expression that suddenly becomes alert. He closes his eyes and shakes his head.

I double-check that Zheglov is dead and turn to

Reynolds. He is breathing strong and steady. There is blood coming from facial wounds. I'm not sure where to start or what to touch with the wicked angle of his fractured jawline.

I breathe him in and lower my lips to his ear.

"I love you."

I have no clue if he heard that. Maybe that's why I said it now. Sirens are getting louder as help draws near. He's hurt bad but he's alive. They'll know what to do. I don't.

"Is Heather alive?" I call to Squires.

"Yes. But it's bad," he answers grimly. "How about Reynolds?"

"I think he's okay. I'm going to head outside and check the uniforms."

Man oh man.

Was this my fault? Did I not take things seriously enough? Did I get four people killed or seriously injured? What if Don had been two minutes earlier and Reynolds two minutes later? No doubt, Don is tough and capable, but no way could he have handled what I suspect Reynolds just did. I might have been attending my partner's funeral and having to look Vanessa in the eyes.

I hate leaving Reynolds, but he's going to live. I walk past Torgerson. There is a lot of blood flowing out, despite Don's makeshift compress using his sweat jacket. I reach over to the couch and grab the first thing I touch, a quilt, and press it to her stomach to help stanch the blood flow. I think my great-grandma made the quilt like a hundred years ago. It's a valuable family heirloom I've been told. Never knew much about great-grandma, but I'm sure she'd understand. Hopefully my mom will too.

I walk outside to the uniforms. I'm afraid to look. The first ambulance pulls in. Hope there's more than a couple EMTs. I'd even welcome Thad, the guy with the knockout syringe, with open arms.

❄ **86** ❄

CPD and the FBI were minutes behind Squires. Then three more ambulances arrived with an army of EMTs. I got a wave and concerned look from Lloyd, an EMT who goes to our church. He lost a hundred pounds last year but I think he's got it all back and more—he looks like himself again. He loves those jumbo hot dogs at Gas and Grub. Then more CPD and FBI arrive. It's turning into a circus. Spencer Doyle showed up, then Czaka. The brass are coming out in force.

Squires finally got control and managed the overall crime scene quite well. He even sent a few of the CPD big wigs home so we had room to work. The tape and barricades were in place before the press started arriving. We'd have to deal with a mob of gawkers outside the tape if the weather hadn't dropped to seven degrees above zero, Fahrenheit.

Whoever questioned my mom played it by the book and was perhaps a little overzealous. I can't believe he threatened to cuff her if she couldn't find her handgun permit. Squires saw what was happening and barked for him to stand down.

At two in the morning I finally got back to my mom's bedroom. I had a few questions to ask her. She was fast asleep with Kendra and James on either side of her. I wonder how the kiddos are doing and if they are going to need counseling. At least James isn't complaining that my mom's house smells funny—though he might be right.

My mom shot a ferocious Russian mobster. Inconceivable.

I shut the door quietly and head upstairs. Jimmy is snoring. Kaylen is just finishing nursing baby Kelsey. I take the baby from her and volunteer to burp her. I breathe in that beautiful scent of innocence until she erupts with a sound loud enough to wake the neighbors—again. I quickly and gently hand her back to Kaylen who puts her in the bassinet Mom keeps in her old room.

"You okay, Kaylen?" I ask.

"Is this normal for you?" she asks back.

"Nah. Being a cop is boring most of the time."

I can tell she doesn't believe me. I'm almost being one hundred percent truthful.

We hug after I tell her to go to bed—and to

consider investing in a sleep apnea machine for Jimmy. That gets a smile out of her.

I can barely move but know where I need to be.

I wake up at six-forty-five—just two hours sleep —step out of the room, and call Blackshear. I wonder if he is up yet.

"Blackshear," he mumbles incoherently.

I guess not.

"Bob, you awake?"

"I am now, Conner."

"You hear about last night?"

"In detail. Konkade and Zaworski were working the phones. I wanted to come over but was told no more bodies in the area."

"It wasn't Bradley."

"What?"

"It wasn't Bradley," I repeat.

"What are you talking about Conner?"

He is skeptical at first, but as he begins to wake up, I can tell what I'm saying is sinking in. I hear a slurp.

"You get a cup of coffee?"

"Thankfully. Tell me again, how'd you think to figure this out?"

"I went back to the scene of the crime one more time and got one of my feelings."

"No way," he says. "No way. What'd it feel like? Did you see a ghost?"

"Bob, if you say I see ghosts one more time, I'm not telling you anything."

"Okay, I won't use the word 'ghost' again."

"I knew something Nancy said felt all wrong. So I walked through the back and side yards and realized she was lying through her teeth about Bradley."

Is there any other way to lie than through your teeth?

"How so?" Bob asks.

"There is no way Bradley is a peeping tom, which Nancy—and Leslie—accused him of being. The houses where I grew up are so small and so close together—not to mention they have small windows—that it would be impossible to look in and see her in her house from his house. Their houses have mirror layouts. The two sides closest to each other are walls and hallways. The angles to see inside her house from his house are all wrong. He would have had to be sitting in Mrs. DeGenares' house to have any hope of seeing her in any of the living spaces. She was lying."

"I'm not sure I understood all your words but I think I know what you're saying."

"I'm not done," I say.

"Keep going," he says.

"That got me thinking, if she lied about him being a peeper, what else did she say that was untrue."

"I'm listening."

"Don't know if you remember, but she also made a point of letting me know that Bradley and Ed weren't spending quality time together—and that Ed didn't think Bradley liked him. But Ed had a special cubby for Bradley in the garage filled with a half-finished project and plans for future projects. Bradley had his name on the cubby and burnished on a tool belt. He had already completed a couple of really nice projects—way too nice to be done without a mentor. She was lying again."

"So you think Nancy did it?"

"I'm not convinced of that."

"Leslie?"

"Absolutely."

"So where does Nancy fit in?"

"She might have been working with Leslie the whole time. But why have divorce papers ready to be served that very day? Why attempt suicide? And why did she about have a seizure when Don asked her if Leslie was there the morning of the murder?"

"Maybe she realized the two of them had been found out."

"Maybe. But maybe Leslie was manipulating her to cover his tracks. He didn't want her to go to jail so he fed her a plausible storyline, knowing she would use it to get us looking another direction."

"But you said she lied. That still sounds like

she's an accomplice to me. Maybe you just don't want her to be guilty."

"You might be right, Bob."

"Heck, I'm so confused I'm not sure what I'm saying."

"Drink another cup of coffee and then get Bradley out of Cook County Juvenile Center. You and the DA can figure out later whether you like Nancy as an accomplice or a stooge."

❄ **87** ❄

I'm not good in hospitals. They wear me out. It is much worse when I'm not the patient. I decide to stay in Reynolds' room again tonight. He's at Northwestern Memorial Medical Center just off Michigan Avenue. I have checked on Torgerson who is still in ICU. Not much I can do there. They've induced a coma and she's going to be unconscious for a while. I'm hoping and praying she makes it all the way back.

I still can't believe my mom saved Reynolds' life. Would I have got there in time if she hadn't acted? Looking at the bruising on his face and his welted swollen neck, I'm not sure. He's beat up to the point it's hard to find his face in there. They reset his jaw tomorrow—if they can get the swelling down enough.

It will be a couple weeks before he can talk. I

wonder if he'll remember what he just had to say to me when I was the one lying in a hospital bed. I wonder if he remembers what I said to him when I found him next to Vladimir Zheglov's dead body.

He really is a handsome man, which is part of the reason I've always been surprised at his persistent interest in me. I'm guessing it will be more than a couple months before he's ready to have his picture taken for the cover of *GQ* magazine, if ever.

I pull apart the chair that doubles as a bed and test it. I think it was invented by a guy who flunked out of Chiropractic College. I brought in my phone charger, plugged in, and set the alarm for seven. Hopefully I'll wake up before it goes off. I don't want to wake Austin. But I need to at least stay in touch with the office, even if I'm not expected to be there. My mind almost let me make a joke about him needing his beauty sleep, but I self-censored.

"How's our soldier?" Willingham asks as he and Van Guten enter the room.

She's cold and severe, but no denying, she is beautiful. She wears expensive clothes that fit and flatter perfectly. Her jewelry, unlike the few baubles I have, is real. She has a way of looking at me that makes me feel very self-conscious. I don't aspire for what she has or how she presents herself. Not by a mile. But I almost . . . only almost . . . feel inferior when she's present.

I'm holding hands with Austin and have been giving him the skinny on everything that happened after he passed out. I might have put him to sleep with my scintillating narrative. It was either that or the drugs. I'm used to having that effect on people when I wax eloquent.

I feel awkward and self-conscience and I'm tempted to let go of his hand. He squeezes tighter. That might mean he wants to stay connected to me. Or it might mean he's having a bad dream about a bear chasing him. He's definitely playing possum with Van Guten present.

"The soldier probably isn't going to be able to say much for a while," I say.

I feel the squeeze again. Good. He wants to be close. Doesn't mean we can talk things through. The internal and external damage to his neck, throat, and jaw is going to ensure he is the strong and silent type.

If he gets better I'll ask him why he's giving me the silent treatment. Sometimes people think my jokes are funny.

A couple days ago I thought he and my sister might be an item. I have to get my thinking back in sync. But what's the hurry?

Willingham comes close to Austin and lightly touches his hair. He leans over and whispers in his ear. Do men tell each other "I love you"? Or is he giving him the score of the Rangers-Bruins hockey game? Heck, he may be giving him his next assignment.

I give them some space.

"You'll do just fine," Van Guten says.

I nod sagely, wondering what she is talking about.

"The Cutter Shark appeal doesn't have a chance."

I nod. He's her subject. I guess she would know what he's up to.

"And with Austin."

Is that her business? I don't think so. Dr. Andrews says I need to take down some of the bricks that I've used to build a wall to keep others from seeing the real me. She might be right or the real me might be so simple and straightforward that what you see is what you get. Probably both. Either way, I'm leaving the bricks up when Van Guten is around.

❄ 88 ❄

Three weeks after the shootout at my mom's house, life feels a little bit like normal. Blackshear had to come over to the Second to prepare for a meeting with the District Attorney to review notes for Leslie Levin's grand jury hearing on charges of first-degree murder and a list of lesser crimes. It's still not decided what to do with Nancy, even though Levin has turned on her. He's painting her as the mastermind and an accomplice from day one. Blackshear agrees. I don't. I think Levin is trying to negotiate a plea bargain that lets him see the light of day before he's sixty. I wonder if his kids will visit him in prison.

Blackshear, Squires, Martinez, the new detectives—Sandy Green and Collin Smith—and me are at Big Mike's on State Street south of the Loop plowing through some gyros. Martinez asked for extra tzatziki, apparently to coat his beard and moustache. He still eats with his mouth half open. I'm not looking his direction.

"*Qué quieres ser el gran jefe?*" he asks Don.

"I haven't decided. Vanessa and I are still talking—which is a good thing. A big improvement. I still think she still wants to move to LA, but me getting promoted is something she's wanted, too."

"And you?" I ask. "What do you want?"

"I always wanted to be an attorney. Now I'm not so sure. I definitely have questions about moving. My sister is in rehab and might be doing well—say a prayer. I've been given two months to let Zaworski and Czaka know if I'll take the job. That's when the Z-man rides back into the sunset. So no hurry."

I've never heard Don mention his sister to our colleagues. I see questioning looks but that's

483

apparently all he's going to say about Debbie. But maybe taking down a single brick is an okay thing.

"If you stick around here, how about you tell your brother about what a great *amigo* I am!" Martinez says, about three chews into an enormous bite of gyro. "Tell him I speak much better Spanish than you. That be very good in California."

We munch our gyros and discuss a range of topics. Zaworski really is going to retire this time. April or May will be his last month. He says we've stolen another ten years from his life. He looked at me when he said that. When we circle back and talk about Squires' job offer some more, I wonder how Blackshear is taking it. I know it about killed him to get demoted. But he seems fine at the moment. Who isn't fine when eating? It always helps me.

We talk about my thrice delayed but upcoming deposition for the Cutter's appeal—I couldn't follow all of Martinez's Spanish when he went on a tirade about it. Gray keeps telling me not to worry. We're solid.

We then hit serious issues, like whether the Blackhawks can win the Stanley Cup again and whether Michael Jordan or Lebron James would win a game of one-on-one basketball. We are all amazed at how incredibly well Bradley Starks seems to be doing—knock on wood and say a prayer. It would be nice if he can keep it going and be one of those all-too-rare success stories we need in Chicago. If the kid makes it as a good, decent, normal adult, he would become a nice part of Ed Keltto's legacy.

I went to Mr. Ed's funeral. I don't know if I was more impressed or sad. He helped a lot of kids. When I got up to leave I saw Nancy heading for the door. It's a strange funeral when the widow isn't invited. Nancy. What were you thinking? What is going to happen to you?

"How's Austin?" Don asks with a wink, knowing he's put me on the hot seat.

I redden and fidget a little—and realize I shouldn't have ordered so much food. I'm having dinner with Austin tonight. He's not able to eat solids yet so I end up eating enough for the both of us. I still meet with Andrews every week, not just because I'm required to, but I figure I need some help opening up to people. Austin is top of the list.

"He's fine," I say. "He still can't talk much so it's working out pretty well for me. I'm not sure if it's working out as well for him because he can't seem to get a word in edgewise."

That gets horrified groans from the three guys—and some of it didn't seem to be play-acting. Green and I look at each other and roll our eyes.

We pay our bills and head out the door. My foot hits a patch of ice and I end up on my butt. I'll give my colleagues credit for trying to look concerned before laughing at me. I join them and even Green can't hold back.

Martinez reaches out a hand and pulls me up.

Life can be cold as ice some days, but the people I love are alive, so I'm not complaining.

❄ **89** ❄

I've been played for the fool. It is so obvious and yet I missed it when she planted the seed.

Dr. Van Guten. You must be taught a lesson. I will let you think you are winning. I will draw you in closer. You'll never see what I have for you coming.

Dear Detective Conner . . . dear Kristen . . . I must find a way to let you know that I have not forgotten you. I still think of you every day. Expect to hear from me soon.

❄ **About the Author** ❄

Mark "M.K." Gilroy is a veteran publisher who has worked with major authors and acquired and created an array of bestselling books and series.

When not writing Detective Kristen Conner novels, he creates book projects for publishers, retailers, organizations, and businesses as a freelance publisher.

Gilroy's debut novel, *Cuts Like a Knife*, quickly garnered critical acclaim from national media, bloggers, and readers—and hit #1 at Barnes & Nobel (BN.com).

The Kristen Conner Mystery series now includes *Every Breath You Take*, *Cold As Ice*, and releasing in February 2016, *Under Pressure*.

Gilroy is a member of the prestigious Mystery Writers of America. He holds the BA in Biblical Literature and Speech Communications, and two graduate degrees, the M.Div. and MBA.

Gilroy is the father of six children. He resides with his wife Amy in Brentwood, Tennessee.

Stay Connected with M.K. at:
www.facebook.com/MKGilroy.Author
www.mkgilroy.com
@markgilroy

Center Point Large Print
600 Brooks Road / PO Box 1
Thorndike, ME 04986-0001 USA

(207) 568-3717

US & Canada:
1 800 929-9108
www.centerpointlargeprint.com